Edward L. Burlingame

Current Discussion

A collection from the chief English essays on questions of the time. Vol. 2

Edward L. Burlingame

Current Discussion
A collection from the chief English essays on questions of the time. Vol. 2

ISBN/EAN: 9783337423896

Printed in Europe, USA, Canada, Australia, Japan

Cover: Foto ©Andreas Hilbeck / pixelio.de

More available books at **www.hansebooks.com**

CURRENT DISCUSSION

A COLLECTION

FROM THE CHIEF ENGLISH ESSAYS ON

QUESTIONS OF THE TIME.

EDITED BY

EDWARD L. BURLINGAME

VOL. II.

QUESTIONS OF BELIEF

———————

NEW YORK

G. P. PUTNAM'S SONS

182 Fifth Avenue

1878.

PREFACE.

THAT highest phase of "Current Discussion," which is ind: the purposely broad title chosen for this volu.. ust of necessity be the most difficult to present fairly or pletely within narrow limits. In the debate upon every other subject, there are many obvious guides as to the importance of different expressions of opinion—as to the degree in which they truly represent the varying directions of thought. Here, there are few such aids, if any ;—selection in this field must unavoidably be a matter of purely individual judgment. In spite of the broad spirit of toleration that marks all recent discussion, there is less here than elsewhere of that common ground, from which the most determined opponents may see and acknowledge the value of each other's arguments as contributions to the whole. In "Questions of Belief" it is still possible that the word. ken upon the one side seem utterly useless, if not absolutely harmful, to the other.

A charge which may naturally be brought against

the choice of material for this volume, is that it favors the expression of what is known as the "radical" school of thinkers upon these subjects. It can only be said that the skeptic first excites discussion ; and that, from whatever point of view we look at it, we must first of all know what he posits, as the very matter in debate ;—that the conservative always speaks least, from the very nature of his position as a resistant, not an aggressor ;—and that the points of attack have been so changed that to many earnest and honest minds *all* schools of thought may now seem radical.

It may fairly be remembered, however, that a single volume gives but very narrow space, much of which must be given to the discussion of a single proposition ; and that it is not intended, should our scheme meet with success, that the present shall be the only selection in this field.

To many the position and the work of all the writers represented here are so thoroughly known, that to repeat the plan adopted in the first volume, of a prefatory note recalling them, may easily seem superfluous. At the same time there appear here many names which may not immediately connect themselves in the minds of all readers with the opinions or the work which they represent. Some of the authors who take part in this discussion have indeed already addressed the largest possible public, and need no explanation of their attitude;—such are Professor Huxley, the Duke of Argyll, Dr. Martineau, and Mr. Hughes, for example; and less can hardly be said of Mr. Lewes. But there are others who, from the very nature of their writings, have spoken to smaller audiences.

Mr. Frederic Harrison, whose remarkable paper—"The Soul and Future Life"—forms the text for so much in this volume, is, it need hardly be said, one of the leaders among English Positivists; and has been for years an untiring and most powerful agent in spreading in England the teachings of his school—a translation (under the title "Social Statics") from Comte's "Positive Polity," being, by the way, one of the latest of his publications. Apart from his many lectures and writings upon philosophical topics, however, he has had an active influence upon affairs which is remarkable for a man of forty-six. Called to the bar in 1859, he quickly became prominent in his profession. Ten years later he was secretary of the "Royal Commission for the Digest of the Law;" in 1873 he was made examiner in Civil and International Law and Jurisprudence, by the Council of

Legal Education ; and he has been very eminent in chancery practice. A special subject of his study has been the education and improvement of the working classes, which he has sought to further in the Working Men's College, the Working Women's College, the Positive School, and· other schemes of which he has been one of the foremost advocates. The greater part of his writings remains in the form of contributions to periodicals—notably to the *Fortnightly Review.*

Mr. R. H. Hutton, as editor of the *Spectator,* occupies one of the foremost positions in English journalism. His contribution in the " Symposium " to the discussion of the "Soul and Future Life" is not the first or only paper that he has written upon the subject, or upon Mr. Harrison's view of it. A series of most noteworthy papers, properly belonging to this literature, but too long to be included here, were contributed by him to early numbers of the *Spectator* for 1877.

Sir James Fitzjames Stephen was best known to the public as a leading jurist, as a codifier of the laws of India, and as the writer of one of the best general works on English criminal law,—until, in 1873, the publication of his " Liberty, Equality and Fraternity " made him famous in a less special field. He has a peculiar title to appear among the representatives of deep and earnest thought upon the first of all speculative questions.

Lord Selborne is better remembered by the general reader as Sir Roundell Palmer; for he was only raised to the peerage in 1872. The political career of a man who has been solicitor-general under Palmerston, attorney-general under Lord John Russell, and Lord Chancellor under Mr. Gladstone, need hardly be recalled here—more especially as his name became familiar to Americans through his representation of Great Britain before the Geneva Arbitrators in 1871. One of the most prominent parts of his purely literary work is his well-known "Book of Praise"—one of the best collections of devotional poetry in the language.

Lord Blachford is a well-known English scholar—like the rest a member of the bar for years, and afterward rising rapidly in political life until his last office—the under-secretaryship for the Colonies—from which he retired in 1871. He has written many striking papers in the Quarterlies and Magazines.

Of the clerical disputants in the "Symposiums," the Reverend Alfred Barry, Canon of Worcester, is a very well-known writer on practical ethics—the character of his work being fairly exemplified, perhaps, by his "Lectures to Men" on "Religion for Every Day"—one of the more recent of his books.

He has gained great distinction not only as a scholar but as a teacher; and has been successively principal of the Leeds Grammar School, Cheltenham College, and King's College, London; and a member of the London School Board. The Dean of St. Paul's (Doctor Richard William Church), less known as a writer than as a preacher, represents fairly in the discussion the conservative element of the Established Church; and Dr. Ward, a well-known contributor to the reviews, performs—not for the only time in the *Nineteenth Century*—the same office for Roman Catholic opinion. The Reverend James Baldwin Brown (the author of "The Higher Life," "The Christian Policy of Life," and other books which have been widely read in his persuasion), is a liberal Independent—the minister of a large London congregation.

Mr. W. R. Greg can need little introduction to any reader of the speculative writing of recent years. His "Enigmas of Life" has passed through many editions, including one at least in this country, and has been unquestionably (in spite of the similarity in its tone to the despondent spirit of his contribution to the Symposium), one of the most widely-read books of its class. His "Political Problems," "Literary and Social Judgments," and "Creed of Christendom" are the chief of his other works, though his "Rocks Ahead, or the Warnings of Cassandra," attracted great attention at the time of its appearance in 1874, and gave rise to a long and vehement discussion.

Professor W. Kingdon Clifford, a man of singularly brilliant and versatile powers, is at the same time one of the most acute thinkers and most attractive writers among the younger generation of English scientific men. He is, I believe, not yet forty. Taking high honors at Cambridge, and especially distinguished both at the University and afterward for the ease with which he mastered the most diverse subjects, he not only devoted himself to his special study,—the higher mathematics,— but soon became known as a writer upon speculative topics. Among his strictly scientific work, that relating to dynamics has been particularly valuable ; and he is the author of one of the first text-books upon the subject. His short papers have generally appeared in the *Fortnightly Review.*

The Hon. Roden Noel has been chiefly known to the general reader through his contributions to a lighter literature, and his name is more easily recalled in connection with his occasional poems and reviews than with speculative essays.

Mr. Mallock, still a young man, and a comparatively recent graduate of Oxford, though his rapidly growing reputation has been chiefly aided with the larger public by his brilliant and capital trifle, " The New Republic " —has shown in his essays a depth and earnestness of thought that place him unquestionably among the most promising writers of the time. A volume like this may fitly close with the work of a pen from which we may certainly hope for further papers as striking and as thoughtful as the one here given.

CONTENTS.

THE SOUL AND FUTURE LIFE.[1]

BY FREDERIC HARRISON.

How many men and women continue to give a mechanical acquiescence to the creeds, long after they have parted with all definite theology, out of mere clinging to some hope of a future life, in however dim and inarticulate a way! And how many, whose own faith is too evanescent to be put into words, profess a sovereign pity for the practical philosophy wherein there is no place for their particular yearning for a Heaven to come! They imagine themselves to be, by virtue of this very yearning, beings of a superior order, and, as if they inhabited some higher zone amidst the clouds, they flout sober thought as it toils in the plain below; they counsel it to drown itself in sheer despair or take to evil living; they rebuke it with some sonorous household word from the Bible or the poets—'Eat, drink, for to-morrow ye die'—'Were it not better not to be?' And they assume the question closed, when they have murmured triumphantly, 'Behind the veil, behind the veil.'

They are right, and they are wrong: right to cling to a hope of something that shall endure beyond the grave; wrong in

1 THE NINETEENTH CENTURY, June, 1877.

their rebukes to men who in a different spirit cling to this hope as earnestly as they. We too turn our thoughts to that which is behind the veil. We strive to pierce its secret with eyes, we trust, as eager and as fearless; and even it may be more patient in searching for the realities beyond the gloom. That which shall come *after* is no less solemn to us than to you. We ask you, therefore, What do you *know* of it? Tell us; we will tell you what we hope. Let us reason together in sober and precise prose. Why should this great end, staring at all of us along the vista of each human life, be forever a matter for dithyrambic hypotheses and evasive tropes? What in the language of clear sense does any one of us hope for after death: what precise kind of life, and on what grounds? It is too great a thing to be trusted to poetic ejaculations, to be made a field for Pharisaic scorn. At least be it acknowledged that a man may think of the Soul and of Death and of Future Life in ways strictly positive (that is, without ever quitting the region of evidence), and yet may make the world beyond the grave the centre to himself of moral life. He will give the spiritual life a place as high, and will dwell upon the promises of that which is after death as confidently as the believers in a celestial resurrection. And he can do this without trusting his all to a *perhaps* so vague that a spasm of doubt can wreck it, but trusting rather to a mass of solid knowledge, which no man of any school denies to be true so far as it goes.

I.

There ought to be no misunderstanding at the outset as to what we who trust in positive methods mean by the word Soul, or by the words 'spiritual,' 'materialist,' and 'future life.' We certainly would use that ancient and beautiful word Soul, provided there be no misconception involved in its use. We assert as fully as any theologian the supreme importance of spiritual life. We agree with the theologians that there is current a great deal of real materialism, deadening to our higher feeling. And we deplore the too common indifference to the world beyond the grave. And yet we find the centre of our religion and our philosophy in Man and man's Earth.

To follow out this use of old words, and to see that there is no paradox in thus using them, we must go back a little to general principles. The matter turns altogether upon habits of thought. What seems to you so shocking will often seem to us so ennobling, and what seems to us flimsy will often seem to you sublime, simply because our minds have been trained in different logical methods; and hence you will call that a beautiful truth which strikes us as nothing but a random guess. It is idle, of course to dispute about our respective logical methods, or to pit this habit of mind in a combat with that. But we may understand each other better if we can agree to follow out the moral and religious temper, and learn that it is quite compatible with this or that mental procedure. It may teach us again that ancient truth, how much human nature there is in men; what fellowship there is in our common aspirations and moral forces; how we all live the same spiritual life; whilst the philosophies are but the ceaseless toil of the intellect seeking again and again to *explain* more clearly that spiritual life, and to furnish it with reasons for the faith that is in it.

This would be no place to expound or to defend the positive method of thought. The question before us is simply, if this positive method has a place in the spiritual world or has anything to say about a future beyond the grave. Suffice it that we mean by the positive method of thought (and we will now use the term in a sense not limited to the social construction of Comte) that method which would base life and conduct, as well as knowledge, upon such evidence as can be referred to logical canons of *proof*, which would place all that occupies man in a homogenous system of *law*. On the other hand, this method turns aside from *hypotheses* not to be tested by any known logical canon familiar to science, whether the hypothesis claim support from intuition, aspiration, or general plausibility. And again, this method turns aside from ideal standards which avow themselves to be *lawless*, which profess to transcend the field of law. We say, life and conduct shall stand for us wholly on a basis of law, and must rest entirely in that region of science (not physical but moral and social science) where we are free to use our intelligence in the methods known to us as intelligible logic, methods which the intellect can analyse. When you confront us with hypotheses, however sublime and however affecting, if they cannot be stated in terms of the rest of our knowledge, if they are disparate to that world of sequence and sensation which to us is the ultimate base of all our real knowledge, then we shake our heads and turn aside. I say, turn aside ; and I do not say, dispute. We cannot *disprove* the suggestion that there are higher channels to knowledge in our aspirations or our presentiments, as there might be in our dreams by night as well as by day ; we courteously salute the hypotheses, as we might love our present dreams; we seek to prove no negatives. We do not pretend there are no mysteries, we do not frown on the poetic splendors of the fancy. There is a world of beauty and of pathos in the vast ether of the Unknown in which this solid ball hangs like a speck. Let all who list, who have true imagination and not mere paltering with a loose fancy, let them indulge their gift, and tell us what their soaring has unfolded. Only let us not waste life in crude dreaming, or loosen the knees of action. For life and conduct, and the great emotions which react on life and conduct, we can place nowhere but in the same sphere of knowledge, under the same canons of proof, to which we entrust all parts of our life. We will ask the same philosophy which teaches us the lessons of civilization to guide our lives as responsible men; and we go again to the same philosophy which orders our lives to explain to us the lessons of death. We crave to have the supreme hours of our existence lighted up by thoughts and motives such as we can measure beside the common acts of our daily existence, so that each hour of our life up to the grave may be linked to the life beyond the grave as one continuous whole, 'bound each to each by natural piety.' And so, wasting no sighs over the incommensurable possibilities of the fancy, we will march on with a firm step till we knock at the gates of Death; bearing always the same human temper, in the same reasonable beliefs, and with the same earthly hopes of prolonged activity amongst our fellows, with which we set out gaily in the morning of life.

When we come to the problem of the human Soul, we simply treat man as man, and we study him in accordance with our human experience. Man is a marvellous and complex being, we may fairly say of complexity past any hope of final analysis of ours, fearfully and wonderfully made to the point of being mysterious. But incredible progress has been won in reading this complexity, in reducing this mystery to order. Who can say that man shall ever be anything but an object of awe and of unfathomable pondering to himself ? Yet he would be false to all that is great in him, if he decried what he already has achieved towards self-knowledge. Man has probed his own corporeal and animal life, and is each day arranging it in more accurate adjustment with the immense procession of animal life around him. He has grouped the intellectual powers, he has traced to their relations the functions of mind, and ordered the laws of thought into a logic of a regular kind. He has analysed and grouped the capacities of action, the moral faculties, the instincts and emotions. And not only is the analysis of these tolerably clear, but the associations and correlations of each with the other are fairly made manifest. At the lowest, we are all assured that every single faculty of man is capable of scientific study. Philosophy simply means, that every part of human nature acts upon a method, and does not act chaotically, inscrutably, or in mere caprice.

But then we find throughout man's knowledge of himself signs of a common type. There is organic unity in the whole. These laws of separate functions, of body, mind, or feeling, have visible relations to each other, are inextricably woven in with each other, act and react, depend and interdepend one on the other. There is no such thing as an isolated phenomenon, nothing *sui generis*, in our entire scrutiny of human nature. Whatever the complexities of it, there is through the whole the solidarity of a single unit. Touch the smallest fibre of the corporeal man, and in some ·infinitesimal way we may watch the effect in the moral man, and we may trace this effect up into the highest pinnacles of the spiritual life. On the other hand, when we rouse chords of the most glorious ecstasy of the soul, we may see the vibration of them visibly thrilling upon the skin. The very animals about us can perceive the emotion. Suppose a martyr nerved to the last sacrifice, or a saint in the act of relieving a sufferer, the sacred passion within them is stamped in the eye, or plays about the mouth, with a connection as visible as when we see a muscle acting on a bone, or the brain affected by the supply of blood. Thus from the summit of spiritual life to the base of corporeal life, whether we pass up or down the gamut of human forces, there runs one organic correlation and sympathy of parts. Man is one, however compound. Fire his conscience, and he blushes. Check his circulation, and he thinks wildly, or thinks not at all. Impair his secretions, and moral sense is dulled, discolored or depraved ; his aspirations flag, his hope, love, faith reel. Impair them still more, and he becomes a brute. A cup of drink degrades his moral nature below that of a swine. Again, a violent emotion of pity or horror makes him vomit. A lancet will restore him from delirium to clear thought. Excess of thought will waste his sinews. Excess of muscular exercise will deaden thought. An emotion will double the strength of his muscles. And at last the prick of a needle or a grain of mineral will in an instant lay to rest forever his body and its unity, and all the spontaneous activities of intelligence, feeling and action, with which that compound organism was charged.

These are the obvious and ancient observations about the human organism. But modern philosophy and science have carried these hints into complete explanations. By a vast accumulation of proof positive thought at last has established a distinct correspondence between every process of thought or of feeling and some corporeal phenomenon. Even when we cannot explain the precise relation, we can show that definite correlations exist. To positive methods, every fact of thinking reveals itself as having functional relation with molecular change. Every fact of will or of feeling is in similar relation with kindred molecular facts. And all these facts again have some relation to each other. Hence we have established an organic correspondence in all manifestations of human life. To think implies a corresponding adjustment of molecular activity. To feel emotion implies nervous organs of feeling. To will implies vital cerebral hemispheres. Observation, reflection, memory, imagination, judgment, have all been analysed out, till they stand forth as functions of living organs in given conditions of the organism, that is in a particular environment. The whole range of man's powers, from the finest spiritual sensibility down to a mere automatic contraction, falls into one coherent scheme : being all the multiform functions of a living organism in presence of its encircling conditions.

But complex as it is, there is no confusion in this whole when conceived by positive methods. No rational thinker now pretends that imagination *is* simply the vibration of a particular fibre. No man can *explain* volition by purely anatomical study. Whilst keeping in view the due relations between moral and corporeal facts, we distinguish moral from biologic facts, moral science from biology. Moral science is based upon biological science ; but it is not comprised in it : it has its own special facts and its own special methods, though always in the sphere of law. Just so, the mechanism of the body is based upon mechanics, would be unintelligible but for mechanics, but could not be explained by mechanics alone, or by anything but a complete anatomy and biology. To explain the activity of the intellect as included in the activity of the body, is as idle as to explain the activity of the body as included in the motion of solid bodies. And it is equally idle to explain the activity of the will, or the emotions, as included in the theory of the intellect. All the spheres of human life are logically separable, though they are organically interdependent. Now the combined activity of the human powers organized around the highest of them we call the Soul. The combination of intellectual and moral energy which is the source of Religion, we call the spiritual life. The explaining the spiritual side of life by physical instead of moral and spiritual reasoning, we call materialism.

The consensus of the human faculties, which we call the Soul, comprises all sides of human nature according to one homogeneous theory. But the intuitional methods ask us to insert into the midst of this harmonious system of parts, as an underlying explanation of it, an indescribable entity ; and to this hypothesis, since the days of Descartes (or possibly of Aquinas), the good old word Soul has been usually restricted.

How and when this entity ever got into the organism, how it abides in it, what are its relations to it, how it acts on it, why and when it goes out of it—all is mystery. We ask for some evidence of the existence of any such entity ; the answer is, we must imagine it in order to explain the organism. We ask what are its methods, its laws, its affinities ; we are told that it simply has none, or none knowable. We ask for some description of it, of its course of development, for some single fact about it, stateable in terms of the rest of our knowledge ; the reply is— mystery, absence of everything so stateable or cognizable, a line of poetry, or an ejaculation. It has no place, no matter, no modes, neither evolution nor decay ; it is without body, parts, or passions : a spiritual essence, incommensurable, incomparable, indescribable. Yet with all this, it is, we are told, an entity, the most real and perfect of all entities short of the divine.

If we ask why we are to assume the existence of something of which we have certainly no direct evidence, and which is so wrapped in mystery that for practical purposes it becomes a nonentity, we are told that we need to conceive it, because a mere organism cannot act as we see the human organism act. Why not ? They say there must be a *principle* within as the cause of this life. But what do we gain by supposing a 'principle?' The 'principle' only adds a fresh difficulty. Why should a 'principle,' or an entity, be more capable of possessing these marvellous human powers than the human organism ? Besides, we shall have to imagine a 'principle' to explain not only why a man can feel affection, but also why a dog can feel affection. If a mother cannot love her child—merely *qua* human organism—unless her love be a manifestation of an eternal soul, how can a cat love her kittens—merely *qua* feline organism—without an immaterial principle or soul ? Nay, we shall have to go on to invent a principle to account for a tree growing, or a thunderstorm roaring, and for every force of nature. Now this very supposition was made in a way by the Greeks, and to some extent by Aquinas, the authors of the vast substructure of *anima* underlying all nature, of which our human Soul is the fragment that alone survives. One by one the steps in this series of hypothesis have faded away. Greek and mediæval philosophy imagined that every activity resulted not from the body which exhibited the activity, but from some mysterious entity inside it. If marble was hard, it had a 'form' informing its hardness ; if a blade of grass sprang up, it had a vegetative spirit mysteriously impelling it ; if a dog obeyed his master, it had an animal spirit mysteriously controlling its organs. The mediæval physicists, as Molière reminds us, thought that opium induced sleep *quia est in eo virtus dormitiva.* Nothing was allowed to act as it did by its own force or vitality. In every explanation of science we were told to postulate an intercalary hypothesis. Of this huge mountain of figment, the notion of man's immaterial Soul is the one feeble residuum.

Orthodoxy has so long been accustomed to take itself for granted, that we are apt to forget how very short a period of human history this sublimated essence has been current. From Plato to Hegel the idea has been continually taking fresh shapes. There is not a trace of it in the Bible in its present sense, and nothing in the least akin to it in the Old Testament.

Till the time of Aquinas theories of a material soul, as a sort of gas, were never eliminated ; and until the time of Descartes, our present ideas of the antithesis of Soul and Body were never clearly defined. Thus the Bible, the Fathers, and the Mediæval Church, as was natural when philosophy was in a state of flux, all represented the Soul in very different ways ; and none of these ways were those of a modern divine. It is a curious instance of the power of words that the practical weight of the popular religion is now hung on a metaphysical hypothesis, which itself has been in vogue for only a few centuries in the history of speculation, and which is now become to those trained in positive habits of thought a mere juggle of ideas.

We have in all this sought only to state what we mean by man's soul, and what we do not mean. But we make no attempt to prove a negative, or to demonstrate the non-existence of the supposed entity. Our purpose now is a very different one. We start out from this—that this positive mode of treating man is in this, as in other things, morally sufficient ; that it leaves no voids and chasms in human life ; that the moral and religious sequelæ which are sometimes assigned to its teaching have no foundation in fact. We say, that on this basis, not only have we an entrance into the spiritual realm, but that we have a firmer hold on the spiritual life than on the basis of hypothesis. On this theory, the world beyond the grave is in closer and truer relation to conduct than on the spiritualist theory. We look on man as man, not as man plus a heterogenous entity. And we think that we lose nothing, but gain much thereby, in the religious as well as in the moral world. We do not deny the conceivable existence of the heterogeneous entity. But we believe that human nature is adequately equipped on human and natural grounds without this disparate nondescript.

Let us be careful to describe the method we employ as that which looks on man as man, and repudiate the various labels, such as materialist, physical, unspiritual methods, and the like, which are used as equivalent for the rational or positive method of treating man. The method of treating man as man insists, at least as much as any other method, that man has a moral, emotional, religious life, but perfectly co-ordinate with that physical life, and to be studied on similar scientific methods. The spiritual sympathies of man are undoubtedly the highest part of human nature ; and our method condemns as loudly as any system physical explanations of spiritual life. We claim the right to use the terms 'soul,' 'spiritual,' and the like, in their natural meaning. In the same way, we think that there are theories which are justly called 'Materialist,' that there are physical conceptions of human nature which are truly dangerous to morality, to goodness, and religion. It is sometimes thought to be a sufficient proof of the reality of this heterogenous entity of the soul, that otherwise we must assume the most spiritual emotions of man to be a secretion of cerebral matter, and that, whatever the difficulties of conceiving the union of Soul and Body, it is something less difficult than the conceiving that the nerves think, or the tissues love. We repudiate such language as much as any one can, but there is another alternative. It is possible to invest with the highest dignity the spiritual life of mankind by treating it as an ultimate fact, without trying to find an explanation for it either in a perfectly unthinkable hypothesis or in an irrational and debasing physicism.

We certainly do reject, as earnestly as any school can, that which is most fairly called Materialism, and we will second every word of those who cry out that civilization is in danger if the workings of the human spirit are to become questions of physiology, and if death is the end of a man, as it is the end of a sparrow. We not only assent to such protests, but we see very pressing need for making them. It is a corrupting doctrine to open a brain, and to tell us that devotion is a definite molecular change in this and that convolution of grey pulp, and that if man is the first of living animals, he passes away after a short space like the beasts that perish. And all doctrines, more or less, do tend to this, which offer physical theories as explaing moral phenomena, which deny man a spiritual in addition to a moral nature, which limit his moral life to the span of his bodily organism, and which have no place for ' religion' in the proper sense of the word.

It is true that in this age, or rather in this country, we seldom hear the stupid and brutal materialism which pretends that the subtleties of thought and emotion are simply this or that agitation in some grey matter, to be ultimately expounded by the professors of grey matter. But this is hardly the danger which besets our time. The true materialism to fear is the prevailing tendency of anatomical habits of mind or specialist habits of mind to intrude into the regions of religion and philosophy. A man whose whole thoughts are absorbed in cuttting up dead monkeys and live frogs has no more business to dogmatize about religion, than a mere chemist to improvise a zoology. Biological reasoning about spiritual things is as presumptious as the theories of an electrician about the organic facts of nervous life. We live amidst a constant and growing usurpation of science in the province of philosophy; of biology in the province of sociology; of physics in that of religion. Nothing is more common than the use of the term science, when what is meant is merely physical and physiological science, not social and moral science. The arrogant attempt to dispose of the deepest moral truths of human nature on a bare physical or physiological basis is almost enough to justify the insurrection of some impatient theologians against science itself. It is impossible not to sympathize with men who at least are defending the paramount claim of the moral laws and the religious sentiment. The solution of the dispute is of course that physicists and theologians have each hold of a partial truth. As the latter insist, the grand problems of man's life must be ever referred to moral and social argument; but then, as the physicists insist, this moral and social argument can only be built up on a physical and physiological foundation. The physical part of science is indeed merely the vestibule to social, and thence to moral science; and of science in all its forms the philosophy of religion alone holds the key. The true Materialism lies in the habit of scientific specialists to neglect all philosophical and religious synthesis. It is marked by the ignoring of religion, the passing by on the other side, and shutting the eyes to the spiritual history of mankind. The spiritual traditions of mankind, a supreme philosophy of life and thought, religion in the proper sense of the word, all these have to play a larger and ever larger part in human knowledge ; not as we are so often told, and so commonly is assumed, a waning and vanishing part. And it is in this field, the field which has so long been abandoned to theology, that Positivism is prepared to meet the theologians. We at any rate do not ask them to submit religion to the test of the scalpel or the electric battery. It is true that we base our theory of society and our theory of morals, and hence our religion itself, on a curriculum of physical, and especially of biological science. It is true that our moral and social science is but a prolongation of these other sciences. But then we insist that it is not science in the narrow sense which can order our beliefs, but Philosophy ; not science which can solve our problems of life, but Religion. And religion demands for its understanding the religious mind and the spiritual experience.

Does it seem to anyone a paradox to hold such language, and yet to have nothing to say about the immaterial entity which many assume to be the *cause* behind this spiritual life ? The answer is that we occupy ourselves with this spiritual life as an ultimate fact, and consistently with the whole of our philosophy, we decline to assign a *cause* at all. We argue, with the theologians, that it is ridiculous to go to the scalpel for an adequate account of a mother's love ; but we do not think it is explained (any more than it is by the scalpel) by a hypothesis for which not only is there no shadow of evidence, but which cannot even be stated in philosophic language. We find the same absurdity in the notion that maternal love is a branch of the anatomy of the *mammæ*, and in the notion that the phenomena of lactation are produced by an immaterial entity. Both are forms of the same fallacy, that of trying to reach ultimate causes instead of studying laws. We certainly do find that maternal love and lactation have close correspondences, and that both are phenomena of certain female organisms. And we say that to talk of maternal love being exhibited by an entity which not only is not a female organism, but is not an organism at all, is to use language which to us, at least, is unintelligible.

The philosophy which treats man as man simply affirms that *man* loves, thinks, acts, not that the ganglia, or the sinuses, or any organ of man, loves and thinks and acts. The thoughts, aspirations, and impulses are not secretions, and the science which teaches us about secretions will not teach us much about them ; our thoughts, aspirations, and impulses are faculties of a man. Now, as a man implies a body, so we say these also imply a body. And to talk to us about a bodyless being thinking and loving is simply to talk about the thoughts and feelings of Nothing.

This fundamental position each one determines according to the whole bias of his intellectual and moral nature. But on the positive, as on the the theological, method there is ample scope for the spiritual life, for moral responsibility, for the world beyond the grave, its hopes and its duties ; which remain to us perfectly real without the unintelligible hypothesis. However much men cling to the hypothesis from old association, if they reflect, they will find that they do not use it to give them any actual knowledge about man's spiritual life ; that all their methodical reasoning about the moral world is exclusively based on the phenomena of this world, and not on the phenomena of any other world. And thus the absence of the hypothesis altogether does not make the serious difference which theologians suppose.

To follow out this into particulars : Analysis of human nature shows us man with a great variety of faculties ; his moral powers are just as distinguishable as his intellectual powers ; and both are mentally separable from his physical powers. Moral and mental laws are reduced to something like system by moral and mental science, with or without the theological hypothesis. The most extreme form of materialism does not dispute that moral and mental science is for logical purposes something more than physical science. So, the most extreme form of spiritualism gets its mental and moral science by observation and argument from phenomena ; it does not, or it does not any longer, build such science by abstract deduction from any proposition as to an immaterial entity. There have been, in ages past, attempts to do this. Plato, for instance, attempted to found, not only his mental and moral philosophy, but his general philosophy of the universe, by deduction from a mere hypothesis. He imagined immaterial entities, the ideas, of things inorganic, as much as organic. But then Plato was consistent and had the courage of his opinions. If he imagined an idea, or soul, of a man, he imagined one also for a dog, for a tree, for a statue, for a chair. He thought that a statue or a chair were what they are, by virtue of an immaterial entity which gave them form. The hypothesis did not add much to the art of statuary or to that of the carpenter ; nor, to do him justice, did Plato look for much practical result in these spheres. One form of the doctrine alone survives,—that man is what he is by virtue of an immaterial entity temporarily indwelling in his body. But, though the hypothesis survives, it is in no sense any longer the basis of the science of human nature with any school. No school is now content to sit in its study and evolve its knowledge of the moral qualities of man out of abstract deductions from the conception of an immaterial entity. All without exception profess to get their knowledge of the moral qualities by observing the qualities which men actually do exhibit or have exhibited. And those who are persuaded that man has, over and above his man's nature, an immaterial entity, find themselves discussing the laws of thought and of character on a common ground with those who regard man as man—*i. e.*, who regard man's nature as capable of being referred to a homogenous system of law. Spiritualists and materialists, however much they may differ in their explanations of moral phenomena, describe their relations in the same language, the language of law, not of illuminism.

Those, therefore, who dispense with a transcendental explanation are just as free as those who maintain it, to handle the spiritual and religious phenomena of human nature, treating them simply as phenomena. No one has ever suggested that the former philosophy is not quite as well entitled to analyse the intellectual faculties of man as the stoutest believer in the immaterial entity. It would raise a smile now-a-days to hear it said that such a one must be incompetent to treat of the canons of inductive reasoning, because he was unorthodox as to the immortality of the Soul. And if, notwithstanding this unorthodoxy, he is thought competent to investigate the laws of thought, why not the moral laws, the sentiments, and the emotions ? As a fact, every moral faculty of man is recognized by him just as much as by any transcendentalist. He does not limit himself, any more than the theologian does, to mere morality. He is fully alive to the spiritual emotions in all their depth, purity, and beauty. He recognizes in man the yearning for a power outside his individual self which he may venerate, a love for the author of his chief good, the need for sympathy with something greater than himself. All these are positive facts which rest on observation, quite apart from any explanation of the hypothetical cause of these tendencies in man. There, at any rate, the scientific observer finds them ; and he is at liberty to give them quite as high a place in his scheme of human nature as the most complete theologian. He may possibly give them a far higher place, and bind them far more truly into the entire tissue of his whole view of life, because they are built up for him on precisely the same ground of experience as all the rest of his knowledge, and have no element at all heterogeneous from the rest of life. With the language of spiritual emotion he is perfectly in unison. The spirit of devotion, of spiritual communion with an ever-present power, of sympathy and fellowship with the living world, of awe and submission towards the material world, the sense of adoration, love, resignation, mystery, are at least as potent with the one system as with the other. He can share the religious emotion of every age, and can enter into the language of every truly religious heart. For myself, I believe that this is only done on a complete as well as a real basis in the religion of Humanity, but we need not confine the present argument to that ground. I venture to believe that this spirit is truly shared by all, whatever their hypothesis about the human soul, who treat these highest emotions of man's nature as facts of primary value, and who have any intelligible theory whereby these emotions can be aroused.

All positive methods of treating man of a comprehensive kind adopt to the full all that has ever been said about the dignity of man's moral and spiritual life, and treat these phenomena as distinct from the intellectual and the physical life. These methods also recognize the unity of consciousness, the facts of conscience, the sense of identity, and the longing for perpetuation of that identity. They decline to explain these phenomena by the popular hypotheses; but they neither deny their existence, nor lessen their importance. Man, they argue, has a complex existence, made up of the phenomena of his physical organs, of his intellectual powers, of his moral faculties, crowned and harmonized ultimately by his religious sympathies, —love, gratitude, veneration, submission, towards the dominant force by which he finds himself surrounded. I use words which are not limited to a particular philosophy or religion— I do not now confine my language to the philosophy or religion of Comte—for this same conception of man is common to many philosophies and many religions. It characterizes such systems as those of Spinosa or Shelley or Fichte as much as those of Confucius or Bouddha. In a word, the reality and the supremacy of the spiritual life have never been carried further than by men who have departed most widely from the popular hypotheses of the immaterial entity.

Many of these men, no doubt, have indulged in hypotheses of their own quite as arbitrary as those of theology. It is characteristic of the positive thought of our age that it stands upon a firmer basis. Though not confounding the moral facts with the physical, it will never lose sight of the correspondence and consensus between all sides of human life. Led by an enormous and complete array of evidences, it associates every fact of thought or of emotion with a fact of physiology, with molecular change in the body. Without pretending to explain the first by the second, it denies that the first can be explained without the second. But with this solid basis of reality to work on, it gives their place of supremacy to the highest sensibilities of man, through the heights and depths of the spiritual life.

Nothing is more idle than a discussion about words. But when some deny the use of the word 'soul' to those who mean by it this consensus, and not any immaterial entity, we may remind them that our use of the word agrees with its etymology and its history. It is the mode in which it is used in the Bible, the well spring of our true English speech. It may, indeed, be contended that there is no instance in the Bible in which Soul does mean an immaterial entity, the idea not having been familiar to any of the writers, with the doubtful exception of St. Paul. But without entering upon Biblical philology, it may be said that for one passage in the Bible in which the word 'soul' can be forced to bear the meaning of immaterial entity, there are ten texts in which it cannot possibly refer to anything but breath, life, moral sense, or spiritual emotion. When the Psalmist says, 'Deliver my soul from death,' 'Heal my soul, for I have sinned,' 'My soul is cast down within me,' 'Return unto my rest, O my soul,' he means by 'soul' what we mean,—the conscious unity of our being culminating in its religious emotions; and until we find some English word that better expresses this idea, we shall continue to use the phraseology of David.

It is not merely that we are denied the language of religion, but we sometimes find attempts to exclude us from the thing. There are some who say that worship, spiritual life, and that exaltation of the sentiments which we call devotion, have no possible meaning unless applied to the special theology of the particular speaker. A little attention to history, a single reflection on religion as a whole, suffice to show the hollowness of this assumption. If devotion mean the surrender of self to an adored Power, there has been devotion in creeds with many gods, with one God, with no gods; if spiritual life mean the cultivation of this temper towards moral purification, there was spiritual life long before the notion of an immaterial entity inside the human being was excogitated; and as to worship, men have worshipped, with intense and overwhelming passion, all kinds of objects, organic and inorganic, material and spiritual, abstract ideas as well as visible forces. Is it implied that Confucius, and the countless millions who have followed him, had no idea of religion, as it is certain that they had none of theology; that Bouddha and the Bouddhists were incapable of spiritual emotion; that the Fire-worshippers and the Sun-worshippers never practised worship; that the pantheists and the humanists, from Marcus Aurelius to Fichte, had the springs of spiritual life dried up in them for want of an Old or New Testament! If this is intended, one can only wonder at the power of a self-complacent conformity to close men's eyes to the native dignity of man. Religion, and its elements in emotion—attachment, veneration, love—are as old exactly as human nature. They moved the first men, and the first women. They have found a hundred objects to inspire them, and have bowed to a great variety of powers. They were in full force long before Theology was, and before the rise of Christianity ; and it would be strange indeed if they should cease with the decline of either. It is not the emotional elements of Religion which fail us. For these, with the growing goodness of mankind, are gaining in purity and strength. Rather, it is the intellectual elements of religion which are conspicuously at fault. We need to-day, not the faculty of worship (that is ever fresh in the heart), but a clearer vision of the power we should worship. Nay, it is not we who are borrowing the privileges of theology : rather it is theology which seeks to appropriate to itself the most universal privilege of man.

II.

The rational view of the Soul (we insisted in a previous paper) would remove us as far from a cynical materialism as from a fantastic spiritualism. It restores to their true supremacy in human life those religious emotions which materialism forgets ; whilst it frees us from the idle figment which spiritualism would foist upon human nature.

We entirely agree with the theologians that our age is beset with a grievous danger of materialism. There is a school of teachers abroad, and they have found an echo here, who dream that victorious vivisection will ultimately win them anatomical solutions of man's moral and spiritual mysteries. Such unholy nightmares, it is true, are not likely to beguile many minds in a country like this, where social and moral problems are still in their natural ascendant. But there is a subtler kind of materialism of which the dangers are real. It does not indeed put forth the bestial sophism, that the apex of philsosphy is to be won by improved microscopes and new batteries. But then it has nothing to say about the spiritual life of man ; it has no particular religion ; it ignores the Soul. It fills the air with pæans to science ; it is never weary of vaunting the scientific methods, the scientific triumphs. But it always means physical, not moral science ; intellectual, not religious conquests. It shirks the question of questions—to what human end is this knowledge—how shall man thereby order his life as a whole— where is he to find the object of his yearnings of spirit ? Of the spiritual history of mankind it knows as little, and thinks as little, as of any other sort of Asiatic devil-worship. At the spiritual aspirations of the men and women around us, ill at ease for want of some answer, it stares blankly, as it does at some spirit-rapping epidemic. "What is that to us ?—see thou to that"—is all that it can answer when men ask it for a religion. It is of the religion of all sensible men, the religion which all sensible men never tell. With a smile or shrug of the shoulders it passes by into the whirring workshops of science (that is, the physical prelude of science) ; and it leaves the spiritual life of the Soul to the spiritualists, theological or nonsensical as the case may be, wishing them both in heaven. This is the materialism to fear.

The theologians and the vast sober mass of serious men and

women who want simply to live rightly are quite right when they shun and fear a school that is so eager about cosmology and biology, whilst it leaves morality and religion to take care of themselves. And yet they know all the while that before the advancing line of positive thought they are fighting a forlorn hope ; and they see their own line daily more and more demoralised by the consciousness that they have no rational plan of campaign. They know that their own account of the Soul, of the spiritual life, of Providence, of Heaven, is daily shifting, is growing more vague, more inconsistent, more various. They hurry wildly from one untenable position to another, like a routed and disorganised army. In a religious discussion years ago we once asked one of the Broad Church, a disciple of one of its eminent founders, what he understood by the third Person of the Trinity ; and he said doubtfully "that he fancied there was a sort of a something." Since those days the process of disintegration and vaporisation of belief has gone on rapidly ; and now very religious minds, and men who think themselves to be religious, are ready to apply this "sort of a something" to all the verities in turn. They half hope that there is "a sort of a something" fluttering about, or inside, their human frames, that there may turn out to be a "something" somewhere after Death, and that there must be a sort of a somebody or (as the theology of Culture will have it) a sort of a something controlling and comprehending human life. But the more thoughtful spirits, not being professionally engaged in a doctrine, mostly limit themselves to a pious hope that there may be something in it, and that we shall know some day what it is.

Now theologians and religious people unattached must know that this will never serve—that this is paltering with the greatest of all things. What then is the only solution which can ultimately satisfy both the devotees of science and the believers in religion? Surely but this, to make religion scientific by placing religion under the methods of science. Let Science come to see that religion, morality, life, are within its field, or rather are the main part of its field. Let Religion come to see that it can be nothing but a prolongation of science, a rational and homogeneous result of cosmology and biology, not a matter of fantastic guessing. Then there will be no true science which does not aim at, and is not guided by, systematic religion. And there will be no religion which pretends to any other basis but positive knowledge and scientific logic. But for this science must consent to add spiritual phenomena to its curriculum, and religion must consent to give up its vapid figments.

Positivism in dealing with the Soul discards the exploded errors of the materialists and the spiritualists alike. On the one hand, it not only admits into its studies the spiritual life of men, but it raises this life to be the essential business of all human knowledge. All the spiritual sentiments of man, the aspirations of the conscious soul in all their purity and pathos, the vast religious experience and potentialities of the human heart seen in the history of our spiritual life as a race—this is, we say, the principal subject of science and of philosophy. No philosophy, no morality, no polity can rest on stable foundations if this be not its grand aim; if it have not a systematic creed, a rational object of worship, and a definite discipline of life. But then we treat these spiritual functions of the Soul, not as mystical enigmas, but as positive phenomena, and we satisfy them by philosophic and historic answers and not by naked figments. And we think that the teaching of history and a true synthesis of science bring us far closer to the heart of this spiritual life than do any spiritualist guesses, and do better to equip us to read aright the higher secrets of the Soul: meaning always by Soul the consensus of the faculties which observation discovers in the human organism.

. On the other hand, without entering into an idle dispute with the spiritualist orthodoxy, we insist on regarding this organism as a perfectly homogeneous unit, to be studied from one end of it to the other by rational scientific methods. We pretend to give no sort of *cause* as lying behind the manifold powers of the organism. We say the immaterial entity is something which we cannot grasp, which explains nothing, for which we cannot have a shadow of evidence. We are determined to treat man as a human organism, just as we treat a dog as a canine organism ; and we know no ground for saying, and no good to be got by pretending, that man is a human organism *plus* an indescribable entity. We say, the human organism is a marvellous thing, sublime if you will, of subtlest faculty and sensibility ; but we, at any rate, can find nothing in man which is not an organic part of this organism ; we find the faculties of mind, feeling, and will, directly dependent on physical organs ; and to talk to us of mind, feeling, and will continuing their functions in the absence of physical organs and visible organisms, is to use language which, to us at least, is pure nonsense.

And now to turn to the great phenomenon of material organisms which we call Death. The human organism, like every other organism, ultimately loses that unstable equilibrium of its correlated forces which we name Life, and ceases to be an organism or system of organs, adjusting its internal relations to its external conditions. Thereupon the existence of the complex independent entity to which we attribute consciousness, undoubtedly—*i.e.* for aught we know to the contrary—comes to an end. But the activities of this organism do not come to an end, except so far as these activities need fresh sensations and material organs. And a great part of these activities, and far the noblest part, only need fresh sensations and material organs in similar organisms. Whilst there is an abundance of these in due relation, the activities go on *ad infinitum* with increasing energy. We have not the slightest reason to suppose that the consciousness of the organism continues, for we mean by consciousness the sum of sensations of a particular organism, and the particular organism being dissolved, we have nothing left whereto to attribute consciousness, and the proposal strikes us like a proposal to regard infinity as conscious. So, of course, with the sensations separately, and with them the power of accumulating knowledge, of feeling, thinking, or of modifying the existence in correspondence with the outward environment. Life, in the technical sense of the word, is at an end, but the activities of which that life is the source were never so potent. Our age is familiar enough with the truth of the persistence of energy, and no one supposes that with the dissolution of the body the forces of its material elements are lost. They only pass into new combinations and continue to work elsewhere. Far less is the energy of the activities lost. The earth, and every country, every farmstead, and every city on it, are standing witnesses that the physical activities are not lost. As century rolls after century, we see every age 'more potent fruits of the labor which raised the Pyramids, or won Holland from the sea, or carved the Theseus out of marble. The bodily organisms which wrought them have passed into gases and earths, but the activity they displayed is producing the precise results designed on a far grander scale in each generation. Much more do the intellectual and moral energies work unceasingly. Not a single manifestation of thought or feeling is without some result so soon as it is communicated to a similar organism. It passes into the sum of his mental and moral being.

But there is about the persistence of the moral energies this special phenomenon. It marks the vast interval between physical and moral science. The energies of material elements, so far as we see, disperse, or for the most part disperse. The energies of an intellectual and moral kind are very largely continued in their organic unities. The consensus of the mental, of the moral, of the emotional powers may go on, working as a whole, producing precisely the same results, with the same individuality, whether the material organism, the source and original base of these powers, be in physical function or not The mental and moral powers do not, it is true, increase and grow, develope and vary within themselves. Nor do they in their special individuality produce visible results, for they are no longer in direct relations with their special material organisms. But the mental and moral powers are not dispersed like gases. They retain their unity, they retain their organic character, and they retain the whole of their power of passing into and stimulating the brains of living men; and in these they carry on their activity precisely as they did, whilst the bodies in which they were formed absorbed and exhaled material substance.

Nay, more; the individuality and true activity of these mental and moral forces is often not manifest, and sometimes is not complete, so long as the organism continues its physical functions. Newton, we may suppose, has accomplished his great researches. They are destined to transform half the philosophy of mankind. But he is old, and incapable of fresh achievements. We will say he is feeble, secluded, silent, and lives shut up in his rooms. The activity of his mighty intellectual nature is being borne over the world on the wings of Thought, and works a revolution at every stroke. But otherwise the man Newton is not essentially distinguishable from the nearest infirm pauper, and has as few and as feeble relations with mankind. At last the man Newton dies—that is, the body is dispersed into gas and dust. But the world, which is affected enormously by his intellect, is not in the smallest degree affected by his death. His activity continues the same; if it were worth while to conceal the fact of his death, no one of the millions who are so greatly affected by his thoughts would perceive it or know it. If he had discovered some means of prolonging a torpid existence till this hour, he might be living now, and it would not signify to us in the slightest degree whether his body breathed in the walls of his lodging or mouldered in the vaults of the Abbey.

It may be said that if it does not signify much to us, it signifies a great deal to Isaac Newton. But is this true? He no
longer eats and sleeps, a burden to himself ; he no longer is
destroying his great name by feeble theology and querulous
pettiness. But if the small weaknesses and wants of the flesh
are ended for him, all that makes Newton (and he had always
lived for his posthumous, not his immediate fame) rises into
greater activity and purer uses. We make no mystical or
fanciful divinity of Death ; we do not deny its terrors or its
evils. We are not responsible for it, and should welcome any
reasonable prospect of eliminating or postponing this fatality,
that waits upon all organic nature. But it is no answer to philosophy or science to retort that Death is so terrible, therefore
man must be designed to escape it. There are savages who
persistently deny that men do die at all, either their bodies or
their souls, asserting that the visible consequences of death are
either an illusion or an artfully contrived piece of acting on
the part of their friends, who have really decamped to the
happy hunting-fields. This seems on the whole a more rational
theory than that of immaterial souls flying about space, as the
spontaneous fancies of savages are sometimes more rational
than the elaborate hypotheses of metaphysics.

But though we do not presume to apologise for death, it is
easy to see that many of the greatest moral and intellectual results of life are only possible, can only begin, when the claims
of the animal life are satisfied ; when the stormy, complex, and
chequered career is over, and the higher tops of the intellectual
or moral nature alone stand forth in the distance of time.
What was the blind old harper of Scio to his contemporaries,

or the querulous refugee from Florence, or even the boon-companion and retired playright of Stratford, or the blind and stern old malignant of Bunhill Fields? The true work of Socrates and his life only began with his resplendent death, to say nothing of yet greater religious teachers, whose names I refrain from citing; and as to those whose lives have been cast in conflicts—the Cæsars, the Alfreds, the Hildebrands, the Cromwells, the Fredericks—it is only after death, oftenest in ages after death, that they cease to be combatants, and become creators. It is not merely that they are only recognised in after-ages; the truth is, that their activity only begins when the surging of passion and sense ends, and turmoil dies away. Great intellects and great characters are necessarily in advance of their age; the care of the father and the mother begins to tell most truly in the ripe manhood of their children, when the parents are often in the grave, and not in the infancy which they see and are confronted with. The great must always feel with Kepler,—' It is enough as yet if I have a hearer now and then in a century.' John Brown's body lies a-mouldering in the grave, but his soul is marching along.

We can trace this truth best in the case of great men; but it is not confined to the great. Not a single act of thought or character ends with itself. Nay, more; not a single nature in its entirety but leaves its influence for good or for evil. As a fact the good prevail; but all act, all continue to act indefinitely, often in ever-widening circles. Physicists amuse us by tracing for us the infinite fortunes of some wave set in motion by force, its circles and its repercussions perpetually transmitted in new complications. But the career of a single intellect and character is a far more real force when it meets with suitable intellects and characters into whose action it is incorporated. Every life more or less forms another life, and lives in another life. Civilization, nation, city, imply this fact. There is neither mysticism nor hyperbole, but simple observation in the belief, that the career of every human being in society does not end with the death of its body. In some sort its higher activities and potency can only begin truly when change is no longer possible for it. The worthy gain in influence and in range at each generation, just as the founders of some populous race gain a greater fatherhood at each succeed- . ing growth of their descendants. And in some infinitesimal degree, the humblest life that ever turned a sod sends a wave— no, more than a wave, a life—through the ever-growing harmony of human society. Not a soldier died at Marathon or Salamis, but did a stroke by which our thought is enlarged and our standard of duty formed to this day.

Be it remembered that this is not hypothesis, but something perfectly real,—we may fairly say undeniable. We are not inventing an imaginary world, and saying it must be real because it is so pleasant to think of ; we are only repeating truths on which our notion of history and society is based. The idea, no doubt, is usually limited to the famous, and to the great revolutions in civilization. But no one who thinks it out carefully can deny that it is true of every human being in society in some lesser degree. The idea has not been, or is no longer, systematically enforced, invested with poetry and dignity, and deepened by the solemnity of religion. But why is that ? Because theological hypotheses of a new and heterogenous existence have deadened our interest in the realities, the grandeur, and the perpetuity of our earthly life. In the best days of Rome, even without a theory of history or a science of society, it was a living faith, the true religion of that majestic race. It is the real sentiment of all societies where the theological hypothesis has disappeared. It is no doubt now in England the great motive of virtue and energy. There have been few seasons in the worlds history when the sense of moral responsibility and moral survival after death was more exalted and more vigorous than with the companions of Vergniaud and Danton, to whom the dreams of theology were hardly intelligible. As we read the calm and humane words of Condorcet on the very edge of his yawning grave, we learn how the conviction of posthumous activity (not of posthumous fame), how the consciousness of a coming incorporation with the glorious future of his race, can give a patience and a happiness equal to that of any martyr of theology.

It would be an endless inquiry to trace the means whereby this sense of posthumous participation in the life of our fellows can be extended to the mass, as it certainly affects already the thoughtful and the refined. Without an education, a new social opinion, without a religion—I mean an organized religion, not a vague metaphysic—it is doubtless impossible that it should become universal and capable of overcoming selfishness. But make it at once the basis of philosophy, the standard of right and wrong, and the centre of a religion, and this will prove, perhaps, an easier task than that of teaching Greeks and Romans, Syrians and Moors, to look forward to a future life of ceaseless psalmody in an immaterial heaven. The astonishing feat was performed; and, perhaps, it may be easier to fashion a new public opinion, requiring merely that an accepted truth of philosophy should be popularized, which is already the deepest hope of some thoughtful spirits, and which does not take the suicidal course of trying to cast out the devil of selfishness by a direct appeal to the personal self.

It is here that the strength of the human future over the celestial future is so clearly pre-eminent. Make the future hope a social activity, and we give to the present life a social ideal. Make the future hope personal beatitude, and personality is stamped deeper on every act of our daily life. Now we make the future hope, in the truest sense, social, inasmuch as our future is simply an active existence prolonged by society. And our future hope rests not in any vague yearning, of which we have as little evidence as we have definite conception: it rests on a perfectly certain truth, accepted by all thoughtful minds, the truth that the actions, feelings, thoughts of every one of us—our minds, our characters, our *souls* as organic wholes—do marvellously influence and mould each other; that the highest part of ourselves, the abiding part of us, passes into other lives and continues to live in other lives. Can we conceive a more potent stimulus to rectitude, to daily and hourly striving after a true life, and this ever-present sense that we are indeed immortal; not that we have an immortal something within us, but that in very truth we ourselves, our thinking, feeling, acting personalities, are immortal; nay, cannot die, but must ever continue what we make them, working and doing, if no longer receiving and enjoying? And not merely we ourselves, in our personal identity, are immortal, but each act, thought, and feeling is immortal ; and this immortality is not some ecstatic and indescribable condition in space, but activity on earth in the real and known work of life, in the welfare of those whom we have loved, and in the happiness of those who come after us.

And can it be difficult to idealize and give currency to a faith, which is a certain and undisputed fact of common sense as well as of philosopy ? As we *live for others* in life, so we *live in others* after death, as others have lived in us, and all for the common race. How deeply does such a belief as this bring home to each moment of life the mysterious perpetuity of ourselves ! For good, for evil, we cannot die ; we cannot shake ourselves free from this eternity of our faculties. There is here no promise, it is true, of eternal sensations, enjoyments, meditations. There is no promise, be it plainly said, of anything but an immortality of influence, of spiritual work, of glorified activity. We cannot even say that we shall continue to love ; but we know that we shall be loved. It may well be that we shall consciously know no hope ourselves ; but we shall inspire hopes. It may be that we shall not think ; but others will think our thoughts, and enshrine our minds. If no sympathies shall thrill along our nerves, we shall be the spring of sympathy in distant generations ; and that, though we be the humblest, and the least of all the soldiers in the human host, the least celebrated and the worst remembered. For our lives live when we are most forgotten ; and not a cup of water that we may have given to an unknown sufferer, or a wise word spoken in season to a child, but has added (whether we remember it, whether others remember it or not) a streak of happiness and strength to the world. Our earthly frames, like the grain of wheat, may be laid in the earth—and this image of our great spiritual Master is more fit for the social than the celestial future—but the grain shall bear spiritual fruit, and multiply in kindred natures and in other selves.

It is a merely verbal question if this be the life of the Soul when the Soul means the sum of the activities, or if there be any immortality where there is no consciousness. It is enough for us that we can trust to a real prolongation of our highest activity in the sensible lives of others, even though our own forces can gain nothing new, and are not reflected in a sensitive body. We do not get rid of Death, but we transfigure Death. Does any religion profess to do more? It is enough for any creed that it can teach *non omnis moriar*; it would be gross extravagance to say *omnis non moriar*, no part of me shall die. Death is the one inevitable law of Life. The business of religion is to show us what are its compensations. The spiritualist orthodoxy, like every other creed, is willing to allow that death robs us of a great deal, that very much of us does die; nay, it teaches that this dies utterly, forever, leaving no trace but dust. And thus the spiritualist orthodoxy exaggerates death, and adds a fresh terror to its power. We, on the contrary, would seek to show that much of us, and that the best of us, does not die, or at least does not end. And the difference between our faith and that of the orthodox is this: we look to the permanence of the activities which give others happiness; they look to the permanence of the consciousness which can enjoy happiness. Which is the nobler?

What need we then to promise or to hope more than an eternity of spiritual influence ? Yet, after all, 'tis no question as to what kind of eternity man would prefer to select. We have no evidence that he has any choice before him. If we were creating a universe of our own and a human race on an ideal mould, it might be rational to discuss what kind of eternity was the most desirable, and it might then become a question if we should not begin by eliminating death. But as we are, with death in the world, and man as we know him submitting to the fatality of his nature, the rational inquiry is this—how best to order his life, and to use the eternity that he has. And an immortality of prolonged activity on earth he has as certainly as he has civilization, or progress, or society. And the wise man in the evening of life may be well content to say : ' I have worked and thought, and have been conscious in the flesh ; I have done with the flesh, and therewith with the toil of thought and the troubles of sensation ; I am ready to pass into the spiritual community of human souls, and when this man's flesh wastes away from me, may I be found worthy to become part of the influence of humanity itself, and so

> Join the choir invisible
> Whose music is the gladness of the world.'

That the doctrine of the celestial future appeals to the essence of self appears very strongly in its special rebuke to the doctrine of the social future. It repeats, ' We agree with all you say about the prolonged activity of man after death, we see of course that the solid achievements of life are carried on, and we grant you that it signifies nothing to those who profit by his work that the man no longer breathes in the flesh : but what is all that to the *man,* to you, and to me ? we shall not *feel* our work, we shall not have the indescribable satisfaction which our souls now have in living, in effecting our work, and profiting by others. What is the good of mankind to me, when I am mouldering unconscious ?' This is the true materialism ; here is the physical theory of another life ; this is the unspiritual denial of the soul, the binding it down to the clay of the body. We say, ' All that is great in you shall not end, but carry on its activity perpetually and in a purer way ;' and you reply, ' What care I for what is great in me, and its possible work in this vale of tears : I want to feel life ; I want to enjoy, I want my personality,'—in other words, ' I want my senses, I want my body.' Keep your body and keep your senses in any way that you know. We can only wonder and say, with Frederic to his runaway soldiers, ' Wollt ihr immer leben ?' But we, who know that a higher form of activity is only to be reached by a subjective life in society, will continue to regard a perpetuity of sensation as the true Hell, for we feel that the perpetual worth of our lives is the one thing precious to care for, and not a vacuous eternity of consciousness.

It is not merely that this eternity of the tabor is so gross, so sensual, so indolent, so selfish a creed ; but its worst evil is that it paralyses practical life, and throws it into discord. A life of vanity in a vale of tears to be followed by an infinity of celestial rapture, is necessarily a life which is of infinitesimal importance. The incongruity of the attempts to connect the two, and to make the vale of tears the ante-chamber or the judgment-dock of heaven, grows greater and not less as ages roll on. The more we think and learn, and the higher rises our social philosophy and our insight into human destiny, the more the reality and importance of the social future impresses us, whilst the fancy of the celestial future grows unreal and incongruous. As we get to know what thinking means, and feeling means, and the more truly we understand what life means, the more completely do the promises of the celestial transcendentalism fail to interest us. We have come to see that to continue to live is to carry on a series of correlated sensations, and to set in motion a series of corresponding forces; to think is to marshal a set of observed perceptions with a view to certain observed phenomena; to feel implies something of which we have a real assurance affecting our own consensus within. The whole set of positive thoughts compels us to believe that it is an infinite apathy to which your heaven would consign us, without objects, without relations, without change, without growth, without action, an absolute nothingness, *nirvána* of impotence,—this is not life; it is not consciousness; it is not happiness. So far as we can grasp the hypothesis, it seems equally ludicrous and repulsive. You may call it paradise; but we call it conscious annihilation. You may long for it, if you have been so taught; just as if you had been taught to cherish such hopes, you might be now yearning for the moment when you might become the immaterial principle of a comet, or as you might tell me, that you really were the ether, and were about to take your place in Space. This is how these sublimities affect us. But we know that to many this future is one of spiritual development, a life of growth and continual upsoaring of still higher affection.

It may be so; but to our mind these are contradictions in terms. We cannot understand what life and affection can mean, where you postulate the absence of every condition by which life and affection are possible. Can there be development where there is no law, thought or affection, where object and subject are confused into one essence? How can that be existence, where everything of which we have experience, and everything which we can define, is presumed to be unable to enter? To us these things are all incoherences; and in the midst of practical realities and the solid duties of life, sheer impertinences. The field is full : each human life has a perfectly real and a vast future to look forward to ; these hyperbolic enigmas disturb our grave duties and our solid hopes. No wonder, then, whilst they are still so rife, that men are dull to the moral responsibility which, in its awfulness, begins only at the grave ; that they are so little influenced by the futurity which will judge them ; that they are blind to the dignity and beauty of death, and shuffle off the dead life and the dead body with such cruel disrespect. The fumes of the celestial immortality still confuse them. It is only when an earthly future is the fulfillment of a worthy earthly life, that we can see all the majesty as well as the glory of the world beyond the grave ; and then only will it fulfill its moral and religious purpose as the great guide of human conduct.

A MODERN "SYMPOSIUM."[1]

THE SOUL AND FUTURE LIFE.

MR. R. H. HUTTON.

. The imaginative glow and rhetorical vivacity which are
visible throughout Mr. Harrison's Essays on "The Soul and
Future Life"[2] are very remarkable, and should guard those of
us who recoil in amazement from its creed or no-creed from
falling into the very common mistake of assuming that the
effect which such ideas as these produce on ourselves is *the*
effect which, apart from all question of the other mental conditions surrounding the natures into which they are received
they naturally produce. It is clear at least that if they ever
tended to produce on the author of these papers the same effect which they not only tend to produce, but do produce, on
myself, that tendency must have been so completely neutral-
ized by the redundant moral energy inherent in his nature, that
the characteristic effect which I should have ascribed to them

[1] THE NINETEENTH CENTURY, September and October, 1877.
[2] P. 1.

is absolutely unverifiable, and, for anything we have the right to assert, non-existent. There is at least but one instance in which I should have traced any shade of what I may call the natural view of death as presented in the light of this creed, and that is the sentence in which Mr. Harrison somewhat superfluously disclaims—and moreover with an accent of hauteur, as though he resented the necessity of admitting that death is a disagreeable certainty—his own or his creed's responsibility for the fact of death. "We make no mystical or fanciful divinity of death," he says; "we do not deny its terrors or its evils. We are not responsible for it, and should welcome any reasonable prospect of eliminating or postponing this fatality that waits upon all organic nature." After reading that admission, I was puzzled when I came to the assertion that "we who know that a higher form of activity is only to be reached by a subjective life in society will continue to regard a perpetuity of sensation as the true Hell,"[1] a sentence in which Mr. Harrison would commonly be understood to mean that he and all his friends, if they had a vote in the matter, would give a unanimous suffrage against this "perpetuity of sensation," and, so far from trying to eliminate or postpone death, would be inclined to cling to and even hasten it. For, in this place at least, it is not the perpetuation of deteriorated energies of which Mr. Harrison speaks, but the perpetuation of life pure and simple. Indeed, nothing puzzles me more in this paper than the diametrical contradictions both of feeling and thought which appear to me to be embodied in it. Its main criticism on the common view of

---

[1] P. 40.

immortality seems to be that the desire for it is a grossly selfish desire. Nay, nicknaming the conception of a future of eternal praise, " the eternity of the tabor," he calls it a conception
" so gross, so sensual, so indolent, so selfish," as to be worthy
of nothing but scorn. I think he can never have taken the
trouble to realize with any care what he is talking of. Whatever
the conception embodied in what Mr. Harrison calls "ceaseless
psalmody" may be—and certainly it is not my idea of immortal life—it is the very opposite of selfish. No conception
of life can be selfish of which the very essence is adoration,
that is, wonder, veneration, gratitude to another. And gross
as the conception necessarily suggested by psalm-singing is,
to those who interpret it, as we generally do, by the stentorian
shoutings of congregations who are often thinking a great
deal more of their own performances than of the object of
their praise, it is the commonest candor to admit that this
conception of immortality owes its origin entirely to men
who were thinking of a life absorbed in the interior contemplation of a God full of all perfections—a contemplation
breaking out into thanksgiving only in the intensity of their
love and adoration. Whatever else this conception of immortality may be, the very last phrase which can be justly applied to it is "gross" or "selfish." I fear that the Positivists have left the Christian objects of their criticism so far
behind that they have ceased not merely to realise what Christians mean, but have sincerely and completely forgotten that
Christians ever had a meaning at all. That Positivists should
regard any belief in the "beatific vision" as a wild piece of
fanaticism, I can understand, but that, entering into the mean-

ing of that fanaticism, they should describe the desire for it as a gross piece of selfishness, I cannot understand ; and I think it more reasonable, therefore, to assume that they have simply lost the key to the language of adoration.   Moreover, when I come to note Mr. Harrison's own conception of the future life, it appears to me that it differs only from the Christian's conception by its infinite deficiencies, and in no respect by superior moral qualities of any kind.   That conception is, in a word, posthumous energy.   He holds that if we could get rid of the vulgar notion of a survival of personal sensations and of growing mental and moral faculties after death, we should consecrate the notion of posthumous activity, and anticipate with delight our " coming incorporation with the glorious future of our race," as we cannot possibly consecrate those great hopes now.

But, in the first place, what is this " glorious future of our race " which I am invited to contemplate ?   It is the life in a better organized society of a vast number of these merely temporary creatures whose personal sensations, if they ever could be "perpetuated," Mr. Harrison regards as giving us the best conception of a " true hell."   Now if an improved and better organized future of ephemerals be so glorious to anticipate, what elements of glory are there in it which would not belong to the immortality looked forward to by the Christian—a far more improved future of endlessly growing natures ?   Is it the mere fact that I shall myself belong to the one future which renders it unworthy, while the absence of any " perpetuity " of my personal " sensations " from the other, renders it unselfish ?   I always supposed selfishness to consist, *not* in the desire for any noble kind of life in which I might share, but in the preference for my own happiness at the *expense* of some one else's. If it is selfish to desire the perpetuation of a growing life, which not only does not, as far as I know, interfere with the volume of moral growth in others, but certainly contributes to it, then it must be the true unselfishness to commit suicide at once, supposing suicide to be the *finis* to personal "sensation." But then universal suicide would be inconsistent with the glorious future of our race, so I suppose it must at least be postponed till our own sensations have been so far " perpetuated " as to leave heirs behind them. If Condorcet is to be held up to our admiration for anticipating on the edge of the grave his " coming incorporation with the glorious future of his race," *i.e.* with ourselves and our posterity, may we not infer that there is something in ourselves, *i.e.* in human society as it now exists, which was worthy of his vision—something in which we need not think it " selfish " to participate, even though our personal " sensations " do form a part of it ? Where then does the selfishness of desiring to share in a glorious future even through personal "sensations," begin ? The only reasonable or even intelligible answer, as far as I can see, is this ;—as soon as that personal " sensation " for ourselves excludes a larger and wider growth for others, but no sooner. But then no Christian ever supposed for a moment that his personal immortality could or would interfere with any other being's growth. And if so, where is the selfishness ? What a Christian desires is a higher, truer, deeper union with God for all, himself included. If his own life drop out of that future, he supposes that there will be so much less that really does glorify the true righteousness, and no compensating equivalent. If it be Mr. Harrison's mission to disclose to us that any perpetuity of sensation on our own parts will positively exclude something much higher which *would* exist if we consented to disappear, he may, I think, prove his case. But in the absence of any attempt to do so, his conception that it is noble and unselfish to be more than content—grateful—for ceasing to live any but a posthumous life, seems to me simply irrational.

But, further, the equivalent which Mr. Harrison offers me for becoming, as I had hoped to become, in another world, an altogether better member of a better society, does not seem to me more than a very doubtful good. My posthumous activity will be of all kinds, some of which I am glad to anticipate, most of which I am very sorry to anticipate, and much of which I anticipate with absolute indifference. Even our best actions have bad effects as well as good. Macaulay and most other historians held that the Puritan earnestness expended a good deal of posthumous activity in producing the license of the world of the Restoration. Our activity, indeed, is strictly posthumous in kind, even before our death, from the very moment in which it leaves our living mind and has begun to work beyond ourselves. What I did as a child is, in this sense, as much producing posthumous effects, *i.e.* effects over which I can no longer exert any control, now, as what I do before death will be producing posthumous effects after my death. Now a considerable proportion of these posthumous activities of ours, even when we can justify the original activity as all that it ought to have been, are unfortunate. Mr. Harrison's papers, for instance, have already exerted a very vivid and very repulsive effect on my mind—an activity which I am sure he will not look upon with gratification, and I do not doubt that what I am now writing will produce the same effect on him, and in that effect I shall take no delight at all. A certain proportion, therefore, of my posthumous activity is activity for evil, even when the activity itself is on the whole good. But when we come to throw in the posthumous activity for evil exerted by our evil actions and the occasional posthumous activity for good which evil also fortunately exerts, but for the good results of which we can take no credit to ourselves, the whole constitutes a *mélange* to which, as far as I am concerned, I look with exceedingly mixed feelings, the chief element being humiliation, though there are faint lights mingled with it here and there. But as for any rapture of satisfaction in contemplating my "coming incorporation with the glorious future of our race," I must wholly and entirely disclaim it. What I see in that incorporation of mine with the future of our race—glorious or the reverse, and I do not quite see why the Positivist thinks it so glorious, since he probably holds that an absolute term must be put to it, if by no other cause, by the gradual cooling of the sun—is a very patchwork sort of affair indeed, a mere miscellany of bad, good, and indifferent without organization and without unity. What I shall be, for instance, when incorporated, in Mr. Harrison's phrase, with the future of our race, I have very little satisfaction in contemplating, except so far, perhaps, as my "posthumous activity" may retard the acceptance of Mr. Harrison's glorious anticipations for the human race. One great reason for my personal wish for a perpetuity of volition and personal energy is, that I may have a better opportunity, as far as may lie in me, to undo the mischief I shall have done before death comes to my aid. The vision of " posthumous activity" ought indeed, I fancy, to give even the best of us very little satisfaction. It may not be, and perhaps is not, so mischievous as the vision of "posthumous fame," but yet it is not the kind of vision which, to my mind, can properly occupy very much of our attention in this life. Surely the right thing for us to do is to concentrate attention on the life of the living moment—to make that the best we can—and then to leave its posthumous effects, after the life of the present has gone out of it, to that Power which, far more than anything in it, transmutes at times even our evil into good, though sometimes, too, to superficial appearance at all events, even our good into evil. The desire for an immortal life—that is, for a perpetuation of the personal affections and of the will—seems to me a far nobler thing than any sort of anticipation as to our posthumous activity ; for high affections and a right will are good in *themselves*, and constitute, indeed, the only elements in Mr. Harrison's "glorious future of our race " to which I can attach much value—while posthumous activity may be either good or evil, and depends on conditions over which he who first puts the activity in motion, often has no adequate control.

And this reminds me of a phrase in Mr. Harrison's paper which I have studied over and over again without making out his meaning. I mean his statement that on his own hypothesis " there is ample scope for the spiritual life, for moral responsibility, for the world beyond the grave, *its hopes and its duties,* which remain to us perfectly real without the unintelligible hypothesis." Now I suppose, by "the hopes" of "the world beyond the grave," Mr. Harrison means the hopes we form *for* the "future of our race," and that I understand. But what does he mean by its "duties?" Not, surely, our duties beyond the grave, but the duties of those who survive us; for he expressly tells us that our mental and moral powers do not increase and grow, develope or vary within themselves—do not, in fact, survive at all except in their effects—and hence duties for *us* in the world beyond the grave are, I suppose, in his creed impossible. But if he only means that there will be duties for those who survive us after we are gone, I cannot see how that is in any respect a theme on which it is either profitable or consolatory for us to dwell by anticipation. One remark more : when Mr. Harrison says[1] that it is quite as easy to learn to long for the moment when you shall become " the immaterial principle of a comet," or that you " really were the ether, and were about to take your place in space," as to long for personal immortality—he is merely talking at random on a subject on which it is hardly seemly to talk at random. He knows that what we mean by the soul is that which lies at the bottom of the sense of personal identity—the thread of the continuity running through all our chequered life ; and how it can be equally unmeaning to believe that this hitherto unbroken continuity will continue unbroken, and to believe that it is to be transformed into something else of a totally different kind, I am not only unable to understand, but even to understand how he could

[1] P. 41

seriously so conceive us.   My notion of myself never had the least connection with the principle of any part of any comet, but it has the closest possible connection with thoughts, affections, and volitions, which, as far as I know, are not likely to perish with my body.   I am sorry that Mr. Harrison should have disfigured his paper by sarcasms so inapplicable and apparently so bitter as these.

PROFESSOR HUXLEY.

Mr. Harrison's striking discourse on the soul and future life has a certain resemblance to the famous essay on the snakes of Ireland.   For its purport is to show that there is no soul, nor any future life in the ordinary sense of the terms. With death, the personal activity of which the soul is the popular hypostasis is put into commission among posterity, and the future life is an immortality by deputy.

Neither in these views, nor in the arguments by which they are supported, is there much novelty.   But that which appears both novel and interesting to me is the author's evidently sincere and hearfelt conviction that his powerful advocacy of soulless spirituality and mortal immortality is consistent with the intellectual scorn and moral reprobation which he freely pours forth upon the " irrational and debasing physicism " of materialism and materialists, and with the wrath with which he visits what he is pleased to call the intrusion of physical science, especially of biology, into the domain of social phenomena.

Listen to the storm :—

We certainly do reject, as earnestly as any school can, that which is most fairly called Materialism, and we will second every word of those who cry out that civilization is in danger if the workings of the human spirit are to become questions of physiology, and if death is the end of a man as it is the end of a sparrow. We not only assent to such protests, but we see very pressing need for making them. It is a corrupting doctrine to open a brain, and to tell us that devotion is a definite molecular change in this and that convolution of grey pulp, and that if man is the first of living animals, he passes away after a short space like the beasts that perish. And all doctrines, more or less, do tend to this, which offer physical theories as explaining moral phenomena, which deny man a spiritual in addition to a moral nature, which limit his moral life to the span of his bodily organism, and which have no place for "religion" in the proper sense of the words.[1]

Now Mr. Harrison can hardly think it worth while to attack imaginary opponents, so that I am led to believe that there must be somebody who holds the "corrupting doctrine" "that devotion is a definite molecular change in this and that convolution of grey pulp." Nevertheless, my conviction is shaken by a passage which occurs at p. 8: "No rational thinker now pretends that imagination *is* simply the vibration of a particular fibre." If no rational thinker pretends this of imagination, why should any pretend it of devotion? And yet I cannot bring myself to think that all Mr. Harrison's passionate rhetoric is hurled at irrational thinkers : surely he might leave such to the soft influences of time and due medical treatment of their "grey pulp" in Colney Hatch or elsewhere.

On the other hand, Mr. Harrison cannot possibly be attacking those who hold that the feeling of devotion is the con-

<hr>

[1] P. 14.

comitant, or even the consequent, of a molecular change in the brain; for he tells us, in language the explicitness of which leaves nothing to be desired, that

To positive methods, every fact of thinking reveals itself as having functional relation with molecular change. Every fact of will or of feeling is in similar relation with kindred molecular facts.

On mature consideration I feel shut up to one of two alternative hypotheses. ˙ Either the " corrupting doctrine " to which Mr. Harrison refers is held by no rational thinker—in which case, surely neither he nor I need trouble ourselves about it— or the phrase, " Devotion *is* a definite molecular change in this and that convolution of grey pulp," means that devotion has a functional relation with such molecular change ; in which case, it is Mr. Harrison's own view, and therefore, let us hope, cannot be a " corrupting doctrine."

I am not helped out of the difficulty I have thus candidly stated, when I try to get at the meaning of another hard saying of Mr. Harrison's, which follows after the " corrupting doctrine " paragraph : " And all doctrines, more or less, do tend to this [corrupting doctrine], which offer physical theories as explaining moral phenomena."

Nevertheless, on pp. 7 and 8, Mr. Harrison says with great force and tolerable accuracy :

Man is one, however compound. Fire his conscience, and he blushes. Check his circulation, and he thinks wildly, or thinks not at all. Impair his secretions, and moral sense is dulled, discoloured, or depraved ; his aspirations flag, his hope, love, faith reel. Impair them still more, and he becomes a brute. A cup of drink degrades his moral nature below that of a swine. Again, a violent emotion of pity or horror makes him vomit. A lancet will restore him from delirium to clear thought. Excess of thought will waste his sinews. Excess of muscular exercise will deaden thought. An emotion will double the strength of his muscles. And at last the prick of a needle or a grain of mineral will in an instant lay to rest for ever his body and its unity, and all the spontaneous activities of intelligence, feeling, and action, with which that compound organism was charged.

These are the obvious and ancient observations about the human organism. But modern philosophy and science have carried these hints into complete explanations. By a vast accumulation of proof, positive thought at last has established a distinct correspondence between every process of thought or of feeling and some corporeal phenomenon.

I cry with Shylock : ·

'Tis very true, O wise and upright judge.

But if the establishment of the correspondence between physical phenomena on the one side, and moral and intellectual phenomena on the other, is properly to be called an *explanation* (let alone a *complete explanation*) of the human organism, surely Mr. Harrison's teachings come dangerously near that tender of physical theories in explanation of moral phenomena which he warns us leads straight to corruption.

But perhaps I have misrepresented Mr. Harrison. For a few lines further on we are told, with due italic emphasis, that "no man can *explain* volition by purely anatomical study."

I should have thought that Mr. Harrison might have gone much further than this. No man ever explained any physiological fact by purely anatomical study. Digestion cannot be so explained, nor respiration, nor reflex action. It would have been as relevant to affirm that volition could not be explained by measuring an arc of the meridian.

I am obliged to note the fact that Mr. Harrison's biologi-

cal studies have not proceeded so far as to enable him to discriminate between the province of anatomy and that of physiology, because it furnishes the key to an otherwise mysterious
utterance :—

A man whose whole thoughts are absorbed in cutting up dead monkeys and live frogs has no more business to dogmatise about religion than
a mere chemist to improvise a zoology.

Quis negavit?   But if, as, on Mr. Harrison's own showing,
is the case, the progress of science (not anatomical, but physiological) has " established a distinct correspondence between
every process of thought or of feeling and some corporeal phenomenon," and if it is true that " impaired secretions " deprave
the moral sense, and make " hope, love, and faith reel," surely
the religious feelings are brought within the range of physiological inquiry. If impaired secretions deprave the moral
sense, it becomes an interesting and important problem to
ascertain what diseased viscus may have been responsible for
the *Priest in Absolution ;* and what condition of the grey pulp
may have conferred on it such a pathological steadiness of faith
as to create the hope of personal immortality, which Mr. Harrison stigmatizes as so selfishly immoral.

I should not like to undertake the responsibility of advis-
ing anybody to dogmatize about anything ; but surely if, as
Mr. Harrison so strongly urges, " the whole range of man's
powers, from the finest spiritual sensibility down to a mere
automatic contraction, falls into one coherent scheme, being
all the multiform functions of a living organism in presence
of its encircling conditions ;" then the man who endeavors

to ascertain the exact nature of these functions, and to determine the influence of conditions upon them, is more likely to be in a position to tell us something worth hearing about them, than one who is turned from such study by cheap pulpit thunder touching the presumption of "biological reasoning about spiritual things."

Mr. Harrison, as we have seen, is not quite so clear as is desirable respecting the limits of the provinces of anatomy and physiology. Perhaps he will permit me to inform him that physiology is the science which treats of the functions of the living organism, ascertains their coordinations and their correlations in the general chain of causes and effects, and traces out their dependence upon the physical states of the organs by which these functions are exercised. The explanation of a physiological function is the demonstration of the connection of that function with the molecular state of the organ which exerts the function. Thus the function of motion is explained when the movements of the living body are found to have certain molecular changes for their invariable antecedents ; the function of sensation is explained when the molecular changes, which are the invariable antecedents of sensations, are discovered.

The fact that it is impossible to comprehend how it is that a physical state gives rise to a mental state, no more lessens the value of the explanation in the latter case, than the fact that it is utterly impossible to comprehend how motion is communicated from one body to another, weakens the force of the explanation of the motion of one billiard ball by showing that another has hit it.

The finest spiritual sensibility, says Mr. Harrison (and I think that there is a fair presumption that he is right), is a function of a living organism—is in relation with molecular facts. In that case, the physiologist may reply, " It is my business to find out what these molecular facts are, and whether the relation between them and the said spiritual sensibility is one of antecedence in the molecular fact, and sequence in the spiritual fact, or *vice versa.* If the latter result comes out of my inquiries, I shall have made a contribution towards a moral theory of physical phenomena ; if the former, I shall have done somewhat towards building up a physical theory of moral phenomena. But in any case I am not outstepping the limits of my proper province : my business is to get at the truth respecting such questions at all risks ; and if you tell me that one of these two results is a corrupting doctrine, I can only say that I perceive the intended reproach conveyed by the observation, but that I fail to recognise its relevance. If the doctrine is true, its social septic or antiseptic properties are not my affair. My business as a biologist is with physiology, not with morals."

This plea of justification strikes me as complete ; whence, then, the following outbreak of angry eloquence ?—

The arrogant attempt to dispose of the deepest moral truths of human nature on a bare physical or physiological basis is almost enough to justify the insurrection of some impatient theologians against science itself.

" That strain again : it has a dying fall ;" nowise similar to the sweet south upon a bank of violets, however, but like the death-wail of innumerable " impatient theologians " as from the high "drum ecclesiastic" they view the waters of science flooding the Church on all hands.   The beadles have long been washed away ; escape by pulpit stairs is even becoming doubtful, without kirtling those outward investments which distinguish the priest from the man so high that no one will see there is anything but the man left. But Mr. Harrison is not an impatient theologian—indeed, no theologian at all, unless, as he speaks of " Soul " when he means certain bodily functions, and of " Future life " when he means personal annihilation, he may make his master's *Grand être suprême* the subject of a theology ; and one stumbles upon this well-worn fragment of too familiar declamation amongst his vigorous periods with the unpleasant surprise of one who finds a fly in a precious ointment.

There are people from whom one does not expect well-founded statement and thoughtful, however keen, argumentation, embodied in precise language.   From Mr. Harrison one does.   But I think he will be at a loss to answer the question, if I pray him to tell me of any representative of physical science who, either arrogantly or otherwise, has ever attempted to dispose of moral truths on a physical or physiological basis. If I am to take the sense of the words literally, I shall not dispute the arrogance of the attempt to dispose of a moral truth on a bare, or even on a covered, physical or physiological basis ; for, whether the truth is deep or shallow, I cannot conceive how the feat is to be performed.   Columbus' difficulty with the egg is as nothing to it.   But I suppose what is meant is, that some arrogant people have tried to upset morality by the help of physics and physiology.   I am sorry if such people exist, because I shall have to be much ruder to them than Mr. Harrison is.   I should not call them arrogant, any more than I should apply that epithet to a person who attempted to upset Euclid by the help of the Rigveda. Accuracy might be satisfied, if not propriety, by calling such a person a fool ; but it appears to me that it would be the height of injustice to term him arrogant.

Whatever else they may be, the laws of morality, under their scientific aspect, are generalisations based upon the observed phenomena of society ; and, whatever may be the nature of moral approbation and disapprobation, these feelings are, as a matter of experience, associated with certain acts.

The consequences of men's actions will remain the same, however far our analysis of the causes which lead to them may be pushed : theft and murder would be none the less objectionable if it were possible to prove that they were result of the activity of special theft and murder cells in that "grey pulp" of which Mr. Harrison speaks so scornfully.   Does any sane man imagine that any quantity of physiological analysis will lead people to think breaking their legs or putting their hands into the fire desirable ?   And when men really believe that breaches of the moral law involve their penalties as surely as do breaches of the physical law, is it to be supposed that even the very firmest disposal of their moral truths upon "a bare physical or physiological basis" will tempt them to incur those penalties ?

I would gladly learn from Mr. Harrison where, in the course of his studies, he has found anything inconsistent with what I have just said in the writings of physicists or biologists. I would entreat him to tell us who are the true materialists, "the scientific specialists" who "neglect all philosophical and religious synthesis," and who "submit religion to the test of the scalpel or the electric battery;" where the materialism which is "marked by the ignoring of religion, the passing by on the other side and shutting the eyes to the spiritual history of mankind," is to be found.

I will not believe that these phrases are meant to apply to any scientific men of whom I have cognizance, or to any recognized system of scientific thought—they would be too absurdly inappropriate—and I cannot believe that Mr. Harrison indulges in empty rhetoric. But I am disposed to think that they would not have been used at all, except for that deep-seated sympathy with the "impatient theologian" which characterizes the Positivist school, and crops out, characteristically enough, in more than one part of Mr. Harrison's essay.

Mr. Harrison tells us that "Positivism is prepared to meet the theologians." I agree with him, though not exactly in his sense of the words—indeed, I have formerly expressed the opinion that the meeting took place long ago, and that the faithful lovers, impelled by the instinct of a true affinity of nature, have met to part no more. Ecclesiastical to the core from the beginning, Positivism is now exemplifying the law that the outward garment adjusts itself, sooner or later, to the inward man. From its founder onwards, stricken with metaphysical incompetence, and equally incapable of appreciating the true spirit of scientific method, it is now essaying to cover the nakedness of its philosophical materialism with the rags of a spiritualistic phraseology out of which the original sense has wholly departed. I understand and I respect the meaning of the word " soul," as used by Pagan and Christian philosophers for what they believe to be the imperishable seat of human personality, bearing throughout eternity its burden of woe, or its capacity for adoration and love. I confess that my dull moral sense does not enable me to see anything base or selfish in the desire for a future life among the spirits of the just made perfect ; or even among a few such poor fallible souls as one has known here below.

And if I am not satisfied with the evidence that is offered me that such a soul and such a future life exist, I am content to take what is to be had and to make the best of the brief span of existence that is within my reach, without reviling those whose faith is more robust and whose hopes are richer and fuller. But in the interests of scientific clearness, I object to say that I have a soul, when I mean, all the while, that my organism has certain mental functions which, like the rest, are dependent upon its molecular composition, and come to an end when I die ; and I object still more to affirm that I look to a future life, when all that I mean is, that the influence of my sayings and doings will be more or less felt by a number of people after the physical components of that organism are scattered to the four winds.

Throw a stone into the sea, and there is a sense in which it is true that the wavelets which spread around it have an effect through all space and all time. Shall we say that the stone has a future life ?

It is not worth while to have broken away, not without pain and grief, from beliefs which, true or false, embody great and fruitful conceptions, to fall back into the arms of a half-breed between science and theology, endowed, like most half-breeds, with the faults of both parents and the virtues of neither. And it is unwise by such a lapse to expose oneself to the temptation of holding with the hare and hunting with the hounds—of using the weapons of one progenitor to damage the other. I cannot but think that the members of the Positivist school in this country stand in some danger of falling into that fatal error; and I put it to them to consider whether it is either consistent or becoming for those who hold that "the finest spiritual sensibility" is a mere bodily function, to join in the view-halloo, when the hunt is up against biological science—to use their voices in swelling the senseless cry that "civilization is in danger if the workings of the human spirit are to become questions of physiology."

LORD BLACHFORD.

Mr. Harrison is of opinion that the difference between Christians and hinself on this question of the soul and the future life "turns altogether on habits of thought." What appears to the Positivist flimsy will, he says, seems to the Christian sublime, and *vice versa,* "simply because our minds have been trained in different logical methods," and this apparently because Positivism "pretends to no other basis than positive knowledge and scientific logic." But if this is so, it is not, I think, quite consistent to conclude, as he does, that " it is idle to dispute about our respective logical methods, or to put this or that habit of minds in a combat with that." As to the combatants this may be true. But it surely is not idle, but very much to the purpose, for the information of those judges to whom the very act of publication appeals, to discuss habits and methods on which, it is declared, the difference altogether turns.

I note therefore *in limine*, what, as I go on, I shall have occasion to illustrate, one or two differences between the methods of Mr. Harrison and those in which I have been trained.

I have been taught to consider that certain words or ideas represent what are called by logicians substances, by Mr. Harrison, I think, entities, and by others, as the case may be, persons, beings, objects, or articles. Such are air, earth, men, horses, chairs, and tables. Their peculiarity is that they have each of them a separate, independent, substantive existence. They *are*.

There are other words or ideas which do not represent existing things, but qualities, relations, consequences, processes, or occurrences, like victory, virtue, life, order, or destruction, which do but belong to substances, or result from them without any distinct existence of their own. A thing signified by a word of the former class cannot possibly be identical or even homogeneous with a thing signified by a word of the second class. A fiddle is not only a different thing from a tune, but it belongs to another and totally distinct order of ideas. To this distinction the English mind at some period of its history must have been imperfectly alive. If a Greek confounded κτίσις with κτίσμα, an act with a thing, it was the fault of the individual. But the English language, instead of precluding or such a confusion, almost, one would say, labors to propagate it. Such words as "building," "announcement," "preparation," or "power," are equally available to signify either the act of construction or an edifice—either the act of proclaiming or a placard—either the act of preparing, or a surgical specimen —either the ability to do something, or the being in which that ability resides. Such imperfections of language infuse themselves into thought. And I venture to think that the slight superciliousness with which Mr. Harrison treats the doctrines which such persons as myself entertain respecting the soul is in some degree due to the fact that positive "habits of thought" and "logical methods" do not recognize so completely as ours the distinction which I have described as that between a fiddle and a tune.

Again, my own habit of mind is to distinguish more pointedly than Mr. Harrison does between a unit and a complex whole. When I speak of an act of individual will, I seem to myself to speak of an indivisible act proceeding from a single being. The unity is not merely in my mode of representation, but in the thing signified. If I speak of an act of the national will—say a determination to declare war—I speak of the concurrence of a number of individual wills, each acting for itself, and under an infinite variety of influences, but so related to each other and so acting in concert that it is convenient to represent them under the aggregate term "nation." I use a term which signifies unity of being, but I really mean nothing more than cooperation, of correlated action and feeling. So, when I speak of the happiness of humanity, I mean nothing whatever but a number of particular happinesses of individual persons. Humanity is not a unit, but a word which enables me to bring a number of units under view at once. In the case of material objects, I apprehend, unity is simply relative and artificial—a grain of corn is a unit relatively to a bushel and an aggregate relatively to an atom. But I, believing myself to be a spiritual being, call myself actually and without metaphor —one.

Mr. Harrison, who acknowledges the existence of no being but matter, appears either to deny the existence of any real unity whatever, or to ascribe that real unity to an aggregate of things or beings who resemble each other, like the members of the human race, or cooperate towards a common result, like the parts of a picture, a melody, or the human frame, and which may thus be conveniently viewed in combination, and represented by a single word or phrase.

I think that the little which I have to say will be the clearer for these preliminary protests.

The questions in hand relate first to the claim of the soul of man to be treated as an existing thing not bound by the laws of matter ; secondly, to the immortality of that existing thing.

The claim of the soul to be considered as an existing and immaterial being presents itself to my mind as follows :

My positive experience informs me of one thing percipient —myself ; and of a multitude of things perceptible—perceptible, that is, not by way of consciousness, as I am to myself, but by way of impression on other things—capable of making themselves felt through the channels and organs of sensation. These things thus perceptible constitute the material world.

I take no account of percipients other than myself, for I can only conjecture about them what I know about myself. I take no account of things neither percipient nor perceptible, for it is impossible to do so. I know of nothing outside me of which I can say it is at once percipient and perceptible. But I inquire whether I am myself so—whether the existing being to which my sense of identity refers, in which my sensations reside, and which for these two reasons I call "myself," is capable also of being perceived by beings outside myself, as the material world is perceived by me.

I first observe that things perceptible comprise not only objects, but instruments and media of perception—an immense variety of contrivances, natural or artificial, for transmitting information to the sensitive being. Such are telescopes, microscopes, ear-trumpets, the atmosphere, and various other media which, if not at present the objects of direct sensation, may conceivably become so—and such, above all, are various parts of the human body—the lenses which collect the vibrations which are the conditions of light ; the tympanum which collects the vibrations which are the conditions of sound ; the muscles which adjust these and other instruments of sensation to the precise performance of their work ; the nerves which convey to and fro molecular movements of the most incomprehensible significance and efficacy. Of all these it is, I understand, more and more evident, as science advances, that they are perceptible, but do not perceive. Ear, hand, eye, and nerves are alike machinery—mere machinery for transmitting the movement of atoms to certain nervous centres—ascertained localities which (it is proper to observe in passing), though small relatively to ourselves and our powers of investigation, may,—since size is entirely relative—be *absolutely* large enough to contain little worlds in themselves.

Here the investigation of things perceptible is stopped, abruptly and completely. Our inquiries into the size, composition, and movement of particles, have been pushed, for the present at any rate, as far as they will go. But at this point we come across a field of phenomena to which the attributes of atoms, size, movement, and physical composition are wholly inapplicable—the phenomena of sensation or animal life.

Science informs me that the movements of these perceptible atoms within my body bear a correspondence, strange, subtle, and precise, to the sensations of which I, as a percipient, am conscious ; a correspondence (it is again proper to observe in passing) which extends not only to perceptions, as in sight or hearing, but to reflection and volition, as in sleep and drunkenness. The relation is not one of similarity. The vibrations of a white, black, or grey pulp are not in any sensible way similar to the perception of colour or sound, or the imagination of a noble act. There is no visible—may I not say no conceivable ?—reason why one should depend on the other. Motion and sensation interact, but they do not overlap. There is no homogeneity between them. They stand apart. Physical science conducts us to the brink of the chasm which separates them, and by so doing only shows us its depth.

I return then to the question, What am I ? My own habits of mind and logical methods certainly require me to believe that I am something—something percipient—but am I perceptible?   I find no reason for supposing it.   I believe myself to be surrounded by things percipient.   Are they perceptible? Not to my knowledge.   Their existence is to me a matter of inference from their perceptible appendages.   Them—their selves—I certainly cannot perceive.   As far as I can understand things perceptible, I detect in them no quality—no capacity for any quality like that of percipiency, which with its homogeneous faculties, intellect, affections, and so on, is the basis of my own nature.   Physical science, while it developes the relation, seems absolutely to emphasise and illuminate the ineradicable difference between the motions of a material and the sensations of a living being.   Of the attributes of a percipient we have, each for himself, profound and immediate experience.   Of the attributes of the perceptible we have, I suppose, distinct scientific conceptions.   Our notions of the one and our notions of the other appear to attach to a different order of being.

It appears therefore to me that there is no reason to believe, and much reason for not believing, that the percipient is perceptible under our present conditions of existence, or indeed under any conditions that our present faculties enable us to imagine.

And this is my case, which of course covers the whole animal creation.   Perception must be an attribute of something, and there is reason for believing that this something is imperceptible.   This is what I mean when I say that I have, or more properly that I am, a soul or spirit, or rather it is the point on which I join issue with those who say that I am not.

I am not, as Mr. Harrison seems to suppose, running about

in search of a "cause."   I am inquiring into the nature of a being, and that being myself.   I am sure I am something.   I am certainly not the mere tangible structure of atoms which I affect, and by which I am affected after a wonderful fashion. In reflecting on the nature of my own operations I find nothing to suggest that my own being is subject to the same class of physical laws as the objects from which my sensations are derived, and I conclude that I am not subject to those laws. The most substantial objection to this conclusion is conveyed, I conceive, in a sentence of Mr. Harrison's : "To talk to us of mind, feeling, and will continuing their functions in the absence of physical organs and visible organisms, is to use language which, to us at least, is pure nonsense."

It is probably to those who talk thus that Mr. Harrison refers when he says that argument is useless.   And in point of fact I have no answer but to call his notions anthropomorphic, and to charge him with want of a certain kind of imagination.   By imagination we commonly mean the creative faculty which enables a man to give a palpable shape to what he believes or thinks possible : and this, I do not doubt, Mr. Harrison possesses in a high degree.   But there is another kind of imagination which enables a man to embrace the idea of a possibility to which no such palpable shape can be given, or rather of a world of possibilities beyond the range of his experience or the grasp of his faculties ; as Mr. John Mill embraced the idea of a possible world in which the connection of cause and effect should not exist.   The want of this necessary though dangerous faculty makes a man the victim of vivid impressions, and disables him from believing what his impressions do not enable him to realise. Questions respecting metaphysical possibility turn much on the presence, or absence, or exaggeration of this kind of imagination. And when one man has said " I can conceive it possible," and another has said " I cannot," it is certainly difficult to get any farther.

To me it is not in the slightest degree difficult to conceive the possible existence of a being capable of love and knowledge without the physical organs through which human beings derive their knowledge, nor in supposing myself to be such a being. Indeed I seem actually to exercise such a capacity (however I got it) when I shut my eyes and try to think out a moral or mathematical puzzle. If it is true that a particular corner of my brain is concerned in the matter, I accept the fact not as a self-evident truth (which would seem to be Mr. Harrison's position), but as a curious discovery of the anatomists. But having said this I have said everything, and as Mr. Harrison must suppose that I deceive myself, so I suppose that in his case the imagination which founds itself on experience is so active and vivid as to cloud or dwarf the imagination which proceeds beyond or beside experience.

Mr. Harrison's own theory I do not quite understand. He derides the idea, though he does not absolutely deny the possibility, of an immaterial entity which feels. And he appears to be sensible of the difficulty of supposing that atoms of matter which assume the form of a grey pulp can feel. He holds accordingly, as I understand, that feeling, and all that follows from it, are the results of an "organism."

If he had used the word "organization," I should have

concluded unhesitatingly that he was a victim of the Anglican confusion which I have above noticed, and that, in his own mind, he escaped the alternative difficulties of the case by the common expedient of shifting, as occasion required, from one sense of that word to the other. If pressed by the difficulty of imagining sensation not resident in any specific sensitive thing, the word organization would supply to his mind the idea of a thing, a sensitive aggregate of organized atoms. If, on the contrary, pressed by the difficulty of supposing that these atoms, one or all, thought, the word would shift its meaning and present the aspect not of an aggregate bulk, but of orderly arrangement—not of a thing, or collection of things, but of a state of things.

But the word "organism" is generally taken to indicate a thing organized. And the choice of that word would seem to indicate that he ascribed the spiritual acts (so to call them) which constitute life, to the aggregate bulk of the atoms organised or the appropriate part of them. But this he elsewhere seems to disclaim. "The philosophy which treats man as man simply affirms that *man* loves, thinks, acts, not that ganglia, or the sinews, or any organ of man loves, and thinks, and acts." Yes, but we recur to the question, what is man? If the ganglia do not think, what is it that does? Mr. Harrison, as I understand, answers that it is a *consensus* of faculties, an harmonious system of parts, and he denounces an attempt to introduce into this collocation of parts or faculties an underlying entity or being which shall possess those faculties or employ those parts. It is then not after all to a being or aggregate of beings, but to a relation or condition of beings, that will and thought and love belong. If this is Mr. Harrison's meaning, I certainly agree with him that it is indeed impossible to compose a difference between two disputants, of whom one holds, and the other denies, that a condition can think. If my opponent does not admit this to be an absurdity, I do not pretend to drive him any further.

With regard to immortality, I have nothing material to add to what has been said by those who have preceded me. I agree with Professor Huxley that the natural world supplies nothing which can be called evidence of a future life. Believing in God, I see in the constitution of the world which He has made, and in the yearnings and aspirations of that spiritual nature which He has given to man, much that commends to my belief the revelation of a future life which I believe Him to have made. But it is in virtue of His clear promise, not in virtue of these doubtful intimations, that I rely on the prospect of a future life. Believing that He is the author of that moral insight which in its ruder forms controls the multitude and in its higher inspires the saint, I revere those great men who were able to forecast this great announcement, but I cannot and do not care to reduce that forecast to any logical process, or base it on any conclusive reasoning. Rather I admire their power of divination the more on account of the narrowness of their logical data. For myself I believe because I am told.

But whether the doctrine of immortality be true or false, I protest, with Mr. Hutton, against the attempt to substitute for what at any rate is a substantial idea, something which can hardly be called even a shadow or echo of it.

The Christian conception of the world is this. It is a world of moral as of physical waste. Much seed is sown which will not ripen, but some is sown that will. This planet is a seat, among other things, of present goodness and happiness. And this our goodness and happiness, like our crime and misery, propagate or fail to propagate themselves during our lives and after our deaths. But, apart from these earthly consequences, which are much to us and all to the Positivist, the little fragment of the universe on which we appear and disappear is, we believe, a nursery for something greater. The capacities for love and knowledge which in some of us attain a certain development here, we must all feel to be capable, with greater opportunities, of an infinitely greater development; and Christians believe that such a development is in fact reserved for those who, in this short time of apprenticeship, take the proper steps for approaching it.

This conception of a glorious and increasing company into which the best of men are continually to be gathered to be associated with each other (to say no more) in all that can make existence happy and noble, may be a dream, and Mr. Harrison may be right in calling it so. In deriding it he cannot be right. " The eternity of the tabor " he calls it ! Has he never felt, or at any rate is he not able to conceive, a thrill of pleasure at a sympathetic interchange of look, or word, or touch with a fellow-creature kind and noble and brilliant, and engaged in the exhibition of those qualities of heart and intellect which make him what he is? Multiply and sustain this—suppose yourself surrounded by beings with whom this interchange of sympathy is warm and perpetual.

Intensify it. Increase indefinitely the excellence of one of those beings, the wonderful and attractive character of his operations, our own capacities of affection and intellect, the vividness of our conception, the breadth and firmness of our mental grasp, the sharp vigor of our admiration; and to exclude satiety, imagine if you like that the operations which we contemplate and our relations to our companions are infinitely varied—a supposition for which the size of the known and unknown universe affords indefinite scope—or otherwise suppose that sameness ceases to tire, as the old Greek philosopher thought it might do if we were better than we are (μεταβολὴ πάντων γλυκύτατον διὰ πονηρίαν τινά), or as it would do, I suppose, if we had no memory of the immediate past. Imagine all this as the very least that may be hoped, if our powers of conception are as slight in respect to the nature of what is to be as our bodies are in relation to the physical universe. And remember that if practical duties are necessary for the perfection of life, the universe is not so small but that in some corner of it its Creator might always find something to do for the army of intelligences whom He has thus formed and exalted.

All this, I repeat, may be a dream, but to characterise it as " the eternity of the tabor " shows surely a feebleness of conception or carelessness of representation more worthy of a ready writer than of a serious thinker. And to place before us as a rival conception the fact that some of our good deeds will have indefinite consequences—to call this scanty and fading chain of effects, which we shall be as unable to perceive or control as we have been unable to anticipate—to call this a "posthumous activity," "an eternity of spiritual influence," and a "life beyond the grave," and finally, under the appellation of "incorporation into the glorious future of our race," to claim for it a dignity and value parallel to that which would attach to the Christian's expectation (if solid) of a sensible life of exalted happiness for himself and all good men, is surely nothing more or less than extravagance founded on misnomer.

With regard to the promised incorporation, I should really like to know what is the exact process, or, event, or condition which Mr. Harrison considers himself to understand by the incorporation of a consentus of faculties with a glorious future ; and whether he arrived at its apprehension by way of "positive knowledge," or by way of "scientific logic."

Mr. Harrison's future life is disposed of by Professor Huxley in a few words : "Throw a stone into the sea, and there is a sense in which it is true that the wavelets which spread around it have an effect through all space and time. Shall we say that the stone has a future life ?"

To this I only add the question whether I am not justified in saying that Mr. Harrison does not adequately distinguish between the nature of a fiddle and the nature of a tune, and would contend (if consistent) that a violin which had been burnt to ashes would, notwithstanding, continue to exist, at least as long as a tune which had been played upon it survived in the memory of any one who had heard it—the *consensus* of its capacities being, it would seem, incorporated into the glorious future of music?

HON. RODEN NOEL.

Death is a phenomenon ; but are we phenomena ?

The question of immortality seems, philosophically speaking, very much to resolve itself into that of personality.   Are we persons, spirits, or are we things?   Perhaps we are a loose collection of successive qualities ?   That seems to be the latest conclusion of Positive, and Agnostic biological philosophy.   The happy thought which, as Dr. Stirling suggests, was probably thrown out in a spirit of persiflage by Hume has been adopted in all seriousness by his followers.   Mr. Harrison is very bitter with those who want to explain mental and moral phenomena by physiology.   But, as Professor Huxley remarks, he seems in many parts of his essay to do the same thing himself. What could Buchner, or Carl Vogt say stronger than this ?   " At last, the prick of a needle, or a grain of mineral, will in an instant lay to rest for ever man's body and its unity, and all the spontaneous activities of intelligence, feeling, and action, *with which that compound organism was charged.*"   Again, he says the spiritual faculties are " directly dependent on physical organs " — " stand forth as functions of living organs in given conditions of the organism."   Again : " At last the man Newton dies, that is, the body is dispersed into gas and dust."   Mr. Harrison then, though a Positivist, bound to know only successive phenomena, seems to know the body as a material entity possessed of such functions as conscience, reason, imagination, perception—to know that Newton's body thought out the Principia, and Shakespeare's conceived Hamlet.   In deed, Agnosticism generally, though with a show of humility, seems rather arbitrary in its selection of what we shall know, and what we shall not : we must know something ; so we shall know that we have ideas and feelings, but not the personal identity that alone makes them intelligible, or we shall use the word, and yet speak as if the idea were a figment ; we shall know qualities, but not substance ; " functions " and " forces," but not the some one or something, of which they must be functions and forces to be conceivable at all. Yet *naturam expellas furca* &c. Common sense insists on retaining the fundamental law of human thought, not being able to get rid of them ; and hence the haphazard, instead of systematic and orderly fashion in which the new philosophy deals with universal convictions, denying even that they exist out of theology and métaphysique.

Thus (in apparent contradiction to the statements quoted) on p. 17, we are told that it is "man who loves, thinks, acts ; not the ganglia, or sinuses, or any organ " that does so. But perhaps the essayist means that all the body together does so. He says a man is " the consensus, or combined activity of his faculties." What is meant by this phraseology? It is just this " *his*," this " *consensus*," or " *combined* acting" that is inconceivable without the focus of unity, in which many contemporaneous phenomena, and many past and present meet to be compared, remembered, identified as belonging to the same self ; so only can they be known phenomena at all. Well, do we find in examining the physical structure of man's body as solid, heavy, extended, divisible, or its living organs and their physical functions, or the rearrangement of molecules of carbon, nitrogen, hydrogen, &c., into living tissue, or its oxidation, anything corresponding to the consciousness of personal moral agency, and personal identity? We put the two classes of conception side by side, and they seem to refuse to be identified—man as one and the same conscious moral agent—and his body, or the bumps on his skull; or is man indeed a function of his own body? Are we right in talking of our bodies as material things, and of ourselves as if we were not things, but persons with mights, rights, and duties? We ought perhaps to talk—theologies and philosophies being now exploded —not of our having bodies, but of bodies having us, and of bodies having rights or duties. Perhaps Dundreary was mistaken, and the tail may wag the dog after all.

Mr. Harrison says: "Orthodoxy has so long been accustomed, to take itself for granted, that we are apt to forget how very short a period of human history this sublimated essence" (the immaterial soul) "has been current. There is not a trace of it in the Bible in its present sense." This reminds one rather of Mr. Matthew Arnold's contention, that the Jews did not believe in God. But really it does not much signify what particular intellectual theories have been entertained by different men at different times about the nature of God or of the soul: the question is whether you do not find on the whole among them all a consciousness or conviction, that there is a Higher Being above them, together with a power of distinguishing themselves from their own bodies, and the world around them—in consequence of this, too, a belief in personal immortality. Many in all ages believe that the dead have spoken to us from beyond the grave. But into that I will not enter. *Are we our bodies?* that seems to be the point. Now I do not think Positivism has any right to assume that we are, even on its own principles and professions.

Mr. Harrison has a very forcible passage, in which he enlarges upon this theme: that "the laws of the separate functions of body, mind, or feeling, have visible relations to each other: are inextricably woven in with each other, act and react." "From the summit of spiritual life to the base of corporeal life, whether we pass up or down the gamut of human forces, there runs one organic correlation and sympathy of parts. Touch the smallest fibre in the corporeal man, and in some infinitesimal way we may watch the effect in the moral man. When we rouse chords of the most glorious ecstasy of the soul, we may see the vibrations of them visibly thrilling upon the skin." Here we are in the region of positive facts as specially made manifest by recent investigation. And the orthodox schools need to recognise the significance of such facts. The close interdependence of body and soul is a startling verity that must be looked in the face ; and the discovery has, no doubt, gone far to shake the faith of many in human immortality, as well as in other momentous kindred truths. It has been so with myself. But I think the old dictum of Bacon about the effect of a little and more knowledge will be found applicable after all. Let us look these facts very steadily in the face. When we have thought for a long time, there is a feeling of pain in the head. That is a feeling, observe, in our own conscious selves. Further, by observation and experiment, it has been made certain that some molecular change in the nervous substance of the brain (to the renewal of which oxygenated blood is necessary), is going on, while the process of thinking takes place—though we are not conscious of it in our own case, except as a matter of inference. The thought itself seems when we reflect on it, partly due to the action of an external world or kosmos upon us; partly to our own "forms of thought," or fixed ways of perceiving and thinking, which have been ours so long as we can remember, and which do not belong to us more than to other individual members of the human family; again partly to our own past experience. But what *is* this material process accompanying thought, which conceivably we might perceive if we could see the inside of our own bodies? Why it too can only seem what it seems by virtue of our own personal past experience, and our own human as well as individual modes of conceiving. Is not that "positive" too? Will not men of science agree with me that such is the fact? In short, our bodies, on any view of them *science herself has taught us* are *percepts and concepts of ours*—I don't say of the "soul," or the mind, or any *bête noire* of the sort, but of *ourselves*, who surely cannot be altogether *betes noires*. They are as much percepts and concepts of ours as is the material world outside them. Are they colored? Color, we are told, is a sensation. Are they hard or soft? These are our sensations, and relative to us. The elements of our food enter into relations we name living; their molecules enter into that condition of unstable equilibrium; there is motion of parts fulfilling definite intelligible and constant uses, in some cases subject to our own intelligent direction. But all this is what appears to our intelligence, and it appears different, according to the stages of intelligence at which we arrive ; a good deal of it is hypothesis of our own minds. Readers of Berkeley and Kant need not be told this ; it is now universally acknowledged by the competent. The atomic theory is a working hypothesis of our minds only. Space and time are relative to our intelligence, to the succession of our thoughts, to our own faculties of motion, motion being also a conception of ours. Our bodies, in fact, as Positivists often tell us, and as we now venture to remind *them*, are *phenomena*, that is, *orderly appearances to us*. They further tell us generally that there is nothing which thus appears, or that we cannot know that there is anything beyond the appearance. What then, according to Positivism itself, is the most we are entitled to affirm with regard to the dead ? Simply that there are *no appearances to us* of a living personality *in connection with* those phenomena which we call a dead body, any more than there are in connection with the used-up materials of burnt tissues that pass by osmosis into the capillaries, and away by excretory ducts. But are we entitled to affirm that the *person* is extinct—is dissolved—the one conscious self in whom these bodily phenomena centred (except so far as they centred in us), who was the focus of them, gave them form, made them what they were ; whose thoughts wandered up and down through eternity ; of whom, therefore, the bodily, as well as mental and spiritual functions were functions, so far as this body entered into the conscious self at all ? We can, on the contrary, only affirm that probably the person no longer perceives, and is conscious, *in connection with this form* we look upon, wherein so-called chemical affinities now prevail altogether over so-called vital power. But even in life the body is always changing and decomposing—foreign substances are always becoming a new body, and the old body becoming a foreign substance. Yet the Person remains one and the same. True, Positivism tries to eliminate persons, and reduce all to appearances; but this is too glaring a violation of common sense, and I do not think from his language Mr. Harrison quite means to do this. Well by spirit, even by "soul," most people, let me assure him, only mean *our own conscious personal selves*. For myself, indeed, I believe that there cannot be appearances without something to appear. But seeing that the material world is in harmony with our intelligence, and presents all the appearance of intelligent cooperation of parts with a view to ends, I believe, with a great English thinker, whose loss we have to deplore (James Hinton), that all is the manifestation of life—of living spirits or persons, not of dead inert matter, though from our own spiritual deadness or inertness it appears to us material. Upon our own moral and spiritual life in fact depends the measure of our knowledge and perception. I can indeed admit with Mr. Harrison that probably there must always be to us the phenomenon, the body, the external; but it may be widely different from what it seems now. We may be made one with the great Elohim, or angels of Nature who create us, or we may still grovel in dead material bodily life. We now appear to ourselves and to others as bodily, as material. Body, and soul or mind, are two opposite phenomenal poles of one Reality, which is self or spirit; but though these phenomena may vary, the creative informing spirit, which underlies all, of which we partake, which is absolute, divine, this can never be destroyed. "In God we live, move, and have our being." It is held indeed by the new philosophy that the temporal, the physical, and the composite (elements of matter and "feeling") are the basis of our higher consciousness : on the contrary, I hold that this is absurd, and that the one eternal consciousness or spirit must be the basis of the physical, composite, and temporal ; is needed to give unity and harmony to the body. One is a little ashamed of agreeing with an old-fashioned thinker, whom an old-fashioned poet pronounced the "first of those who know," that the spirit is organizing vital principle of the body, not *vice versa*. The great difficulty, no doubt, is that apparent irruption of the external into the personal, when, as the essayist says, "impair a man's secretions, and moral sense is dulled, discolored, depraved." But it is our spiritual deadness that has put us into this physical condition ; and probably it is *we* who are responsible in a fuller sense than we can realize now for this effect upon us, which must be in the end too for purposes of discipline ; it belongs to our spiritual history and purpose. Moreover, this external world is not so foreign to us as we imagine ; it is spiritual, and between all spirit there is solidarity.

Mr. Hinton observes (and here I agree with him rather than with Mr. Harrison), that the defect and falseness of our knowing must be in the knowing by only part of ourselves. Whereas sense had to be supplemented by intellect, and proved misleading without it, so intellect, even in the region of knowledge, has to be supplemented by moral sense, which is the highest faculty in us. We are at present misled by a false view of the world, based on sense and intellect only. Death is but a hideous illusion of our deadness—

> Death is the veil which those who live call life .
> We sleep, and it is lifted.

The true definition of the actual is that which is true for, which satisfies the whole Being of humanity. We must ask of a doctrine: does it answer in the moral region? if so, it is as true as we can have it with our present knowledge ; but, if the moral experiment fails, it is not true. Conscience has the highest authority about knowledge, as it has about conduct. Now apply this to the negations of Positivism, and the belief Comte would substitute for faith in God, and personal immortality. Kant sufficiently proved that these are postulates required by Practical Reason, and on this ground he believed them. I am not blind to the beauty and nobleness of Comte's moral ideal (not without debt to Christ's) as expounded by himself, and here by Mr. Harrison. Still I say : the moral experiment fails. Some of us may seek to benefit the world, and then desire rest. But what of the maimed and broken and aimless lives around us? What of those we have lost, who were dearer to us than our own selves, full of fairest hope and promise, unaware annihilated in earliest dawn, whose dewy bud yet slept unfolded? If they were *things*, doubtless we *might* count them as so much manure, in which to grow those still more beautiful, though still brief-flowering human aloes, which Positivism, though knowing nothing but present phenomena, and denying God, is able confidently to promise us in some remote future. But alas! they *seemed* living spirits, able to hope for infinite love, progressive virtue, the beatific vision of God Himself! And they really *were*—so much manure? Why, as has already been asked, are such ephemerals worth living for, however many of them there may be, whose lives are as an idle flash in the pan, always promising, yet failing to attain any substantial or enduring good? What of these agonising women and children, now the victims of Ottoman blood-madness? What of all the cramped, unlovely, debased, or slow-tortured, yet evanescent lives of myriads in our great cities? These cannot have the philosophic aspirations of culture. They have too often none at all. Go proclaim to them this gospel, supplementing it by the warning that in the end there will remain only a huge block of ice in a " wide, grey, lampless, deep, unpeopled world!" I could believe in the pessimism of Schopenhauer, not in this jaunty optimism of Comte.

Are we then indeed orphans? Will the tyrant go ever unpunished, the wrong ever unredressed, the poor and helpless remain always trampled and unhappy? Must the battle of good and evil in ourselves and others hang always trembling in the balance, for ever undecided ; or does it all mean nothing more than we see now, and is the glorious world but some ghastly illusion of insanity? When " the fever called living is over at last," is all indeed over? Thank God that through this Babel of discordant voices modern men can still hear His accents who said : " Come unto me, all ye that are weary and heavy laden, and I will give you rest."

II.

LORD SELBORNE.

I am too well satisfied with Lord Blachford's paper, and with much that is in the other papers of the September number, to think that I can add anything of importance to them. The little I would say has reference to our actual knowledge of the soul during this life ; meaning by the soul what Lord Blachford means, viz., the conscious being, which each man calls " himself."

It appears to me, that what we know and can observe tends to confirm the testimony of our consciousness to the reality of the distinction between the body and the soul. From the necessity of the case, we cannot observe any manifestations of the soul, except during the time of its association with the body. This limit of our experience applies, not to the " ego," of which alone each man has any direct knowledge, but to the perceptible indications of consciousness in others. It is impossible, in the nature of things, that any man can ever have had experience of the total cessation of his own consciousness ; and the idea of such a cessation is much less natural, and much more difficult to realize, than that of its continuance. We observe the phenomena of death in others, and infer, by irresistible induction, that the same thing will also happen to ourselves. But these phenomena carry us only to the dissociation of the " ego " from the body, not to its extinction.

Nothing else can be credible, if our consciousness is not ; and I have said that this bears testimony to the reality of the distinction between soul and body.   Each man is conscious of using his own body as an instrument, in the same sense in which he would use any other machine.   He passes a different moral judgment on the mechanical and involuntary actions of his body, from that which he feels to be due to its actions resulting from his own free will.   The unity and identity of the " ego," from the beginning to the end of life, is of the essence of his consciousness.

In accordance with this testimony are such facts as the following : that the body has no proper unity, identity, or continuity through the whole of life, all its constituent parts being in a constant state of flux and change ; that many parts and organs of the body may be removed, with no greater effect upon the " ego " than when we take off any article of clothing ; and that those organs which cannot be removed or stopped in their action without death, are distributed over different parts of the body, and are homogeneous in their material and structure with others which we can lose without the sense that any change has passed over our proper selves.   If, on the one hand, a diseased state of some bodily organs interrupts the reasonable manifestations of the soul through the body, the cases are, on the other, not rare, in which the whole body decays, and falls into extreme age, weakness, and even decrepitude, while vigor, freshness, and youthfulness are still characteristics of the mind.

The attempt, in Butler's work, to reason from the indivisibility and indestructibility of the soul, as ascertained facts, is less satisfactory than most of that great writer's arguments, which are, generally, rather intended to be destructive of objections, than demonstrative of positive truths. But the modern scientific doctrine, that all matter, and all force, are indestructible, is not without interest in relation to that argument. There must at least be a natural presumption from that doctrine, that, if the soul during life has a real existence distinct from the body, it is not annihilated by death. If, indeed, it were a mere " force " (such as heat, light, &c., are supposed by modern philosophers to be, though men who are not philosophers may be excused, if they find some difficulty in understanding exactly what is meant by the term, when so used), it would be consistent with that doctrine, that the soul might be transmuted, after death, into some other form of force. But the idea of "force," in this sense (whatever may be its exact meaning), seems wholly inapplicable to the conscious being, which a man calls "himself."

The resemblances in the nature and organization of animal and vegetable bodies seem to me to confirm, instead of weakening, the impression, that the body of a man is a machine under the government of his soul, and quite distinct from it. Plants manifest no consciousness ; all our knowledge of them tends irresistibly to the conclusion, that there is in them no intelligent, much less any reasonable, principle of life. Yet they are machines very like the human body, not indeed in their formal development or their exact chemical processes, but in the general scheme and functions of their organism— in their laws of nutrition, digestion, assimilation, respiration, and especially reproduction. They are bodies without souls, living a physical life, and subject to a physical death. The inferior animals have bodies still more like our own ; indeed, in their higher orders, resembling them very closely indeed ; and they have also a principle of life quite different from that of plants, with various degrees of consciousness, intelligence, and volition. Even in their principle of life, arguments founded on observation and comparison (though not on individual consciousness), more or less similar to those which apply to man, tend to show that there is something distinct from, and more than, the body. But, of all these inferior animals, the intelligence differs from that of man, not in degree only, but in kind. Nature is their simple, uniform, and sufficient law ; their very arts (which are often wonderful) come to them by nature, except when they are trained by man ; there is in them no sign of discourse of reason, of morality, or of the knowledge of good and evil. The very similarity of their bodily structure to that of man tends, when these differences are noted, to add weight to the other natural evidence of the distinctness of man's soul from his body.

The immortality of the soul seems to me to be one of those truths, for the belief in which, when authoritatively declared, man is prepared by the very constitution of his nature.

CANON BARRY.

Any one who from the ancient positions of Christianity looks on the controversy between Mr. Harrison and Professor Huxley on "The Soul and Future Life" (to which I propose mainly to confine myself) will be tempted with Faulconbridge to observe, not without a touch of grim satisfaction, how, "from North to South, Austria and France shoot in each other's mouth." The fight is fierce enough to make him ask, *Tantæne animis sapientibus iræ?* But he will see that each is far more effective in battering the lines of the enemy than in strengthening his own. Nor will he be greatly concerned if both from time to time lodge a shot or two in the battlements on which he stands, with some beating of that "drum scientific," which seems to me to be in these days always as resonant, sometimes with as much result of merely empty sound, as "the drum ecclesiastic," against which Professor Huxley is so fond of warning us. Those whom Mr. Harrison calls "theologians," and whom Professor Huxley less appropriately terms "priests" (for of priesthood there is here no question), may indeed think that, if the formidable character of an opponent's position is to be measured by the scorn and fury with which it is assailed, their ground must be strong indeed ; and they will possibly remember an old description of a basis less artificial than "pulpit stairs," from which men may look without much alarm, while "the floods come and the winds blow." Gaining from this conviction courage to look more closely, they will perceive, as I have said, that each of the combatants is far stronger on the destructive than on the constructive side.

Mr. Harrison's earnest and eloquent plea against the materialism which virtually, if not theoretically, makes all that we call spirit a mere function of material organization (like the ἁρμονία of the *Phædo*), and against the exclusive "scientism" which, because it cannot find certain entities along its line of investigation, asserts loudly that they are either non-existent or "unknowable," is strong, and (*pace* Professor Huxley) needful; not, indeed, against him (for he knows better than to despise the metaphysics in which he is so great an adept), but against many adherents, prominent rather than eminent, of the school in which he is a master. Nor is its force destroyed by exposing, however keenly and sarcastically, some inconsistencies of argument, not inaptly corresponding (as it seems to me) with similiar inconsistencies in the popular exposition of the views which it attacks. If Professor Huxley is right (as surely he is) in pleading for perfect freedom and boldness in the investigation of the phenomena of humanity from the physical side, the counter plea is equally irresistible for the value of an independent philosophy of mind, starting from the metaphysical pole of thought, and reasoning positively on the phenomena, which, though they may have many connections with physical laws, are utterly inexplicable by them. We might, indeed, demur to his inference that the discovery of "antecedence in the molecular fact" necessarily leads to a "physical theory of moral phenomena," and *vice versa*, as savoring a little of the *Post hoc, ergo propter hoc.* Inseparable connection it would imply; but the ultimate causation might lie in something far deeper, underlying both "the molecular" and "the spiritual fact." But still, to establish such antecedence would be an important scientific step, and the attempt might be made from either side.

On the other hand, Professor Huxley's trenchant attack on the unreality of the Positivist assumption of a right to take names which in the old religion at least mean something firm and solid, and to sublime them into the cloudy forms of transcendental theory, and on the arbitrary application of the word " selfishness," with all its degrading associations, to the consciousness of personality here and the hope of a nobler personality in the future, leaves nothing to be desired. I fear that his friends the priests would be accused of the crowning sin of " ecclesiasticism " (whatever that may be) if they used denunciations half so sharp. Except with a few sarcasms which he cannot resist the temptation of flinging at them by the way, they will have nothing with which to quarrel ; and possibily they may even learn from him to consider these as claps of " cheap thunder " from the " pulpit," in that old sense of the word in which it designates the professorial chair.

The whole of Mr. Harrison's two papers may be resolved into an attack on the true individuality of man, first on the speculative, then on the moral side ; from the one point of view denouncing the belief in it as a delusion, from the other branding the desire of it as a moral degradation. The connection of the two arguments is instructive and philosophical. For no argument merely speculative, ignoring all moral considerations, will really be listened to. His view of the soul as " a consensus of human faculties " reminds us curiously of the Buddhist " groups ; " his description of " a perpetuity of sensation as the true Hell " breathes the very spirit of the longing for *Nirvana.* Both he and his Asiatic predecessors are certainly right in considering the " delusion of individual existence " as the chief delusion to be got rid of on the way to a perfect Agnosticism, in respect of all that is not merely phenomenal. It is true that he protests in terms against a naked materialism, ignoring all spiritual phenomena as having a distinctive character of their own ; but yet, when he tells us that "to talk about a bodiless being thinking and loving is simply to talk of the thoughts and feelings of Nothing," he certainly appears to assume substantially the position of the materialism he denounces, which (as has been already said) holds these spiritual energies to be merely results of the bodily organization, as the excitation of an electric current is the result of the juxtaposition of certain material subtances.   If a bodiless being is Nothing, there can be no such thing as an intrinsic or independent spiritual life ; and it is difficult for ordinary minds to attach any distinct meaning to the declaration that the soul is " a conscious unity of being," if that being depends on an organization which is unquestionably discerptible, and of which (as Butler remarks) large parts may be lost without affecting this consciousness of personality.

Now this is, after all, the only point worth fighting about. Mr. Hutton has already said with perfect truth that by " the Soul " we mean that " which lies at the bottom of the sense of personal identity—the thread of the continuity running through all our chequered life," and which remains unbroken amidst the constant flux of change both in our material body, and in the circumstances of our material life.   This belief is wholly independent of any " metaphysical hypothesis " of modern " orthodoxy," whether it is, or is not, rightly described as a " juggle of ideas," and of any examination of the question (on which Lord Blachford has touched) whether, if it seem such to "those trained in positive habits of thought," the fault lies in it or in them.   I may remark in passing, that in this broad and simple sense it certainly runs through the whole

Bible, and has much that is "akin to it in the Old Testament." For even in the darkest and most shadowy ideas of the *Sheôl* of the other world, the belief in a true personal identity is taken absolutely for granted ; and it is not a little curious to notice how in the Book of Job the substitution for it of "an immortality in the race " (although there not in the whole of humanity, but simply in the tribe or family) is offered, and rejected as utterly insufficient to satisfy either the speculation of the intellect or the moral demands of the conscience.[1] Now it is not worth while to protest against the caricature of this belief, as a belief in " man plus a heterogeneous entity " called the soul, which can be only intended as a sarcasm. But we cannot acquiesce in any statement, which represents the belief in this immaterial and indivisible personality as resting simply on the notion that it is needed to explain the acts of the human organism. For as a matter of fact, those who believe in it conceive it to be declared by a direct consciousness, the most simple and ultimate of all acts of consciousness. They hold this consciousness of a personal identity and individ-uality, unchanging amidst material change, to be embodied in all the language and literature of man ; and they point to the inconsistencies in the very words of those who argue against it, as proofs that man cannot divest himself of it. No doubt they believe that so the acts of the organism are best explained, but it is not on the necessity of such explanation that they base their belief : and this fact separates altogether their belief in the human soul, as an immaterial entity, from those conceptions of a soul, in animal, vegetable, even inor-

1 See Job xiv. 21, 22.

ganic substances, with which Mr. Harrison insists on confounding it. Of the true character of animal nature we know nothing (although we may conjecture much), just because we have not in regard to it the direct consciousness, which we have in regard of our own nature. Accordingly we need not trouble our argument for a soul in man with any speculation as to a true soul in the brute creatures.

In what relation this personality stands to the particles which at any moment compose the body, and which are certainly in a continual state of flux, or to the law of structure which in living beings, by some power to us unknown, assimilates these particles, is a totally different question. I fear that Mr. Harrison will be displeased with me if I call it "a mystery." But, whatever future advances of science may do for us in the matter—and I hope they may do much—I am afraid I must still say that this relation is a mystery, which has been at different times imperfectly represented, both by formal theories and by metaphors, all of which by the very nature of language are connected with original physical conceptions. Let it be granted freely that the progress of modern physiological science has rendered obsolete the old idea that the various organs of the body stand to the true personal being in a purely instrumental relation, such as (for example) is described by Butler in his *Analogy*, in the celebrated chapter on the Future Life. The power of physical influences acting upon the body to affect the energies of thought and will is unquestionable. The belief that the action of all these energies is associated with molecular change is, to say the least, highly probable. And I may remark that Christianity has no

quarrel with these discoveries of modern science ;, for its
doctrine is that for the perfection of man's being a bodily
organisation is necessary, and that the "intermediate state"
is a state of suspense and imperfection, out of which, at the
word of the Creator, the indestructible personality of man
shall rise, to assimilate to itself a glorified body. The doctrine of the Resurrection of the Body boldly faces the perplexity as to the connection of a body with personality, which
so greatly troubled ancient speculation on the immortality of
the soul. In respect of the intermediate " state," it only extends (I grant immeasurably) the experience of those suspen-
sions' of the will and the full consciousness of personality,
which we have in life, in sleep, swoon, stupor, dependent on
normal and abnormal conditions of the bodily organization ;
and in respect of the Resurrection, it similarly extends the
action of that mysterious creative will, which moulds the
human body of the present life slowly and gradually out of the
mere germ, and forms, with marvellous rapidity and exuberance
of prolific power, lower organisms of high perfection and
beauty.

But while modern science teaches us to recognise the influence of the bodily organization on mental energy, it has,
with at least equal clearness, brought out in compensation
the distinct power of that mental energy, acting by a process
wholly different from the chain of physical causation, to alter
functionally, and even organically, the bodily frame itself.
The Platonic Socrates (it will be remembered) dwells on the
power of the spirit to control bodily appetite and even passion
(τὸ θυμοειδές,), as also on its having the power to assume

qualities, as a proof that it is not a mere ἁρμονία. Surely modern science has greatly strengthened the former part of his argument, by these discoveries of the power of mind over even the material of the body. This is strikingly illustrated (for example) to the physician, both by the morbid phenomena of what is called generally "hysteria," in which the belief in the existence of physical disease actually produces the most remarkable physical effects on the body ; and also by the more natural action of the mind on the body, when in sickness a resolution to get well masters the force of disease, or a desire to die slowly fulfils itself. Perhaps even more extraordinary is the fact (I believe sufficiently ascertained) that during pregnancy the presentation of ideas to the mind of the mother actually affects the physical organization of the offspring. Hence I cannot but think that, at least as distinctly as ever, our fuller experience discloses to us two different processes of causation acting upon our complex humanity—the one wholly physical, acting sometimes by the coarser mechanical agencies, sometimes by the subtler physiological agencies, and in both cases connecting man through the body with the great laws ruling the physical universe—the other wholly metaphysical, acting by the simple presentation of ideas to the mind (which may, indeed, be so purely subjective that they correspond to no objective reality whatever), and, through them, secondarily acting upon the body, producing no doubt the molecular changes in the brain and the affections of the nervous tissue, which accompany and exhibit mental emotion. In the normal condition of the earthly life, these two powers act and react upon each other, neither being absolutely independent of the other. In the perfect state of the Hereafter we believe that it shall be so still. But we do know of cases in which the metaphysical power is apparently dormant or destroyed, in which accordingly all emotions can be produced automatically by physical processes only, as happens occasionally in dreams (whether of the day or night), and morbid conditions, as of idiocy, which may themselves be produced either by physical injury or by mental shock. I cannot myself see any difficulty in conceiving that the metaphysical power might act, though no doubt in a way of which we have no present experience, and (according to the Christian doctrine) in a condition of some imperfection, when the bodily organization is either suspended or removed. For to me it seems clear that there is something existent, which is neither material nor even dependent on material organization. Whether it be stigmatized as a "heterogeneous entity," or graciously designated by the "good old word soul," is a matter of great indifference. There it is ; and, if it is, I cannot see why it is inconceivable that it should survive all material change. For here, as in other cases, there seems to be a frequent confusion between conceiving that a thing may be, and conceiving how it may be. Of course we cannot figure to ourselves the method of the action of a spiritual energy apart from a bodily organization ; in the attempt to do so the mind glides into quasi-corporeal conceptions and expressions, which are a fair mark for satire. But that there may be such action is to me far less inconceivable, than that the mere fact of the dissolution of what is purely physical should draw with it the destruction of a soul, that can think, love, and pray.

I do not think it necessary to dwell at any length on the second of Mr. Harrison's propositions, denouncing the desire of personal and individual existence as "selfishness," with a vigor quite worthy of his royal Prussian model. But history, after all, has recognized that the poor grenadiers had something to say for themselves. Mr. Hutton has already suggested that, if Mr. Harrison had studied the Christian conception of the future life, he could not have written some of his most startling passages, and has protested against the misapplication of the word "selfishness," which in this, as in other controversies, quietly begs the question proposed for discussion. The fact is that this theory of "Altruism," so eloquently set forth by Mr. Harrison and others of his school, simply contradicts human nature, not in its weakness or sins, but in its essential characteristics. It is certainly not the weakest or ignoblest of human souls, who have felt, at the times of deepest thought and feeling, conscious of but two existences—their own, and the Supreme Existence, whether they call it Nature, Law, or God. Surely this Humanity is a very unworthy deity, at once a vague and shadowy abstraction, and, so far as it can be distinctly conceived, like some many-headed idol, magnifying the evil and hideousness, as well as the good and beauty, of the individual nature. But if it were not so, still that individuality, as well as unity, is the law of human nature, is singularly indicated by the very nature of our mental operations. In the study and perception of truth, each man, though he may be guided to it by others, stands absolutely alone ; in love, on the other hand, he loses all but the sense of unity ; while the conscience holds the balance, recognizing at once individuality and unity. Indeed, the sacredness of individuality is so guarded by the darkness which hides each soul from all perfect knowledge of man, so deeply impressed on the mind by the consciousness of independent thought and will, and on the soul by the sense of incommunicable responsibility, that it cannot merge itself in the life of the race. Self-sacrifice, or unselfishness, is the conscious sacrifice, not of our own individuality, but of that which seems to minister to it, for the sake of others. The law of human nature, moreover, is such that the very attempt at such sacrifice inevitably strengthens the spiritual individuality in all that makes it worth having. To talk of "a perpetuity of sensation as a true Hell" in a being supposed capable of indefinite growth in wisdom, righteousness, and love, is surely to use words which have no intelligible meaning.

No doubt, if we are to take as our guiding principle either Altruism or what is rightly designated "selfishness," we must infinitely prefer the former. But where is the necessity ? No doubt the task of harmonizing the two is difficult. But all things worth doing are difficult ; and it might be worth while to consider whether there is not something in the old belief, which finds the key to this difficult problem in the consciousness of the relation to One Supreme Being, and, recognizing both the love of man and the love of self, bids them both agree in conscious subordination to a higher love of God. What makes our life here will, we believe, make it up hereafter, only in a purer and nobler form. On earth we live at once in our own individuality and in the life of others. Our

heaven is not the extinction of either element of that life—
either of individuality, as Mr. Harrison would have it, or of
the life in others, as in that idea of a selfish immortality which
he has, I think, set up in order to denounce it—but the continued harmony of both under an infinitely increased power of
that supreme principle.

MR. W. R. GREG.

It would seem impossible for Mr. Harrison to write anything that is not stamped with a vigor and racy eloquence
peculiarly his own ; and the paper which has opened the present discussion is probably far the finest he has given to the
world. There is a lofty tone in its imaginative passages
which strikes us as unique among Negationists, and a vein of
what is almost tenderness pervading them, which was not observed in his previous writings. The two combined render
the second portion one of the most touching and impressive
speculations we have read. Unfortunately, however, Mr.
Harrison's innate energy is apt to boil over into a vehemence
approaching the intemperate ; and the antagonistic atmosphere is so native to his spirit that he can scarcely enter the
lists of controversy without an irresistible tendency to become
aggressive and unjust ; and he is, too, inclined to forget the
first duty of the chivalric militant logician, namely, to select
the adversary you assail from the nobler and not the lower
form and rank of the doctrine in dispute. The inconsistencies and weaknesses into which this neglect has betrayed him
in the instance before us have, however, been so severely,

dealt with by Mr. Hutton and Professor Huxley, that I wish rather to direct attention to two or three points of his argument that might otherwise be in danger of escaping the appreciation and gratitude they may fairly claim.

We owe him something, it appears to me, for having inaugurated a discussion which has stirred so many minds to give us on such a question so much interesting and profound, and more especially so much suggestive, thought. We owe him much, too, because, in dealing with a thesis which it is specially the temptation and the practice to handle as a theme for declamation, he has so written as to force his antagonists to treat it argumentatively and searchingly as well. Some gratitude, moreover, is due to the man who had the moral courage boldly to avow his adhesion to the negative view, when that view is not only in the highest degree unpopular, but is regarded for the most part as condemnable into the bargain, and when, besides, it can scarcely fail to be painful to every man of vivid imagination and of strong affections. It is to his credit, also, I venture to think, that, holding this view, he has put it forward, not as an opinion or speculation, but as a settled and deliberate conviction, maintainable by distinct and reputable reasonings, and to be controverted only by pleas analogous in character. For if there be a topic within the wide range of human questioning in reference to which tampering with mental integrity might seem at first sight pardonable, it is that of a future and continued existence. If belief be ever permissible—perhaps I ought to say, if belief be ever possible—on the ground that " there is peace and joy in believing," it is here, where the issues are so vast, where the conception in its highest form is so ennobling, where the practical influences of the Creed are, in appearance at least, so beneficent. But faith thus arrived at has ever clinging to it the curse belonging to all illegitimate possessions. It is precarious, because the flaw in its title-deeds, barely suspected perhaps and never acknowledged, may any moment be discovered ; misgivings crop up most surely in those hard and gloomy crises of our lives when unflinching confidence is most essential to our peace ; and the fairy fabric, built up not on grounded conviction but on craving need, crumbles into dust, and leaves the spirit with no solid sustenance to rest upon.

Unconsciously and by implication Mr. Harrison bears a testimony he little intended, not indeed to the future existence he denies, but to the irresistible longing and necessity for the very belief he labors to destroy. Perhaps no writer has more undesignedly betrayed his conviction that men will not and cannot be expected to surrender their faith and hope without at least something like a compensation; certainly no one has ever toiled with more noble rhetoric to gild and. illuminate the substitute with which he would fain persuade us to rest satisfied. The nearly universal craving for posthumous existence and enduring consciousness, which he depreciates with so harsh a scorn, and which he will not accept as offering even the shadow or *simulacrum* of an argument for the Creed, he yet respects enough to recognize that it has its foundation deep in the framework of our being, that it cannot be silenced and may not be ignored. Having no precious metal to pay it with, he issues paper money instead, skilfully

engraved and gorgeously gilded to look as like the real coin
as may be. It is in vain to deny that there is something
touching and elevating in the glowing eloquence with which
he paints the picture of lives devoted to efforts in the service
of the race, spent in laboring, each of us in his own sphere,
to bring about the grand ideal he fancies for humanity, and
drawing strength and reward for long years of toil in the anticipation of what man will be when those noble dreams shall
have been realized at last—even though we shall never see
what we have wrought so hard to win. It is vain to deny,
moreover, that these dreams appear more solid and less wild
or vague when we remember how close an analogy we may
detect in the labors of thousands around us who spend their
whole career on earth in building up, by sacrifice and painful
struggles, wealth, station, fame and character for their children, whose enjoyment of these possessions they may never
live to see, without their passionate zeal in the pursuit being
in any way cooled by the discouraging reflection. Does not
this oblige us to confess that the posthumous existence Mr.
Harrison describes is not altogether an airy fiction? Still,
somehow, after a few moments spent in the thin atmosphere
into which his brilliant language and unselfish imagination
have combined to raise us, we—ninety-nine out of every hundred of us at the least—sink back breathless and wearied after
the unaccustomed soaring amid light so dim, and craving as
of yore after something more personal, something more solid,
and more *certain.*

To that more solid certainty I am obliged to confess,
sorrowfully, and with bitter disappointment, that I can contrib-

ute nothing—nothing, I mean, that resembles evidence, that can properly be called argument, or that I can hope will be received as even the barest confirmation. Alas ! *can* the wisest and most sanguine of·us all bring anything beyond our own sentiments to swell the common hope ? We have aspirations to multiply, but who has any *knowledge* to enrich our store ? I have of course read most of the pleadings in favor of the ordinary doctrine of the Future State ; naturally, also, in common with all graver natures, I have meditated yet more ; but these pleadings, for the most part, sound to anxious ears little else than the passionate outcries of souls that cannot endure to part with hopes on which they have been nurtured, and which are intertwined with their tenderest affections. Logical reasons to *compel* conviction, I have met with none— even from the interlocutors in this actual Symposium. Yet few can have sought for such more yearningly. I may say I share in the anticipations of believers ; but I share them as aspirations, sometimes approaching almost to a faith, occasionally and for a few moments perhaps rising into something like a trust, but never able to settle into the consistency of a definite and enduring creed. I do not know how far even this incomplete state of mind may not be merely the residuum of early upbringing and habitual associations. But I must be true to my darkness as courageously as to my light. I cannot rest in comfort on arguments that to my spirit have no cogency, nor can I pretend to respect or be content with reasons which carry no penetrating conviction along with them. I will not make buttresses do the work or assume the posture of foundations. I will not cry " Peace, peace, when there is no peace."

I have said elsewhere, and at various epochs of life why the ordinary "proofs" confidently put forward and gorgeously arrayed "have no help in them;" while, nevertheless, the pictures which imagination depicts are so inexpressibly alluring. The more I think and question, the more do doubts and difficulties crowd around my horizon and cloud over my sky. Thus it is that I am unable to bring aid or sustainment to minds as troubled as my own, and perhaps less willing to admit that the great enigma is, and must remain, insoluble. Of two things, however, I feel satisfied—that the negative doctrine is no more susceptible of proof than the affirmative, and that our opinion, be it only honest, can have no influence whatever on the issue, nor upon its bearing on ourselves.

Two considerations that have been borne in upon my mind while following this controversy may be worth mentioning, though neither can be called exactly helpful. One is that we find the most confident, unquestioning, dogmatic belief in heaven (and its correlative) in those whose heaven is the most unlikely and impossible, the most entirely made up of mundane and material elements, of gorgeous glories and of fading splendors[1]—just such things as uncultured and

---

[1] "There may be crowns of material splendour, there may be trees of unfading loveliness, there may be pavements of emerald, and canopies of the brightest radiance, and gardens of deep and tranquil security, and palaces of proud and stately decoration, and a city of lofty pinnacles, through which there unceasingly flows a river of gladness, and where jubilee is ever sung by a concord of seraphic voices."—*Dr. Chalmers' Sermons.*

"Poor fragments all of this low earth—
Such as in dreams could hardly soothe
A soul that once had tasted of immortal truth."—*Christian Year.*

undisciplined natures most envied or pined after on earth, such as the lower order of minds could best picture and would naturally be most dazzled by. The higher intelligences of our race, who need a spiritual heaven, find their imaginations fettered by the scientific training which, imperfect though it be, clips their wings in all directions, forbids their glowing fancy, and annuls that gorgeous creation, and bars the way to each successive local habitation that is instinctively wanted to give reality to the ideal they aspire to; till, in the effort to frame a future existence without a future world, to build up a state of being that shall be worthy of its denizens, and from which everything material shall be excluded, they at last discover that in renouncing the "physical" and inadmissible they have been forced to renounce the "conceivable" as well; and a dimness and fluctuating uncertainty gathers round a scene, from which all that is concrete and definable, and would therefore be incongruous, has been shut out. The next world cannot, it is felt, be a material one; and a truly "spiritual" one even the saint cannot conceive so as to bring it home to natures still shrouded in the garments of the flesh.

The other suggestion that has occurred to me is this :—It must be conceded that the doctrine of a future life is by no means as universally diffused as it is the habit loosely to assert. It is not always discoverable among primitive and savage races. It existed among pagan nations in a form so vague and hazy as to be describable rather as a dream than a religious faith. It can scarcely be determined whether the Chinese, whose cultivation is perhaps the most ancient existing in the world, can be ranked among distinct believers; while the conception of *Nirvana*, which prevails in the meditative minds of other Orientals, is more a sort of conscious non-existence than a future life. With the Jews, moreover, as is well known, the belief was not indigenous, but imported, and by no means an early importation. But what is not so generally recognised is that, even among ourselves in these days, the conviction of thoughtful natures varies curiously in strength and in features at different periods of life. In youth, when all our sentiments are most vivacious and dogmatic, most of us not only cling to it as an intellectual creed, but are accustomed to say and feel that, without it as a solace and a hope to rest upon, this world would be stripped of its deepest fascinations. It is from minds of this age, whose vigor is unimpaired and whose relish for the joys of earth is most expansive, that the most glowing delineations of heaven usually proceed, and on whom the thirst for felicity and knowledge, which can be slaked at no earthly fountains, has the most exciting power. Then comes the busy turmoil of our mid career, when the present curtains off the future from our thoughts, and when a renewed existence in a different scene is recalled to our fancy chiefly in crises of bereavement. And finally, is it not the case that in our fading years—when something of the languor and placidity of age is creeping over us, just when futurity is coming consciously and rapidly more near, and when one might naturally expect it to occupy us more incessantly and with more anxious and searching glances—we think of it less frequently, believe in it less confidently, desire it less eagerly than in our youth? Such, at least, has been my observation and experience, especially among the more reflective and inquiring order of men. The life of the hour absorbs us most completely, as the hours grow fewer and less full ; the pleasures, the exemptions, the modest interests, the afternoon peace, the gentle affections of the present scene, obscure the future from our view, and render it, curiously enough, even less interesting than the past. To-day, which may be our last, engrosses us far more than to-morrow, which may be our FOREVER ; and the grave into which we are just stepping down troubles us far less than in youth, when half a century lay between us and it.

What is the explanation of this strange phenomenon? Is it a merciful dispensation arranged by the Ruler of our life to soften and to ease a crisis which would be too grand and awful to be faced with dignity or calm, if it were actually *realized* at all? Is it that thought—or that vague substitute for thought which we call time—has brought us, half unconsciously, to the conclusion that the whole question is insoluble, and that reflection is wasted where reflection can bring us no nearer to an issue ? Or finally, as I know is true far oftener than we fancy, is it that threescore years and ten have quenched the passionate desire for life with which at first we stepped upon the scene? .We are tired, some of us, with unending and unprofitable toil ; we are satiated, others of us, with such ample pleasures as earth can yield us ; we have had enough of ambition, alike in its successes and failures ; the joys and blessings of human affection on which, whatever their crises and vicissitudes, no righteous or truthful man will cast a slur, are yet so blended with pains which partake of their intensity ; the thirst for knowledge is not slaked, indeed, but the capacity for the labor by which alone it can be gained has consciously died out ; the appetite for life, in short, is gone, the frame is worn and the faculties exhausted ; and— possibly this is the key to the phenomenon we are examining —*age* CANNOT, from the very law of its nature, *conceive itself endowed with the bounding energies of youth*, and without that vigor both of exertion and desire, renewed existence can offer no inspiring charms. Our being upon earth has been enriched by vivid interests and precious joys, and we are deeply grateful for the gift ; but we are wearied with one life, and feel scarcely qualified to enter on the claims, even though balanced by the felicities and glories, of another. It may be the fatigue which comes with age—fatigue of the fancy as well as of the frame ; but somehow, what we yearn for most instinctively at last is *rest*, and the peace which we can imagine the easiest because we know it best is that of sleep.

REV. BALDWIN BROWN.

The theologians appear to have fallen upon evil days. Like some of old, they are filled with rebuke from all sides. They are bidden to be silent, for their day is over. But some things, like Nature, are hard to get rid of. Expelled, they "recur" swiftly. Foremost among these is theology. It seems as if nothing could long restrain man from this, the loftiest exercise of his powers. The theologians and the Comtists have met in the sense which Mr. Huxley justly in- dicates ; he is himself working at the foundations of a larger, nobler, and more complete theology. But for the present, theology suffers affliction, and the theologians have in no small measure themselves to thank for it. The protest rises from all sides, clear and strong, against the narrow, formal, and, in these last days, selfish system of thought and expectation, which they have presented as their kingdom of Heaven to the world.

I never read Mr. Harrison's brilliant essays, full as they always are of high aspiration and of stimulus to noble endeavor, without finding the judgment which I cannot but pass in my own mind on his unbeliefs and denials, largely tempered by thankfulness. I rejoice in the passionate earnestness with which he lifts the hearts of his readers to ideals which it seems to me that Christianity—that Christianity which as a living force in the Apostles' days turned the world upside down, that is, right side up, with its face towards heaven and God—alone can realize for man.

I recall a noble passage written by Mr. Harrison some years ago. " A religion of action, a religion of social duty, devotion to an intelligible and sensible Head, a real sense of incorporation with a living and controlling force, the deliberate effort to serve an immortal Humanity—this, and this alone, can absorb the musings and the cravings of the spiritual man." [1] It seems to me that it would be difficult for any one to set forth in more weighty and eloquent words the kind of object which Christianity proposes, and the kind of help towards the attainment of the object which the Incarnation affords. And in the matter now under debate, behind the stern denunciation of the selfish striving towards a per-

---

[1] *Fortnightly Review*, vol. xii. p. 529.

sonal immortality which Mr. Harrison utters with his accustomed force, there seems to lie not only a yearning for, but a definite vision of, an immortality which shall not be selfish, but largely fruitful to public good. It is true that, as has been forcibly pointed out, the form which it wears is utterly vain and illusory, and wholly incapable, one would think, of accounting for the enthusiastic eagerness with which it appears to be sought. May not the eagerness be really kindled by a larger and more far-reaching vision — the Christian vision, which has become obscured to so many faithful servants of duty by the selfishness and vanity with which much that goes by the name of the Christian life in these days has enveloped it ; but which has not ceased and will not cease, in ways which even consciousness cannot always trace, to cast its spell on human hearts ?

Mr. Harrison seems to start in his argument with the conviction that there is a certain baseness in this longing for immortality, and he falls on the belief with a fierceness which the sense of its baseness alone could justify. But surely he must stamp much more with the same brand. Each day's struggle to live is a bit of the baseness, and there seems to be no answer to Mr. Hutton's remark that the truly unselfish action under such conditions would be suicide. But at any rate it is clear from history that the men who formulated the doctrine and perfected the art of suicide in the early days of Imperial Rome, belonged to the most basely selfish and heartless generation that has ever cumbered this sorrowful world. The love of life is on the whole a noble thing, for the staple of life is duty. The more I see of classes in which at first sight selfishness seems to reign, the more am I struck with the measure in which duty, thought for others, and work for others, enters into their lives. The desire to live on, to those who catch the Christian idea, and would follow Him who "came, not to be ministered unto, but to minister," is a desire to work on, and by living to bless more richly a larger circle in a wider world.

I can even cherish some thankfulness for the fling at the eternity of the tabor in which Mr. Harrison indulges, and which draws on him a rebuke from his critics the severity of which one can also well understand. It is a last fling at the *laus perennis*, which once seemed so beautiful to monastic hearts, and which, looked at ideally, to those who can enter into Mr. Hutton's lofty view of adoration, means all that he describes. But practically it was a very poor, narrow, mechanical thing; and base even when it represented, as it did to multitudes, the loftiest form of a soul's activity in such a sad suffering world as this. I, for one, can understand, though I could not utter, the anathema which follows it as it vanishes from sight. And it bears closely on the matter in hand. It is no dead mediæval idea. It tinctures strongly the popular religious notions of heaven. The favourite hymns of the evangelical school are set in the same key. There is an easy, self-satisfied, self-indulgent temper in the popular way of thinking and praying, and above all of singing, about heaven, which, sternly as the singers would denounce the cloister, is really caught from the monastic choir. There is a very favourite verse which runs thus :—

> There, on a green and flowery mount,
>   Our weary souls shall sit,
> And with transporting joys recount
>   The labors of our feet. [1]

It is a fair sample of the staple of much pious forecasting of the occupations and enjoyments of heaven. I cannot but welcome very heartily any such shock as Mr. Harrison administers to this restful and self-centered vision of immortality. Should he find himself at last endowed with the inheritance which he refuses, and be thrown in the way of these souls mooning on the mount, it is evident that he would feel tempted to give them a vigorous shake, and to set them with some stinging words about some good work for God and for their world. And as many of us want the shaking now badly enough, I can thank him for it, although it is administered by an over-rough and contemptuous hand.

I feel some hearty sympathy, too, with much which he says about the unity of the man. The passage to which I refer commences on page 17 with the words "The philosophy which treats man as man simply affirms that man loves, thinks, acts, not that the ganglia, the senses, or any organ of man, loves, thinks, and acts."

So far as Mr. Harrison's language and line of thought are a protest against the vague, bloodless, bodiless notion of the life of the future, which has more affinity with Hades than with Heaven, I heartily thank him for it. Man is an embodied spirit, and wherever his lot is cast he will need and

---

[1] Mr. Martin's picture of the Plains of Heaven exactly presents it, and it is a picture greatly admired in the circles of which we speak.

will have the means of a spirit's manifestation to and action on its surrounding world. But this is precisely what is substantiated by the Resurrection. The priceless value of the truth of the Resurrection lies in the close interlacing and interlocking of the two words which it reveals. It is the life which is lived here, the life of the embodied spirit, which is carried through the veil and lived there. The wonderful power of the Gospel of "Jesus and the Resurrection" lay in the homely human interest which it lent to the life of the immortals. The risen Lord took up life just where He left it. The things which He had taught His disciples to care about here, were the things which those who had passed on were caring about there, the reign of truth, righteousness, and love. I hold to the truth of the Resurrection, not only because it appears to be firmly established on the most valid testimony, but because it alone seems to explain man's constitution as a spirit embodied in flesh which he is sorely tempted to curse as a clog. It furnishes to man the key to the mystery of the flesh on the one hand, while on the other it justifies his aspiration and realises his hope.

Belief in the risen and reigning Christ was at the heart of that wonderful uprising and outburst of human energy which marked the age of the Advent. The contrast is most striking between the sad and even despairing tone which breathes through the noblest heathen literature, which utters perhaps its deepest wail in the cry of Epictetus, "Show me a Stoic— by heaven I long to see a Stoic," and the sense of victorious power, of buoyant exulting hope, which breathes through the word and shines from the life of the infant Church. "As dying, and behold we live ; as sorrowful, yet always rejoicing ; as poor, yet making many rich ; as having nothing, and yet possessing all things." The Gospel which brought life and immortality to light won its way just as dawn wins its way, when "jocund day stands tiptoe on the misty mountain tops," and flashes his rays over a sleeping world. Everywhere the radiance penetrates ; it shines into every nook of shade ; and all living creatures stir, awake, and come forth to bask in its beams. Just thus the flood of kindling light streamed forth from the Resurrection, and spread like the dawn in the morning sky ; it touched all forms of things in a dark, sad world with its splendour, and called man forth from the tomb in which his higher life seemed to be buried, to a new career of fruitful, sunlit activity ; even as the Saviour prophesied, " The hour is coming, and now is, when the dead shall hear the voice of the Son of God, and they that hear shall live."

The exceeding readiness and joyfulness with which the truth was welcomed, and the measure in which Christendom—and that means all that is most powerful and progressive in human society—has been moulded by it, are the most notable facts of history. Be it truth, be it fiction, be it dream, one thing is clear : it was a baptism of new life to the world which was touched by it, and it has been near the heart of all the great movements of human society from that day until now. I do not even exclude " the Revolution," whose current is under us still. Space is precious, or it would not be difficult to show how deeply the Revolution was indebted to the ideas which this gospel brought into the world. I entirely agree with Lord Blachford that Revelation is the ground on which faith securely rests. But the history of the quickening and the growth of Christian society is a factor of enormous moment in the estimation of the arguments for the truth of immortality. We are assured that the idea had the dullest and even basest origin. Man has a shadow, it suggested the idea of a second self to him! he has memories of departed friends, he gave them a body and made them ghosts! Very wonderful surely, that mere figments should be the strongest and most productive things in the whole sphere of human activity, and should have stirred the spirit and led the march of the strongest, noblest, and most cultivated peoples; until now, in this nineteenth century, we think that we have discovered, as Miss Martineau tersely puts it, that " the theological belief of almost everybody in the civilized world is baseless." Let who will believe it, I cannot.

It may be urged that the idea has strong fascination, that man naturally longs for immortality, and gladly catches at any figment which seems to respond to his yearning and to justify his hope. But this belief is among the clearest, broadest, and strongest features of his experience and history. It must flow out of something very deeply embedded in his constitution. If the force that is behind all the phenomena of life is responsible for all that is, it must be responsible for this also. Somehow man, the masterpiece of Creation, has got himself wedded to the belief that all things here have relations to issues which lie in a world that is behind the shadow of death. This belief has been at the root of his highest endeavor and of his keenest pain; it is the secret of his chronic unrest. Now Nature through all her orders appears to have made all creatures contented with the conditions of their life. The brute seems fully satisfied with the resources of his world. He shows no sign of being tormented by dreams; his life withers under no blight of regret. All things rest, and are glad and beautiful in their spheres. Violate the order of their nature, rob them of their fit surroundings, and they grow restless, sad, and poor. A plant shut out from light and moisture will twist itself into the most fantastic shapes, and strain itself to ghastly tenuity; nay, it will work its delicate tissues through stone walls or hard rock, to find what its nature has made needful to its life. Having found it, it rests and is glad in its beauty once more. Living things, perverted by human intelligent effort, revert swiftly the moment that the pressure is removed. This marked tendency to reversion seems to be set in Nature as a sign that all things are at rest in their natural conditions, content with their life and its sphere. Only in ways of which they are wholly unconscious, and which rob them of no contentment with their present, do they prepare the way for the higher developments of life.

What then means this restless longing in man for that which lies beyond the range of his visible world? Has Nature wantonly and cruelly made man, her masterpiece, alone of all the creatures restless and sad? Of all beings in the Creation must he alone be made wretched by an unattainable longing, by futile dreams of a visionary world? This were an utter breach of the method of Nature in all her operations. It is impossible to believe that the harmony that runs through all her spheres fails and falls into discord in man. The very order of Nature presses us to the conviction that this insatiable longing which somehow she generates and sustains in man, and which is unquestionably the largest feature of his life, is not visionary and futile, but profoundly significant ; pointing with firm finger to the reality of that sphere of being to which she has taught him to lift his thoughts and aspirations, and in which he will find, unless the prophetic order of the Creation has lied to him, the harmonious completeness of his life.

And there seems to be no fair escape from the conclusion by giving up the order, and writing Babel on the world and its life. Whatever it is, it is not confusion. Out of its disorder, order palpably grows ; out of its confusion arises a grand and stately progress. Progress is a sacred word with Mr. Harrison. In the progress of humanity he finds his longed-for immortality. But, if I may repeat in other terms a remark which I offered in the first number of this Review, while progress is the human law, the world, the sphere of the progress, is tending slowly but inevitably to dissolution. Is there discord again in this highest region? Mr. Harrison writes of an immortal humanity. How immortal, if the glorious progress is striving to accomplish itself in a world of wreck? Or is the progress that of a race born with a sore but joyful travail from the highest level of the material creation into a higher region of being, whence it can watch with calmness the dissolution of all the perishable worlds?

The belief in immortality is so dear to man because he grasps through it the complement of his else unshaped and imperfect life. It seems to be equally the complement of this otherwise hopelessly jangled and disordered world.　It is asked triumphantly : Why of all the hosts of creatures does man alone lay claim to this great inheritance ?　Because in man alone we see the experiences, the strain, the anguish, that demand it, as the sole key to what he does and endures. There is to me something horrible in the thought of such a life as ours, in which for all of us, in some form or other, the Cross must be the most sacred symbol, lived out in that bare, heartless, hopeless world of the material, to which Professor Clifford so lightly limits it.　And I cannot but think that there are strong signs in many quarters of an almost fierce revulsion from the ghastly drearihood of such a vision of life.

There seems to me to run through Mr. Harrison's utterances on these great subjects—I say it with honest diffidence of one whose large range of power I so fully recognize, but one must speak frankly if this Symposium is to be worth anything—an instinctive yearning towards Christian ideas, while that faith is denied which alone can vivify them and make them a living power in our world.　There is everywhere a shadowy image of a Christian substance ; but it reminds one of that formless form, wherein " what seemed a head, the likeness of a kingly crown had on."　And it is characteristic of much of the finest thinking and writing of our times.　The saviour Deronda, the prophet Mordecai, lack just that living heart of faith which would put blood into their pallid lineaments, and make them breathe and move among men. Again I say that we have largely ourselves to thank for this saddening feature of the higher life of our times—we who have narrowed God's great kingdom to the dimensions of our little theological sphere. I am no theologian, though intensely interested in the themes with which the theologians occupy themselves. Urania, with darkened brow, may perhaps rebuke my prating. But I seem to see quite clearly that the sad strain and anguish of our life, social, intellectual, and spiritual, is but the pain by which great stages of growth accomplish themselves. We have quite outgrown our venerable, and in its time large and noble, theological shell. We must wait, not fearful, far less hopeless, while by the help of those who are working with such admirable energy, courage, and fidelity, outside the visible Christian sphere, that spirit in man which searches and cannot but search "the deep things of God," creates for itself a new instrument of thought which will give to it the mastery of a wider, richer, and nobler world.

DR. W. G. WARD.

Mr. Harrison considers that the Christian's conception of a future life is "so gross, so sensual, so indolent, so selfish," as to be unworthy of respectful consideration. He must necessarily be intending to speak of this conception in the shape in which we Christians entertain it; because otherwise his words of reprehension are unmeaning. But our belief as to the future life is intimately and indissolubly bound up with our belief as to the present; with our belief as to what is the true measure and standard of human action in this world. And I would urge that no part of our doctrine can be rightly apprehended, unless it be viewed in its connection with all the rest. This is a fact which (I think) infidels often drop out of sight, and for that reason fail of meeting Christianity on its really relevant and critical issues.

Of course I consider Catholicity to be exclusively the one authoritative exhibition of revealed Christianity. I will set forth therefore the doctrine to which I would call attention, in that particular form in which Catholic teachers enounce it ; though I am very far indeed from intending to deny, that there are multitudes of non-Catholic Christians who hold it also. What then, according to Catholics, is the true measure and standard of human action ? This is in effect the very first question propounded in our English elementary Catechism. " Why did God make you ? " The prescribed answer is, " To know Him, serve Him, and love Him in· this world, and to be happy with Him for ever in the next." And St. Ignatius's *Spiritual Exercises*—a work of the very highest authority among us— having laid down the very same " foundation," presently adds, that " we should not wish on our part for health rather than for sickness, wealth rather than poverty, honor rather than ignominy ; desiring and choosing those things alone, which are more expedient to us for the end for which we were created." Now what will be the course of a Christian's life in proportion as he is profoundly imbued with such a principle as this, and vigorously aims at putting it into practice ? The number of believers, who apply themselves to this task with reasonable consistency, is no doubt comparatively small. But in proportion as any given person does so, he will in the first place be deeply penetrated with a sense of his moral weakness ; and (were it for that reason alone) his life will more and more be a life of prayer. Then he will necessarily give his mind with great earnestness and frequency to the consideration, what it is which at this or that period God desires at his hands. On the whole (not to dwell with unnecessary detail on this part of my subject) he will be ever opening his heart to Almighty God ; turning to Him for light and strength under emergencies, for comfort under affliction ; pondering on His adorable attributes ; animated towards Him by intense love and tenderness. Nor need I add how singularly—how beyond words—this personal love of God is promoted and facilitated by the fact, that a Divine Person has assumed human nature, and that God's human acts and words are so largely offered to the loving contemplation of redeemed souls.

In proportion then as a Christian is faithful to his creed, the thought of God becomes the chief joy of his life. "The thought of God," says F. Newman, "and nothing short of it, is the happiness of man ; for though there is much besides to serve as subjects of knowledge, or motive for action, or instrument of excitement, yet the *affections* require a something more vast and more enduring than anything created. He alone is sufficient for the heart who made it. The contemplation of Him, and nothing but it, is able fully to open and relieve the mind, to unlock, occupy, and fix our affections. We may indeed love things created with great intenseness ; but such affection, when disjoined from the love of the Creator, is like a stream running in a narrow channel, impetuous, vehement, turbid. The heart runs out, as it were, only at one door ; it is not an expanding of the whole man. Created natures cannot open to us, or elicit, the ten thousand mental senses which belong to us, and through which we really love. None but the presence of our Maker can enter us ; for to none besides can the whole heart in all its thoughts and feelings be unlocked and subjected. It is this feeling of simple and absolute confidence and communion, which soothes and satisfies those to whom it is vouchsafed. We know that even our nearest friends enter into us but partially, and hold intercourse with us only at times ; whereas the consciousness of a perfect and enduring presence, and it alone, keeps the heart open. Withdraw the object on which it rests, and it will relapse again into its state of confinement and constraint ; and in proportion as it is limited, either to certain seasons or to certain affections, the heart is straitened and distressed."

Now Christians hold, that God's faithful servants will enjoy hereafter unspeakable bliss, through the most intimate imaginable contact with Him whom they have here so tenderly loved. They will see face to face Him, whose beauty is dimly and faintly adumbrated by the most exquisitely transporting beauty which can be found on earth ; Him whose adorable perfections they have in this life imperfectly contemplated, and for the fuller apprehension of which they have so earnestly longed here below. I by no means intend to imply, that the hope of this blessedness is the sole or even the chief inducement which leads saintly men to be diligent in serving God. Their immediate reason for doing so is their keen sense of His claim on their allegiance ; and, again, the misery which they would experience, through their love of Him, at being guilty of any failure in that allegiance. Still the prospect of that future bliss, which I have so imperfectly sketched, is doubtless found by them at times of invaluable service, in stimulating them to greater effort, and in cheering them under trial and desolation.

Such is the view taken by Christians of life in heaven; and surely any candid infidel will at once admit, that it is profoundly harmonious and consistent with their view of what should be man's life on earth. To say that their anticipation of the future, *as it exists in them*, is gross, sensual, indolent, and selfish, is so manifestly beyond the mark, that I am sure Mr. Harrison will, on reflection, retract his affirmation. Apart, however, from this particular comment, my criticism of Mr. Harrison would be this. He was bound, I maintain, to consider the Christian theory of life *as a whole;* and not to dissociate that part of it which concerns eternity, from that part of it which concerns time.

And now as to the merits of this Christian theory. For my own part I am, of course, profoundly convinced that, as on the one hand it is guaranteed by Revelation, so on the other hand it is that which alone harmonizes with the dicta of reason and the facts of experience, so far as it comes into contact with these. Yet I admit that various very plausible objections may be adduced against its truth. Objectors may allege very plausibly, that by the mass of men it cannot be carried into practice; that it disparages most unduly the importance of things secular; that it is fatal to what they account genuine patriotism; that it has always been, and will always be, injurious to the progress of science; above all, that it puts men (as one may express it) on an entirely wrong scent, and leads them to neglect many pursuits which, as being sources of true enjoyment, would largely enhance the pleasurableness of life. All this, and much more, may be urged, I think, by antitheists with very great superficial plausibility; and the Christian controversialist is bound on occasion steadily to confront it. But there is one accusation which has been brought against this Christian theory of life—and that the one mainly (as would seem) felt by Mr. Harrison—which to me seems so obviously destitute of foundation, that I find difficulty in understanding how any infidel can have persuaded himself of its truth : I mean the accusation that this theory is a *selfish* one. There is no need of here attempting a philosophical discussion on the respective claims of what are now called "egoism" and "altruism:" a discussion in itself (no doubt) one of much interest and much importance, and one moreover in which I should be quite prepared (were it necessary) to engage. Here, however, I will appeal, not to philosophy but to history. In the records of the past we find a certain series of men, who stand out from the mass of their brethren, as having pre-eminently concentrated their energy on the love and service of God, and pre-eminently looked away from earthly hopes to the prospect of their future reward. I refer to the Saints of the Church. And it is a plain matter of fact, which no one will attempt to deny, that these very men stand out no less conspicuously from the rest in their self-sacrificing and (as we ordinary men regard it) astounding labours, in behalf of what they believed to be the highest interests of mankind.

Before I conclude I must not omit a brief comment on one other point, because it is the only one on which I cannot concur with Lord Blachford's masterly paper.   I cannot agree with him, that the doctrine of human immortality fails of being supported by " conclusive reasoning."   I do not, of course, mean that the dogma of the Beatific Vision is discoverable apart from Revelation ; but I do account it a truth cognizable with certitude by reason, that the human soul is naturally immortal, and that retribution of one kind or another will be awarded us hereafter, according to what our conduct has been in this our state of probation.   Here, however, I must explain myself.   When theists make this statement, sometimes they are thought to allege that human immortality is sufficiently proved by *phenomena ;* and sometimes they are thought to allege that it is almost intuitively evident.   For myself, however, I make neither of these allegations.   I hold that the truth in question is conclusively established by help of certain premisses ; and that these premisses themselves can previously be known with absolute certitude, on grounds of reason or experience.

They are such as these : (1) There exists that Personal Being, infinite in all perfections, whom we call God.   (2) He has implanted in His rational creatures the sense of right and wrong ; the knowledge that a deliberate perpetration of certain acts intrinsically merits penal retribution.   (3) Correlatively, He has conferred freedom on the human will ; or, in other words, has made acts of the human will exceptions to that law of uniform sequence, which otherwise prevails throughout the phenomenal world.[1]   (4) By the habit of prayer to God

---

[1] I shall not, of course, be understood to deny the existence and frequency of miracles.

we obtain augmented strength for moral action, in a degree which would have been quite incredible antecedently to experience. (5) Various portions of our divinely given nature clearly point to an eternal destiny. (6) The conscious self or ego is entirely heterogeneous to the material world : entirely heterogeneous, therefore, to that palpable body of ours, which is dissolved at the period of death.

I do not think any one will account it extravagant to hold, that the doctrine of human immortality is legitimately deducible from a combination of these and similar truths. The antitheist will of course deny that they *are* truths. Mr. Greg, who has himself "arrived at no conviction" on the subject of immortality, yet says that considerations of the same kind as those which I have enumerated "must be decisive" in favor of immortality "to all to whose spirits communion with their Father is the most absolute of verities." Nor have I any reason to think that even Mr. Huxley and Mr. Harrison, if they could concede my premisses, would demur to my conclusion.

MR. FREDERIC HARRISON.

[I have now, not so much to close a symposium, or general discussion, as to reply to the convergent fire of nine separate papers, extending over more than fifty pages.[1] Neither time, nor space, nor the indulgence of the reader, would enable me to do justice to the weight of this array of criticism, which reaches me in fragments whilst I am otherwise occupied abroad. I will ask those critics, whom I have not been able to notice, to believe that I have duly considered the powerful

---

[1] See his letter in the *Spectator* of August 25.

appeals they have addressed to me. And I will ask those who are interested in this question, to refer to the original papers in which my views were stated. And I will only add, by way of reply, the following remarks which were, for the most part, written and printed, whilst I had nothing before me but the first three papers in this discussion. They contain what I have to say on the theological, the metaphysical, and the materialist aspect of this question. For the rest, I could only repeat what I have already said in the two original essays.]

Whether the preceding discussion has given much new strength to the doctrine of man's immaterial Soul and Future existence I will not pretend to decide. But I cannot feel that it has shaken the reality of man's posthumous influence, my chief and immediate theme. It seemed to me that the time had come, when, seeing how vague and hesitating were the prevalent beliefs on this subject, it was most important to re-member that, from a purely earthly point of view, a man had a spiritual nature, and could look forward after death to some-thing that marked him off from the beasts that perish. I can-not see that what I urged has been in substance displaced; though much criticism (and some of it of a verbal kind) has been directed at the language which I used of others. My object was to try if this life could not be made richer ; not to destroy the dreams of another. But has the old doctrine of a future life been in any way strengthened ? Mr. Hutton, it is true, has a "personal wish" for a perpetuity of volition. Lord Blachford "believes because he is told." And Professor Huxley knows of no evidence that "such a soul and a future life exist ;" and he seems not to believe in them at all.

Philosophical discussion must languish a little, if, when we ask for the philosophical grounds for a certain belief, we find one philosopher believing because he has a "personal wish" for it, and another "believing because he is told." Mr. Hutton says that, as far as he knows, "the thoughts, affections, and volitions are not likely to perish with his body." Professor Huxley seems to think it just as likely that they should. Arguments are called for to enable us to decide between these two authorities. And the only argument we have hitherto got is Mr. Hutton's "personal wish," and Lord Blachford's *ita scriptum est.* I confess myself unable to continue an argument which runs into believing "because I am told." It is for this reason that the lazzarone at Naples believes in the blood of St. Januarius.

My original propositions may be stated thus.

1. Philosophy as a whole (I do not say specially biological science) has established a functional relation to exist between every fact of thinking, willing, or feeling, on the one side, and some molecular change in the body on the other side.

2. This relation is simply one of correspondence between moral and physical facts, not of assimilation. The moral fact does not become a physical fact, is not adequately explained by it, and must be mainly studied as a moral fact, by methods applicable to morals—not as a physical fact, by methods applicable to physics.

3. The moral facts of human life, the laws of man's mental, moral, and affective nature, must consequently be studied, as they have always been studied, by direct observation of

these facts ; yet the correspondences, specially discovered by biological science between man's mind and his body, must always be kept in view. They are an indispensable, inseparable, but subordinate part of moral philosophy.

4. We do not diminish the supreme place of the spiritual facts in life and in philosophy by admitting these spiritual facts to have a relation with molecular and organic facts in the human organism—provided that we never forget how small and dependent is the part which the study of the molecular and organic phenomena must play in moral and social science.

5. Those whose minds have been trained in the modern philosophy of law cannot understand what is meant by sensation, thought, and energy, existing without any basis of molecular change ; and to talk to them of sensation, thought, and energy, continuing in the absence of any molecules whatever, is precisely such a contradiction in terms as to suppose that civilization will continue in the absence of any men whatever.

6. Yet man is so constituted as a social being, that the energies which he puts out in life mould the minds, characters, and habits of his fellow-men ; so that each man's life is, *in effect*, indefinitely prolonged in human society. This is a phenomenon quite peculiar to man and to human society, and of course depends on there being men in active association with each other. Physics and biology can teach us nothing about it ; and physicists and biologists may very easily forget its importance. It can be learnt only by long and refined observations in moral and mental philosophy as a whole, and in the history of civilization as a whole.

7. Lastly, as a corollary, it may be useful to retain the words Soul and Future Life for their associations ; provided we make it clear that we mean by Soul the combined faculties of the *living* organism, and by future life the subjective effect of each man's objective life on the actual lives of his fellow-men.

I. Now I find in Mr. Hutton's paper hardly any attempt to disprove the first six of these propositions. He is employed for the most part in asserting that his hypothesis of a future state is a more agreeable one than mine, and in earnest complaints that I should call his view of a future state a selfish or personal hope. As to the first, I will only remark that it is scarcely a question whether his notion of immortality is beautiful or not, but whether it is true. If there is no rational ground for expecting such immortality to be a solid fact, it is to little purpose to show us what a sublime idea it would be if there were anything in it. As to the second, I will only say that I do not call his notion of a future existence a selfish or personal hope. In the last paragraph of my second paper I speak with respect of the opinion of those who look forward to a future of moral development instead of to an idle eternity of psalm-singing. My language as to the selfishness of the vulgar ideas of salvation was directed to those who insist that unless they are to *feel* a continuance of pleasure they do not care for any continuance of their influence at all. The vulgar are apt to say that what they desire is the sense of personal satisfaction, and if they cannot have this they care for nothing else. This, I maintain, is a selfish and debasing idea. It is the common notion of the popular religion, and its tendency to concentrate the mind on a merely personal salvation does exert an evil effect on practical conduct. I once heard a Scotch preacher dilating on the narrowness of the gate, &c., exclaim, " O dear brethren, who would care to be saved *in a crowd ?* "

I do not say this of the life of grander activity in which Mr. Hutton believes, and which Lord Blachford so eloquently describes. This is no doubt, a fine ideal, and I will not say other than an elevating hope. But on what does it rest? Why this ideal rather than any other? Each of us may imagine, as I said at the outset, his own Elysian fields, or his own mystic rose. But is this philosophy? Is it even religion? Besides, there is this other objection to it. It is not Christianity, but Neo-Christianity. It is a fantasia with variations on the orthodox creed. There is not a word of the kind in the Bible. Lord Blachford says he believes in it, " because he is told." But it so happens that he is not told this, at any rate in the creeds and formularies of orthodox faith. If this view of future life is to rest entirely on revelation, it is a very singular thing that the Bible is silent on the matter. Whatever kind of future ecstasy may be suggested in some texts, certain it is that such a glorified energy as Lord Blachford paints in glowing colours is nowhere described in the Bible. There is a constant practice nowadays, when the popular religion is criticised, that earnest defenders of it come forward exclaiming: "Oh! that is only the vulgar notion of our religion. My idea of the doctrine is so and so," something which the speaker has invented without countenance from official authority. For my part I hold Christianity to be what is taught in average churches and chapels to the millions of professing Christians. And I say it is a very serious fact when philosophical defenders of religion begin by repudiating that which is taught in average pulpits.

Perhaps a little more attention to my actual words might have rendered unnecessary the complaints in all these papers as to my language about the hopes which men cherish for the future. In the first place I freely admit that the hopes of a grander energy in heaven are not open to the charge of vulgar selfishness. I said that they are unintelligible, not that they are unworthy. They are unintelligible to those who are continually alive to the fact I have placed as my first proposition—*that every moral phenomenon is in functional relation with some physical phenomenon.* To those who deny or ignore this truth, there is doubtless no incoherence in all the ideals so eloquently described in the papers of Mr. Hutton and Lord Blachford. But once get this conception as the substratum of your entire mental and moral philosophy, and it is as incoherent to talk to us of your immaterial development as it would be to talk of obtaining redness without any red thing.

I will try to explain more fully why this idea of a glorified activity implies a contradiction in terms to those who are imbued with the sense of correspondence between physical and moral facts. When we conceive any process of thinking, we call up before us a complex train of conditions ; objective facts outside of us or the revived impression of such facts ; the molecular effect of these facts upon certain parts of our organism, the association of these with similar facts recalled by memory, an elaborate mechanism to correlate these im-

pressions, an unknown to be made known, and a difficulty to
be overcome.   All systematic thought implies relations with
the external world present or recalled, and it also implies
some shortcoming in our powers of perfecting those relations.
When we meditate, it is on a basis of facts which we are observing, or have observed and are now recalling, and with a
view to get at some result which baffles our direct observation
and hinders some practical purpose.

The same holds good of our moral energy.   Ecstasy and
mere adoration exclude energy of action. Moral development
implies difficulties to be overcome, qualities balanced against
one another under opposing conditions, this or that appetite
tempted, this or that instinct tested by proof. Moral development does not grow like a fungus ; it is a continual struggle
in surrounding conditions of a specific kind, and an active
putting forth of a variety of practical faculties in the midst of
real obstacles.

So, too, of the affections, they equally imply conditions.
Sympathy does not spurt up like a fountain in the air ; it implies beings in need of help, evils to be alleviated, a fellowship
of giving and taking, the sense of protecting and being protected, a pity for suffering, an admiration of power, goodness,
and truth.   All of these imply an external world to act in,
human beings as objects, and human life under human conditions.

Now all these conditions are eliminated from the orthodox
ideal of a future state.   There are to be no physical impressions, no material difficulties, no evil, no toil, no struggle, no
human beings, and no human objects.   The only condition is

a complete absence of all conditions, or all conditions of which we have any experience. And we say, we cannot imagine what you mean by your intensified sympathy, your broader thought, your infinitely varied activity, when you begin by postulating the absence of all that makes sympathy, thought, and activity possible, all that makes life really noble.

A mystical and inane ecstasy is an appropriate ideal for this paradise of negations, and this is the orthodox view; but it is not a high view. A glorified existence of greater activity and development may be a high view, but it is a contradiction in terms ; exactly, I say, as if you were to talk of a higher civilization without any human beings. But this is simply a metaphysical afterthought to escape from a moral dilemma. Mr. Hutton is surely mistaken in saying the Positivists have forgotten that Christians ever had any meaning in their hopes of a " beatific vision." He must know that Dante and Thomas à Kempis form the religious books of Positivists, and they are, with some other manuals of Catholic theology, amongst the small number of volumes which Comte recommended for constant use. We can see in the celestial "visions " of a mystical and unscientific age much that was beautiful in its time, though not the highest product even of theology. But in our day these visions of paradise have lost what moral value they had, whilst the progress of philosophy has made them incompatible with our modern canons of thought.

Mr. Hutton supposes me to object to any continuance of sensation as an evil in itself. My objection was not that consciousness should be prolonged in immortality, but that nothing else but consciousness should be prolonged. All real human life, energy, thought, and active affection, are to be made impossible in your celestial paradise, but you insist on retaining consciousness. To retain the power of feeling, whilst all means and object are taken away from thinking, all power of acting, all opportunity of cultivating the faculties of sympathy are stifled: this seems to me something else than a good. It would seem to me, that simply to be conscious, and yet to lie thoughtless, inactive, irresponsive, with every faculty of a man paralyzed within you, as if by that villanous drug which produces torpor whilst it intensifies sensation: such a consciousness as this must be a very place of torment.

I think some contradictions which Mr. Hutton supposes he detects in my paper are not very hard to reconcile. I admitted that Death is an evil, it seems ; but I spoke of our posthumous activity as a higher kind of influence. We might imagine, of course, a Utopia, with neither suffering, waste, nor loss ; and compared with such a world, the world as we know it, is full of evils, of which Death is obviously one. But relatively, in such a world as alone we know, Death becomes simply a law of organized nature, from which we draw some of our guiding motives of conduct. In precisely the same way the necessity of toil is an evil in itself; but, with man and his life as we know them, we draw from it some of our highest moral energies. The grandest qualities of human nature, such as we know it at least, would become for ever impossible, if Labor and Death were not the law of life.

Mr. Hutton again takes but a pessimist view of life when

he insists how much of our activity is evil, and how questionable is the future of the race. I am no pessimist, and I believe in a providential control over all human actions by the great Power of Humanity, which indeed brings good out of evil, and assures, at least for some thousands of centuries, a certain progress towards the higher state. Pessimism as to the essential dignity of man and the steady development of his race, is one of the surest marks of the enervating influence of this dream of a celestial glory. If I called it as wild a desire as to go roving through space in a comet, it is because I can attach no meaning to a *human* life to be prolonged without a human frame and a human world; and it seems to me as rational to talk of becoming an angel as to talk of becoming an ellipse.

By "duties" of the world beyond the grave, I meant the duties which are imposed on us in life, by the certainty that our action must continue to have an indefinite effect. The phrase may be inelegant, but I do not think the meaning is obscure.

II. I cannot agree with Lord Blachford that I have fallen into any confusion between a substance and an attribute. I am quite aware that the word Soul has been hitherto used for some centuries as an entity. And I proposed to retain the term for an attribute. It is a very common process in the history of thought. Electricity, Life, Heat, were once supposed to be substances. We now very usefully retain these words for a set of observed conditions or qualities.

I agree with Mr. Spencer that the unity of the social organism is quite as complete as that of the individual organism.   I do not confuse the two kinds of unity ; but I say that man is in no important sense a unit that society is not also a unit.

With regard to the " percipient " and the " perceptible," I cannot follow Lord Blachford. He speaks a tongue that I do not understand.   I have no means of dividing the universe into " percipients " and " perceptibles."   I know no reason why a " percipient " should not be a " perceptible," none why I should not be " perceptible," and none why beings about me should not be " perceptible."   I think we are all perfectly " perceptible "—indeed some of us are more " perceptible " than " percipient "—though I cannot say that Lord Blachford is always " perceptible " to me.   And how does my being " perceptible," or not being "perceptible," prove that I have an immortal soul ? Is a dog " perceptible," is he " percipient ? "   Has he not some of the qualities of a " percipient," and if so, has he an immortal soul? Is an ant, a tree, a bacterium, percipient, and has any of these an immortal soul ; for I find Lord Blachford declaring there is an " ineradicable difference between the motions of a material and the sensations of a living being," as if the animal world were percipient, and the inorganic perceptible ? But surely in the sensations of a living being the animal world must be included. Where does the vegetable world come in ?

I used the word " organism " advisedly, when I said that will, thought, and affection, are functions of a living organism. I decline exactly to localise the organ of any function of mind or will.   When I am asked, What are *we ?* I reply we are *men.*   When I am asked, Are *we* our bodies ? I say no, nor

are we our minds.   Have we no sense of personality, of unity ?
I am asked.   I say certainly ; it is an acquired result of our
nervous organization, liable to be interrupted by derange-
ments of that nervous organization.   What is it that makes
us think and feel?   The facts of our human nature ; I cannot get behind this, and I need no further explanation.   We
are men, and can do ' what men can do.   I say the tangible
collection of organs known as a " man " (not the consensus
or the condition, but the *man*) thinks, wills, and feels, just as
much as that visible organism lives and grows.   We do not
'say that this or that ganglion in particular lives and grows ;
we say the *man* grows.   It is as easy to me to imagine that
we shall grow fifteen feet high, when we have no body, as that
we shall grow in knowledge, goodness, activity, &c., &c., &c.,
when we have no organs.   And the absence of all molecular
attributes would be, I should think, particularly awkward in
that life of cometary motion in the interstellar spaces with
which Lord Blachford threatens us.   But as the poet
says :—

   Trasumanar significar per verba.
   Non si porria—

" *If*," says he, " practical duties are necessary for the perfection of life," we can take a little interstellar exercise.   Why,
practical duties are the sum and substance of life ; and life
which does not centre in practical duties is not Life, but a
trance.

Lord Blachford, who is somewhat punctilious in terms,
asks me what I consider myself to understand " by the incorporation of a consensus of faculties with a glorious future."

Well! it so happens that I did not use that phrase. I have never spoken of an immortal Soul anywhere, nor do I use the word Soul of any but the living man. I said a man might look forward to incorporation with the future of his race, explaining that to mean his "posthumous activity." And I think at any rate the phrase is quite as reasonable as to say that I look forward, as Mr. Hutton does, to a "union with God." What does Mr. Hutton, or Lord Blachford, understand himself to mean by that?

Surely Lord Blachford's epigram about the fiddle and the tune is hardly fortunate. Indeed, that exactly expresses what I find faulty in the view of himself and the theologians. He thinks the tune will go on playing when the fiddle is broken up and burned. I say nothing of the kind. I do not say the man will continue to exist after death. I simply say that his influence will; that other men will do and think what he taught them to do or to think. Just so, a general would be said to win a battle which he planned and directed, even if he had been killed in an early part of it. What is there of fiddle and tune about this? I certainly think that when Mozart and Beethoven have left us great pieces of music, it signifies little to art if the actual fiddle or even the actual composer continue to exist or not. I never said the tune would exist. I said that men would remember it and repeat it. I must thank Lord Blachford for a happy illustration of my own meaning. But it is *he* who expects the tune to exist without the fiddle. *I* say, you can't have a tune without a fiddle, nor a fiddle without wood.

III. I have reserved the criticism of Professor Huxley,

because it lies apart from the principle discussion, and turns mainly on some incidental remarks of mine on "biological reasoning about spiritual things."

I note three points at the outset. Professor Huxley does not himself pretend to any evidence for a theological soul and future life. Again, he does not dispute the account I give of the functional relation of physical and moral facts. He seems surprised that I should understand it, not being a biologist; but he is kind enough to say that my statement may pass. Lastly, he does not deny the reality of man's posthumous activity. Now these three are the main purposes of my argument; and in these I have Professor Huxley with me. He is no more of a theologian than I am. Indeed, he is only scandalized that I should see any good in priests at all. He might have said more plainly that, when the man is dead, there is an end of the matter. But this clearly is his opinion, and he intimates as much in his paper. Only he would say no more about it, bury the carcase, and end the tale, leaving all thoughts about the future to those whose faith is more robust and whose hopes are richer; by which I understand him to mean persons weak enough to listen to the priests.

Now this does not satisfy me. I call it materialism, for it exaggerates the importance of the physical facts, and ignores that of the spiritual facts. And the object of my paper was simply this: that as the physical facts are daily growing quite irresistible, it is of urgent importance to place the spiritual facts on a sound scientific basis at once. Professor Huxley implies that his business is with the physical facts, and the spiritual facts must take care of themselves. I cannot agree with him. That is precisely the difference between us. The spiritual facts of man's nature are the business of all who undertake to denounce priestcraft, and especially of those who preach Lay Sermons.

Professor Huxley complains that I should join in the view-halloo against biological science. Now I never have supposed that biological science was in the position of the hunted fox. I thought it was the hunter, booted and spurred and riding over us all, with Professor Huxley leaping the most terrific gates and cracking his whip with intense gusto. As to biological science, it is the last thing that I should try to run down; and I must protest, with all sincerity, that I wrote without a thought of Professor Huxley at all. He insists on knowing, in the most peremptory way, of whom I was thinking, as if I were thinking of him. Of whom else could I be thinking, forsooth, when I spoke of Biology? Well! I did not bite my thumb at him, but I bit my thumb.

Seriously, I was not writing at Professor Huxley, or I should have named him. I have a very great admiration for his work in biology; I have learned much from him; I have followed his courses of lectures years and years ago, and have carefully studied his books. If, in questions which belong to sociology, morals, and to general philosophy, he seems to me hardly an authority, why need we dispute? Dog should not bite dog; and he and I have many a wolf that we both would keep from the fold.

But if I did not mean Professor Huxley, whom did I mean? Now my paper, I think clearly enough, alluded to two very different kinds of Materialism. There is systematic Materialism, and there is the vague Materialism. The eminent example of the first is the unlucky remark of Cabanis that the brain secretes thought, as the liver secretes bile ; and there is much of the same sort in many foreign theories—in the tone of Moleschott, Buchner, and the like. The most distinct examples of it in this country are found amongst phrenologists, spiritualists, some mental pathologists, and a few communist visionaries. The far wider, vaguer, and more dangerous school of Materialism is found in a multitude of quarters—in all those who insist exclusively on the physical side of moral phenomena—all, in short, who, to use Professor Huxley's phrase, are employed in "building up a physical theory of moral phenomena." Those who confuse moral and physical phenomena are indeed few. Those who exaggerate the physical side of moral phenomena are many.

Now, though I did not allude to Professor Huxley in what I wrote, his criticism convinces me that he is sometimes at least found among these last. His paper is an excellent illustration of the very error which I condemned. The issue between us is this :—We both agree that every mental and moral fact is in functional relation with some molecular fact. So far we are entirely on the same side, as against all forms of theological and metaphysical doctrine which conceive the possibility of human feeling without a human body. But then, says Professor Huxley, if I can trace the molecular facts which are the antecedents of the mental and moral facts, I have *explained* these mental and moral facts. That I deny ; just as much as I should deny that a chemical analysis of the body could ever lead to an explanation of the physical organism. Then, says the Professor, when I have traced out the molecular facts, I have built up a *physical theory of moral phenomena.* That again I deny. I say there is no such thing, or no rational thing, that can be called a physical theory of moral phenomena ; any more than there is a moral theory of physical phenomena. What sort of a thing would be a physical theory of history—history *explained* by the influence of climate or the like? The issue between us centres in this. I say that the physical side of moral phenomena bears about the same part in the moral sciences that the facts about climate bear in the sum of human civilisation. And, that to look to the physical facts as an explanation of the moral, or even as an independent branch of the study of moral facts, is perfectly idle ; just as it would be if a mere physical geographer pretended to give us, out of his geography, a climatic philosophy of history. Yet Professor Huxley has not been deterred from the astounding paradox of proposing to us a *physiological theory of religion.* He tells us how "the religious feelings may be brought within the range of physiological inquiry." And he proposes as a problem—" *What diseased viscus may have been responsible for the 'Priest in Absolution?'*" I will drop all epithets ; but I must say that I call that materialism, and materialism not very nice of its kind. One might as reasonably propose as a problem—What barometrical readings are responsible for the British Constitution? and suggest a congress of meteorologists to do the work of Hallam, Stubbs, and Freeman. No doubt there is *some* connection between the House of Commons and the English climate, and so there is no doubt *some* connection between religious theories and physical organs. But to talk of "bringing religion within the range of physiological inquiry" is simply to stare through the wrong end of the telescope, and to turn philosophy and science upside down. Ah! Professor Huxley, this is a bad day's work for scientific progress—

ἦ κεν γηθήσαι Πρίαμος, Πριάμοιό τε παῖδες.

Pope Pius and his people will be glad when they read that fatal sentence of yours. When I complained of "the attempt to dispose of the deepest moral truths of human nature on a bare physical or physiological basis," I could not have expected to read such an illustration of my meaning by Professor Huxley.

. Perhaps he will permit me to inform him (since that is the style which he affects) that there once was—and indeed we may say still is—an institution called the Catholic Church ; that it has had a long and strange history, and subtle influences of all kinds ; and I venture to think that Professor Huxley may learn more about the *Priest in Absolution* by a few weeks' study of the Catholic system than by inspecting the diseased *viscera* of the whole human race. When Professor Huxley's historical and religious studies "have advanced so far as to enable him to explain" the history of Catholicism, I think he will admit that "Priestcraft" cannot well be made a chapter in a physiological manual. It may be cheap pulpit thunder, but this idea of his of inspecting a "diseased viscus" is precisely what I meant by "biological reasoning about spiritual things." And I stand by it, that it is just as false in science as it is deleterious in morals. It is an attempt (I will not say arrogant, I am inclined to use another epithet) to explain, by physical observations, what can only be explained by the most subtle moral, sociological, and historical observations. It is to think you can find the golden eggs by cutting up the goose, instead of watching the goose to see where she lays the eggs.

I am quite aware that Professor Huxley has elsewhere formulated his belief that Biology is the science which " includes man and all his ways and works." If history, law, politics, morals, and political economy, are merely branches of biology, we shall want new dictionaries indeed ; and biology will embrace about four-fifths of human knowledge. But this is not a question of language ; for we here have Professor Huxley actually bringing religion within the range of *physiological* inquiry, and settling its problems by references to " diseased viscus." But the differences between us are a long story ; and since Professor Huxley has sought me out, and in somewhat monitorial tone has proposed to set me right, I will take an early-occasion to try and set forth what I find paradoxical in his notions of the relations of Biology and Philosophy.

I note a few special points between us, and I have done. Professor Huxley is so well satisfied with his idea of a "physical theory of moral phenomena," that he constantly attributes that sense to my words, though I carefully guarded my language from such a construction. Thus he quotes from me a passage beginning, "Man is one, however compound," but he breaks off the quotation just as I go on to speak of the direct analysis of mental and moral faculties by mental and moral science, not by physiological science. I say: "philosophy and science" have accomplished explanations; I do not say biology; and the biological part of the explanation is a small and subordinate part of the whole. I do not say that the correspondence between physical and moral phenomena is an *explanation* of the human organism. Professor Huxley says that, and I call it materialism. Nor do I say that "spiritual sensibility is a *bodily* function." I say, it is a moral function; and I complain that Professor Huxley ignores the distinction between moral and physical functions of the human organism.

As to the distinction between anatomy and physiology, if he will look at my words again, he will see that I use these terms with perfect accuracy. Six lines below the passage he quotes, I speak of the human mechanism being only explained by a "complete anatomy *and biology*," showing that anatomy is merely one of the instruments of biology.

He might be surprised to hear that he does not himself give an accurate definition of physiology. But so it is. He says: "Physiology is the science which treats of the functions of living organism." Not so; for the finest spiritual sensibility is, as Professor Huxley admits, a function of a living organism; and physiology is not the science which treats of the spiritual sensibilities. They belong to moral science. There are mental, moral, affective functions of the living organism; and they are not within the province of physiology. Physiology is the science which treats of the *bodily* functions of the living organism; as Professor Huxley says in his admirable

Elementary Lessons, it deals with the facts "concerning the action of the *body*." I complain of the pseudo-science which drops that distinction for a minute. He says: "The explanation of a physiological function is the demonstration of the connection of that function with the molecular state of the organ which exerts that function." That I dispute. It is only a small part of the explanation. The explanation substantially is the demonstration of the laws and all the conditions of the function. The explanation of the circulation of the blood is the demonstration of all its laws, modes, and conditions ; and the molecular antecedents of it are but a small part of the explanation. The principal part relates to the molar (and not to the molecular) action of the heart and other organs. " The function of motion is explained," he says, " when the movements of the living body are found to have certain molecular changes for their invariable antecedents." Nothing of the kind. The function of bodily motion is explained when the laws, modes, and conditions of that motion are demonstrated ; and molecular antecedents are but a part of these conditions. The main part of the explanation, again, deals with molar, not molecular, states, of certain organs. " The function of sensation is explained," says Professor Huxley, " when the molecular changes, which are the invariable antecedents of sensations, are discovered." Not a bit of it. The function of sensation is only explained when the laws and conditions of sensation are demonstrated. And the main part of this demonstration will come from direct observation of the sensitive organism organically, and by no molecular discovery whatever. All this is precisely the materialism which I condemn; the fancying that one science can do the work of another, and that any molecular discovery can dispense with direct study of organisms in their organic, social, mental, and moral aspects. Will Professor Huxley say that the function of this Symposium is explained, when we have chemically analysed the solids and liquids which are now effecting molecular change in our respective digestive apparatus? If so, let us ask the butler if he cannot produce a less heady and more mellow vintage. What irritated *viscus* is responsible for the *Materialist in Philosophy?* We shall all philosophise aright, if our friend Tyndall can hit for us the exact chemical formula for our drinks.

It does not surprise me, so much as it might, to find Professor Huxley slipping into really inaccurate definitions in physiology, when I remember that hallucination of his about questions of science becoming questions of molecular physics. The molecular facts are valuable enough; but we are getting molecular-mad, if we forget that molecular facts have only a special part in physiology, and hardly any part at all in sociology, history, morals, and politics; though I quite agree that there is no single fact in social, moral, or mental philosophy, that has not its correspondence in some molecular fact, if we only could know it. All human things undoubtedly depend on, and are certainly connected with, the general laws of the solar system. And to say that questions of human organisms, much less of human society, tend to become questions of molecular physics, is exactly the kind of confusion it would be, if I said that questions of history tend to become questions of astronomy, and that the more refined calculations of planetary movements in the future will explain to us the causes of the English Rebellion and the French Revolution.

There is an odd instance of this confusion of thought at the close of Professor Huxley's paper, which still more oddly Lord Blachford, who is so strict in his logic, cites with approval. " Has a stone a future life," says Professor Huxley, " because the wavelets it may cause in the sea persist through space and time ? " Well ! has a stone a *life* at all ? because if it has no present life, I cannot see why it should have a future life. How is any reasoning about the inorganic world to help us here in reasoning about the organic world ? Professor Huxley and Lord Blachford might as well ask if a stone is capable of civilisation because I said that man was. I think that man is wholly different from a stone ; and from a fiddle ; and even from a dog ; and that to say that a man cannot exert any influence on other men after his death, because a dog cannot, or because a fiddle, or because a stone cannot, may be to reproduce with rather needless affectation the verbal quibbles and pitfalls which Socrates and the sophists prepared for each other in some wordy symposium of old.

Lastly, Professor Huxley seems to think that he has disposed of me altogether, so soon as he can point to a sympathy between theologians and myself. I trust there is great affinity and great sympathy between us ; and pray let him not think that I am in the least ashamed of that common ground. Positivism has quite as much sympathy with the genuine theologian as it has with the scientific specialist. The former may be working-on a wrong intellectual basis, and often it may be by most perverted methods ; but in the best types he has a high social aim and a great moral cause to maintain amongst men. The latter is usually right in his intellectual basis as far as it goes; but it does not go very far, and in the great moral cause of the spiritual destinies of men he is often content with utter indifference and simple nihilism. Mere raving at priestcraft, and beadles, and outward investments, is indeed a poor solution of the mighty problems of the human soul and of social organisation. And the instinct of the mass of mankind will long reject a biology which has nothing for these but a sneer. It will not do for Professor Huxley to say that he is only a poor biologist and careth for none of these things. His biology, however, "includes man and all his ways and works." Besides, he is a leader in Israel; he has preached an entire volume of Lay Sermons; and he has waged many a war with theologians and philosophers on religious and philosophic problems. What, if I may ask him, is his own religion and his own philosophy? He says that he knows no scientific men who "neglect all philosophical and religious synthesis." In that he is fortunate in his circle of acquaintance. But since he is so earnest in asking me questions, let me ask him to tell the world what is his own synthesis of philosophy, what is his own idea of religion? He can laugh at the worship of Priests and Positivists; whom, or what, does he worship? If he dislikes the word Soul, does he think man has anything that can be called a spiritual nature? If he derides my idea of a Future life, does he think that there is anything which can be said of a man, when his carcase is laid beneath the sod, beyond a simple final *Vale?*

P.S.—And now space fails me to reply to the appeals of so many critics. I cannot enter with Mr. Roden Noel on that great question of the materialisation of the spirits of the dead; I know not whether we shall be "made one with the great Elohim, or angels of Nature, or if we shall grovel in dead material bodily life." I know nothing of this high matter: I do not comprehend this language. Nor can I add anything to what I have said on that sense of personality which Lord Selborne and Canon Barry so eloquently press on me. To me that sense of personality is a thing of somewhat slow growth, resulting from our entire nervous organisation and our composite mental constitution. It seems to me that we can often trace it building up and trace it again decaying away. We feel ourselves to be *men*, because we have human bodies and human minds. Is that not enough? Has the baby of an hour this sense of personality? Are you sure that a dog or an elephant has not got it? Then has the baby no soul; has the dog a soul? Do you know more of your neighbor, apart from inference, than you know of the dog? Again, I cannot enter upon Mr. Greg's beautiful reflections, save to point out how largely he supports me. He shows, I think with masterly logic, how difficult it is to fit this new notion of a glorified activity on to the old orthodoxy of beatific ecstasy. Canon Barry reminds us how this orthodoxy involved the resurrection of the body, and the same difficulty has driven Mr. Roden Noel to suggest that the material world itself may be the *débris* of the just made perfect. But Dr. Ward, as might be expected, falls back on the beatific ecstasy as conceived by the mystics of the thirteenth century. No word here about moral activity and the social converse, as in the Elysian fields, imagined by philosophers of less orthodox severity.

One word more. If my language has given any believer pain, I regret it sincerely. It may have been somewhat obscure, since it has been so widely arraigned, and I think misconceived. My position is this. The idea of a glorified energy in an ampler life is an idea utterly incompatible with exact thought, one which evaporates in contradictions, in phrases which when pressed have no meaning. The idea of beatific ecstasy is the old and orthodox idea ; it does not involve so many contradictions as the former idea, but then it does not satisfy our moral judgment. I say plainly that the hope of such an infinite ecstasy is an inane and unworthy crown of a human life. And when Dr. Ward assures me that it is merely the prolongation of the saintly life, then I say the saintly life is an inane and unworthy life. The words I used about the "selfish" view of futurity, I applied only to those who say they care for nothing but personal enjoyment, and to those whose only aim is "to save their own souls," Mr. Baldwin Brown has nobly condemned this creed in words far stronger than mine. And here let us close with the reflection that the language of controversy must always be held to apply not to the character of our opponents, but to the logical consequences of their doctrines, if uncorrected and if forced to their extreme.

A MODERN "SYMPOSIUM."[1]

THE INFLUENCE UPON MORALITY OF A DECLINE IN RELIGIOUS BELIEF.

SIR JAMES STEPHEN.

Many persons regard everything which tends to discredit theology with disapprobation, because they think that all such speculations must endanger morality as well. Others assert that morality has a basis of its own in human nature, and that, even if all theological belief were exploded, morality would remain unaffected.

My own view is that each party is to a considerable extent right, but that the true practical inference is often neglected.

Understanding by the theology of an age or country the theory of the universe generally accepted then and there, and by its morality the rules of life then and there commonly regarded as binding, it seems to me extravagant to say that the one does not influence the other. The difference between

---

[1] THE NINETEENTH CENTURY, April and May, 1877.

living in a country where the established theory is that exis·
tence is an evil, and annihilation the highest good, and living
in a country where the established theory is that the earth is
the Lord's and the fulness thereof, the round world and they
that dwell therein, has surely a good deal to do with the other
differences which distinguish Englishmen from Buddhists.

Even if it be said that such differences are merely a way
of expressing the result of a difference of temperament and
constitution otherwise caused, this does not diminish the
effect of a belief in the truth of the theory. Kali, Bhowanee,
and other malevolent deities worshipped in India are probably phantoms engendered by fear working on a rank fancy ;
but this does not make the belief in their real existence less
influential in those who hold it. A man who cuts off the end
of his tongue to propitiate Kali would let it alone if he
ceased to believe in her existence, though the temper of
mind which created her might still remain, and show itself in
other ways.

The belief that the course of the world is ordered by a
good God, that right and wrong are in the nature of a divine
law, that this world is a place of trial, and part only of a
wider existence—in a word, the belief in God and a future
state—may be accounted for in various ways. Now that in
this country (to go no further) the vast majority of people believe these doctrines to be true in fact just as they believe it
to be true in fact that ships and carriages can be driven by
steam, and that their conduct is in innumerable instances as
distinctly influenced by the one belief as by the other, appear
to me to be propositions too plain to be proved.

On the other hand, it seems at least equally evident that morality has a basis of its own quite independent of all theology whatever. It is difficult to imagine any doctrine about theology which has not prevailed at some time or place ; but no one ever heard of men living together without some rules of life—that is, without some sort of morality. Given human action and human passion, and a vast number of people all acting and feeling, moral rules of conduct of some sort are a necessary consequence. The destruction of religion would, I think, involve a moral revolution; but it would no more destroy morality than a political revolution destroys law. It would substitute one set of moral rules and sentiments for another, just as the establishment of Christianity and Mohammedanism did when they superseded various forms of paganism.

It would be scarcely worth while to write down these common-places, if it were not for the sake of the practical inference. It is that theology and morality ought to stand to each other in precisely the same relation as facts and legislation.

No one would propose to support by artificial means a law passed under a mistake, for fear it should have to be altered. To say that the truth of a theological doctrine must not be questioned, lest the discovery of its falsehood should produce a bad moral effect, is in principle precisely the same thing. It is at least as unlikely that false theology should produce good morals as that legislation based on a mistaken view of facts should work well in practice.

I will give two illustrations of this—any number might be

given. Suicide is commonly regarded as wrong; and this moral doctrine is defended on theological grounds, which are summed up in the old saying that the soldier must not leave his post till he is relieved. I will not inquire whether any other argument can be produced forbidding suicide to a person laboring under a disease which converts his whole life into one long scene of excruciating agony, and which must kill him in the course of a few useless months, during which he is a source of misery, and perhaps danger, to his nearest and dearest friends. I confine myself to saying that, if it could be shown that there is no reason to suppose that God has in fact forbidden such an act, its morality might be discussed and decided upon on different grounds from those on which it must be considered and decided upon on the opposite hypothesis.

Take again the law of marriage. Suppose a man's wife is hopelessly insane—ought he to be allowed to marry again? Ought divorce to be permitted in any case? These questions will be discussed in a very different spirit, though it is possible that they might be answered in the same way, by persons who do and by persons who do not believe in sacraments, and that marriage is a sacrament.

Now let us suppose for the sake of argument that it could be shown that if all theological considerations were set aside, it would be desirable that a person dying of cancer should be permitted to commit suicide, and that a man whose wife was incurably mad should be allowed to marry again; and that on the other hand, if theological considerations were taken into account, the opposite was desirable. Upon these suppositions the question whether the theological beliefs which make the difference are beneficial or not will depend on the question whether they are true or not. Applied generally, this shows that the support which an existing creed gives to an existing system of morals is irrelevant to its truth, and that the question whether a given system of morals is good or bad cannot be fully determined until after the determination of the question whether the theology on which it rests is true or false. The morality is good if it is founded on a true estimate of the consequences of human actions. But if it is founded on a false theology, it is founded on a false estimate of the consequences of human actions ; and, so far as that is the case, it cannot be good ; and the circumstance that it is supported by the theology to which it refers is an argument against, and not in favor of, that theology.

LORD SELBORNE.

I begin by observing that (putting special cases aside, and looking at the question in a general way) morality has not flourished, amongst either civilised or uncivilised men, when religious belief has been generally lost, or utterly debased. Not to dwell upon the case of savage races, the modern Hindoos and Chinese have long been civilised, but are certainly not moral ; nor can anything worse be conceived than the morality of the Greeks and Romans, at the height of their civilisation. The morality of the Romans, in the old republican times when they knew nothing of Greek philosophy, was praised by Polybius, who connected it directly, and emphatically, with the influence among them of religious belief. After their intellectual cultivation had taken its tone from the irreligious or agnostic materialism of Epicurus (hardly distinguishable, I think, from that sort of philosophy which some persons think destined to supplant religious belief in the present day), their morality became what is described in the first chapter of the Epistle to the Romans and in the Satires of Juvenal; nor does it seem to have been worse than that of the other civilised races on the shores of the Mediterranean, over whom, at the same time, religion had equally lost its influence.

On the other hand, it seems to me certain, as an historical fact, that the place which the principles of love and benevolence, humility and self-abnegation, have assumed in the morality of the Christian nations (with a wide-spreading influence which has been advancing till the present time with the growth of civilisation) is specifically due to Christianity. To Christianity are specifically due (1) our respect for human life, which condemns suicide, infanticide, political assassination, and I might almost say homicide generally, in a way previously unknown, and still unknown where Christianity does not prevail; (2) our recognition of such moral and spiritual relations between man and man as are inconsistent with the degradation of women, and with the practice of slavery; (3) our reverence for the bond of marriage; and (4) our abhorrence of some particular forms of vice. I do not mean to deny that traces of a state of opinion, more or less similar upon some of these points, are discoverable in what we know of the manners of some non-Christian nations: but it is historically true to say, that the prevalence of each of these principles, as manifested amongst ourselves, is specifically due to Christianity. Of Christianity I speak in a sense inclusive of all that it derives from the antecedent Jewish system; of which it claims to be the true continuation and development.

If freedom of inquiry is not to be stopped, after the rejection of religious belief, it must gradually extend itself to the whole circle of morality: most, if not all, of which is as little capable of demonstrative proof through the evidence of the senses as any of the doctrines of religion. Those who reject religion will not voluntarily submit to moral restraints founded upon the religion which they reject, unless they can be placed upon some other intellectual basis, sufficiently cogent to themselves to resist the attractions of appetite or self-interest. That large part of mankind who are always too much under the government of their inclinations and passions will be quicker in drawing moral corollaries from irreligious principles than the philosophers by whom those principles are propounded; and the advanced posts of morality, in which the influence of religion culminates, and of which the necessity may not be so evident on natural or social grounds, are not likely to be very strenuously defended by those philosophers themselves.

If the religious foundations and sanctions of morality are given up, what is to be substituted for them?

First; will the modern notion of a duty to act so as may conduce to the greatest happiness of the greatest number of men be sufficient? I think, certainly not. The idea of duty is not, to my mind, practical or intelligible without religious conceptions; and this particular conception of duty depends entirely upon a test extrinsic, and not personal, to the individual—a test too, which it is difficult (not to say impossible) for each individual to verify for himself; though it may be verified, to their own satisfaction, by philosophical students of casuistry or political economy. Those motives are of necessity strongest which directly concern the man himself : and a moral principle which attempts to counteract influences operating directly and immediately upon the will by others which are speculative and remote, without any higher sanctions realised by and reacting upon the individual, must necessarily be weak.

But, secondly ; will this idea be sufficient, if so modified as to present to the man the pursuit of his own happiness in this world as the rule of life, but teach him to discover it by observing and doing those things which most conduce to the happiness of men in general? In this form it is older and more plausible ; but the difficulties of making it practical are really very much the same. This doctrine, as Aristotle observes, depends upon a general induction : it deals only with general truths, and general conclusions, to which there are many apparent and (if there was no law of moral retribution and adjustment behind) many real exceptions. The foundations of a man's moral character and habits must be laid in his youth : when (as Aristotle also says) he is inexperienced, naturally inclined to follow his passions, and not predisposed to accept the disquisitions of philosophers as proof that his own happiness will not be promoted by seeking it in his own way. The temperament most likely to act consciously on such a rule of life is not the most generous ; it is rather that which is cold and calculating, and which values the reputation more than the reality of virtue. Upon such men, at the best, its influence is to establish a low standard of virtue ; perhaps only to check and impose limits on their tendencies to vice. Over others it can have little or no power, except when operating in combination with, and subordination to higher principles.

Not only did the ethical systems of the ancients which were based upon this principle fail to make men moral, but we see its impotence constantly exemplified amongst those whom we call " men of the world "—a class of persons who are by no means indifferent to their own happiness, or to the good opinion of the world, but by whom the influence of religious belief is not practically felt ;—exemplified, too, on points of morality of which the reasonableness seems most manifest. There are no virtues, I suppose, which can more readily be shown to be conducive to happiness, whether particular or general, than that which the Greeks called ἐγκράτεια, and that of benevolence. What can be more contrary, to both at once of these, than the irregular indulgence of sensual appetite at the cost of the permanent degradation, and almost certain misery, of human beings who are its instruments and victims, and of innumerable physical as well as moral evils to individuals, families, and mankind at large ? Yet how very common is this sort of immorality even among cultivated men, living on good terms with society ! How little it is reproved, how seldom restrained, except by the authority, or through the influence, direct or indirect, of religion ! All readers of Horace remember the *sententia dia Catonis*, and I doubt whether non-religious opinion among ourselves is much stricter on this subject, though it may be less freely expressed.   If it is otherwise as to some of the more abnormal forms of ἀκρασία, I have already said that this is specifically due to Christianity. The cultivated Greeks and Romans spoke and wrote lightly and familiarly of vices of which we do not speak at all : they regarded them, indeed, as effeminate, but not as infamous, and certainly did not visit them with grave social penalties. So tainted was their moral atmosphere, that even such really religious men among them as Socrates and Plato (to whom, however, a religion teaching morals with definiteness and authority was unknown) surprise us by their want of sensitiveness on these points, as manifested in some passages of the Socratic Dialogues.

I will next inquire whether a sufficient rule of morality is to be found, when religion is set aside, in any law of our nature ;—first, regarding the constitution of our nature apart from—and, secondly, taking into account—the existence in it of a moral instinct or sense.

If any one calls the application of right reason to human conduct generally, a law of our nature, from which such a rule is to be derived, without taking into account the moral sense,—this, as it seems to me, would be only a different and more indefinite mode of expressing substantially the same theories, which have been already dealt with.

But it may, perhaps, be suggested that laws of our nature from which such a rule may be derived, are to be found in the

final causes and purposes of the several organs and powers
which exist in that nature ; and that the use of any of those
organs or powers in a manner aberrant from their proper
causes and purposes is a breach of natural morality. I do
not pause to inquire whether the idea of "cause" and "purpose," which is involved in such a view, can be verified apart
from religion. But such a rule would, at best, be far from
coextensive with the whole field of morality : some most
necessary parts of a moral code (such *e.g.* as the regulation of
the relations between the sexes) being incapable of being
deduced, with any approach to certainty, from the mere
constitution of our nature. As to some of our faculties, the
determination, with sufficient accuracy to furnish a rule of
life, of their final causes and purposes, might involve difficult
philosophical inquiries. As to others, though there might be
no such difficulty, it is to be remembered that we have a
complex nature, in which the forces which operate, either
mechanically or in a way resembling the mechanical, upon the
will are constantly in practical antagonism to the regulative
faculty. The faculties of which the final causes are most
obvious exist, not apart from, but in combination with, other
elements of our nature which (either generally or often) result
in tendencies to their use without any direct view to the fulfilment of their proper purposes. The gratification of some of
those tendencies (such *e.g.* as eating and drinking for the
mere pleasure of taste, and not for nourishment) can hardly
be condemned as immoral, on natural grounds, unless carried
so far as to overpower reason, or impair strength or health.
When it is carried to that excess (as in the case of intem-

perance), it is still true that the origin of the vice has been in the natural constitution of men's bodies, by which a sensible gratification has been found in its indulgence: which (as it seems to me) goes far to prove that this conception of a physical law cannot be relied upon, even in the cases to which it is most directly applicable, as a practical basis of morality—a view of which is confirmed by the actual prevalence among men of that class of vices, even when, to all natural safeguards, is superadded the external influence of religion.

When we proceed to take into account the moral instinct or sense, we come upon the border-ground, if not into the proper territory, of Religion. To a man who believes in a moral government of the Universe, in the distinctness of the *Ego*, the real man, from his bodily organisation, and in the doctrines of moral responsibility and moral adjustment in a future state, nothing can be more real, nothing more intelligible, than this moral instinct or sense, with its suggestions of right and wrong, of duty, guilt, and sin, and its judicial conscience. But, if all these postulates are denied, what is then to be thought of this moral instinct or sense? Why is it, on that hypothesis, less a mere accident of the nervous system, or of some other part of the bodily organisation, than the religious instinct, which is already supposed to set aside, as resting upon no demonstrable ground? As a phenomenon, and in some sense a fact, it exists, just as the religious instinct does (if they be not really the same); but those principles of thought which explain away the one, as having no proper objective cause, and as indicative of no objective truth, may as easily explain away the other also. The one is not more susceptible of sensible and experimental demonstration than the other. If a man were merely a higher order of the organisation of matter, homogeneous with, and produced by spontaneous development from, inorganic substances, plants, and inferior animals, and under no responsibility to any moral intelligence greater than his own, what reality would there be in the conception of a moral law of obligation, inapplicable to all other known forms of matter, and applicable only to man.

These questions are practical. Experience, on the large scale, shows that men who disregard the religious, cannot generally be trusted to pay regard to the moral, sense. A moral sense, not believed in, can never supply a practical foundation for morality. On the other hand, a moral sense, believed in, is (in reality) itself religion—possibly inarticulate, but religion still. Such a belief cannot exist, without accepting the evidence of the moral sense as equally trustworthy concerning those things of which it informs us, as the evidence of the bodily sense is concerning those things of which they inform us. It is, of course, only from the impressions made upon our own minds that we can know anything about any of the subjects, either of physical, or of intellectual, or of moral sensation : their intrinsic nature, abstracted from those impressions, is to us, in each case alike, an inaccessible mystery. But belief in the sense is belief in the truth of the information which the sense gives to us : that is, that this information, if rightly apprehended, is trustworthy, as far as it goes ; that there are objective realities corresponding with it.   The moral sense, believed in, is not merely a possible, but I suppose it to be the only possible, human foundation of morality.   An intelligent belief in the moral sense naturally takes the man beyond himself, to a higher source of his moral conceptions, which it really presupposes ; and any truths correlative to it, which are either ascertainable by the processes of reason, or capable of being otherwise made known, will naturally, when they become known, be recognised, in their proper relation to it, and cannot be rejected without doing it violence.   Any such correlative knowledge of the higher truths (to the existence of which the moral sense testifies, though it does not fully reveal them) must enlighten, inform, and strengthen it.   It is the office of such knowledge to answer authoritatively those questions, as to the real nature, the proper work, the true happiness, the true place in the Universe, of man, which philosophy has always been asking, and has never, by itself, been able to solve.   It harmonises, accounts for, and enforces by authoritative sanctions, the concurrent testimonies of the moral sense, the religious instinct, nature interpreted by reason, and reason enlightened by experience.   On the other hand, the want, and still more the rejection, of such knowledge (supposing it to be attainable, and true) must, in a corresponding degree, obscure, perplex, or discredit, the moral sense.

I am well aware that some who seem to reject all dogmatic theology, and even the principles of natural religion. do nevertheless live up to a high moral standard ; just as there are too many others, professing (not always insincerely) to believe in religion, who do the reverse.   The moral sense never has been, and never will be, extinguished among mankind ; and in all ages and countries, of which we have any real historical knowledge, there have been conspicuous examples of men who have made it their rule of life. Doubtless there have been many more who did so, of whom we know nothing : nor is it unreasonable to believe that there may be many such, even among very degraded races. But these facts do not invalidate general conclusions as to the general moral tendency of a decline of religious belief. Those examples of exceptional goodness have not been sufficient to prevent, or to arrest, a progressive deterioration of general morality, when the light of religion has been absent or obscured ; and the best ancient schemes of philosophy, which were founded upon the moral sense, failed to compete practically with that of materialism, which did all that was possible to destroy it. " Live while we may "—" let us eat and drink, for to-morrow we die "—are natural corollaries from the doctrine of Epicurus ; whatever more refined conceptions that philosopher, or any of his followers, may have propounded. Such will ever be the effect, in the world generally, of a popular disbelief in the doctrines of immortality and retribution : not because the hope of rewards, or the fear of punishments, is the foundation of religious morality (which, to fulfil the requirements either of religion or of the moral sense, must ascend much higher), but because our nature is so constituted, that the destiny of the individual, for good or evil, for happiness or the reverse, is inseparably bound up with the moral law of his being ; and because those aids and defences, which result from the recognition of this truth, are necessary for the ascendency of the higher over the lower elements of our nature, and for the education of man to virtue. A boy, whose mainsprings of right action are conscience and love, will not endeavor to fulfil the objects for which he is sent to school more selfishly, or from less worthy motives, when he is informed of their relation to his future life, than if he were left in ignorance of it; but the knowledge of that relation, by making him understand the importance of the future as compared with the present, and the meaning and reasonableness of his present duties, may enable him better to fulfil them.

All that has been said assumes, of course, that there is such a thing as religious truth : nor is it possible to deny that, if this could really be disproved, the morality founded upon it would fail. But it cannot be without importance, whenever the proper evidences of the truth of religion are considered, to take into account, as one of them, its relation to morality : the certainty that, if it were displaced, the system of morality now received among men would, to a great extent, fall with it ; and the extreme intellectual difficulty of maintaining in that event the supremacy of the moral sense, or placing the morality of the future upon a new basis, likely to acquire general authority among mankind. If it should be suggested that a sufficient moral code for practical purposes might be maintained by increasing the stringency of human laws in proportion to the failure of religious sanctions, I should reply, that the power of human laws depends upon morality, and not morality upon human laws ; and that any legislation, greatly in advance of the moral sentiment of the community, would certainly not be effectual, and could not long be maintained.

It has been no part of my purpose to enter into an examination of any questions as to particular doctrines of religion. I have throughout used the word "religion" in a sense exclusive of all systems, usurping that name, which take no cognisance of morality, or which are repugnant, in their practical precepts, to the general moral sense of mankind ; and I have not dissembled my belief, that Christianity (regarded in its general aspect, with reference to the points of agreement rather than those of difference among Christians) does fulfil the conditions necessary for moral efficacy. Error, inconsistency, incompleteness, or admixture of foreign elements, in particular modes of apprehending or representing it, must, no doubt, as far as they prevail, and in proportion to their importance, detract from the authority, or deteriorate the quality, of its influence. So also must the mere fact of disagreement. But, notwithstanding all these drawbacks, Christianity is the great moral power of the world. It has often been supposed to be declining, but has, as often, renewed its strength ; nor has any other power been found to take its place, where it has seemed to lose ground. As to other forms of religion, it may, without difficulty, be admitted, that such elements as they have in common with Christianity may be expected (except so far as they are neutralised or counteracted by other contrary elements) to tend in their measure towards the same standard of morality. It is proper (as I suppose) to Christianity, rightly understood, to assert the identity of its own essential principles with those of natural religion, while teaching that the moral government of the world has been so conducted as not to leave mankind dependent upon natural religion only ; and it refers to a common origin with itself all the elements of religious belief, consistent with its own doctrines, which have been, at any time or place, accepted among the nations of the world. These propositions, and also that of the presence of the religious principle in any practical belief of the moral sense, appear to be in accordance with what is said by St. Paul in the 19th and 20th verses of the first, and the 14th and 15th verses of the second, chapters of the Epistle to the Romans.

REV. DR. MARTINEAU.

In order to estimate aright the moral influence of declining religious belief, the relation between morals and religion must be accurately conceived. They may be regarded as independent, or as identical, or, again, either may be taken to be the foundation of the other. The following positions will serve as a sufficient ground for the opinion which I shall offer.

A sense of duty is inherent in the constitution of our nature, and cannot be escaped till we can escape from ourselves. It does not wait on any ontological conditions, and incur the risk of non-existence should no assurance be gained with regard to a being and a life beyond us. Even though we came out of nothing, and returned to nothing, we should be subject to the claim of righteouness so long as we are what we are. Morals have their own base, and are second to nothing.

Apart from this intrinsic consciousness of ethical distinctions, no ontological discoveries would avail to set up a law of duty, and give us the characteristics of moral beings. A Supreme Power might dictate an external rule, and break us in to obedience by hopes and fears of unlimited extent. But by this sway of preponderant interests we are not carried beyond prudence; and in the absence of a law within, responding to the demands from without, we do not reach the confines of moral obligation; and, in case of failure, we incur the sense only of error, not of sin. Theology cannot supply a base for morals that have lost their own.

Does it follow that because morals are indigenous, they are therefore self-sufficing? By no means. Though religion is not their foundation, it is assuredly their crown—related to them as Plato says dialectic is to the sciences, ὥσπερ θριγκὸς τοῖς μαθήμασιν [1]—the *coping* that consummates them. Be the genesis of the conscience what it may, we learn from it at last that there is a better and a worse in the springs of action which contend for us; and that, whilst it is open to us as a possibility, it is closed against us as a right, to follow the lower when the higher calls. The *authority* which stamps the one as a temptation, and the other as a peremptory claim, is not, we are well aware, of our own making; for it masters us with compunction, and defies all repeal. Nor is it the mere expression of public self-interest; for it extends beyond the range of social action, and covers the whole voluntary field. Speaking with a voice before which our whole personality bows, and which equally gives law to other men, it issues from a source transcending human life, and infusing into it

[1] *Rep.* vii. 534 E.

a moral order from a more comprehensive sphere. It postulates a superior will in communion with ours, and administering this world as a school of character.

To this result our moral experience naturally runs up, and stops short of it only where its course is artificially arrested. Till it is reached, the ethical demands upon us seem to address us in tones too portentous for their immediate significance; remorse clings to us with a tenacity, aspiration returns upon us with a power, which reason cannot adequately justify. But in the presence of an objective moral law pervading the universe, administered by a Mind wherein it perfectly lives, and continued for man beyond his present term of years, the scale of the ethical passions, and the intensity of admiration and reverence for the good, fall into proportionate place, and escape the irony of being at once the ultimate nobleness and the supreme extravagance of our nature. Religion, on this. side, is but the open blossom of the moral germs implanted within us—the explicit form, developed in thought, of faiths implicitly contained in the sense of responsibility and the forebodings of guilt. Its effect, therefore, is to suffuse with a divine light relations and duties which before were simply personal and social.

A similar transfiguration befalls the pleasures and pains attending voluntary conduct, and constituting its natural "sanctions." Treated as ultimate facts, they can never acquire more than a prudential significance. Treated as symbolical lineaments of a world under moral government they are invested with an expression of character, and look into us with living eyes. Their appeal alights no longer on self-regarding hope and fear, but on the springs of sympathy and shame :—they pass from sensitive to ethical phenomena. The new and ideal meaning thus given to a large portion of actual human experience cannot pause there ; it completes itself in the congenial anticipation of a further and invisible store of awards consummating the incipient justice of this world. The faith in a future life—where it is more than a belief at second hand—has its sheet-anchor in the moral affections. But for the felt interval between what we are and what we ought to be, for the indignation at wrong, for compassion towards innocent suffering, and reverence for high excellence, vaticinations of renewed existence would have no origin and no support.

In assigning this method of growth to religion, I do not mean to deny that it may have other lines of formation. The nature-worship which plays so great a part in ancient civilisation has a different history, and stands in much less intimate relations with the moral life of its votaries. We pay, I am disposed to think, too great a compliment to the Greek mythology when we attribute the ethical decay of later Athens and Corinth to the growing skepticism about its gods. The public life was dead. The theatre of great passion and great action was closed. The calls for sacrifice, the opportunities for national expansion, were gone, and the political school for the discipline of character was no longer there. With the loss of a progressive history, the springs of heroic emulation suffered atrophy, a sickly hue passed over literature, philosophy, and art; and the subsidence of human loves and cares upon low Epicurean levels was inevitable though the Olympian deities had never been dethroned. In the *absence* of any moral religion, no efficacious resistance could be set up, with or without a pantheistic polytheism, against the canker of social degeneracy.

In dealing with the present problem, however, we confine our attention to the Christian type of religion, which has its hold upon our nature from the moral side. The question is, what practical effect might be expected from a decay of that religion.

Under that change morality would lose, not its base, but its summit. The ground and principles of duty would remain ; the means for deducing rules of action, estimating the worth of conflicting impulses, and measuring the grades of obligation, would in the main be unaffected ; so that the moral code which would emerge from the labors of a mere philosopher need not materially differ from that recognized by a Christian. This is only an inverse method of saying that the Christian ethics are true to human life and the expression of right reason. I do not think, therefore, that the form and contents of a moral system would be essentially modified by the decline of religious belief. It may, no doubt, happen that particular problems of conduct, as in the case of suicide and of marriage, have become the subjects of ecclesiastical legislation, and so have passed into preoccupation of religious feeling, and, on the disappearance of that feeling, may be flung back into an indeterminate condition. But to the real solution of such problems it would be difficult to show that religion contributes any new elements, so as to turn into duty that which was not duty before. Its ministers and temporary interpreters can give an historical consecration to all sorts of ungrounded opinions, and these will in any case have to look out for an adequate base, whether or not the religious view of life is still upheld. But it is quite possible that a rule of life, once thoughtfully constituted, should be acknowledged in common over the whole range of social duty by persons simply ethical and by those who are also religious.

But though the decay of religion may leave the institutes of morality intact, it drains off their inward power. The devout faith of men expresses and measures the intensity of their moral nature, and it cannot be lost without a remission of enthusiasm and, under this low pressure, and successful reentrance of the importunate desires and clamorous passions which had been driven back. To believe in an ever-living and perfect Mind, supreme over the universe, is to invest moral distinctions with immensity and eternity, and lift them from the provincial stage of human society to the imperishable theatre of all being. When planted thus in the very substance of things, they justify and support the ideal estimates of the conscience; they deepen every guilty shame; they guarantee every righteous hope; and they help the will with a divine casting-vote in every balance of temptation. The sanctity thus given to the claims of duty, and the interest that gathers around the play of character, appear to me more important elements in the power of religion than its direct sanctions of hope and fear. Yet to these also it is hardly possible to deny great weight, not only as extending the range of personal interests, but as the answer of reality to the retributory verdicts of the moral sense. Cancel these beliefs, and morality will be left reasonable still, but paralysed; possible to tem-peraments comparatively passionless, but with no grasp on vehement and poetic natures; and gravitating towards the simply prudential wherever it maintains its ground.

Historical experience appears to confirm this estimate. In no race (notwithstanding conspicuous individual exceptions) have the excesses of sensual passion been so kept in check as among the Jews. There is no more striking feature in their literature during the moral declension of Greek and Roman society (*e.g.* in the Sibylline Oracles) than the horror which it expresses of the pervading dissoluteness of the pagan world. It certainly cannot be said that the problem was rendered easy by the coolness of the Jewish temperament. The phenom-ena of Christendom present a more complicated tissue. But a just analysis yields, I believe, the same result, and attests the force of religious conviction as the only successful antagonist, on any large scale, of the animal impulses. True it is that, in the very presence of the Church, and even among its rep-resentatives, gross vices have at times prevailed. But these have been hollow times, in which, with large classes of per-sons, the outer shell of religion sheltered no sincere life, and the private habits betrayed the inward disintegration which policy or indifference concealed. To test the power of re-ligion, we must limit ourselves to cases where that power is not effete. In the Puritan families of the seventeenth cen-tury, among the present Catholic peasantry of Ireland, through-out the Society of Friends, and in the Wesleyan classes, it can hardly be denied that the control of irregular desires has been attained with an exceptional ease and completeness.

One source of this distinctive power yet remains to be indicated. A simply conscientious man may surrender himself unreservedly to the sense of moral obligation, and be so possessed by it as to feel it more than reasonable, and own a certain sacredness in its appeal. Duty, honour, self-forgetfulness in others' good, may obtain the real command of such a one. But the persuasive force with which the right speaks to him is beyond all intellectual measure ; it stirs him in depths he cannot reach ; its heat is in excess of its light ; it is something mystic which must have him, but of which he can render no account. Here, in truth, is religion pressing into life, only with form still indistinct, and its organism of thought not yet differentiated and articulate. Let it complete its development and what change will ensue ? Once rendered conscious of the Supreme Source of his moral perceptions, the responsible agent no longer obeys a pressure out of the dark, but rather a drawing towards higher light ; for an impersonal drift of nature is substituted a profound personal veneration, and enthusiasm turned from a blind nobleness into the clear allegiance of living affection. It is not without reason that this change has been treated as an emergence into new life. Its vast influence is attested by the whole literature of devotion, and especially by its most popular element, the hymns of every age from the Psalter to the *Christian Year*.

Though in theory the contents of morality are not altered by acquiring divine obligation, the efficacy of religion is more immediately felt in some parts of the character than in others. The scene to which it introduces the mind is one which throws it instantly into the attitude of looking up to wards an Infinite Perfection, whose presence it never quits, and thus supplies the true conditions of humility, of aspiration, and of felt equality of moral trust for all men before God. These moods of thought are specifically induced by the contact of higher excellence and a more capacious rule of righteousness ; and they are but poorly simulated by the mere sense of personal insignificance amid the immensity of nature, and the awe of the unknown, and the conscious partnership of us all in the human liabilities. The moral characteristics of the Christian temper are nothing but the natural posture of a mind standing face to face with the invisible reality of the highest ideals of its conscience and its love. If that presence departs, they cannot survive.

MR. FREDERIC HARRISON.

And all this, to me, describes the moral characteristics, not of the Christian, but of the religious temper. With what has been so finely said in the preceding discourse we ought, I think, most cordially to join. Only for the words "Theology" and "Christian" we must put the wider and more ancient terms "Religion" and "Human ; " and again, for the intrinsic consciousness and emotional intuitions, whereby these are said to prove themselves, we must substitute the reasonable proof of science, philosophy, and positive psychology.

We have before us three distinctive views as to the relations of Religion and Morality. Each of the three has pressed on us a very powerful thought. The reconciliation is obscure, yet I hold on to the hope that it may one day be found ;

that we shall have to surrender neither Religion nor Science, neither demonstration on the one hand, nor Dogma, Worship, and Discipline on the other; that we shall end by accepting a purely human base for our Morality, and withal come to see our Morality transfigured into a true Religion.

It is the purport of the first of the arguments before us to establish : that morality has a basis of its own quite independent of all theology whatever, but that since morality must be deeply affected by any theology, the morality will be undermined if based on a theology which is not true. We must all agree, I think, to that.

The second argument insists that if the religious foundations and sanctions of morality be given up, human life runs the risk of sinking into depravity, since morality without religion is insufficient for general civilisation. For my part I entirely assent to that.

The third argument rejoins that Theology cannot supply a base for morals that have lost their own ; but that morals, though they have their own base, and are second to nothing, are not adequate to direct human life until they be transfused into that sense of resignation, adoration, and communion with an overruling Providence which is the true mark of Religion. I assent entirely to that.

We, who follow the teaching of Comte, humbly look forward to an ultimate solution of all such difficulties by the force of one common principle. That we acknowledge a religion, of which the creed shall be science ; of which the Faith, Hope, Charity, shall be real, not transcendental, earthly, not heavenly—a religion, in a word, which is entirely human, in its evi-

dences, in its purposes, in its sanctions and appeals. Write
the word "Religion" where we find the word "Theology,"
write the word "Human" where we find the word "Christian,"
or the word "Theist," "Mussulman," or "Buddhist," and
these discussions grow practical and easily reconciled ; the
aspirations and sanctions of Religion burst open to us anew
in greater intensity, without calling on us to surrender one
claim of reality and humanity ; the realm of Faith and Adoration becomes again conterminous with Life, without disturb-
ing, nay, whilst sanctifying, the invincible resolve of modern
men to live *in* this world, *for* this world, *with* their fellow-men.

And this brings us to the source of all difficulties about
the relations of Morality and Religion. We place our morality—we are compelled by the conditions of all our positive
knowledge to place it—in a strictly human world. But it is
the mark of every theology (the name of Theology assumes it)
to place our religion in a non-human world. And thus our
human system of morals may possibly be distorted—it cannot be supported—by a non-human religion. But, on the
other hand, it is dwarfed and atrophied for want of being duly
expanded into a truly human religion. Our morality with its
human realities, our theology with its non-human hypotheses,
will not amalgamate. Their methods are in conflict. In
their base, in their logic, in their aim, they are heterogeneous. They do not lie *in pari materiâ*. Give us a religion as
truly human, as really scientific, as is our moral system, and
all is harmony. Our morals, based as they must be on our
knowledge of Life and of Society, are then ordered and inspired by a religion which belongs, just as truly as our moral

science does, to the world of science and of man. And then religion will be no longer that quicksand of Possibility which two thousand years of debate have still left it to so many of us. It becomes at last the issue of our knowledge, the meaning of our science, the soul of our morality, the ideal of our imagination, the fulfilment of our aspirations, the lawgiver, in short, of our whole lives. Can it ever be this whilst we still pursue Religion into the bubble world of the Whence and the Whither?

That morality is dependent on theology ; that morality is independent of religion : each of these views presents insuperable difficulties, and brings us to an alternative from which we recoil. To assert that there is no morality but what is based on Theology is to assert what experience, history, and philosophy flatly contradict, nay that which revolts the conscience of all manly purpose within us. History teaches us that some of the best types of morality, in men and in races, have been found apart from anything that Christians can call theology at all. Morality has been advancing for centuries in modern Europe, whilst theology, at least in authority, has been visibly declining. The morality of Confucius and of Sakya Mouni, of Socrates and Marcus Aurelius, of Vauvenargues, Turgot, Condorcet, Hume, was entirely independent of any theology. The moral system of Aristotle was framed without any view to theology, as completely as that of Comte or of our recent moralists. We have experience of men with the loftiest ideal of life and of strict fidelity to their ideal, who expressly repudiate theology, and of many more whom theology never touched. Lastly, there is a spirit within us which will not believe that to know and to do the right, we must wait until the mysteries of existence and the universe are resolved, its origin, its government, and its future. To make right conduct a corollary of a theological creed, is not only contrary to fact, but shocking to our self-respect. We know that the just spirit can find the right path, even whilst the judgment hangs bewildered amidst the Churches.

To hold, as would seem to require of us the second argument, that, though theology is necessary as a base for morality, yet almost any theology will suffice—Polytheist, Mussulman, or Deist—so long as some imaginary being is postulated, this is indeed to reduce theology to a minimum; since, in this case, it does not seem to matter in which God you may believe. To say that morality is dependent on *one* particular theology, is to deny that men are moral outside your peculiar orthodoxy; to say that morality is dependent merely on *some* form of theology, is to say that it matters little to practical virtue which of a hundred creeds you may profess. And when we shrink from the arrogance of the first and the looseness of the second position, we have no alternative but to admit that our morality must have a human, and not a superhuman, base.

It does not follow that morality can suffice for life without religion. Morality, if we mean by that the science of duty, after all, can supply us only with a knowledge of what we should do. Of itself it can neither touch the imagination, nor satisfy the thirst of knowledge, nor order the emotions. It tells us of human duty, but nothing of the world without us ; it prescribes to us our duties, but it does not kindle the feelings which are the impulse to duty. Morality has nothing to tell us of a paramount Power outside of us, to struggle with which is confusion and annihilation, to work with which is happiness and strength ; it has nothing to teach us of a communion with a great Goodness, nor does it touch the chords of Veneration, Sympathy, and Love within us. Morality does not profess to organise our knowledge and give symmetry to life. It does not deal with Beauty, Affection, Adoration. If it order conduct, it does not correlate this conduct with the sum of our knowledge, or with the ideals of our imagination, or with the deepest of our emotions. To do all this is the part of Religion, not of morality ; and inasmuch as the sphere of this function is both wider and higher, so does Religion transcend Morality. Morality has to do with conduct, Religion with life. The first is the code of a part of human nature, the second gives its harmony to the whole of human nature. And morality can no more suffice for life than a just character would suffice for any one of us without intellect, imagination, or affection, and the power of fusing all these into the unity of a man.

The lesson, I think, is twofold. On the one hand, morality is independent of theology, is superior to it, is growing whilst theology is declining, is steadfast whilst theology is shifting, unites men whilst theology separates them, and does its work when theology disappears. There is something like a civilised morality, a standard of morality, a convergence about morality. There is no civilised theology, no standard of theology, no convergence about it. On the other hand, morality will never suffice for life; and every attempt to base our existence on morality alone, or to crown our existence with morality alone, must certainly fail.   For this is to fling away the most powerful motives of human nature.   To reach these is the privilege of Religion alone.   And those who trust that the Future can ever be built upon science and civilisation, without religion, are attempting to build a Pyramid of bricks without straw.   The solution, we believe, is a non-theological religion.

There are some who amuse themselves by repeating that this is a contradiction in terms, that religion implies theology. Yet no one refuses the name of religion to the systems of Confucius and Buddha, though neither has a trace of theology.   But disputes about a name are idle.   If they could debar us from the name of Religion, no one could disinherit us of the thing.   We mean by religion a scheme which shall explain to us the relations of the faculties of the human soul within, of man to his fellowmen beside him, to the world and its order around him; next, that which brings him face to face with a Power to which he must bow, with a Providence which he must love and serve, with a Being which he must adore—that which, in fine, gives man a doctrine to believe, a discipline to live by, and an object to worship.   This is the ancient meaning of religion, and the fact of religion all over the world in every age.   What is new in our scheme is merely that we avoid such terms as Infinite, Absolute, Immaterial, and vague negatives altogether, resolutely confining ourselves to the sphere of what can be shown by experience, of what is relative and not absolute, and wholly and frankly, *human.*

THE DEAN OF ST. PAUL'S.

It seems to me difficult to discuss this question till it is set-tled, at least generally, what morality is influenced, and what religious belief is declining.

The morality generally acknowledged in Europe differs in most important points from that of the Hebrews in the days of Moses, of the Greeks in the days of Socrates, of the Romans under the Empire, of the monks of Egypt, of the Puritans of the seventeenth century. All of these had among them high types of character, higher, it may be, than any types among us ; but who among us would accept their morality as a whole? Our morality has come to be recognised as it is by a definite progress of which the steps may be traced. It is plain that one form of religious thought and religious faith might aid this progress of morality by its decline, and another might, by its decline, impede or reverse it. On such a morality as we acknowledge, whencesoever derived, the decline of Buddhist belief or ancient Roman religious belief might act as a stimulus and a help. The decline of another kind of relig-ious belief might, on the other hand, act most injuriously.

It seems to me, therefore, that till the question is pre-sented in a concrete and historical form, nothing can be made of it. I do not understand the two terms of the comparison. Before I can attempt to answer it, I must know, at least ap-proximately, *what* morality and *what* religion.

If by morality is meant the morality generally recognised in Europe on the points of truthfulness, honesty, humanity, purity, self-devotion, kindness, justice, fellow-feeling, and not

only recognised, but judged by a conscious superiority of reason and experience to be the right standard, as compared
with other moralities—such as those of the Puritans, the monks,
the Romans, the Hebrews—then I observe that, as a matter
of fact and history, which to me seems incontrovertible, this
morality has synchronised in its growth and progress with an
historical religion, viz. Christianity. We are come to the end
of eighteen of the most eventful and fruitful centuries of all,
at least, that are known to us ; and we are landed in what we
accept as a purer morality than any which has been known
in the world before, and one which admits itself not to be
perfect, but contains in itself principles of improvement and
self-purification. With this progress from the first, sometimes, I quite admit, with gross and mischievous mistakes,
but always with deliberate aim and intention of good, Christianity has been associated. And in proportion as Christian
religious belief has thrown off additions not properly belonging to it, and has aimed at its own purification and at a
greater grasp of truth, the standard and ideas of morality
have risen with it. The difficulty at this moment is to determine how much of our recognised morality, both directly and
much more indirectly, has come from Christianity, and could
not conceivably have come at all, supposing Christianity
absent.

I do not here, in these few lines, assume that in Christianity and its long association with human morality we have a
vera causa of its improved and improving character. But
with this immense fact of human experience before me,
unique, it seems to me, in its kind, and in its broad outlines

undeniable, no abstract reasonings can reassure me as to the probability that with the failing powers of what has hitherto been, directly or indirectly, the source of much, and the support and sanction of still more, of our morality, our morality will fail too. It seems to me quite as easy to be skeptical about morality as it is about religion. If the religion has been proved to be not true, then of course it is no use talking about the matter. But if not, a declining belief in it may, with our present experience, be thought at least by those who believe in it, to be attacking the roots of morality, if not in our own generation, at least in those which come after.

It is matter of history that in what we now generally accept as true morality there are two factors :—(1) On the one hand, human experience, human reasonableness, human good feeling, human self-restraint ; and (2) on the other, the belief, the laws, the ideas, the power of Christianity. It is difficult to conceive what reason there is to expect that if one factor is taken away the result will continue the same : that the removal or weakening of such an important one as Christianity would not seriously affect such departments of morals as purity, the relations of the strong to the weak, respect for human life, slavery.

THE DUKE OF ARGYLL.

Considering that these papers are contributed by men belonging to very different schools of thought, and that they deal with a question very abstract and very ill defined, it is surely very remarkable that so much agreement should emerge on certain fundamental points.

Most remarkable of all, in this respect, is the paper emanating from one of those who "follow the teaching of Comte."

In that paper I find the following propositions :

I. That morality is independent of theology ; but

II. That it is not independent of religion, inasmuch as morality without religion cannot "suffice for life."

III. That religion means a scheme which (among other things) "brings man face to face with a Power to which he must bow, with a Providence which he must love and serve, with a Being which he must adore—that which, in fine, gives man a doctrine to believe, a discipline to live by, and an object to worship."

IV. That this scheme or conception of religion is "new," and differs from mere theology in the following distinctive points :—

(1) That it avoids certain words or phrases, such as "infinite," "absolute," "immaterial."

(2) That it avoids also all "vague negatives."

(3) That it resolutely confines us to the sphere of what can be shown by experience—"of what is relative and not absolute," and "of what is wholly and frankly human."

I will examine these propositions in their order.

Proposition I. clearly depends entirely on what is meant by theology, and on the distinction which is drawn in the propositions which follow between theology and religion. Two things, however, may be said of this proposition : First, that, as a matter of historical fact, men's conceptions of moral obligation have been deeply influenced by their conceptions and beliefs about theology, or about the " whence and whither." Secondly, that, as all branches of truth are and must be closely related to each other, it cannot possibly be true that morality is independent of theology, except upon the assumption that there is no truth in any theology. But this is an assumption which cannot be taken for granted, being very different indeed from the assumption (which may be reasonable) that no existing theology is unmixed with error. The absolute independence of morality as regards theology, assumes much more than this ; it assumes that there is no theology containing even any important element of truth.

Proposition II. is, I think, perfectly true.

Proposition III. contains a definition of religion which might probably be accepted by any theological professor in any of our schools of divinity as good and true, if not in all respects adequate or complete.

Proposition IV. defines the elements in all theologies which constitute their fundamental errors, and which distinguish them from religion as defined in Proposition III. In short, Proposition III. defines affirmatively what religion is ; and Proposition IV. defines negatively what it is not. It adds also a few more affirmative touches to complete the picture of what it is.

Looking now at the erroneous theological elements which are to be thrown away, we find three words fixed upon as specimens of what is vicious. One of them is " the Absolute." Most heartily do I wish it were abolished. More nonsense has been talked and written under cover of it than under cover of any other of the voluminous vocabulary of unintelligible metaphysics. It is admitted that the Absolute is "unthinkable," and things which are unthinkable had better be considered as also unspeakable, or at least be left unspoken.

Next, "immaterial" is another word to be cast away. The worst of this demand is, that the words material and im-material express a distinction of which we cannot get rid in thought. I do know that the pen with which I now write is made of that which to me is known as matter; but I do not know that the ideas which are expressed in this writing are made of any like substance, nor even of any substance like the brain. On the contrary, it seems to me that these ideas cannot be so made and that there is an absolute difference between thought and the external substances which it thinks about. This may be my ignorance, but until that ignorance is removed I must accept those distinctions which are founded on the experience and observation of my own na-ture, and I must retain words which are necessary to express them.

Then, as regards the word "infinite," in like manner, I cannot dispense with it, for the simple reason that the idea of infinity is one of which I cannot get rid, and which all science teaches me is an idea inseparable from our highest concep-tions of the ·realities·of nature. Infinite time and infinite space, and the infinite duration of matter and of force, are conceptions which are part of my intellectual being, and I cannot "think them away." Metaphysicians may tell me that they are "forms of thought." But if so they are at least all the more "frankly human," and I accept them as such.

Next we are to avoid "vague negatives altogether." Well, but surely a definition of religion as distinguished from theology, which consists in "avoiding" certain terms, such as we have now examined, is a definition consisting of "vague negatives" and of nothing else.

But then we come next to an affirmative definition : "confining ourselves resolutely to the sphere of what can be shown by experience." To this I assent, provided experience be not confined to the sphere of sense, and provided everything which any man has ever felt, or known, or conceived, be accepted as in its own place and rank, coming within the sphere which is thus described.

Again, it is demanded of us that we confine ourselves resolutely within " what is relative and not absolute." To this I assent. All knowledge is relative—relative both to the mind which knows, and relative also to all other things which remain to be known. Absolute goodness, and absolute power, and absolute knowledge are all conceivable, but they are all relative ; and to talk of any object of knowledge, or of any subject of knowledge as non-relative, is, or seems to me to be, simply nonsense.

Lastly, it is demanded of us to confine ourselves to what " is wholly and frankly human." If this means that we are not to think of any Power or any being who is not related to our human faculties in a most definite and intelligible sense, I accept the limitation. But if it means that we are not to think of any such Power or Being except under all the imperfections, weaknesses, and vices of humanity, then the limitation is one which I cannot accept either as conceivable in itself, or as consistent with what I can see or understand of nature.

But ought we not to be agreed in this? If there is a Power to which man " must bow," "a Being which he must adore," and a " Providence which he must love and serve," it is clearly impossible that this Being, Power, or Providence can be wholly human," in the sense of being no greater, no wiser, no better than man himself.

The whole of this language is the language of theology and of nothing else—language, indeed, which may be held consistently with a vast variety of theological creeds, but which is inseparable from those fundamental conceptions which all such creeds involve, which is borrowed from them, and without which it has to me no intelligible sense.

With these explanations I accept the tenth paragraph of Paper No. IV., and that part of the last paragraph which has been already quoted, as expressing, with admirable force and truth at least one aspect of the connection between morals and religion.

PROFESSOR CLIFFORD.

In the third of the preceding discourses there is so much which I can fully and fervently accept, that I should find it far more grateful to rest in that feeling of admiration and sympathy than to attend to points of difference which seem to me to be of altogether secondary import. But for the truth's sake this must first be done, because it will then be more easy to point out some of the bearings of the position held in that discourse upon the question which is under discussion.

That the sense of duty in a man is the prompting of a self other than his own, is the very essence of it. Not only would morals not be self-sufficing, if there were no such prompting of a wider self, but they could not exist; one might as well suppose a fire without heat. Not only is a sense of duty inherent, in the constitution of our nature, but the prompting of a wider self than that of the individual is inherent in a sense of duty. It is no more possible to have the right without unselfishness than to have man without a feeling for the right.

We may explain or account for these facts in various ways, but we shall not thereby alter the facts. No theories about heat and light will ever make a cold fire. And no doubt or disproof of any existing theory can any more extinguish that self other than myself, which speaks to me in the voice of conscience, than doubt or disproof of the wave-theory of light can put out the noonday sun.

One such theory is defended in the discourse here dealt with, and, if I may venture to say so, is not quite sufficiently distinguished from the facts which it is meant to explain. The theory is this : that the voice of conscience in my mind is the voice of a conscious being external to me and to all men, who has made us and all the world. When this theory is admitted, the observed discrepancy between our moral sense and the government of the world as a whole makes it necessary to suppose another world and another life in it for men, whereby this discord shall be resolved in a final harmony.

I fully admit that the theistic hypothesis, so grounded, and considered apart from objections otherwise arising, is a reasonable hypothesis and an explanation of the facts. The idea of an external conscious being is unavoidably suggested, as it seems to me, by the categorical imperative of the moral sense; and moreover, in a way quite independent, by the aspect of nature, which seems to answer to our questionings with an intelligence akin to our own. It is more reasonable to assume one consciousness than two, if by that one assumption we can explain two distinct facts; just as if we had been led to assume an ether to explain light, and an ether to explain electricity, we might have run before experiment and guessed that these two ethers were but one. But since there is a discordance between nature and conscience, the theory of their common origin in a mind external to humanity has not met with such acceptance as that of the divine origin of each. A large number of theists have rejected it, and taken refuge in Manichæism and the doctrine of the Demiurgus in various forms; while others have endeavoured, as aforesaid, to redress the balance of the old world by calling into existence a new one.

It is, however, a very striking and significant fact, that the very great majority of mankind who have thought about these questions at all, while acknowledging the existence of divine beings and their influence in the government of the world, have sought for the spring and sanction of duty in something above and beyond the gods. The religions of Brahmanism and of Buddhism, and the moral system of Confucius, have together ruled over more than two-thirds of the human race during the historic period; and in all of these the moral sense is regarded as arising indeed out of a universal principle, but not as personified in any conscious being. This vast body of dissent might well, it should seem, make us ask if there is anything unsatisfying in the theory which represents the voice of conscience as the voice of a god.

Although, as I have said, the idea of an external conscious being is unavoidably suggested by the moral sense, yet, if this idea should be found untrue, it does not follow that nature has been fooling us. The idea is not in the facts, but in our inference from the facts. A mirror unavoidably suggests the idea of a room behind it ; but it is not our eyes that deceive us ; it is only the inference we draw from their testimony. Further consideration may lead to a different inference of far greater practical value.

Now, whether or no it be reasonable and satisfying to the conscience, it cannot be doubted that theistic belief is a comfort and a solace to those who hold it, and that the loss of it is a very painful loss. It cannot be doubted, at least, by many of us in this generation, who either profess it now, or received it in our childhood and have parted from it since with such searching trouble as only cradle-faiths can cause. We have seen the spring sun shine out of an empty heaven, to light up a soulless earth ; we have felt with utter loneliness that the Great Companion is dead. Our children, it may be hoped, will know that sorrow only by the reflex light of a wondering compassion. But to say that theistic belief is a comfort and a solace, and to say that it is the crown or coping of morality, these are different things.

For in what way shall belief in God strengthen my sense

of duty ? *He is a great one working for the right.* But I already know so many, and I know these so well. *His righteousness is unfathomable ; it transcends all ideals.* But I have not yet fathomed the goodness of living men whom I know ; still less of those who have lived, and whom I know. And the goodness of all these is a striving for something better ; now it is not the goal, but the striving for it, that matters to me. The essence of their goodness is the losing of the individual self in another and a wider self ; but God cannot do this ; his goodness must be something different. *He is infinitely great and powerful, and he lives for ever.* I do not understand this mensuration of goodness by foot-pounds and seconds and cubic miles. A little field-mouse, which busies itself in the hedge, and does not mind my company, is more to me than the longest ichthyosaurus that ever lived, even if he lived a thousand years. When we look at a starry sky, the spectacle of whose awfulness Kant compared with that of the moral sense, does it help out our poetic emotion to reflect that these specks are really very very big, and very very hot, and very very far away ? Their heat and their bigness oppress us ; we should like them to be taken still further away, the great blazing lumps. But when we think of the unseen planets that surround them, of the wonders of life, of reason, of love that may dwell therein, then indeed there is something sublime in the sight. Fitness and kinship ; these are the truly great things for us, not force and massiveness and length of days.

Length of days, said the Old Rabbi, is measured, not by their number, but by the work that is done in them. We are all to be swept away in the final ruin of the earth. The thought of that ending is a sad thought; there is no use in trying to deny this. But it has nothing to do with right and wrong; it belongs to another subject. Like All-father Odin, we must ride out gaily to do battle with the wolf of doom, even if there be no Balder to come back and continue our work. At any rate the right will have been done, and the past is safer than all storehouses.

The conclusion of the matter is that belief in God and in a future life is a source of refined and elevated pleasure to those who can hold it. But the foregoing of a refined and elevated pleasure, because it appears that we have no right to indulge in it, is not in itself, and cannot produce as its consequence, a decline of morality.

There is another theory of the facts of the moral sense set forth in the succeeding discourse, and this seems to me to be the true one. The voice of conscience is the voice of our Father Man who is within us; the accumulated instinct of the race is poured into each one of us, and overflows us, as if the ocean were poured into a cup.[1] Our evidence for this explanation is that the cause assigned is a *vera causa*, it undoubtedly exists; there is no *perhaps* about that. And those who have tried tell us that it is sufficient; the explanation, like the fact, "covers the whole voluntary field." The lightest and the gravest action may be consciously done in and for Man. And the sympathetic aspect of Nature is explained to us in the same way. In so far as our concep-

[1] Schopenhauer. There is a most remarkable article on the " Natural History of Morals " in the *North British Review*, Dec. 1867.

tion of nature is akin to our minds that conceive it, Man made it ; and Man made us, with the necessity to conceive it in this way.[1]

I do not, however, suppose that morality would practically gain much from the wide acceptance of true views about its nature, except in a way which I shall presently suggest. I neither admit the moral influence of theism in the past, nor look forward to the moral influence of humanism in the future. Virtue is a habit, not a sentiment or an -ism. The doctrine of total depravity seems to have been succeeded by a doctrine of partial depravity, according to which there is hope for human affairs, but still men cannot go straight unless some tremendous all-embracing theory has a finger in the pie. Theories are most important and excellent things when they help us to see the matter as it really is, and so to judge what is the right thing to do in regard to it. They are the guides of action, but not the springs of it. Now the spring of virtuous action is the social instinct, which is set to work by the practice of comradeship. The union of men in a common effort for a common object—*band-work*, if I may venture to translate co-operation into English—this is, and always has been, the true school of character. Except in times of severe struggle for national existence, the practice of virtue by masses of men has always been coincident with municipal freedom, and with the vigor of such unions as are not large enough to take from each man his conscious share in the work and in the direction of it.

[1] For an admirable exposition of the doctrine of the social origin of our conceptions, see Professor Croom Robertson's Paper, " How we come by our Knowledge," in the first number of the *Nineteenth Century.*

What really affects morality is not religious belief, but a practice which, in some times and places, is thought to be religious—namely, the practice of submitting human life to clerical control. The apparently destructive tendency of modern times, which arouses fear and the foreboding of evil in the minds of many of the best of men, seems to me to be not mainly an intellectual movement. It has its intellectual side, but that side is the least important, and touches comparatively few souls. The true core of it is a firm resolve of men to know the right at first hand, which has grown out of the strong impulse given to the moral sense by political freedom. Such a resolve is a necessary condition to the existence of a pure and noble theism like that of the third discourse, which learns what God is like by thinking of man's love for man. Although that doctrine has been prefigured and led up to for many ages by the best teaching of Englishmen, and—what is far more important—by the best practice of Englishmen, yet it cannot be accepted on a large scale without what will seem to many a decline of religious belief. For assuredly if men learn the nature of God from the moral sense of man, they cannot go on believing the doctrines of popular theology. Such change of belief is of small account in itself, for any consequences it can bring about ; but it is of vast importance as a symptom of the increasing power and clearness of the sense of duty.

On the other hand there is one "decline of religious belief," inseparable from a revolution in human conduct, which would indeed be a frightful disaster to mankind. A revival of any form of sacerdotal Christianity would be a matter of practice and not a matter of theory. The system which snapped the foundations of patriotism in the old world; which well nigh eradicated the sense of intellectual honesty, and seriously weakened the habit of truth-speaking; which lowered men's reverence for the marriage-bond by placing its sanctions in a realm outside of nature instead of in the common life of men, and by the institutions of monasticism and a celibate clergy; which stunted the moral sense of the nations by putting a priest between every man and his conscience; this system, if it should ever return to power, must be expected to produce worse evils than those which it has worked in the past. The house which it once made desolate has been partially swept and garnished by the free play gained for the natural goodness of men. It would come back accompanied by social diseases perhaps worse than itself, and the wreck of civilized Europe would be darker than the darkest of past ages.

II.

DR. WARD.

I agree with the Dean of St. Paul's, that the wording of our question is unfortunately ambiguous; and I think that this fact has made the discussion in several respects less pointed and less otherwise interesting than it might have been.

For my present purpose, I understand the term "religious belief" as including essentially belief in a Personal God and in personal immortality. Less than this is not worthy the name of religious belief; and, on the other hand, I will not refer to any other religious truths than these. I am to inquire, therefore, what would be the influence on morality of a decline in these two beliefs.

But next, what is meant by "morality?" I will explain as clearly as brevity may permit what I should myself understand by the term ; though I am, of course, well aware, that this is by no means the sense in which Sir J. Fitzjames Stephen, or Mr. Harrison, or Professor Clifford, understands it.

I consider that there is a certain authoritative Rule of life,[1] necessarily not contingently existing, which may be regarded under a twofold aspect. It declares that certain acts (exterior or interior) are intrinsically and necessarily evil ; it declares again that some certain act (exterior or interior), even where not actually evil, is by intrinsic necessity, under the circumstances of some given moment, less morally excellent than some certain other act. Any given man, therefore, more effectively practises "morality," in proportion as he more energetically, predominantly, and successfully aims at adjusting his whole conduct, interior and exterior, by this authoritative Rule. Accordingly, when I am asked what is the bearing of some particular influence on morality,—I understand myself to be asked how far such influence affects for good or evil the prevalence of that practical habit which I have just described ; how far such influence disposes men (or the contrary) to adjust their conduct by this authoritative Rule.

These explanations having been premised, my answer to

---

[1] To prevent misapprehension I may explain that, in my view, those various necessary truths which collectively constitute this rule are, like all other necessary truths, founded on the Essence of God : they are what they are because He is what He is.

the proposed question is this. The absence of religious belief —of belief in a Personal God and personal immortality—does not simply *injure* morality, but, if the disbelievers carry their view out consistently, utterly *destroys* it. I affirm—which, of course requires proof, though I have no space here to give it —that no one except a Theist can, in consistency, recognize the necessarily existing authoritative Rule of which I have spoken. But for practical purposes there is no need of this affirmation, because in what follows I shall refer to no other opponents of religion, except that antitheistic body—consisting of Agnostics, Positivists, and the like—which in England just now heads the speculative irreligious movement. Now it is manifest on the very surface of philosophical literature that, as *a matter of fact*, these men deny in theory the existence of any such necessary authoritative Rule, as that on which I have dwelt. A large proportion of Theists accept it, and call it " the Natural Law;"[1] an Agnostic or Positivist denies its existence. It is very clear that he who denies that there is such a thing as a necessarily existing authoritative Rule of life cannot consistently aim at adjusting any, even the smallest part of his conduct by the intimations of that Rule ; or, in other words, cannot consistently do so much as one act, which (on the theory which I follow) can be called morally good.

[1] The Natural Law more strictly includes only God's *prohibition* of acts intrinsically evil, and his *preception* of acts which cannot be omitted *without* doing what is intrinsically evil. But we may with obvious propriety so extend the term as to include under it God's *counselling* of those acts which, as clothed in their full circumstances, are by intrinsic necessity the more morally excellent.

Here, however, a most important explanation must be made. It continually happens that some given philosopher holds some given doctrine speculatively and theoretically, while he holds the precisely contradictory doctrine implicitly and unconsciously; insomuch that it is the latter, and not the former, which he applies to his estimate of events as they successively arise. Now the existence of the Natural Law,—so I would most confidently maintain,—is a truth so firmly rooted by God Himself in the conviction of every reasonable creature, that practically to leaven the human mind with belief of its contradictory is, even under the circumstances most favorable to that purpose, a slow and uphill process. In the early stages, therefore, of antitheistic persuasion, there is a vast gulf between the antitheist's speculative theory and his practical realization of that theory. Mr. Mallock has set forth this fact, I think, with admirable force, in an article contributed by him to the *Contemporary* of last January. When antitheists say,—such is his argument,—that the pursuit of truth is a " sacred," "heroic," " noble " exercise—when they call one way of living mean, and base, and hateful, and another way of living great, and blessed, and admirable — they are guilty of most flagrant inconsistency. They therein use language and conceive thoughts, which are utterly at variance with their own speculative theory. If it be admitted (1) that the idea expressed by the term "moral goodness" is a simple idea, an idea incapable of analysis ; and (2) that to this idea there corresponds a necessary objective reality *in rerum naturâ ;*—if these two propositions be admitted, the existence of the Natural Law is a truth which irresistibly results from the admission.   On the other hand, if these two propositions be *not* postulated, then to talk of one human act being " higher " or " nobler " than another, is as simply unmeaning as to talk of a bed being nobler than a chair, or a plough than a harrow.   Whether it be the bed, or the plough, or the human act, it may be more *useful* than the other articles with which it is brought into comparison ; but to speak in either case of " nobleness," is as the sound of a tinkling cymbal. Or rather, which is my present point, the fact of antitheists using such language shows, that their practical belief is so far essentially opposed and (as I, of course, should say) immeasurably superior to their speculative theory. To my mind there is hardly any truth which needs more to be insisted on than this, in the present crisis of philosophical thought: when antitheism successfully conceals its hideous deformity from its own votaries, by dressing itself up in the very garments of that rival creed which it derides as imbecile and obsolete.   I heartily wish I had space for setting forth in full and clear light the argument on which I would here insist.   I may refer, however, to Mr. Mallock's article, for an excellent exposition of it from his own point of view ; and, in particular, I cannot express too strongly my concurrence with the following remarks :—

All the moral feelings (he says) at present afloat in the world depend, as I have already shown, on the primary doctrines of religion ; but that the former would *outlive* the latter is nothing more than we should naturally expect: just as water may go on boiling after it is taken off the fire, as flowers keep their scent and color after we have plucked them, or as a tree whose roots have been cut may yet put out green leaves for one spring more.   But a time must come when all this will be over, and when the true effects of what has been done will begin to show themselves. Nor can there be any reason brought forward to show why, if the creed of unbelief was once fully assented to by the world, all morality—a thing always attended by some pain and struggle—would not gradually wither away, and give place to a more or less successful seeking after pleasure, no matter of what kind.

I would also recall to Sir J. Fitzjames Stephen's remembrance an admirable statement of his, which occurs in the work on "Liberty, Equality, and Fraternity." "We cannot judge of the effects of Atheism," he says, "from the conduct of persons who have been educated as believers in God, and in the midst of a nation which believes in God. If we should ever see a generation of men, especially a generation of Englishmen, to whom the word 'God' has no meaning at all, we should get a light on the subject which might be lurid enough."[1]

So far I have used the word "morality" in that sense which I account the true one. But a different acceptation of the word is very common; and it will be better perhaps briefly to consider our proposed question in the sense which that acceptation would give it. Morality, then, is often spoken of as consisting in a man's sacrifice of his personal desires for the public good; so that each man more faithfully practises "morality," in proportion as he more effectively postpones private interests to public ones. I have always been extremely surprised that any Theist can use this terminology; though I am well aware, of course, that may do so. To mention no other of its defects, it excludes from the sphere of morality precisely what a Theist must consider the

---

[1] Second edition, p. 326.

most noble and elevating branch thereof—viz., men's duties to their Creator. Constant remembrance of God's presence, prayer to Him for moral strength, purging the heart from any such worldly attachment as may interfere with His sovereignty over the affections—these, and a hundred others, which are man's highest moral actions, are excluded by this strange terminology from being moral actions at all. Still in one respect there is great agreement between the two "moralities" in question, for under either of them morality very largely consists in self-denial and self-sacrifice.

Now, if it be asked in what way morality, as so understood, would be affected by the absence of religious belief,—I think the true reply is one which has so often been drawn out that I need do no more than indicate it. Firstly, apart from Theistic motives there is no sufficient moral leverage ; men would not have the moral strength required for sustained self-denial and self-sacrifice. Secondly and more importantly, if Theistic sanctions were away, no theory could be drawn out explaining why it should be *reasonable* that a man sacrifice his personal interest to that of his fellows.

On this matter I am glad that I have the opportunity of drawing attention to a very fine passage of Mr. Goldwin Smith's, published in the *Macmillan* of last January :—

Materialism has in fact already begun to show its effects on human conduct and on society. They may perhaps be more visible in communities where social conduct depends greatly on individual conviction and motive than in communities which are more ruled by tradition and bound together by strong class organizations ; though the decay of morality will perhaps be more complete and disastrous in the latter than in the former. God and future retribution being out of the question, it is difficult to see what can restrain the selfishness of an ordinary man, and induce him, in the absence of actual coercion, to sacrifice his personal desires to the public good. The service of humanity is the sentiment of a refined mind conversant with history ; within no calculable time is it likely to overrule the passions and direct the conduct of the mass. And after all, without God or spirit, what is "humanity?" One school of science reckons a hundred and fifty different species of man. What is the bond of unity between all these species, and wherein consists the obligation to mutual love and help ? A zealous servant of science told Agassiz that the age of real civilization would have begun when you could go out and shoot a man for scientific purposes ; and in the controversy respecting the Jamaica massacre we had proof enough that the ascendency of science and a strong sense of human brotherhood might be very different things. "Apparent diræ facies." We begin to perceive, looming through the mist, the lineaments of an epoch of selfishness compressed by a government of force.

In fact, even in the present early stage of English anti-theistic philosophy, if its adherents are directly asked what is man's reasonable rule of life, I know of no other answer they will theoretically give except one. They will say that any given person's one reasonable pursuit on earth is to aim at his own earthly happiness—to obtain for himself out of life the greatest amount he can of gratification. No doubt they will make confident statements, on the indissoluble connection between happiness and "virtue." Still, according to their speculative theory, the only reasonable ground for practising "virtue" is its conduciveness to the agent's happiness.

Now let us suppose a generation to grow up, profoundly imbued with this principle, carrying it consistently into detail, emancipated from the unconscious influence of (what I must be allowed to call) a more respectable creed. What would be the result? Evidently a man so trained, in calculating for himself the balance of pleasure and pain, will give no credit on the former side to such gratifications as might arise from consciousness of conquest over his lower nature, or from the pursuit of lofty and generous aims.   These, I say, will have no place in his list of pleasures ; because he will have duly learned his lesson, that there is no "lower" or "higher" nature ; that no one aim can be "loftier" than any other ; that there is nothing more admirable in generosity than in selfishness.   On the other hand, neither will he include, under his catalogue of *pains*, any feeling of remorse for evil committed, or any dread of possible punishment in some future life ; for he will look 'with simple contempt on those doctrines, which are required as the foundation for such pains.   His common-sense course will be to make this world as comfortable a place as he can, by bringing every possible prudential calculation to bear on his purpose.   Before all things he will keep his digestion in good order.   He will keep at arm's-length (indeed at many arms'-lengths) every disquieting considera-tion, such, *e.g.*, as might arise from a remembrance of other men's misery, or from a thought of that repulsive spectre which the superstitious call moral obligation.

It is plain that duly to pursue the subject thus opened would carry me indefinitely beyond my limits ;[1] and I will only therefore make one concluding observation.   If the term "virtue" be retained by those of whom I am speaking, it will be used, I suppose, to express any habitual practice, which solidly conduces to the agent's balance of earthly enjoyment.   I am confident that,—should this be the recognized terminology, and should the new school be permitted to arrive at its legiti-

[1] I have treated it at somewhat greater length in an article which I con-tributed to the *Dublin Review* of last January, pp. 15-21.

mate development,—there is one habit which would be very prominent among its catalogue of " virtues."   The habit to which I refer is indulgence in licentiousness—licentiousness practised no doubt prudently, discreetly, calculatingly, but at the same time habitually, perseveringly, and with keen zest.

PROFESSOR HUXLEY.

We are led to do this thing, and to avoid that, partly by instinct and partly by conscious motives ; and our conduct is said to be moral or the reverse, partly on the ground of its effects upon other beings, partly upon that of its operation upon ourselves.

Social morality relates to that course of action which tends to increase the happiness or diminish the misery of other beings ; personal morality relates to that which has the like effect upon ourselves.

If this be so, the foundation of morality must needs lie in the constitution of nature, and must depend on the mental construction of ourselves and of other sentient beings.

The constitution of man remaining what it is, his capacity for the pleasures and pains afforded by sense, by sympathy, or by the contemplation of moral beauty and ugliness, is obviously in no way affected by the abbreviation of the prolongation of his conscious life ; nor by the mere existence or non-existence of anything not included in nature ; nor, so long as he believes that actions have consequences, does it matter to him what connection there may be between these actions and other phenomena of nature.

The assertion that morality is in any way dependent upon the views respecting certain philosophical problems a person may chance to hold, produces the same effect upon my mind as if one should say that a man's vision depends on his theory of light; or that he has no business to be sure that ginger is hot in the mouth unless he has formed definite views, in the first place, as to the nature of ginger, and, secondly, as to whether he has or has not a sensitive soul.

Social morality belongs to the realm of inductive and deductive investigation. Given a society of human beings under certain circumstances; and the question whether a particular action on the part of one of the members of that society will tend to the increase of the general happiness or not, is a question of natural knowledge, and, as such, is a perfectly legitimate subject of scientific inquiry. And the morality or immorality of the action will depend upon the answer which the question receives.

If it can be shown by observation or experiment that theft, murder, and adultery do not tend to diminish the happiness of society, then, in the absence of any but natural knowledge, they are not social immoralities.

It does not follow, however, that they might not be personal immoralities. Without committing myself to any theory of the origin of the moral sense, or even as to the existence of any such special sense, I may suggest that it is quite conceivable that discords and harmonies may affect the congeries of feelings to which we give the name, as they do others.

I see no reason for doubting that the beauty of holiness

and the ugliness of sin are, to a great many minds, no mere metaphors, but feelings as real and as intense as those with which the beauty or ugliness of form or color fills the artist mind, and that they are as independent of intellectual beliefs, and even of education, as are all the true æsthetic powers and impulses.

On the other hand, I do not doubt the existence of persons, like the hero of the *Fatal Boots*, devoid of any sense of moral beauty or ugliness, and for them personal morality has no existence. They may offend, but they cannot sin; they may be sorry for having stolen or murdered, because society punishes them for their social immoralities, but they are incapable of repentance.

Before going further, I think it may be needful to discriminate between religion and theology.

I object to the very general use of the terms Religion and Theology as if they were synonymous, or indeed had anything whatever to do with one another. Religion is the affair of the affections, theology of the intellect. The religious man loves an ideal perfection, which may be natural or non-natural ; the theologian expounds the attributes of what he terms " supernatural " Being as so many scientific truths, the consequences of which work into the general scheme of nature, and are there discernible by ordinary methods of investigation. What the theologian affirms may be put in this way that beyond the *natura naturata*, mirrored or made by the natural operations of the human mind, there is a *natura naturans*, sufficient knowledge of which is attainable only through the channel of revelation.

Now I think it cannot be doubted that both religion and theology, as thus defined, have exercised, and must exercise, a profound influence on morality. For it may be that the object of a man's religion—the ideal which he worships—is an ideal of sensual enjoyment, or of domination, or of the development of all his faculties towards perfection, or of self-annihilation, or of benevolence; and his personal morality will, in part, contribute largely to the formation of his ideal, and will, in part, be swayed and bent until it harmonizes with that ideal.

Moreover, it is clear that a man's theology may give him such views of the action of the *natura naturans* as will profoundly modify or even reverse his social morality.

He may see ground for believing that conduct of evil effect upon society, which is part of the *natura naturata*, is in harmony with the laws of action of the *natura naturans;* and that, as the rewards and punishments of men are but slight and temporary, while those inflicted by the greater power behind the *natura naturata* are grievous and endless, common prudence may dictate obedience to the stronger. And history proves that there is no social crime that man can commit which has not been dictated by theology and committed on theological grounds. On the other hand, the belief that the divine commands are identical with the laws of social morality has lent infinite strength to the latter in all ages.

In like manner it seems to me impossible to overestimate the influence of speculative beliefs as to the nature of the Deity, apart from all idea of rewards and punishments, upon personal morality. The lover of moral beauty, struggling through a world full of sorrow and sin, is surely as much the stronger for believing that sooner or later a vision of perfect peace and goodness will burst upon him, as the toiler up a mountain for the belief that beyond crag and snow lies home and rest.   For the other side of the picture, who shall exaggerate the deadly influence on personal morality of those theologies which have represented the Deity as vainglorious, irritable, and revengeful—as a sort of pedantic drill-sergeant of mankind, to whom no valor, no long-tried loyalty, could atone for the misplacement of a button of the uniform, or the misunderstanding of a paragraph of the "regulations and instructions?"

While no one can dare history, or even look about him, without admitting the enormous influence of theology on morality, it would perhaps be hard to say whether it has been greater or less than the influence of morality on theology. But the latter topic is not at present under discussion ; and the only further remark I would venture to add is this—that the intensity and reality of the action of theological beliefs upon morality are precisely measured by the conviction of those who hold them that they are true.   That such and such a doctrine conduces to morality, and disbelief in it to immorality, may be demonstrated by an endless array of convincing syllogisms ; but unless the doctrine is true, the practical result of this expenditure of logic is not apparent.   I have not the slightest doubt that if mankind could be got to believe that every socially immoral act would be instantly followed by three months' severe toothache, such acts would soon cease to be perpetrated.   It would be a faith charged with most beneficent works, but unfortunately this faith can so easily be shown to be disaccordant with fact that it is not worth while to become its prophet.

For my part I do not for one moment admit that morality is not strong enough to hold its own. But if it is demonstrated to me that I am wrong, and that without this or that theological dogma the human race will lapse into bipedal cattle, more brutal than the beasts by the measure of their greater cleverness, my next question is to ask for the proof of the truth of the dogma.

If this proof is forthcoming, it is my conviction that no drowning sailor ever clutched a hencoop more tenaciously than mankind will hold by such dogma, whatever it may be. But if not, then I verily believe that the human race will go its evil way; and my only consolation lies in the reflection that, however bad our posterity may become, so long as they hold by the plain rule of not pretending to believe what they have no reason to believe because it may be to their advantage so to pretend, they will not have reached the lowest depths of immorality.

MR. R. H. HUTTON.

That has happened to us which happened to the disputants in that Attic Symposium from which, I suppose, the name for our discussion was taken. We have been interrupted by a "great knocking at the door" and the entrance of an unbidden guest, who, however, shows no sign either of Alcibiades' intoxication, or of that generous disposition to crown the most deserving with garlands, which may perhaps have had some connection with the excesses of the brilliant Athenian's potations. The *Saturday* Reviewer, who, without dropping his mask, has thrust upon us his own criticism on our discussion,[1] has certainly not conferred the most meagre of wreaths on any one, unless indeed it may be said that he grudgingly crowns the Dean of St. Paul's and the Duke of Argyll with a withered sprig or two of parsley, for pointing out that our subject is much too vague, and for trying to narrow a discussion so "abstract and ill-defined." His general criticism is contained in the harsh remark that " all the fine talk of the chosen *illuminati* is a mass of words with very little meaning," and that "the deliberations of the Symposium bear a very strong resemblance to those of the diplomatists who have been lately concocting protocols ; that is, they consist of empty phrases to which all the parties can agree because they do not touch any of the points on which the co-signataries would be likely to differ." That is a much crueller interruption than any caused by Alcibiades to the guests assembled at the Symposium of Plato, nor do I think it is quite just, though there is enough justice in it to make me try to bring out what seem to me the clearly understood issues between us a little more distinctly, in the few words I have to say. To limit the subject as much as possible, I will speak of nothing but the effect likely to be produced on morality by any decline in the belief in a righteous God independent of, and external to, the human race—in one, that is, whose leading purpose in relation to us is believed to be to mould

<hr>

[1] See *Saturday Review* for March 31, art. " A Modern Symposium."

our motives and characters into the likeness of his own. Now it seems to me that all the previous speakers except two, Mr. Frederic Harrison and Professor Clifford, believe, for different reasons, and in different degrees, that such a decline in such a belief in God would probably result in parallel decline in human morality though some insist most, like Sir James Stephen and Professor Huxley, on the point that any attempt to bolster up the belief artificially *for the sake* of its moral consequences, by discountenancing free discussion, would result in a worse decline of morality, and others insist most, like Dr. Martineau, Lord Selborne, and Dean Church, on the point that the same causes which result in a decline in this belief (especially as it is represented in Christianity) are likely to result also in a decline in the force of the ethical principles so closely associated with it. But I do not understand any one to differ with Professor Huxley that if the belief can be shown to be false, be the moral consequence what it may, it ought to go. On the other hand, I understand both Mr. Harrison and Professor Clifford to assert that the causes which, as they think, have under-mined and are undermining the belief in a righteous God, external to the human race, have no tendency to undermine the binding power of the highest human ethics, but, on the contrary, have a direct tendency to elevate and refine them, though Professor Clifford regards this tendency as, on the whole, slight, and confined chiefly to the blow which such a change in belief will have in diminishing the control of the clergy, while Mr. Harrison expects very much indeed from it, if only through its tendency to concentrate on the desirable aims of a real world, an enthusiasm now so much dissipated, in his opinion, by lavishing it on imaginary objects.

Now, while I heartily admit with Professor Huxley the conceivability that a gross delusion—like the belief "that every socially immoral act would instantly be followed by three months, severe toothache "—if it could be palmed off successfully upon our race, would have *some* very beneficial consequences—(some also by no means beneficial)—and should not a bit the less regard a conspiracy, even if one were practicable, to impose such a delusion on our race, as a great sin, I cannot the more on that account see how to disentangle the question whether there be a righteous God external to men from the question whether there would be a great moral loss to human nature in the dissipation of the belief in such a God. It is quite conceivable—nay, it has often happened—that a sincere delusion has produced the best results. The belief in an imaginary danger of death, for instance, has often made a man take life more seriously ; and the belief in an imaginary danger of invasion has probably often bound a divided nation together and given it a greater nervous strength and manliness. But though it is easy to conceive a belief, in some respects beneficial, which is wholly false, it seems to me, in the case before us, that the very element in the belief we are discussing which makes it beneficial, is also a clear note of its truth. What makes the belief in such a God as I have spoken of beneficial, is that this belief, and this only, gives to the attitude of man's mind, in relation to right motive and right action, that mixture of courage and cheerful irresponsibility for the result, characteristic of a *faith*.

Luther's great saying, " We say to our Lord God that if He will have his Church, He must uphold it, for we cannot uphold it, and, even if we could, we should become the proudest asses under heaven," [1] would be of course simply untranslatable into any humanist or Positivist dialect at all. I do not indeed quite know what Mr. Harrison means when he talks of a " frankly human " religion which shall provide us with a " Providence " whom we are " to love and serve ; " but I suppose he must mean that we are to love that law of the universe which produces a certain amount of correspondence between our nature and its " environment," and that we are to cooperate with that law. At least this is the only meaning I am able to attach to " loving and serving " a Providence without believing in God. Now for myself I am incapable of loving a mere law of any kind, whether it be a law of gravitation, a law of assimilation between my organism and its environment, or any other; and as for " serving " it, I like to judge for myself, and, instead of allowing myself always to be assimilated to my " environment," I sometimes prefer what is called, in the language of the same philosophy, " differentiating " myself from it. But I think even Mr. Harrison would hardly justify language of trust like Luther's towards a " Being " of whom we are supposed to know nothing except that it has given rise to the earth we live on, and will most likely, in a few thousand years, also put a final end to it. You cannot trust a being of whose purposes, or capacity for having purposes, you know nothing, because trust implies approving those purposes and believing them to be accompanied by a

---

[1] *Tischreden*, ed. Förstemann, Leipzig, 1844, vol. ii. p. 330.

-far higher range of knowledge and foresight than your own. Yet has not all the benefit of trust in God arisen from that humility and courage, that self-abandonment to a higher will, that sense of complete irresponsibility for the result when the right thing is once done, which constitute moral heroism? Could such moral heroism survive the belief in a divine will which is shaping all right action to a perfect end? Suppose we believed in unknown causes which produce indeed such moral phenomena as those of human life for a moment in the long ages of evolution—which bring them like a ripple to the surface, but quench them, like that ripple, for evermore, and which are as certain so to quench them as the sun is one day to be burnt out,—is it possible we could cast ourselves on such unknown causes with the sort of faith in God that has "moved mountains," and that will move mountains again, that will say, for instance, to this huge dead weight of Secularism and Positivism, "Be thou cast into the sea," and it will obey?

Nor can I see any better help in Professor Clifford's substitute for God—namely, the higher self represented by "the voice of our Father Man who is within us," *i.e.* by "the accumulated instinct of the race poured into each one of us", and overflowing us, "as if the ocean were poured into a cup." The "accumulated instinct of our race" includes a great deal of evil as well as good, and is often unaccompanied by any accumulation of instinct for the suppressing of the evil by the good. I quite agree with those who have urged that it was the "accumulated instinct" of the Athenian people which taught them the necessity of putting down Socrates as one who was undermining the social order to which he belonged.

I do not doubt that Socrates shared that accumulated instinct not less—nay, probably, much more—than the rest of his countrymen. Probably it overflowed him "as an ocean might overflow a cup." Nevertheless the solitary voice within him, which he attributed to his "dæmon," though it could not drown the voice of this "accumulated instinct," was heard above it, and prevailed over the pleas of comradeship, and over what Professor Clifford deems the only "spring of virtuous action," the impulse which invites men to make individual sacrifices to promote the greater efficiency of the social bond.

Some one may wonder (says Socrates in Plato's *Apology*) why I go about in private giving advice and busying myself with the concerns of others, but do not venture to come forward in public and advise the State. I will tell you the reason of this. You have often heard me speak of an oracle or sign which comes to me, and is the divinity which Meletus ridicules in the indictment. This sign I have had ever since I was a child. The sign is a voice which comes to me and always forbids me to do something which I am going to do, but never commands me to do anything, and this is what stands in the way of my being a politician. And rightly, as I think. For I am certain, O men of Athens, that if I had engaged in politics I should have perished long ago and done no good either to you or to myself. And don't be afraid of my telling you the truth, for the truth is that no man who goes to war with you or any other multitude, honestly struggling against the commission of unrighteousness and wrong in the State, will save his life ; he who will really fight for the right, if he would live even for a little while, must have a private station and not a public one.[1]

This is unsocial doctrine enough, and of course Professor Clifford will say that, though fatal to the existing Athenian State, it had its source in instincts essential to a higher political virtue and to the cohesion of a nobler kind of State.

[1] Professor Jowett's *Plato*, vol. i. p. 346, 1st ed.

Grant it for a moment. Yet how can we expect moral heroism of the same type as that which is convinced that invisible Power is on its side, and trusts to the vindication of the future, if instead of ascribing the origin of its impulses to a divine Power which is the same yesterday, to-day, and for ever—a Power above it and beyond it,—he who has to evince this moral heroism believes that there is no inspiring mind higher than his own, and holds, therefore, that he must rely on himself, and on himself alone, for the fine faculty to discriminate between the inchoate order of a new society, and the worn-out guarantees of an order which is passing away? How is one who is fully aware that he is dissolving the ancient bonds of a venerable society and polity, but who only *hopes* that he is creating the germs of something better, to set his face against the brotherhood among whom he lives, and to defy the wrath of the fellow-citizens whom he sees, and all without the whisper of approval from any spiritual being behind the veil? Surely the hesitating inspiration of that long-buried ancestor, "our Father Man"—to admit, for a moment, Professor Clifford's assumption—when it spells out dubious and unaccustomed lessons which the voices of our brother-men join, in loud chorus, to decry, would not be very likely to triumph over fears and scruples which "our Father Man" also authenticates, and authenticates much more positively than he ever can authenticate the first faintly uttered principles of a new kind of social union against the old. What was it, as I asked before, which stimulated Luther to his gigantic enterprise? Not the doubtful guess that buried generations had transmitted to him the glimpse of a reform which would transfigure society, but the belief that he could honestly use the language of that psalm that he so much delighted to appropriate to himself: "They came about me like bees, and are extinct even as the fire among the thorns, for in the name of the Lord I will destroy them." Whether the belief in "our Father Man" and in a tentative Providence which does not *foresee*, but only accommodates the individual to his "environment," as the only guides of our moral life, be wild or sober, this, I think, is clear, that it does not provide the martyr or the reformer with the stimulating power of a *faith;* that it can give no confidence like that in an inspiration of far wider grasp and far deeper purpose than any which the reformer himself commands; that it leaves him a mere *pioneer* amidst dangers and difficulties to which it may turn out that both he and his race are quite unequal, instead of a humble follower obeying the beckoning of one who holds both past and future in his hand.

And now as to my second point—that the very element which gives so beneficial a character to the belief that conscience is the inspiration of God—the very element which makes it a useful and practically stimulating belief, and not, as Professor Clifford calls it, a mere source of "refined and elevated pleasure"—is also a note of its *truth.* I hold this to be so because the very experience which produces the trust is an experience of life, and of life morally higher than one's self. Surely, if we are competent, as we are, to say when our friends and our favorite books tempt us, and when they raise us above temptation, we are also competent to say when thoughts that strike with a living power upon the heart come from a higher, and when they come from a lower source than that of our own habitual principles of action—when they come with promise and command, and when they come with discordant sneers, discouragement, and enervation. When we grasp dimly at a great moral principle which is full, to use Professor Tyndall's language, of "the promise and potency" of all forms of life—when the more we consider it, the less we see where it is leading us, and yet only feel the more confidence in it on that account—when we recognize a clue and a guide without recognizing where that clue and that guide are pointing to—when we know that it is our duty to defy the world in the name of a principle of which we cannot gauge the full meaning, or measure even the immediate effects (and this is, as I maintain, the true phenomenon visible in all great moral, as in all great intellectual, origination) —then it does seem to me to be a sober and wholesome conviction that that which *we* do not know, there is one who puts the clue into our hands, who does know ; that what we cannot foresee, there is one who does foresee ; that we are grasping the hand of a Power which knows the way before as well as behind ; that we are following the glimmer of a ray which will lead us on to the dayspring from which it descended. I cannot but believe that we have as secure a faculty to discriminate the superiority of the life in which a moral impression originates, as we have to discriminate its rightness itself —that it is one and the same act of discrimination which says "This is obligatory," and which says "This is instinct with divine life and promise." To suppose that a dead ancestry are flashing through us these commands which at once repudiate their principles and nerve us against the wrath of their descendants, seems to me, I confess, a degrading superstition. If "we boast to be better than our fathers," it must be some one better than our fathers who is giving us our watchword. This is why I hold that to lose the faith in God would be to lose a great inheritance of moral order and moral progress, and also to lose at the same moment a truth in comparison with which all other truths are as dim and isolated sparks beside a pillar of fire that can guide us through a wilderness that we have never even explored.

SIR JAMES STEPHEN.

The paper which began this discussion was entitled "The Influence upon Morality of a Decline in Religious Belief." The Dean of St. Paul's remarks : "It seems to me difficult to discuss this question till it is settled, at least generally, what morality is influenced, and what religious belief is declining." The Duke of Argyll observes that these papers "deal with a question very abstract and ill-defined." Dr. Ward says that " the wording of our question is unfortunately ambiguous, and I think that this fact has made the discussion in several respects less pointed and less otherwise interesting than it might have been."

To these criticisms I reply that the title of my paper contains no questions at all, and was not intended to do so. It is simply an indication, in the most general terms, of the subject to which the paper of which it is the title relates. Anyone who will take the trouble to read the paper will see that its principal object was to assert the proposition with which it concludes, which is in these words :—

> This [*i.e.* the whole of the preceding argument] shows that the support which an existing creed gives to an existing system of morals is irrelevant to its truth, and that the question whether a given system of morals is good or bad cannot be fully determined until after the determination of the question whether the theology on which it rests is true or false. The morality is [I should have said "may be "] good if it is founded on a true estimate of the consequences of human actions. But if it is founded on a false theology it is founded on a false estimate of the consequences of human actions; and so far as that is the case it cannot be good ; and the circumstance that it is supported by the theology to which it refers is an argument against, and not in favour of, that theology.

The only "question" which my paper was intended to raise is the question wl ether that proposition is true or not? . I do not see how its truth can depend (as the Dean of St. Paul's suggests) upon further particulars as to "what morality is influenced," or "what theology is declining." I said nothing about the decline of any particular theological belief, or its influence on any particular system of morals. My proposition would apply to all creeds and all forms of morality.

As to the Duke of Argyll's statement that "the question is very abstract and ill-defined," I should admit its justice if the title of the paper were taken as the statement of a question. But this is not the case. The proposition which I put forward, in the hope that it would be discussed, is no doubt general in its terms, but it seemed, and still seems to me, definite enough to be discussed. As to the "ambiguity" of which Dr. Ward complains, I cannot see how my proposition can have more meanings than one.

The papers which have been written subsequently to my

paper raise a great variety of points which I feel much tempted to discuss, but I hardly feel at liberty to do so, as they do not in any way qualify anything said by me. Each paper, indeed, is an illustration of the truth of some part of my proposition or of the assertions by which it is introduced ; for each shows in various ways how very close is the connection in the writer's mind between the theological system which he believes to be true and the moral system which he considers to be good ; and this again shows that the question of truth must precede the question of goodness, and cannot be determined by any answer which may be given to the latter question. I cannot help thinking that if this were generally understood it would affect very deeply the character of a great proportion of current theological speculation.

THE COURSE OF MODERN THOUGHT.[1]

BY G. H. LEWES.

MODERN Philosophy has moved along two increasingly divergent lines. One traversed by Galileo, Descartes, Newton, and Laplace, had for its goal the absolute disengagement of the physical from the mental, *i.e.* the objective from the subjective aspect of phenomena, so that the physical universe, thus freed from all the complexities of Feeling, might be interpreted in mechanical terms. As a preliminary simplification of the problem this was indispensable ; only by it could the First Notion of primitive speculation be replaced by the Theoretic Conception of scientific speculation.[2] The early thinker inevitably invested all external objects with properties and qualities similar to those he assigned to human beings, their actions he assigned to human motives. Sun, moon, and stars seemed living beings ; flames, streams, and winds were supposed to be moved by feelings such as those known to move animals and men. Nor was any other conception then possible : men could only interpret the unknown by the known,

---

[1] THE FORTNIGHTLY REVIEW, MARCH, 1877. This essay is to form part of a forthcoming volume on *The Physical Basis of Mind.*

[2] On the distinction between first notions and theoretic conceptions, see Mr. Lewes' *Problems of Life and Mind*, vol. ii. p. 251.

and their standard of all action was necessarily drawn from their own actions. Not having analyzed Volition and Emotion, above all, not having localized these in a neuro-muscular system, men could not suspect that the movements of planets and plants, and of streams and stones, had motors of a different kind from the movements of animals. The scientific conception of inert insensible Matter was only attained through a long education in abstraction; and is assuredly never attained by animals, or by savages. But no sooner were vital conditions recognized, than the difference between vital and mechanical movements emerged. When men learned that many of their own actions were unaccompanied either by Love or Hate, by Pleasure or Pain, and that many were unprompted by conscious intention, while others were unaccompanied by conscious sensation, they easily concluded that wherever the special conditions of Feeling were absent, the actions must have some other motors. Intelligence, Emotion, Volition, and Sensation being one by one stripped away from all but a particular class of bodies, nothing remained for the other bodies but insensible Matter and Motion. This was the Theoretic Conception which science substituted for the First Notion. It was aided by the observation of the misleading tendency of interpreting physical phenomena by the human standard, substituting our fancies in the place of facts, manipulating the order of the universe according to our imagination of what it might be, or ought to be. Hence the vigilance of the new school in suppressing everything pertaining to the subjective aspect of phenomena, and the insistance on a purely objective classification, so that by this means we might attain to a knowledge of things as they are. By thus withdrawing Life and Mind from Nature, and regarding the universe solely in the light of Motion and the laws of Motion, two great scientific ends were furthered, namely, a classification of conceptions, and a precision of terms. Objective phenomena made a class apart, and the great aim of research was to find a mathematical expression for all varieties under this class. Masses were conceived as aggregates of Atoms, and these were reduced to mathematical points. Forces were only different modes of Motion. All the numberless differences which perception recognized as *qualities* in things were reduced to mere variations in *quantity.* Thus all that was particular and concrete became resolved by analysis into what was general and abstract. The Cosmos then only presented a problem of mechanics.

During this evolution, the old Dualism (which conceived a material universe sharply demarcated from the mental universe) kept its ground, and attained even greater precision. The logical distinction between Matter and Mind was accepted as an essential distinction, *i.e.* representing distinct reals. There was on one side a group of phenomena, Matter and Force ; on the other side an unallied group, Feeling and Thought ; between them an impassable gulf. How the two were brought into relation, each acting and reacting on the other, was dismissed as an " insoluble mystery "—or relegated to Metaphysics for such minds as chose to puzzle over questions not amenable to experiment. Physics, confident in the possession of mathematical and experimental methods which yielded definite answers to properly restricted questions, peremptorily refused to listen to any suggestion of the kind.

And the career of Physics was so triumphant that success seemed to justify its indifference.

In our own day this analytical school has begun to extend its methods even to the mental group. Having reduced all the objective group to mathematical treatment, it now tries to bring the subjective group also within its range. Not only has there been more than one attempt at a mathematical Psychology, but also attempts to reduce Sensibility, in its subjective no less than in its objective aspect, to molecular movement. Here also the facts of Quality are translated into facts of Quantity; and all diversities of Feeling are interpreted as simply quantitative differences.

Thus far the one school. But while this Theoretic Conception stripped Nature of consciousness, motive, and passion, rendering it a mere aggregate of mathematical relations, a critical process was going on, which, analyzing the nature of Perception, was rapidly moving toward another goal. Locke, Berkeley, Hume, and Kant, directing their analysis exclusively to the subjective aspect of phenomena, soon broke down the barriers between the physical and mental, and gradually merged the former in the latter. Matter and its qualities, hitherto accepted as independent realities, existing where no Mind perceived them, were now viewed as the creations of Mind — their existence was limited to a state of the percipient. The old Dualism was replaced by Idealism. The Cosmos, instead of presenting a problem of Mechanics, now presented a problem of Psychology. Beginning with what are called the secondary qualities of Matter, the psychological analysis resolved these into modes of feeling. "The heat which the vulgar imagine to be in the fire and the color they imagine in the rose are not there at all, but are in us —mere states of our organism." Having gained this standing-place, there was no difficulty in extending the view from the secondary to the primary qualities. These also were perceptions, and only existed in the percipient. Nothing then remained of Matter save the hypothetical unknown x — the postulate of speculation. Kant seemed for ever to have closed the door against the real Cosmos when he transformed it into a group of mental forms—Time, Space, Causality, Quantity, &c. He propounded what may be called a theory of mental Dioptrics, whereby a pictured universe became possible, as Experience by its own *à priori* laws moulded *itself* into a consistent group of appearances, which produced the illusion of being a group of realities. He admitted, indeed, that by the operation of Causality we are compelled to believe in a Real underlying the appearances ; but the very fact that this Causality is a *subjective law* is proof, he said, of its not being an *objective truth.* Thus the aim of the mechanical conception was to free research from the misleading complexities of subjective adulterations, and view *things as they are* apart from their *appearances ;* but this aim seemed illusory when Psychology showed that Time, Space, Matter, and Motion were themselves not objective reals except in so far as they represented subjective necessities ; and that, in short, things *are* just what they *appear,* since it is only in the relation of external reals to internal feelings that objects exist for us.

Idealism has been the outcome of the psychological method. It has been of immense service in rectifying the dualistic conception, and in correcting the mechanical conception. It has restored the subjective factor, which the mechanical conception had eliminated. It has brought into incomparable clearness the fundamental fact that all our knowledge *springs from*, and is *limited by*, Feeling. It has shown that the universe represented in that knowledge can only be a picture of the system of things as these exist in relation to our Sensibility. But equally with the mechanical conception it has erred by incomplete analysis. For a complete theory of the universe or of any one phenomenon, those elementary conditions which analysis has provisionally set aside must finally be restored. When Quality is replaced by Quantity, this is an artifice of method, which does not really correspond with fact. The quality is the fact given in feeling, which we analytically refer to quantitative differences, but which can never be wholly resolved into them, since it must be presupposed throughout. One color, for example, may be distinguished from another as having more or fewer undulations ; and so we may by abstraction, letting drop all qualitative characters, make a scale of undulations to represent a scale of colors. But this is an ideal figment. It is the representation of one series of feelings by another series of different feelings. No variation of undulations will really correspond with variation in color, unless we re-introduce the suppressed *quality* which runs through all color. Attempt to make one born blind feel, or even understand, Color by describing to him the kind of wave-movement which it is said to be, and the vanity of the effort will be manifest. Movement he knows, and varieties of movement as given in *tactile and muscular sensations ;* but no combination and manipulation of such experiences can give him the specific sensation of color. That is a purely sub-jective state which he is incapable of experiencing, simply be-cause one of the essential factors is absent. One set of ob-jective conditions is present, but the other set (his sense-organ) is defective. Without the "greeting of the spirit" un-dulations cannot become colors (nor even undulations, for there also are forms of feeling). Besides the sense-organ there is needed the feeling of Difference, which is itself the pro-duct of past and present feelings. The reproduction of other colors, or other shades of color, is necessary to this perception of difference ; and this involves the element of Likeness and Unlikeness between what is produced and reproduced. So that a certain mental co-operation is requisite even for the simplest perception of quality. In fact, psychological analysis shows that even Motion and Quantity, the two objective terms to which subjective Quality is reduced, are themselves Funda-mental Signatures of Feeling ;[1] so that here, as elsewhere, it is only by analytical artifice that the objective can be divorced from the subjective. Matter *is* for us the Felt ; its Qualities are differences of feeling.

Not that this result is to be interpreted as freeing our Theoretic Conception from its objective side, and landing us in Idealism, which suppresses the real universe. The denial of all reality apart from our minds is a twofold mistake ; it confounds the conception of general relations with particular relations, declaring that because the External in its relation to the sentient organism can only be what it is felt to be, there-

---

[1] Not transcendental and *à priori*, as Kant teaches, but immanent in Feeling

fore it can have no *other* relations to other individual reals. This is the first mistake. The second is the disregard of the constant presence of the objective real in every fact of Feeling : the Not-Self is emphatically present in every consciousness of Self.

The legitimate conclusion is neither that of Dualism nor of Idealism, but what I have named Reasoned Realism ("Problems," vol. i. p. 176), which reconciles Common Sense with Speculative Logic, by showing that although the *truth* of things (their *Wahrheit*) is just what we perceive in them (our *Wahrnehmung*), yet their *reality* is this, and much more than this. *Things* are what they are felt to be; and what they are thought to be, when thoughts are symbols of the perceptions. Idealism declares that they are *nothing but* this. It is against this *nothing but* that Common Sense protests; and the protest is justified by Reasoned Realism, which, taking a comprehensive survey of the facts, thus answers the idealist : "Your synthesis is imperfect, since it does not include *all* the data—notably it excludes the fact of an objective or Not-Self element in every feeling. You may, conceivably, regard the whole universe as nothing but a series of changes in your consciousness ; but you cannot hope to convince me that I myself am simply a change in yourself, or that my body is only a fleeting image in your mind. Hence, although I conclude that the Not-Self is to you, as to me, undivorceable from Self, inalienable from Feeling, in so far as it is felt, yet there must nevertheless be for both of us an existence not wholly coextensive with our own. *My* world may be my picture of it ; *your* world may be your picture of it ;

but there is something common to both which is more than either—an existent which has different relations to each. *You* are not *me*, nor is the pictured Cosmos *me*, although I picture it. Looking at you and it, I see a vast whole of which you are a small part ; and such a part I conclude myself to be. It is at once a picture and the pictured ; at once subjective and objective. To me all your modes of existence are objective aspects, which, drawn from my own experience, I believe to have corresponding subjective aspects ; so that your emotions, which to me are purely physical facts, are to you purely mental facts. And psychological analysis assures me that all *physical facts are mental facts expressed in objective terms*, and *mental facts are physical facts expressed in subjective terms*."

But while Philosophy thus replaces the conceptions of Dualism and Idealism by the conception of the Twofold Aspect, the special sciences in their analytical career have disregarded the problem altogether. The mechanical theory of the universe not only simplified research by confining itself solely to the objective aspect of phenomena, but by a further simplification set aside all vital and chemical relations, to deal exclusively with mechanical relations. In ascertaining the mathematical relations of the planetary system, no elucidation could possibly be gained from biological or chemical conceptions ; the planets therefore were provisionally stripped of everything not mechanical. In systematizing the laws of motion, it was necessary to disengage the abstract relations from everything in any way resembling spontaneity, or extra mechanical agency : Matter was therefore, by a bold fiction, declared to be inert, and its motion regarded as something superadded from without.

And this was indispenable for the construction of those ideal laws which are the objects of scientific research. Science, as we often say, is the systematization of Experience under the forms of ideal constructions. Experience implies Feeling and certain fundamental Signatures, all reducible to the primary discernment of Likeness and Unlikeness. Hence Science is first a *classification* of qualities or discerned likenesses and differences ; next a *measurement* of quantities of discerned likenesses and differences. Although measurement is itself a species of classification, it is distinguished by the adoption of a standard unit of comparison, which, being precise and unvarying, enables us to express the comparisons in precise and unvarying symbols. Whether the unit of length adopted be an inch, a foot, a yard, a mile, the distance of the earth from the sun, or the distances of the fixed stars, the quantities thus measured are symbols admitting of one invariable interpretation. The exactness of the mathematical sciences is just this precision and invariability of their symbols, and is not, as commonly supposed, the source of any superior certainty as to the facts. The classificatory sciences, which deal with qualities rather than with quantities, may be equally *certain*, and represent fuller *knowledge*, because involving more varied feelings, but they cannot pretend to exactness. Even on the quantitative side, certainty is not identical with exactness. I may be quite certain that one block of marble is larger than another—meaning that it affects me more voluminously—but I cannot know how much larger it is without interpreting my feelings by the standard of quantity—the how-muchness as represented by that standard. The immense advantages of exact measurement need not be insisted on. The Biological Sciences, which are predominantly classificatory, can never rival the Cosmological Sciences in exactness ; but they may reach a fuller knowledge ; and their certainty will assume more and more the character of exactness as methods of measurement are applied to their classifications of qualities. The qualitative and quantitative aspects of phenomena are handled by the two great instruments, Logic and Mathematics, the second being only a special form of the first. These determine the general conceptions which are derived from our perceptions, and the whole constitute Experience.

What is the conclusion to which these considerations lead ? It is that the separation of the quantitative from the qualitative aspect of phenomena—the objective mechanical from the subjective psychological—is a logical artifice indispensable to research ; but it is only an artifice.[1] In pursuance of this artifice, each special science must be regarded as the search after special analytical results ; and meanwhile this method should be respected, and no confusion of the boundaries between one science and another should be suffered. Mechanical problems must not be confused by the introduction of biological relations. Biological problems must not be restricted to mechanical relations. I do not mean that

---

[1] The reader will understand that although mechanical relations are modes of Feeling, as all other relations are, yet their aspect is exclusively objective, referring to objects ideally detached from subjects.

the mechanical relations present in biological phenomena are not to be sought, and, when found, to be expressed in mechanical terms; I mean that such an inquiry must be strictly limited to mechanical relations. Subjective relations are not to be denied, because they are provisionally set aside, in an inquiry into objective relations; but we must carefully distinguish which of the two orders we are treating of, and express each in its appropriate terms. This is constantly neglected. For example, nothing is more common than to meet such a phrase as this: " A *sensory impression* is transmitted as a *wave* of *motion* to the brain, and there being transformed into a state of *consciousness*, is again reflected as a *motor* impulse."

The several sciences having attained certain analytical results, it remains for Philosophy to co-ordinate these into a doctrine which will furnish general conceptions of the World, Man, and Society. On the analytical side a mechanical theory of the universe might be perfected, but it would still only be a theory of mechanical relations, leaving all other relations to be expressed in other terms. We cannot accept the statement of Descartes that Nature is a vast mechanism, and Science an universal application of mathematics. The equation of a sphere, however valuable from a geometrical point of view, is useless as an explanation of the nature and properties of the spherical body in other relations. And so a complete theory of the mechanical relations of the organism, however valuable in itself, would be worthless in the solution of a biological problem, unless supplemented by all that mechanical terms are incompetent to express.

The course of biological speculation has been similar to the cosmological. It also began with a First Notion, which compendiously expressed the facts of Experience. Nor can any Theoretic Conception be finally adopted which does away with these facts, known with positive certainty, and popularly expressed in the phrase: "I have a body, and a soul." We may alter the phrase either into, "I *am* a body, and I *am* a soul;" or into "My body is only the manifestation of my soul;" or, "My soul is only a function of my body;" but the fundamental experiences which are thus expressed are of absolute authority, no matter how they may be interpreted. That I have a body, or am a body, is not to be speculatively argued away. That I move my arm to strike the man who has offended me, or stretch out my hand to seize the fruit which I see, is unquestionable; that these movements are determined by these feelings, and are never thus effected unless thus determined, is also unquestionable. Here are two sets of phenomena, having well-marked differences of aspect; and they are grouped respectively under two general heads, Life and Mind. Life is assigned to the physical organism, or Body—all its phenomena are objective. Mind is assigned to the psychical organism, or Soul—all its phenomena are subjective. Although what is called my Body is shown to be a group of qualities which are feelings —its color, form, solidity, position, motion—all its physical attributes being what is felt by us in consequence of the laws of our organization; yet inasmuch as these feelings have the characteristic marks of objectivity, and are thereby referred to some objective existence, we draw a broad line of demarcation between them and other feelings having the characteristic marks of subjectivity, and referring to ourselves as subjects. Psychological analysis shows us that this line of demarcation is artificial, only representing a diversity of aspect; but as such it is indispensable to science. We cannot really separate in a sensation what is objective from what is subjective, and say how much belongs to the Cosmos apart from Sensibility, and how much to the subject pure and simple; we can only view the sensation alternately in its objective and subjective aspects. What belongs to extramental existence in the phenomena of color, and what to the "greeting of the spirit," is utterly beyond human knowledge; for the ethereal undulations which physicists presuppose as the cosmic condition are themselves subjected to this same greeting of the spirit; they too are ideal forms of sensible experiences.

This conclusion, however, was very slowly reached. The distinction of aspects was made the ground of a corresponding distinction in agencies. Each group was personified and isolated. The one group was personified in Spirit—an existent in every respect opposed to Matter, which was the existent represented in the other group. One was said to be simple, indestructible; the other compound, destructible. One was invisible, impalpable, beyond the grasp of Sense; the other was visible, tangible, sensible. One was of heaven, the other of earth. Thus a biological Dualism, analogous to the cosmological, replaced the First Notion. It was undermined by advances in two directions. Psychology began to disclose that our conception of matter was, to say the least,

saturated with Mind, its Atoms confessedly being ideal figments ; and that all the terms by which we expressed *material qualities* were terms which expressed *modes of Feeling ;* so
that whatever remained over and above this was the unknown
x, which speculation required as a postulate.   Idealism, re-
jecting this postulate, declared that Matter was simply the
projection of Mind, and that our Body was the objectivation
of our Soul.   Physiology began to disclose that all the mental processes were (mathematically speaking) *functions* of
physical processes, *i. e.* varying with the variations of bodily
states ; and this was declared enough to banish forever the
conception of a Soul, except as a term simply expressing
certain functions.

Idealism and Materialism are equally destructive of Dualism. The defects of particular idealist and materialist
theories we will not here touch upon ; they mainly result
from defects of Method. Not sufficiently recognizing the
primary fact testified by Consciousness, namely, that Experience expresses both physical and mental aspects, and
that a Not-Self is everywhere indissolubly interwoven with
Self, an objective factor with a subjective factor, the idealist
reduces Existence to a mere panorama of mental states, and
the Body to a group in this panorama.   He is thus incapable
of giving a satisfactory explanation of all the objective phenomena which do not follow in the same order as his feelings, which manifest a succession unlike his expectation, and
which he cannot class under the order of his mental states
hitherto experienced.   He conceives that it is the Mind
which *prescribes* the order in Things ; whereas experience as-

sures us that the order is *described*, not prescribed by us: described in terms of Feeling, but determined by the laws of Things. The genesis of subjective phenomena is determined by the action of the Cosmos on our Sensibility, and the reaction of our Sensibility. He overlooks the evidence that the mental forms or laws of thought which determine the character of particular experiences, were themselves evolved through a continual action and reaction of the Cosmos and the Soul, precisely as the laws of organic action which determine the character of particular functions were evolved through a continual adaptation of the organism to the medium. These immanent laws are declared to be transcendental, antecedent to all such action and reaction.

A similar exclusiveness vitiates the materialist doctrine. Overlooking the primary fact that Feeling is indissolubly interwoven with processes regarded as purely physical because they are considered solely in their objective aspect, the materialist fails to recognize the operation of psychological laws in the determination of physiological results; he hopes to reduce Biology to a problem of Mechanics. But Vitality and Sensibility are coefficients which must render the mechanical problem insoluble, if only on the ground that mechanical principles have reference to quantitative relations, whereas vital relations are qualitative. His error is the obverse of the vitalist's error. The vitalist imagines that the speciality of organic phenomena proves the existence of a cause which has no community with the forces operating elsewhere; so turning his back on all the evidence, he attempts to explain organic phenomena without any aid from Physics and Chemistry. The materialist, turning his back on all the evidence of quite special conditions, only found at work in living organisms, tries to explain the problem solely by the aid of Physics and Chemistry. It is quite certain that physiological and psychological problems are not to be solved if we disregard the laws of Evolution through Epigenesis. The mental structure is evolved, as the physical structure is evolved. It is quite certain that no such evolution is visible in an organism, nor will any one suppose it to be possible in machines. From the biological point of view we must therefore reject both Idealism and Materialism. We applaud the one when it says, " Don't confuse mental facts by the introduction of physical hypotheses ; " and the other when it says, " Don't darken physical facts with metaphysical mists." We say to both : " By all means make clear to yourselves which aspect of the phenomena you are dealing with, and express each in its own terms. But in endeavoring to understand a phenomenon you must take into account all its ascertainable conditions. Now these conditions are sometimes only approachable from the objective side ; at other times only from the subjective side."

While it is necessary to keep the investigation of a process on its objective side limited to objective conditions, and to express the result in objective terms, we must remember that this is an artifice ; above all, we must remember that even within the objective limits our analyses are only provisional, and must be finally rectified by a restoration of all the elements we have provisionally set aside. Thus rectified, the objective interpretation of vital and mental phenomena has the incomparable advantage of simplifying research, keeping it fixed on physical processes, instead of being perturbed by suggestions of metaphysical processes. And as all physical investigation naturally tends to reduce itself to a mechanical investigation, because Mechanics is the science of Motion, and all physical processes are motions, we may be asked, Why should not the mechanical point of view be the rational standing-point of the biologist? Our answer is, Because Mechanics concerns itself with abstract relations, and treats of products without reference to modes of production, *i. e.* with motions without reference to all the conditions on which they depend. Every physical change, if expressed in physical terms, is a change of position, and is determined by some preceding change of position. It is a movement having a certain velocity and direction, which velocity and direction are determined by the velocity and direction of a force (a pressure or a tension) compounded with the forces of resistance, *i. e.* counter-pressures. Clearly, the nature of the forces in operation must be taken into account; and it is this which the mechanical view disregards, the biological regards. The mechanical view is fixed on the ascertained adjustment of the parts, so that the working of the organism may be explained as if it were a machine, a movement here liberating a movement there. The biological view includes this adjustment of parts, but takes in also the conditions of molecular change in the parts on which the adjustment dynamically depends. Mechanical actions may be expressed as the enlargement or diminution of the angle of two levers;

but chemical actions are not thus expressible ; still less vital and mental actions.

The organism is on the physical side a mechanism, and so long as the mechanical interpretation of organic phenomena is confined to expressing the mechanical principles involved in the mechanical relations, it is eminently to be applauded. But the organism is something more than a mechanism, even on the physical side ; or, since this statement may be misunderstood, let me say, what no one will dispute, that the organism is a mechanism of a very special kind, in many cardinal points unlike all machines. This difference of kind brings with it a difference of causal conditions. In so far as the actions of this mechanism are those of a dependent sequence of material positions, they are actions expressible in mechanical terms ; but in so far as these actions are dependent on vital processes, they are not expressible in mechanical terms. Vital facts, especially facts of sensibility, have factors neither discernible in machines nor expressible in mechanical terms. We cannot ignore them, although for analytical purposes we may provisionally set them aside.

In the course of the development of the mechanical theory, the history of which has just been briefly sketched, biological problems have more and more come under its influence. There has always been a fierce resistance to the attempt to explain vital and sentient phenomena on mechanical, or even physical principles, but still the question has incessantly recurred, How far is the organism mechanically interpretable ? And while the progress of Biology has shown more and more the machine-like adjustment of the several parts of which the organism is composed, it has also shown more and more the intervention of conditions not mechanically interpretable.

THE CONDITION AND PROSPECTS OF THE CHURCH OF ENGLAND.[1]

BY THOMAS HUGHES.

I think that many of those whom I am about to address in this College [2] on the condition and prospects of our National Church, may very probably be asking themselves at this moment what possible claim I can have to do so, or what possible good can come of anything I may say. I, at any rate, very readily admit that such questions would be most reasonable, so perhaps a few preliminary words of explanation may not be out of place.

It was some months ago, before the late occurrences at Hatcham and all that has followed on them, that the proposal was made to me. Even then I had serious doubt as to accepting, and ultimately did so with some reluctance. The doubt arose from a genuine belief that I had much more to learn from than to teach the members of Sion College on such a subject. It is true that I had been asked to speak or lecture on the Church question at Birmingham, Norwich, and else-

[1] THE CONTEMPORARY REVIEW, MAY, 1877.

[2] This article was delivered as an address, at Sion College, March 13th.

where: but those addresses were delivered to popular audiences, to whom I had been asked to speak as a politician, and at times when this great controversy was in a very different phase. But in this place I knew that I should be addressing an audience of experts, the metropolitan representatives of the great profession (or "calling," to use the better word) of ordained ministers of the National Church—a very different and much more serious matter. Hence my doubt.

My reluctance arose from a dislike to stir still waters, and raise discussion upon grave matters at a time when there seemed no pressing need for action or decision with regard to them. And I own that the earlier part of the past year appeared to me to bear many signs of such a time; for the usual motions, pointing to a severance of Church and State, or to reconstruction or reform of one kind or another, had not been made in the House of Commons. In the addresses of members and candidates to constituencies last autumn, when reference was made to the Church question, it was generally treated as a kind of neutral territory in politics, even advanced Liberals, like Mr. Leonard Courtney, declaring, that though they were theoretically in favor of the entire severance of Church and State when the proper time might come, yet they saw no sign of its coming, and deprecated any attempt to force it. On the other hand, one most important Church reform, the full meaning of which has never been popularly appreciated, — I mean the subdivision of dioceses and the appointment of Suffragan Bishops who should not be Peers of Parliament,— had made great progress, almost without opposition from the non-conforming bodies or the Liberation Society. Thus far the time seemed one for letting well alone, and I should certainly have desired to do so then, but for the smouldering discontent already too apparent in one extreme wing of the National clergy. In view of this, however, it seemed to me possibly worth while to put forward at Sion College a lay view of the matters which were causing such discontent amongst a section of Churchmen. So with this view I overcame my reluctance, never dreaming that before I should address you here, this smouldering fire would have burst into a blaze ; that we should have, on the one hand, the Church Union publicly denying the right of the nation to control the clergy, and clergymen declaring that they "will labor night and day to set the Church of England free from a persecuting State ;" on the other hand, the Liberationists, reassured at hearing their own war-cries issuing from within what they are used to regard as the hostile camp, openly preparing for a campaign which they seem to think may be the final one.

Had I been able to foresee such a state of things, I candidly confess that I should have declined this invitation. The prospect is to me altogether too sad and too confusing, and the issues are at present so undefined, and the forces on either side so undeveloped, that I would very gladly have been silent, at any rate till I could see more clearly how the great controversy was shaping itself, and what it behoved one to say or do in this matter who looks upon the connection of Church and State—of the spiritual and temporal life of the nation, as it exists, and has existed in England ever since we were a nation—as a part of our national inheritance which it would be a grievous misfortune, and an irreparable misfortune, to lose.

I am here, however, to speak to you on the subject, and must do so to the best of my ability, glad at any rate that you will hear the views frankly expressed of what I believe to be a much larger proportion than is generally supposed of ordinary English Churchmen—laymen who have no strong bias for or against any party in the Church ; who have neither time nor taste for the lamentable party wrestling-matches got up by the (so-called) religious press and societies ; but only desire to use themselves in peace, and to hand down to their children, the opportunities for Christian worship and Christian living which have served their forefathers for so many generations — improved and reformed to suit the needs of a new time, but still an inalienable part of the birthright of every English child. I repeat that I believe—and, as one who has had much intercourse with all classes of our society, and has for years been much exercised by this question, have broad grounds for my belief—that this class is a far larger one than is commonly allowed. And it would be a great mistake to suppose, because they make no strife or fuss about their religion, that they do not really care about it. It is often assumed, nowadays, that the bulk of our Church laity are mere formalists, supporting religion because they believe the parson to be the most powerful kind of policeman ; and ready to welcome whatever form of new worship, or no-worship, may come next, when criticism and science shall have dealt finally with the supernatural and Christianity, so long only as some form or other be left to keep the common folk in order, and their own wives and children quiet. On the contrary, we (for I must rank myself in their number) are thoroughly satisfied that Christianity is in no more real danger now than it was a hundred and fifty years ago, when Dean Swift, and many other greater wits than we have amongst us nowadays, thought and said that it was doomed. We hold in perfect good faith that the good news our Lord brought is the best the world will ever hear; that there has been a revelation in the Man Jesus Christ, of God the Creator of the world as our Father, so that the humblest and poorest man can know God for all purposes for which men need to know Him in this life, and can have his help in becoming like him, the business for which they were sent into it ; and that there will be no other revelation, though this one will be, through all time, unfolding to men more and more of its unspeakable depth and glory and beauty, in external nature, in human society, in individual men. That I believe to be a fair statement of the positive religious belief of average Englishmen, if they had to think it out and to put it in words ; and all who hold it must of course look upon Christ's gospel as the great purifying, reforming, redeeming power in the world, and desire that it shall be free to work in their own country on the most favorable conditions which can be found for it.

On the other hand, there are a number of matters which have been commonly insisted upon in England as part of Christianity, as to many of which the kind of Englishmen I am speaking of have come to have no belief at all one way or the other. They have no time to spare for such subjects, and do not feel it needful for their higher life that they should make up their minds, for instance, as to the exact quality of the inspiration of Scripture, the origin of evil, the method of the Atonement, the nature and effect of sacraments, justification, conversion, and other much-debated matters. As to another class of ecclesiastical subjects, such as Apostolical succession, and all the priestly and mediatorial claims which are founded on it, they have indeed made up their minds thoroughly, and believe them to be men's fables, mischievous and misleading to those who teach and those who learn—to priests and people alike.

Probably many of my hearers will consider such a belief as this too vague to be of any practical value ; but at any rate, as a fact, there it is, and it has to be acknowledged and accounted with as a fact in dealing with this Church question. And, as a rule, while it hinders those who hold it from attaching any exaggerated or superstitious importance to one form or another of Church organization, it inclines them to respect and value that which they find to have been thought out and beaten out by successive generations, and to have brought the nation safely at least, and not without honour, so far. Such a man is therefore generally an attached, though not an enthusiastic Churchman, and in the main for the following reasons :—

First, the historical. Our time is not one in which any institution is able to stand on its pedigree only, but it is also one in which we are bound to be specially careful of any wholesome links which bind us to the past, and make our history one of steady and connected life and progress. And from this point of view the national Church is beyond all question the most venerable of our institutions, and as intimately bound up with the national life as the Monarchy or the Houses of Parliament. The latest and best historian of the Conquest describes the England of 1066 as "a land where the Church and nation were but different names for the same community; a 'land where priests and prelates were subject to the law like other men; a land where the King and the witan gave away the staff of the bishop;" adding that "such a land was more dangerous in the eyes of Rome than one of Jews or Saracens."

And through the long four hundred years' struggle with the Papacy, the same description holds good; and in every great crisis the Church and nation has held together as one community. When à Becket backed the Pope's claim to make Church Courts supreme over the clergy, and to exempt them from the national tribunals, the King answered by the Constitutions of Clarendon, which declared the Church to be part and parcel of the nation, and the clergy amenable to the civil law like all other citizens; and those Constitutions were supported by clergy and laity alike.

When the King, backed by the Pope, refused the demands of the nation for the Great Charter, it was Archbishop Langton who headed the barons. Two of the three sureties to whom John was bound for its fulfilment were bishops, and the first nine names are those of Church dignitaries. Again and again the identity of the Church of England with the nation was upheld; sometimes by bishops, as when Robert Grostete flatly refused to institute Innocent IV's Genoese nominee to an English benefice; sometimes by the King or his Courts of Law, as when the King's Bench outlawed the members of the assembly of clergy, who had come together without the King's writ, and, in deference to a Papal Bull produced by Archbishop Winchelsea, refused to grant a subsidy to Edward I. for his Scotch campaign. The statutes of mortmain, of provisors, of prohibition, of præmunire, all aimed at some encroachment of Rome on the national character of the English Church, were all passed with the assent and by the help of that Church, which, by its very divisions in such crises, proved its national character. It is not necessary to follow the history since the Reformation, for it is part of the case of those of the clergy who seek to sever the connection that has existed in full force from that time. Even when Episcopacy was abolished during the Commonwealth and Protectorate, the national principle was upheld, and the established Presbyterian Church was even more intimately allied with the State than its predecessor had been. Cromwell had no more thought of severing the connection than Edward or Henry, but desired to make the Church as broad and tolerant as possible.

And so the Church has continued to our own day in theory, and still is to a very great extent in fact, the nation organized for spiritual purposes, and in striking sympathy with and faithfully mirroring the nation in all its varying moods—at times no doubt persecuting, apathetic, unfaithful—but on the whole faithful to her great mission, and exercising a noble and purifying influence on the national conscience and the national life.

If this is at all a true view of the history of the Church of England, the fallacy of the main argument of the English Church Union at recent meetings becomes clear. Appeal is made to some supposed compact between the State and the Church, and it is contended that the Church never conceded to the State the right of control in spiritual matters when that compact was made. This assumes that the State and the Church of England were at some time two distinct corporate bodies, in part at least composed of different persons, and capable of contracting with one another. But there never was such a time in England; State and Church never stood in such relations to each other; there never was any such formal contract between them as the Church Union argument starts from. Between the officers of the Church for the time being and the State, there can of course be, and always has been, a contract of service, as there is between the officers of the army and the State. But it is placing matters on a false issue to represent the Church of England as a power bound by treaty or compact with the State of England for certain definite purposes, and competent to annul that treaty when she pleases. A Church with the pretensions of Rome, or a voluntary Church, such as the Methodists, if the nation were to come to them now to make terms, might assume such an attitude and make such claims, but they contradict the very idea of our national Church, as those words have always been understood in England.

Before quitting the historical ground I would just remind you that this modern cry for disestablishment, or the absolute severance of the State from religion, has really no English tradition at all behind it, at any rate since the Long Parliament. In that celebrated assembly it was indeed mooted, but with no success.   Dr. Owen, the brother-in-law of Cromwell, and a famous Nonconformist minister, was its most vigorous opponent, and evidently expressed the sense of the House and the country when he protested in the most solemn and earnest words against the notion that they, as rulers of the nation, had nothing to do with religion.   From that time to our own the effort has never been repeated, while the greatest names amongst the Nonconformists may be cited as supporters of the direct and avowed connection of the State with religion. Thus Matthew Henry thanks God "for the national establishment of our religion with that of our peace and civil liberty ;" and Bunyan, Wesley, Baxter, may all be quoted on the same side ; even the leading Nonconformists and the reformers of the very last generation had no such policy.   Mr. Grote, who may be taken as their representative man on this question in the first Reformed Parliament, advocated indeed sweeping and stringent reforms within the Church, but, so far as I am aware, never hinted at severing the connection between the Church and the civil Government.   I need not say that the cry from within the Church herself for this divorce is of even more recent origin.

It may of course be replied to all this, that however strong the historical argument may be, it is after all mainly a sentimental one which can be allowed little weight in the changed and changing conditions and aims of our time.   And I would not press it beyond this, that if thirty generations of Englishmen, who have given us our country as we enjoy it, have insisted on a national profession of Christianity by the State, those who now oppose it shall at least give us some grounds for believing that the nation will become nobler and better for renouncing that profession.

The second reason for which such men as I am speaking of value the connection, may also possibly be called a sentimental one, but, has I believe, a very important practical side to it. It is that that connection is a constant and powerful protest against the desire and effort to divide human life sharply into two parts, one of which is concerned with the visible and the other with the invisible, or as the commoner phrase goes, one with secular the other with religious affairs. Notwithstanding the experience of many failures, that desire and effort were never more active than in our time. And, however firmly convinced we may be from the experience of our own lives, and from our observation of all that is going on around us, that no such severance is possible,—that the two realms will assert their independence sooner or later, whatever rules we may lay down for keeping them apart,— still the mere attempt to sever them will always work mischief ; and we cannot afford to part, or to tamper with, any witness that they have been joined together from the beginning of time, and will remain so joined to the end, by a law which man cannot set aside. And the connection of Church and State is a standing witness to this law in the highest places, a protest against the notion that the nation can repudiate its highest functions and duties, any more than one of its own citizens can do so. Were the present connection severed, the only result would be, that, sooner or later, probably after much national deterioration and humiliation, the law would have to be reasserted, and the duty accepted again by the nation under new conditions. Therefore, those in whom the love of their country is deepest and strongest, should be foremost in insisting that we shall not give up the highest national ideal because we find it hard to realize.

It is scarcely possible to contend that the ideal is not lowered by severance of the connection. An abandonment of important functions may be expedient, or convenient, or even necessary, but it must remain a proof of a more stunted and narrower life. And without dwelling on the many ways in which such an abandonment might probably act in England, I think no one will deny that, in any case, it is certain to lessen the interest which religious men take in politics and public life. There is, I know, a school of politicians, not wanting influential representatives in the press, who will exclaim at once, " What a blessing ! How smoothly public business would run on in future if we could only get rid of them altogether ! They are the bane of public life, at least just so far as they will insist on bringing religious considerations to bear on it. A nation to be great and prosperous can't afford to keep a religious conscience." But I venture to think, notwithstanding, from all I have seen of public life in England, that precisely the contrary is true, that men who are avowedly religious are the best politicians, and that it is of the highest moment for the national character, and therefore in the end for national prosperity, that they should be kept interested in politics. It is not easy to do this now, and I am at a loss to see how it will become easier when we declare that henceforth the nation will take no cognizance of, and will cease in its corporate capacity to have anything to do with, religion. If it is replied by some sections of Liberationists (as I presume some at least of the nonconforming bodies would reply) that this is not their meaning—that they never intended to bring about such a result, and they do not believe that disestablishment will effect it — I can only ask, how they propose to avert it? By what machinery can the national supervision and control of religion be made less irksome to them than the present arrangement?

Again, such a man finds himself born to a certain religious inheritance as an Englishman. He can go and settle in any remotest hamlet of this island of ours, and there he shall find provided for him and his family a public place of worship, an officer of the State, and all the machinery necessary for enabling him to enjoy every office and ministration of religion, if, and so far only as, he desires them. This, I say, is part of his and of my birthright, and of every man's birthright as an Englishman, in this year 1877. I have the right to all these things, not because I hold any particular religious opinions, but simply because I am an Englishman, and claim them. If I am too poor or too miserly to pay for them, I can claim them without payment.

Now, to put it no higher, this particular portion of our birthright can do us no harm, for this if for no other reason, that we need not use it unless we please. If we do not want to worship God ourselves, or to be baptized, married, buried, consoled, aided, instructed—if we want none of these things for our wives and children—there is no compulsion whatever upon us in the matter. It is not easy, therefore, to see how we or our families can be injured by this option, and by no means clear how any one else can be. Again, another reason why such men as I am trying to describe are attached to and desire to maintain the connection between Church and State, as the religious condition of things most favourable to national life, is that they see that the principle which underlies the National Church is inclusiveness. Every Englishman born is assumed to be a member, and continues to be so without question, until he leaves it by his own act, by his own free will ; whereas the principle which underlies all voluntary Churches is exclusiveness—they are essentially a section gleaned out of the nation, and whereas an Englishman cannot get out of the National, he cannot get into any voluntary Church without an effort of will. It follows, or at any rate is the fact, that the National Church is the most liberal in spirit ; for by its very nature and constitution it is bound to protest against the sectarian spirit, the spirit of division. Whenever the National Church is not bearing this protest faithfully, it is untrue to itself. The wide divergences of opinion allowed within its ranks, so triumphantly cited in some quarters as signs of weakness, seem to such men proofs of strength.

They see also that the National is the only organization by which the gospel can be carried to the very poor and the outcasts—to those, in short, who need it most, but who do not value it, and cannot or will not pay for it. For voluntary Churches cannot live in the poorest districts, but must follow those who can maintain them, and are only bound to minister to these.

They see, lastly, that the National Church is best adapted to the tone and circumstances of the people of England, as is proved by the fact that the voluntary Churches are all imitating her in so many ways, by using more and more of her Liturgy, by copying her architecture and music, till it is often difficult to tell as you pass a place of worship whether it is National or Nonconformist—by even adopting for their ministers the titles by which the National clergy have always been distinguished.

I have had to dwell at some length, though I trust so as not to weary you, on the sort of views which are held by a large number of quiet lay Churchmen who think about such subjects at all. And now, if there be the least ground of truth in my picture, if I am not dreaming when I say that such men are numerous in England, I would ask any clergyman here to try to put himself in the place of such a layman, and consider how he would regard the doings of the last few months within the Church, and the position which a section of the clergy are taking up and the language they are using—I say a section of the *clergy*, not meaning for a moment to deny that they have a following of laymen (not really so numerous as they suppose, but genuine as far as it goes) with them, but only to place the burthen on the right back. No laity would be there but for them ; it is idle to talk of offences coming mainly from the newly-aroused zeal of boys and girls. It is a portion of the National clergy who are responsible, and must answer for the present state of things, be it for good or for evil.

Now this extreme section are deliberately breaking the law, and, to our astonishment, are applauded and upheld in doing so, not only by newspapers and unions from which nothing better could be expected, but by considerable numbers of their brethren upon whom we had been accustomed to look with respect as honest and faithful ministers, however much we might differ from them.   They do not indeed pretend to agree with the extreme Ritualists, but they support them openly and warmly, on the plea that they are suffering for conscience sake.   Well, let the plea pass—admit that they are making these things matters of conscience—but we must be allowed to ask, as Englishmen, whether this is the kind of conscience which we desire to cultivate in ourselves, or to see cultivated in this nation.   Poor conscience ! to what pitiful uses is that sacred name turned !   The stolid Essex peasant, one of the Peculiar people, lets his child die because he will not allow it to take medicine, and believes himself to be suffering for conscience sake because he is summoned before a magistrate to answer for its life.   And he has far more reason on his side than these Ritualist martyrs—I desire neither to speak nor think scornfully or bitterly of them, but this at least I must say, that men who can make matters of conscience of such trivialities as the shape and color of vestments, the burning of candles and incense, the position of tables, and the like, and in defence of these things are prepared to defy authority, and break what they know to be the law of their country, are not fit to be trusted with the spiritual guidance of any portion of our people.   This nation has a great work still to do in the world, for which she needs children with quite other kind of consciences than these—consciences which shall be simple, manly, obedient, qualities which must disappear under such examples and teachings as these men are giving. It is with reluctance that one has to come to such a conclusion, but there is no use in blinding ourselves any longer as to their meaning. They have resolved to try their strength with the nation ; to throw off all civil control as well as to disobey and defy their spiritual superiors, and they will have to abide the consequences, which will assuredly be that they will not be allowed to minister any longer in the National Church which they are doing all they can to destroy.

Were it only a question of these extreme men, there would be small cause for anxiety ; but, as already stated, they have been backed—at any rate, ever since the judgment in the Hatcham case—by a large number of High Church clergy, from whom we had a right to look for very different things. I have heard friends of my own speaking of these men as martyrs, and echoing the claptrap cries of the (so-called) religious press, such as that of " The interference of the State with the Church has increased, is increasing, and ought to be diminished." A martyr I have always understood to be one who suffers willingly for his faith ; it is abusing an almost sacred word to apply it to such suffering as is possible here in England nowadays, for any opinion (I will not speak of faith) about what postures of the body, or shape or color of garments, have been in use in churches since Edward the Sixth's time. And as to the interference of the State having increased, it is notoriously untrue in any sense except that offences against the law have increased, and so that law has had to be (with extreme reluctance) enforced by the heads of the Church against the offenders.

I willingly admit, however, that they have more reasonable arguments than these. They urge, for instance, that (apart from the extreme Ritualists, whose proceedings they do not approve,) they have been the moving power of the great Church revival of our time, the evidences of which lie broadcast over the whole country, in restored cathedrals and churches, frequent and reverent services, and the widespread zeal for all social reform and philanthropic effort, which has become the honorable and distinguishing characteristic of the nation in our day. In return for these services they have met with abuse, distrust, misrepresentation, and now at last are the subjects of direct attack on the part of the nation, both in the Law Courts and in Parliament, the crowning act of aggression being the Public Worship Regulation Act, which has been aimed at them, and at them only.

Now even those who distrust the High Church party most, must admit their plea as to the zealous, and in many respects admirable, work which they have done since the revival begun by the "Tracts for the Times" forty years ago. They have deserved well of the nation in many ways, and have possibly some grounds for their complaints as to the suspicion with which they have no doubt been always regarded, though they have certainly taken no pains to avoid it. But it is impossible to admit that they have any reason to complain of harsh or unjust treatment, either from the national Executive or from the Legislature. The judgment in Mr. Bennet's case shows how far the Law Courts have been disposed to go in construing their obligations in the largest and widest sense. It is only when there has been an obvious and scandalous disregard and defiance of the law (as in the case of Mr. Purchas and Mr. Tooth) that it has been enforced against any of their number. Indeed, another proof of the advantage of the national principle may be found in the reluctance with which the Courts have intervened; and the steadiness with which they have upheld the principle of a large toleration and inclusiveness in the face of strong popular excitement.

Again, as respects the Legislature, so far from showing any readiness or eagerness to follow the popular cry, it has been only when the open defiance of the law had become a public scandal that Parliament could be induced to interfere at all, and then by an Act which I venture to think has been greatly misunderstood and misrepresented.

Let me just remind you of a fact or two with respect to this Act. In the first place, remember it was a church measure. Whereas the custom had prevailed for years, until it had almost become a rule, that such Bills should be introduced by the Government of the day in consultation with the Bishops, this Bill was not a Government measure. I have never heard why it was that the rule was broken, but broken it was, and it was not until after the Bill had passed the Lords, and been debated for three long nights in the Commons, that it was at length adopted by the Government.

It was introduced by the Archbishop of Canterbury, and received the general support of the whole Bench, though the Bishops of Lincoln and Oxford took some objections to small matters of detail.

At the end of the long and able debate in the Commons, the feeling of the House, and of the nation, had been so clearly expressed that the second reading was carried without a division.

I scarcely remember a question which has stirred the House or the country more deeply in the last twenty years. It was discussed all over the country, in meetings held chiefly, I believe, under the auspices of the Church Association and the Church Union (as to which bodies the Bishop of Lichfield has well said that there will be no peace in the Church till they cease to exist). I would only ask any fair man who is inclined to join in the attempt to take the Church from under State control, to compare the speeches in Parliament and those of the members of these ecclesiastical organizations, during the spring and summer of 1874, and then say which yoke (as the phrase goes) he would honestly desire to be under.

As for the Act itself, it was well said by Mr. Goschen— himself I believe a High Churchman—that it would prove either a small or a large measure, a small one if the clergy meant to obey it, otherwise most likely a large and searching one.

By its provisions the clergy of every school are protected against any malicious or arbitrary use of the Act, by the interposition of the chief of their own body in the diocese in which it is sought to put it in motion, whose leave must be obtained before the institution of proceedings. The bishop practically becomes an arbiter in the case if both parties are willing to accept him ; if not, an impartial tribunal is provided for the decision of the questions at issue.

I trust there are even yet hopes that it may prove a small

Act ; for I cannot believe that, in spite of all the goading of the religious press, and of the semi-ecclesiastical societies, a body of high-principled English gentlemen will continue to maintain the attitude of defiance to the law, and to the clearly expressed will of the nation.

The often repeated cry that the Act is one-sided, and aimed against one party only in the Church, may serve the purpose of excited speakers, but will not bear examination. For it makes no alteration in the law, but only simplifies and cheapens the processes by which the law is administered. Whatever was lawful in the fabric or arrangement of conse-crated buildings, or in vestments, postures, or decorations, remains still lawful—whatever was required before the pass-ing of the Act is still required, the neglect to use that which is prescribed standing in precisely the same category as the use of that which is forbidden.

If it be one-sided, every efficient law in the Statute Book is one-sided ; for every such law inflicts penalties, not on those who keep within, but on those who break it.

The objection to the constitution of the Court which takes cognizance of these offences, when the parties will not submit to the bishop, can scarcely be regarded as serious. It is said that the authority of this Court " is not derived from the rightful royal supremacy exercised ' under God,' but of the Sovereign in council by authority of Parliament." , But surely those who make this protest are aware that the Queen has no authority by virtue of her mere supremacy to constitute any court apart from Parliament.

On the whole, it is not easy to see how, if order is to be

preserved, and the law enforced at all in the National Church, any more moderate or fair method could have been found than that adopted by the Act in question.

But let us pass from the late Act to the remedies for the present state of things, which have been suggested by those who are taking part in this agitation. These are not at present very definite. They are indeed vaguely pledging themselves to " work night and day to set the Church of England free from a persecuting State ; " but we are not told, with any distinctness, what they desire to substitute for the yoke of the nation. If the words of some of their number are to be taken literally, it would seem as though our history of seven hundred years ago had been rolled back, and that England is again face to face with the monks who followed à Becket in his attempt to sever the clergy from the nation, and set them as a caste outside and above the law of the land. I do not of course mean that the present contention is that the clergy shall not be amenable to the law for civil offences, like all other citizens ; but apparently there *is* a section of them who do claim, that as regards all matters connected with their position and functions as clergy, they shall be subject to Church Courts only. And by Church Courts they cannot mean any courts constituted in our national manner, and under the jurisdiction of Parliament ; for then their grievance comes to nothing. It is reduced to a mere question of names, and it does not matter a straw by what name the Courts which try ecclesiastical causes are known, if they are constituted, and their judges appointed, by the head of the State on the advice of responsible Ministers, and under the control of Parliament.

One is driven, therefore, to the conclusion that they mean a tribunal independent of State control, the judges of which are elected by, and responsible to, the clergy, or some purely ecclesiastical organization. There was some strength and meaning in à Becket's proposal, because he had the Pope to put in the place of King and King's Council, as the head and fountain of authority for the Courts which he proposed to substitute for the national Courts. But as the Ritualists have not that resource, they should either cease beating about the bush and make their demands clear and precise, telling us who is to be the fountain on earth of ecclesiastical authority, or leave the National Church, and set up a sect of their own, in which they may place themselves as priests in whatever position they please, as they find themselves unable to accept the grandest of all positions, that of simple citizens, called and appointed to minister to the nation, whose sons they are, in spiritual things.

There is another course advocated by many High Churchmen as an escape from our present difficulties, which is advanced temperately and reasonably, and has the public sanction of at least one bishop. I think I shall state it most fairly perhaps in his own words :—" I am of opinion," the Bishop of Lincoln writes, " that for the sake of the State as well as for that of the Church much more liberty ought to be given, and much more weight attached, to the judgment of the spirituality in ecclesiastical causes, and to the action of the Church of England in her synods, diocesan and provincial." I am glad to be able to quote his further words of warning :—" But we shall never obtain these benefits by violent resistance to constitutional authority ; on the contrary, we shall provoke violent reprisals, and shall greatly injure the cause we desire to mantain."

I presume that these words point to investing Convocation with some legislative powers in ecclesiastical affairs ; and with every desire to concede whatever can be conceded for the sake of peace, I' am bound to say plainly that I do not think it can be found in this direction.   Convocation has now for some years been sitting and discussing all questions upon which legislation is needed, or which seriously affect the religious condition of the nation.   But I fear that the reports of the debates in both Houses have not had a reassuring effect on the country ; indeed, they have been characterized by timidity and narrowness, and an apparent want of appreciation of the forces which are working in the outside world, which has disappointed those who looked most hopefully towards this experiment.   I am not aware of any recommendation of practical value which has as yet come from that body.   Indeed, it seems to me that the main result of the recent revival of Convocation has been to strengthen the convictions of all those who value the national character of the Church, that that character cannot be maintained if its direction and government is to be entrusted to any ecclesiastical body.   It may be said that the proposal is to reform Convocation by the admission of the laity.   But this would not remove the objection.   Such laymen as would have a chance of election would not represent the nation, besides which they would be powerless in such a body.   When professionals and amateurs meet, we know which side is likely to go to the wall.

Convocation was no doubt two hundred years ago a sort of fourth estate of the realm, representing not the National Church but the clergy, even for purposes of taxation. It was at their own request that for those purposes they were merged in the nation, and taxed by the same machinery as the laity. From that time Convocation was practically without functions, and when summoned, as in 1698, the disputes between the Low Church bishops appointed by the Crown and the Jacobite clergy ran so high as to create scandal and render their debates fruitless; and from 1717 till our own day, though formally summoned, they were always at once prorogued.

But even if the traditions of Convocation were far more satisfactory, the chief objection remains that to hand over the control of the Church to that body would be an infringement of the national principle, and an imitation of the practice of the sects, without any compensating advantage. For what ground from recent experience have we for believing that the various parties in the Church would agree better in Convocation than they did in 1698?

To give the powers that are claimed to Convocation would be a certain step towards a severance of all connection with the State, and consequently (in words probably familiar to many here) would inevitably lead to that "degradation which by an almost universal law overtakes religion when, even while attaining a purer form, it loses the vivifying and elevating spirit breathed into it by close contact with the great historic and secular influences, which act like fresh air on a contracted atmosphere, and are thus the divine antiseptics against the spiritual corruption of merely ecclesiastical communities " (Dean Stanley).

I am not aware of any other proposal to which the same objection does not attach. They are one and all aimed at a further severance of the clergy from the Church and from the nation, whereas what we need is precisely the reverse of this —that the clergy should be brought into closer contact with the nation, and should learn to feel more and more the worth and nobleness of their common citizenship.

That they have a higher citizenship is of course true, but only in the same sense in which it is true of every one of their lay brethren. That Christ is the only head of the Church is also true, but is He not also the only head of the nation? He is no more visible to the Church than to the nation, to the priest than to the crossing-sweeper. They hold their commission from Him no doubt, but they must receive it, with some visible seal, from some human hands; and what seal can be so worthy, so noble, as that of the nation whose children they are?

But if none of the suggestions yet made seem to offer relief, what is the outlook? Dark enough, I admit, but still by no means so dark as it has often been before, for all these struggles and controversies are, after all, but the signs of a vigorous life. All that is needed—and surely England will not now for the first time need it in vain—is some small share of the self-restraint, the patience, and the courage which have never yet failed her under God's blessing. That there must be a great reform in our National Church is clear, but she is strong enough to bear it. What has been done in our day in this direction should be encouraging instead of depressing to any one who will look at it steadily and fairly; but it is only a fraction of what is needed.

The readjustment of Church property, the establishment of the Ecclesiastical Commission, the abolition of tests, the relaxation of subscription, the reorganization of parishes, the appointment of bishops without seats in the House of Lords, the subdivision of dioceses, the Church Discipline Acts, the revision of the Bible, and, lastly, this Public Worship Act, are all measures passed within my own memory. And surely such a list (and it might be doubled) may well give heart of grace to the most desponding, for these reforms have been made in a time peculiarly unfavourable to the development of the Church. The commercial spirit, with its utilitarian and materialistic Gospel, has been in the ascendant, with the result that the friends of the National Church have been afraid of touching a brick of the old fabric lest the whole should come about their ears, while her enemies have looked upon every effort for reform with watchful jealousy, fearing lest it should strengthen the old walls and foundations. No one can have been in the House of Commons without becoming aware of the strength of these two antagonist forces, both however working in the same direction, that of making any resolute action in Church reform all but impossible. And yet all these things I have just referred to have been done in such a time.

Why then should we despair of greater and better things, when a time has come in which there are unmistakable signs that, whatever the controlling spirit may prove to be, it will not be the utilitarian or materialistic? If the Church has emerged from such a time as the one which is expiring, fuller than ever of spiritual life and zeal, and without having as yet lost anything of her national character, what fear is there that she will be false to her own and her country's history in the time which is coming? It was in a crisis in several respects as serious as the present that the wisest as well as the most observant and best-informed of foreign critics of our national habits and institutions, wrote :—" To this country belongs the honour of having, so far as the State is concerned, succeeded in the mighty task of reconciling individual liberty with allegiance and submission to the will of the community, whilst other nations are still wrestling with it ; and I feel persuaded that the same earnest zeal and practical wisdom which have made her political constitution an object of admiration to other nations will, under God's blessing, make her Church also a model to the world " (Prince Albert).

It is in this hope and with this belief that I have ventured to speak to you this evening. I know that I must have said things which may have roused painful, and possibly indignant feelings in the minds of persons for whom individually, and for much of whose work, I should desire only to express respect and gratitude. If there should be any such here, I can only ask them to believe that it is from love to the Church, of which we are all members, not less sincere, I trust, and loyal than their own—from an estimate not lower, at any rate, though in some respects differing from theirs, of the mission of that Church, and of the work she has been called to do for the nation and for the world—that one is constrained to be perfectly outspoken, and not to ignore or explain away facts, or to call things by any other than their plainest names at such a time as this.

There is no danger for our Church that I can see, except from her own children, indeed from her own officers. There is no deeper feeling on this subject of disestablishment in the House of Commons than irritated jealousy, having its root in social and political soil, and its expression in clever flippancy and bitterness, and the House in this matter very fairly represents the people. Those who express anything more serious are, I think, constantly finding it more and more difficult to persuade themselves or any one else that they are working for the highest good of the country, and with a single view of placing religion under the absolutely best conditions for doing the nation's work. It is only within her own ranks that there is zeal and fire enough to be dangerous.

Before going further on these new and perilous ways, the discontented in her own ranks should at least count the cost more carefully than they seem yet to have done. Can any one of them say deliberately that in his conscience he believes the conditions and prospects of the religious life of this nation will be improved by the withdrawal of religion altogether from the cognizance and control of the nation? If he can answer yes, there is no more to be said, and there can be neither peace nor even truce possible between us. If not there is scarcely any point, short of the intrusion of outside influence in the National Church, or disobedience to the law, to which we would not go to help them. We will join them in efforts to obtain thorough Church reform, the deeper and wider the better. We have no fear of touching formularies, or canons, or rubrics, or liturgies ; indeed are anxious they should be touched, inasmuch as they are in not a few respects obsolete and unfitted to our time. Whenever the clergy are prepared for this necessary work, which cannot be long deferred—though in the midst of the present agitation it is difficult to see how or by whom it can be taken in hand—they will find lay Churchmen cordial and strenuous helpers. All we ask of them is, that in one of the great crises of the world—the days of the Lord, as they are so well called —they shall not wantonly destroy that example of the conditions on which the Gospel and the nations can live together, which, with all its faults, is the best hitherto seen in the world, and the only one which gives us even a distant hint of how, in God's good time, the kingdoms of this world may become the kingdoms of our Lord and of His Christ.

IS LIFE WORTH LIVING ? [1]

By W. H. Mallock.

I.

THE apostles of modern progress claim many virtues for the present, which the unenlightened observer may be somewhat slow to detect in it. But it has one distinctive feature at any rate, the reality of which can be denied by nobody, and which has needed but little heightening from the imagination of the optimist. That feature is the singular toleration of its temper amongst all that, apparently, can most excite intolerance. Every belief that life was once supposed to rest upon we see men calmly questioning and preparing to cast aside, and yet we most of us keep our tempers ; we are neither afraid nor angry. Doctrines are swinging before us in the balance that seemed but yesterday to be fixed as mountains, not to be weighed at all ; and yet no Brennus adds a sword to make his own scale heavier. There is, in fact, a greater intellectual struggle going on now about us, than the world in its whole history has ever before witnessed ; the difference that is at the heart of it is wider and more profound. And yet never in any past period has the philosophic and the theological hatred

<hr>

[1] THE NINETEENTH CENTURY, SEPTEMBER, 1877, and JANUARY, 1878.

been felt so little or been so well suppressed by the disputants ; whilst amongst the world at large that intelligently watches the movement, and with interest abides the result of it, prejudice seems almost completely to be laid to sleep, and to have given place to a true judicial calm.   Our avowed desire is simply to discover where truth lies, not to discover that it lies either here or there.   Truth is the pearl we want, and the divers may seek for it either in cesspools or in crystal seas. Let them only prove to us satisfactorily where it is to be found. It is not by its locality that we shall judge of its value.

A toleration so catholic and so complete as this seems doubtless a very attractive thing, and is hailed by many wise and worthy men as the fairest and surest sign of a really enlightened age.   It is to be feared, however, that in this view we flatter ourselves too much.   In some small measure our toleration may indeed be a sign of our enlightenment, but in a far greater measure it is a sign and an effect of our ignorance. We are tolerant of various views, because we have grasped the full meaning of none of them.   We are calm as we watch the battle, because we are happily unconscious of what hangs on the issue of it.

This unconsciousness is as easy to explain as it is difficult to excuse.   It lies in the following fact.   The seat of war, so to speak, is at present in a distant country.   Our homes, our families, and the course of our daily lives are not disturbed by it.   The questions now dividing the intellectual world are as yet unpractical and remote ones.   They deal with the most distant things of the past, or the most elusive things of the present—with the connection of mind and body, with the foundations of morality, with the descent of man, with the origin of life, with the composition of matter, with the existence or non-existence of a first cause. Such questions as these hardly ever occur to us, much less do we seriously think them over, except in times of leisure or retirement. When we are engaged in action, or when we are stirred by feeling, they recede entirely from us ; we forget that we have ever known them. No questions, however, are simply abstract that are of any importance to the world at large, or that the world at large takes any genuine interest in. They may seem to be so, but they are not so ; and the world by a keen instinct feels that they are not so, long before this feeling has become conscious knowledge, and before conscious knowledge has produced wisdom. Sooner or later, directly or indirectly, such questions will show their bearing on life. They will become capable of being expressed in terms of action ; and we shall discuss the distant premisses under the form of the near conclusion. And not this only ; not only shall we thus discuss them, but it is this last discussion, this discussion of the conclusion, that will really be the decisive one. It may reverse in a moment all former judgments, and from it there will be no appeal. Philosophies, let us remember, exist for the world, not the world for philosophies ; and philosophies can only rule the world by guiding it in directions which it is willing itself to take. Let them try to do it violence, and to force it, no matter on what grounds : it will argue back from the practical conclusions to the theoretical premises ; and if it rejects the latter as repulsive, it will wisely and inevitably condemn the former as false.

. The world, then, is tolerant at present of all the rival theories that so much engage its attention, because it is not yet aware of the rival practical meanings which lurk below, but only a little below, the surface of them. I have no wish to pronounce on these any judgment of my own. To do so would be quite beside my point. My aim is a far humbler one. It is simply to awake others, and enable them to pass judgment for themselves. It is my aim to make them see what in these days we are really all debating about, and to show them that it is not only first causes, and natural selection, and the condition of the universe millions of years ago ; but the tone and character of our human existence now—our hopes, our fears, our affections, even our amusements, our relations with our wives and parents, and the education of our children. It is all under debate—the entire scheme and conduct of our lives, the complexion of each short day of them from sunrise to sunset. But of this the world seems quite ignorant ; and, being ignorant it can easily afford to be tolerant.

Let us examine the matter more particularly, but first let us make our minds clear about one important point.

The schools of thought that are being now developed about us seem from some points of view to be very various. Theologies, moral philosophies, and materialisms distract our attention with their endless details, and, seen through a dim intellectual twilight, look even more confused and numerous than they really are. But there is one grand division to be made between them, at which they at once form into order, and are forced to group themselves into two classes, between which there is no sympathy and no connection, and between

which the line of separation is sharp, distinct, and insuperable, and between which, if their difference have any meaning
at all, accounts must first be settled before we can with profit
proceed an inch further. The one of these classes is distinguished by the affirmation, the other by the denial, of two
dogmas—the existence of a personal God, and the personal
immortality of man. The distinct affirmation of these I shall
call Religion, or Belief ; the distinct denial of them I shall
call Atheism, or Unbelief. I need not pause to defend this
use of the words. For the present it is enough that I explain it.

It is true that Religion and Atheism represent opposite
poles of thought, and that between these two certainties
there are all gradations of doubt. But with none of these
forms of doubt need we now concern ourselves ; and for this
reason. My aim is not now to deal with conditions of mind,
but with the practical, with the active results which such conditions produce. If neither Religion nor Atheism have any
practical effect on the conduct and character of life, if their
axioms are mere barren propositions beginning and ending
with themselves, without any significance, be it ever so small,
to the human race at large, it is a foolish waste of time to
affirm or to deny either of them. They may serve to amuse the
barbarous leisure of pedants, but all except pedants will wisely
refuse a thought to them. If, however, on the other hand, they
have any effect at all, then, in so far as certainty either way
can direct or stimulate action, doubt in a like degree must
paralyse and arrest it. But it is in action that man's life and
health consist ; what tends to hinder action is the beginning

of death.   The philosophy of complete doubt therefore stands self-condemned.   It still exists, it is true ; the sentence upon it has never been fully executed ; but it exists as a disease— a disease, indeed, from which some of us may ourselves be suffering, but which it seems hardly conceivable that any one in his senses should boast of, still less try to propagate ; whilst, if the doubt be not complete, if it be not balanced perfectly in the centre, it must be always tending either to one pole or the other, and its right name would be incomplete religion or incomplete atheism, neither of which stages is final ; and, the incompleteness being in each case an imperfection, it must be got rid of before we can do any justice to either side.

The matter, then, is thus far simplified.   All minor differences, of whatever magnitude, for the present may be quite dropped.   We will but busy ourselves with the greatest difference of all.   As far as we are concerned, there are but two parties now contending, and these parties are Religion and Atheism, Belief and Unbelief, those fundamental opposites, those irreconcilable enemies.   Such being the case, we may indeed find matter for wonder in the extreme forbearance with which the contest is conducted, and the impartiality, despite the interest, with which it is watched.

In former times, when Atheism was vague and stammering, incomplete and unorganized, it was condemned and suppressed with horror, anger and indignation.   Its apostles were execrated as monsters doomed to eternal torments.   The world cast them out, and the Church burnt them.   But now that Atheism is complete and organized, without concealment and without shame, its name is not even a term of mild reproach. On the contrary, its most notorious professors are honored and looked up to by the world in general, and are listened to with respectful patience by even their professed opponents. Deans avow friendship for men compared with whom Voltaire is orthodox, and cardinals with such men gravely discuss beliefs which Voltaire would have thought it horrible to question.

The reason of this is obvious. Atheism has come forward under changed conditions. It is based upon new foundations; it is animated with a new temper. For the first time it rests itself not on the private speculations of a rebellious intellect, not on the ravings of a vile Parisian populace drunk with the wine of politics, and suffering from political delirium tremens, but on the deep and broad foundations of research, experiment, and proof. It has thus lost all that insolence of private passion and of private judgment, which used to make it as offensive to men's practical instincts as it was hostile to their theoretical convictions. Our modern atheists in profession, and to a great measure in fact are entirely free of the old personal bravado; they claim to teach with authority, because they have been content to learn with humility. For they, too, have their church, their infallible teacher, to whom they profess an implicit and devout obedience. And this teacher is undoubtedly an august one. It is none other than Nature herself, as our powerful science compels her answers from her—Nature, in the widest sense of the word, including the history of the universe and the history of the human race, and the laws in obedience to which this history has developed itself. Here, we are told, is our one source of knowledge ; here we learn the truth, and the whole truth. Nature bears witness about every conceivable subject ; there is no rational question which, if we do but ask it properly, she will not answer. She will require no faith from us ; she will ask us to take nothing on trust. Everything that she teaches us she will prove and verify ; and there is no variableness in her, nor any shadow of turning. " Come, then "—this is the appeal that our modern atheists make to us—" and let us learn of Nature ; let us listen to the voice of Truth ! " And what does Truth tell us ? Among many things Truth tells us two, which are of prime importance, and which are universally intelligible to the human race. There is no God, and there is no future life. The notion of the first is unnecessary, and that of the second is ridiculous. In the name of Truth, then, let us cast these lies away from us, however painfully for the moment we may feel their loss, however closely they may be bound up for us with memories of the past. But we are not left with this exhortation only. Something more is added to sustain and stimulate us. These lies, we are told, if we will but look them boldly in the face, instead of blinking at them out of deference to their supposed divinity, we shall see to be not lies only, but profoundly immoral lies. It is, therefore, in the name not of selfish indulgence, not of license and free-living, but of sacred truth and all the severest principles, that we are invited to accept the creed of Atheism, and to cast out Religion. Thus the Atheism of to-day, though theoretically destructive, is practically conservative. It no longer assails society as it is, or any of those rules that sustain it, or the chastened affections that are supposed to make it worth sustaining. It is associated no longer with any dissolute wit, with any cruel and brilliant cynicism, or with the fascinations of lawless love. On the contrary, it is on the whole somewhat dull; and, to say the least of it, it is eminently respectable. It is the Atheism of the vigil, not of the orgy; and its character when developed is solemn, almost puritanical. Study the language, the conduct, even the faces of its most eminent exponents, and signs will be apparent everywhere of gravity and of severe earnestness. These are men, we see in a glance, who hold life a serious thing—a thing not to be trifled away in idleness, however harmless, or in licentious self-indulgence, however refined or graceful. What is really of value in life, what men should really strive for, are things to be reached only by self-denial and labor, and a vigilant rigor in the guidance and control of our passions. Those who pay no heed to the better part, but who saunter, who lounge, who smile, who sneer through life, are condemned by the atheists even more grimly than by the believers.

Here, then, is the explanation of our modern tolerance. Both the opposing schools unite in one point; and this is the only point on which difference could not be forgotten, and on which agreement must be hourly felt and remembered. Both agree in their determination to enforce morality, to enjoin strictly on men one certain line of conduct, and by some means or other to persuade or constrain them to follow it. The two schools may differ as to minor details; this comparatively is of small moment. All that we need now remember is that they agree about the great premiss, which, though often not expressed, is implied in all moral systems whatsoever, and without which it is manifest they must all fall to the ground. That premiss is this:—*Human life is a thing of solemn importance; it is of the utmost matter how we live it. Lived in one way, it is a hateful failure; lived in another, it is a beautiful success.* In other words, there is something in it of such consummate and incomparable value that its attainment will repay every possible cost to us of weariness, of patience, and of torture, and, once attained, will make us feel truly that we have not lived in vain. Thus human endeavor has a meaning, and, rightly directed, is sure of its own reward. Life is not vanity, it is not vexation of spirit. Of the existence of this precious something that gives life its value there is no question; that, by both parties, is taken for granted. The only question is as to its analysis—what are its component parts, on what is its value founded? Thus the rival parties are agreed to share the treasure; their only contest is as to who shall protect the treasury.

There is one fact, however, which the unbelievers pass by. They are sometimes so ignorant that they do not know of it; they are sometimes so preoccupied that they forget it; they are often of what we should most of us call so fine a nature that they can but imperfectly understand it. At any rate, from whatever cause, they one and all ignore it; or when for a moment sometimes it is actually forced upon their notice, they only put it aside with anger and irritation. They will not even examine it. This fact, however, is one that must be dealt with—that we must look fully in the face. Sooner or later we shall have to do so. We cannot dispose of it either by ill-temper or forgetfulness. Let us try to consider it, and calmly value its importance.

We can most of us, we can probably all of us, remember times in the course of our lives, when we have felt like Macbeth or Hamlet in their most desponding moods. We have heard the rumor of life as it were an idiot's tale in our ears, full of sound and fury, signifying nothing ; all the uses of the world have seemed weary, stale, flat, and unprofitable to us. We have thought that there was nothing worth striving for, that there was no profit under the sun. The splendor has gone from the grass, the glory from the flower. Knowledge, life, affection—all these have ceased to appeal to us. We have felt that we must do something, but that it was no matter what we did. To some of us suicide has no doubt suggested itself ; and to others the more popular philosophy, so tersely expressed by Byron, that—

Man, *being reasonable*, must get drunk.

This view, however, even by most of those who hold it, has been felt to be really but a half-view in the guise of a whole one. It has else been intentionally adopted as a kind of solemn affectation, or it has else been lamented as a miserable sad disease. It is a view, indeed, that healthy intellects have hitherto declined even to consider. Its advocates have met with neglect, contempt, or castigation, not with arguments ; they have been pitied as insane, condemned as cynical, or passed over as frivolous. And yet but for one reason, this view would have been to the whole modern world not only not untenable, but even obvious. The emptiness of the things of this life, their utter powerlessness to make us really happy, has been the theme equally of saints and sages. Commerce with the world and meditation in the cloister seemed to teach all of them the same lesson, seemed to preach to them the same sermon *de contemptu mundi.* The view which the eager monk began with, the sated monarch ended with. But matters did not end here. There was something more to come, by which this view was completely changed and transmuted, and which made the wilderness and the waste place at once blossom as the rose. Judged of by itself, this life would indeed be vanity; but it was not to be judged of by itself. All its ways seemed to break short aimlessly in precipices, or to be lost hopelessly in deserts; they led to no visible end. True; but they led instead to ends that were invisible—to spiritual and eternal destinies, to triumphs exceeding every hope, to terrible failures exceeding every fear. This, all men might see if they would only choose to see. The most trivial of our daily actions became thus invested with an immeasurable meaning. Life was thus evidently not vanity, not an idiot's tale, not unprofitable; and those who affected to think it was were naturally disregarded by the world as either insane or insincere.

But now with the unbelievers all this is changed. They, too, hold that life is serious; as serious, they say, as the believers hold it—nay, even more so. But they must base this faith of theirs upon quite new reasons; they must find quite a new answer with which to confute objectors. It is, in fact, their boast that they are obliged to do so. Not only do they think the old answers to be insufficient or beside the point, but they think them to be lies, to be groundless lies, to be immoral lies. To destroy them, to cast them out, to cleanse the world of them, is with our new teachers the very beginning of progress. What then is the practical result, or rather the practical meaning, of this ? An extreme value to life, we have seen, they are resolved—indeed, being moralists, they are obliged—to give ; they will not tolerate those who deny this value. But they are obliged to find the value in a new place—in the very place where hitherto it has been thought most conspicuous by its absence. It is to be found in no better and wider future, where injustice shall be turned to justice, trouble into rest, and blindness into clear sight ; for no such future awaits us. It is to be found in life itself, in this earthly life, this life between the cradle and the grave—there or nowhere ; and within these limits they imply it assuredly is to be found—found and attained also, for it is nothing if not attainable. Here, then, is a distinct intelligible task that the unbelievers have unintentionally set themselves ; and when they realize what it is, they may perhaps be startled at its boldness. They have taken everything away from life that to wise men hitherto has seemed to redeem it from vanity. They have to prove to us that they have not left it vain. They have to prove those things to be solid which their predecessors thought hollow, those things serious which their predecessors thought contemptible ; they must prove to us that we shall be content with that which has never yet contented us, and that the widest minds will thrive within limits that have hitherto been thought too narrow for the narrowest. They may be able to prove this ; there is nothing on the face of it that is impossible. But at all events it requires to be proved. They must not beg the very point which is most open to contradiction, and which, when once duly apprehended, will be most sure to provoke it. If this life is not of itself incapable of satisfying us, let them show us conclusively that it is not. But they can hardly expect that, without any such showing at all, the world will suddenly repel as a blasphemy what it has hitherto accepted as a commonplace.

If we consider the matter a little further, this will become more evident.

All systems of morality, we have seen, must postulate some end of action—an end that is worth living for—an end that is supremely good for us to gain, and supremely ill for us to lose—an end that we can only gain by virtue, and that we must lose by vice. We have seen also that every system of morality that is not religious must place this end wholly within the present life. Life, this terrestrial human life, it premises, contains something in it that can satisfy man ; and this *something* is to be reached only in certain ways—ways that can be prescribed, and taught, and which are named morality. Now let us reflect a little about this *something*, and see generally what sort of *something* it must be, if it is to satisfy all the demands that will necessarily be made upon it.

In the first place, it is of course a *something* whose value can be, and is, recognized by those who follow it. Virtuous men are virtuous because virtue brings them something which they wish to be brought to them—because the end it aims at seems to them the highest aim. But this is not all. It is not enough that to those who already know it, and who are already seeking and finding it, the *something* in question appears an adequate end of action. It must be capable of being put as such before those who already do not know it, and who have never sought it, but who have, on the contrary, always turned away from everything that is supposed to lead to it. It must be able, in other words, not only to satisfy the virtuous of the wisdom of their virtue; it must be able to convince the vicious of the folly of their vice. If it cannot fulfil this condition, the atheistic moralist can make no converts. Vice is only bad in his eyes because of the precious *something* we lose by it. He can only convince us of our error by giving us some picture of our loss. And this, if his moral system be worth anything, he must be able to do, and, in promulgating his system, he professes to be able to do. The physician's work is to heal the sick. His skill must not end in explaining his own health.

Here, then, is an important fact about the supreme *something*—that *something* that alone makes life serious, and that is of necessity postulated by every unbelieving moralist. It is nothing, as we have already said, if not attainable. We now see that it is next to nothing if not describable.

Let us go a little farther.

One term of description we may at once apply to it, as about that there has been no question. The *something* we are in search of is some form of happiness. But it is not enough to call it happiness. For of happiness there are countless kinds; and one or other of these all men follow, and take very different paths in doing so. But it is plain that they are not for this reason moral. Else there would be an indefinite number of moralities, and we might multiply them at our own caprice. But this plainly is not the case. Of moralities, unless we give the word an entirely new meaning, there is fundamentally only one, and this is equally applicable to all varieties of men. Morality, then, is the art of one single kind of happiness; and this happiness will, when once known, be attractive to all alike, despite every difference of situation, taste, and temper. It will be attractive, too, in so superlative a degree, that every pleasure will be gladly sacrificed, and every pain gladly suffered for it, by those who have once seen it in its true colors.

It thus appears, then, that all those who, dispensing with religion, would yet maintain morality stand committed to the following statement—that human life contains for those who seek it a certain kind of happiness so supreme and satisfying that if a man gain the whole world and yet lose this, his entire career is but a calamitous failure. And this supreme kind of happiness is the same for all; it is within the reach of all; when once fully known it is irresistibly attractive to all; and, by some means or other, it is describable or presentable to all.

And now let us dwell once again on this last characteristic, and see a little more clearly how essential it is.

A code of morals is a number of restraining orders; it rigorously bids us walk in certain paths. But why? What is the use of bidding us? Because there are a variety of other paths that we are naturally inclined to walk in. The right paths are right because they lead to the highest kind of happiness; the wrong paths are wrong because they lead to lower kinds of happiness. But when men choose vice instead of virtue, what is happening? They are considering the lower happiness better than the highest; they are making a mistake as to the value of the end. It is this mistake that is the essence and the cause of immorality; it is this mistake that mankind is for ever inclined to make; and it is the great *raison d'être* of a moral system that it can bring this mistake home to us, and so cure us of it; that it can open our mind's eyes, and show us that the highest happiness is indeed the highest, and so make us sharply conscious of what we lose by losing it. This highest happiness must, then, be describable or presentable; and the men to whom we shall chiefly want to present it are not men who desire to see it, and will seek for it of their own accord, but men who are turned away from it, and on whose sight it must be thrust. And not this only. Not only must it be thus presentable, but when presented it must be able to stand the inveterate criticism of those who fear being allured by it, who are content as they are, and have no wish to be rendered discontented. These men will submit it to every test by which they may hope to prove that its attractions are delusive. They will ask what it is based upon, and of what it is compounded. They will submit it to an analysis as merciless as that by which their atheistic advisers and censors have destroyed religion. They will test it with reason, as we test a metal by acid. It must, therefore, be able to bear this fiery and fierce ordeal, and come out none the worse for it. Not only must it have a bloom of beauty on it at first sight, but this beauty must bear handling, and must be insoluble by reason, with which it is sure to be tested.

Now is this happiness a reality, or is it a myth? That is the great question. Can human life, cut off utterly from every hope beyond itself—can human life supply it? If it cannot, then evidently there can be no morality without religion. But perhaps it can. But perhaps life has greater capacities than we have hitherto given it credit for. Perhaps this happiness may be really not far from any one of us, and we have only overlooked it hitherto because it was too directly before our eyes. If so, let it be pointed out to us. It is useless, as we have seen, if not presentable. To those who most need it, it is useless until presented. Indeed, until it is presented, we are but acting on our teacher's maxim by refusing to believe in it. And as yet it never has been presented. No image of any kind of terrestrial happiness has as yet been put before the world that can at all bear the weight that will be put upon it, as the foundation of morality, unless we give morality an entirely new and, in many points, an entirely inverted meaning.

I know that this statement will be contradicted by many, and, till it is explained further, it is only natural that it should be. It will be said that a terrestrial happiness, just of the kind needed, has been put by the unbelieving moralists before the world again and again. Is not virtue, it has been asked us, its own reward? Shall we only be generous, be kind, be brave, be true, for the hope of future payment, or the fear of future pain? Shall we not rather be all these things for the simple sake of being them? and shall not we find ample blessedness in this? I know that all this has been urged upon us, and that it is being urged upon us daily now. But with what results?　With none, or rather with far worse than none. Not only has it done absolutely nothing towards clearing up the matter, but it has, on the contrary, completely disordered and confused it.　It has reduced it to a state in which it is impossible to pass any judgment on it.　And the reason why is simple.　It begs the answer in the very terms in which it propounds the question.

This hitherto has been the fault of all the unbelieving moralists.　They will never state their own position clearly. I have said they will not, but it must be more true to say they cannot.　They apparently only mystify others, because they have first honestly mystified themselves.　At any rate, the first thing to be done, before we proceed further, is to extricate the question from all those irrelevant surroundings which so completely hide its features as it is at present presented to us.

As it is necessary before all things that this be done thoroughly, I will not contend with the vague representative generalities which I just now put into the mouths of the unbelievers. I will take the very words of one of themselves, and these words shall be the most favorable and complete specimen I am able to find of their way of putting the case.　They shall show in its best and most alluring light the code of atheistic ethics as it is offered to us by our modern atheists.　We shall then see distinctly with that we have first to deal.

The following verses are George Eliot's:

> Oh may I join the choir invisible
> Of those immortal dead, who live again
> In minds made better by their presence . . .

So to live is heaven . . .
To make undying music in the world,
Breathing us beauteous order that controls
With growing sway the growing life of man.
So we inherit that sweet purity
For which we struggled, groaned, and agonised
With widening retrospect that bred despair . . .
That better self shall live till human time
Shall fold its eyelids, and the human sky
Be gathered like a scroll within the tomb,
Unread for ever. This is life to come,
Which martyred men have made more glorious
For us who strive to follow. May I reach
That purest heaven, and be to other souls
That cup of strength in some great agony,
Enkindle generous ardour, feed pure love,
Beget the smiles that have no cruelty,
Be the sweet presence of a good diffused,
And in diffusion ever more intense ;
So shall I join that choir invisible,
Whose music is the gladness of the world.

In these remarkable verses we have the whole gospel of atheistic ethics, as it is now preached to us, presented in an impassioned epitome. All that our unbelieving moralists say we have condensed here, and condensed in such a way that it shall look at its very best, that it shall look as beautiful and as alluring as it possibly can be made to look. Indeed, the objection might readily suggest itself that it was too beautiful, too highly strung—that it was fit only for saints and heroes. This objection, however, is a completely false one. It would apply equally well to any system of morality that tended to raise men. Our professions must be above our practice, else our practice would soon sink below our professions. We are only not worse than we are, because we know we ought to be better. A morality will never save sinners that will not satisfy saints, and the

sentiments of a system must be always suited to the most exalted of those that live by it.   In fact it is these that, before
all others, it must suit; for it is they, though in numbers a
minority, that are the primary sources of all moral power.
The world may be divided into two classes.   The first is composed of the great mass of men without strong ambitions,
without strong principles, without either the need or power
to think things out for themselves.   They are content to live,
as it were, from hand to mouth—in so far as they are virtuous
doing their duties, in so far as they are vicious avoiding them,
with no inquiry into the deeper reasons of things, and the
fundamental difference between vice and virtue.   The second
class is a comparatively small one, though its limits cannot be
defined with any great exactness.   It consists of men with
minds and wills so active that they cannot take things thus
quietly.   There are two questions, one of which they will ask,
and very often both of them.   What meaning can be wrung
out of life? and how can we ourselves wring out this meaning?
These are the men who, in a greater or less degree, approach
the ideals of sanctity, of heroism, or of genius.   These are
the salt of the earth, the little leaven hid in a barrel of meal
—the men who have subdued kingdoms, escaped the edge of
the sword, out of weakness been made strong, and have put
to flight the armies of the aliens.   These are the Pauls of the
world, and the Voltaires also, the Loyolas and the Benthams.
These are that gifted minority by whom men's blind instincts
are converted into clear governing principles, and principles
shown in action by example, by whom the world is taught,
and whom the world follows.   To such men George Eliot's

verses could not be in any way unsatisfactory on the score of
their elevation.   And such men, let us remember, are all that
we need now consider.   For it is these a system must first
move and satisfy, before it can move and satisfy any others.
If the morality of atheism cannot attract them, we may be
quite sure it will attract nobody else.   If they are convinced
that religion is false, that without religion there can be no
power to enable us to overcome temptation, and no reason
for desiring to do so, that in a moral sense life is worthless,
and that wisdom and folly are all one, much more will the
world at large be convinced, to whom wisdom is naturally
irksome, and folly easy.

And now, before recurring to George Eliot's verses let us
notice carefully one essential characteristic of the conduct of
this minority to whom the verses are primarily addressed.
Every human action must have a motive, it must aim at some
end which the agent desires to attain.   But with the sort of
men we are now considering it is not enough that the act has
a *motive*, it must have also a *justification*.   They must be assured that the ends they aim at are right and worthy ones.
This being the case, we may divide their actions into three
classes.   In the first the motive and the justification are essentially inseparable.   The former supplies the latter.   The
motive is its own justification.   The end, in other words, is
good for its own sake.   That is all we can say.   We can defend our desire for it no further.   In the second class of actions the motive and the justification are inseparable also.
But here matters are reversed.   The latter supplies the former.   The justification is the only motive.   The end, in other

words, is in no sense good for its own sake, but only as leading to some other good that is.   Lastly, there is a third class
in which the motive and the justification are separate and distinct things.   Here the reasons for which we choose an act
are different from the reasons for which we allow ourselves to
choose it.   It is specially important that this should be understood rightly ; I will therefore give a few examples of
what I mean.   Let us take the matter of politics.   A political
career has for many men an irresistible fascination.   They
pursue it with an appetite and an eagerness that seems utterly
unconnected with anything else beyond.   The only motives
they are conscious of are excitement and ambition.   But these
strong motives are not sufficient.   They need a justification
to clench their power.   The justification is that politics are
not absorbing only, but necessary; not exciting only, but
useful.   Once let this justification go, once disconnect the
success of the statesman from the improvement of the State,
once make it self-evident that in following his own interests
he is ministering to no interests beyond them, and the whole
charm of politics will be gone.   They will have become nothing
but a game, and a foolish vapid game at which no one will care
to play.   There is, to take another instance, a certain set of
excellent women, who are continually being moved to giving
advice and telling the whole truth to their friends.   What can
be more distinct than motive and justification here ?   The
justification is the good they do, the motive is the annoyance
they give.   Or, to come to a commoner matter yet, let us
take the matter of eating.   Nine times out of ten our immediate motive for eating is the immediate pleasure which the

process gives us. As far as we are conscious at the moment eating is for the most part a simple self-indulgence. But if eating were nothing more than that, conscientious men would never devote the time to it which they do at present. It has, however, a justification ; it is necessary for maintaining life. We do not remember this each time we eat ; we do not perhaps remember it so often as once a twelvemonth ; but the knowledge is always latent, and by this knowledge the self-indulgence is justified.

Here then are three distinct classes of action. In the *first* the motive supplies its own justification ; in the *second* the justification is the only motive ; in the *third* the motive and the justification are distinct and separate. If we lived to eat, eating would belong to the first class ; since we eat to live, eating does belong to the third class. But there is this exception : nauseous food is sometimes taken medicinally, and then eating belongs to the second class. To one or other of these classes every act must belong which any moral man can desire to practise, and every act which any moralist can enjoin. It will be seen further that the whole justification, the whole moral character in fact, of the last two classes of acts is derived ultimately from their connection with the first. In other words, every moral act that we can do is either an act that aims at some end good for its own sake, and that thus stands solely and simply on its own merits ; or else it is only moral in so far as it tends to produce, to facillitate, or to multiply such acts. Such acts then, acts of the first class, acts of which the motive supplies the only justification, are the only acts that are of themselves good, or virtuous, or high, or moral. It is from them that the others derive their whole ethical character. And accordingly, in testing the soundness of ethical systems, it is with them only that our first concern lies. Everything else will stand or fall with these.

And now, remembering this, let us turn to George Eliot's verses, and get rid of every act commended in them which is not in itself moral, of which the motive is not its own justification. In this way the matter will be rapidly simplified, and we shall see somewhat more clearly what is the real point at issue. Now the principle and the virtue that George Eliot most dwells upon, and upon which she relies mainly for exciting our sympathies and enlisting them in her cause, is self-sacrifice and heroism, and a losing of our individual lives in the larger life of our own beloved race. It is thus that she professes to offer us a higher kind of morality altogether than the old religious kind, which was, compared with this, a selfish hireling thing, bought by a splendid promise of future heavenly wages. George Eliot herself, it is true, offers us a reward; but her reward is quite different. Though our own, it will yet not be our own. Our good will be the good of others ; our life will be the life of others. For us will be agony, and groans, and struggling ; but we shall welcome them as glorious, we shall choose them gladly ; for by them we mix ourselves with the better self of the whole great world, we become notes in its undying music. All this, no doubt, sounds very fine indeed. A class of actions is here commended to us that are in many ways very powerfully attractive. But to what class do they belong? They belong all of them to those two classes we have been just considering, of which the motive is entirely distinct from the justification, or else for its force altogether depends upon it. They are not actions which stand on their own merit. They are not self-luminous. It is quite true that men will often suffer and die, and earn the name of heroes, because it seems *dulce et decorum* to them so to do. That is the motive. But there must also be the latent justification, that to themselves at least the end has seemed a worthy one. Else, if the end have not so seemed, if they have undergone suffering for ends which they themselves recognized to be frivolous, we shall certainly not call them heroes ; on the contrary we shall call them fools and madmen. If a Christian were to be crucified that he might turn the world from vice to virtue, he might well be called a hero, or something yet higher ; if he were to be crucified that the world might prefer dry champagne to sweet, he might well be called a fool, or anything lower. It is evident, then, that all this groaning, this agony, this sacrifice of ourselves for others, depends for its value on the results it is designed to compass. No unbeliever would pretend that agony was good for itself, that groaning was good for itself, or that heroism without an object was heroism at all. It is on the object that the whole matter depends. Granted that the object is good, the paths that lead to it are of course good also; and the harder and more rugged they are, the more shall we admire those who traverse them, and who assist others to traverse them. About this there is no question. What do these paths lead to ? That is the only point there can be any serious dispute about. And I here take occasion to protest, with all the emphasis I may, against a certain practice of our unbelieving moralists which, if its deceit were not evidentally unintentional, and if they themselves were not the first victims of it, would demand the hardest epithet that the moral vocabulary can supply. They always speak, they apparently always contrive to think, of this self-abnegating heroism, to which they give such prominence, as a virtue that is something new and peculiar to their own systems ; that it is cherished by unbelief, and that religion stunts it. It is difficult to conceive an assumption more utterly untrue than this, and not only more untrue, but more groundless. Indeed it can only have imposed on any one by its inconceivable audacity. Heroism and self-abnegation, as a moment's unruffled thought will show us, are parts of religious morality just as much as of atheistic. It is about the object only of the heroism that the two systems differ. Both have for their end true human welfare, the truest human happiness ; but the one connects such happiness with something beyond this life—with something higher, purer, and more complete ; the other explicitly bounds it by this life, which contains, it teaches, all the elevation, purity, and completeness of which the loftiest human nature is capable. Here is the only difference. George Eliot says, " I desire to be immortal in the beneficial effects of my life ; I desire to live on in the higher lives of others." Well and good ; so she may desire it. But the desire is not peculiar to those who desire nothing more than this. The believer has just the same desire. He would just as gladly spend and·be spent for humanity. He only connects humanity with something better than itself, and so makes it better worth his being spent for. Let us then, for the present at least, quite put out of our heads all these providing, these provisional virtues, these virtues not self-luminous, not self-justified, which are common to both systems. There need be no discussion where there is no disagreement. Let us consider only the self-justified object which the unbelievers give their virtues, and from which alone they gain their virtuous character. For here it is that the heart of the difference lies. And what on this point does George Eliot tell us? What is all her heroism, all her self-devotion to conduce to? To making men better, to making undying music and beauteous order in the world, to diffusing sweet purity, and smiles that have no cruelty in them. Here we come to the point. This is the thing we want to know. We want to know what is the precious thing we are to strive for, not to be told again and again that we must heroically strive for something precious. The foundation, then, of the unbeliever's ethics is not the fact that heroism is good, and that self-sacrifice is good, but that kind smiles are, and sweet purity is, and the world's better self is.

Such is George Eliot's answer ; and such, in substance, is the answer of all her school of moralists. But this is not enough. This sort of answer practically is absolutely value-less. We have here a lot of fine phrases. But what do these fine phrases mean? They may mean anything, or they may mean nothing. They name a *something*, it is true ; but, in the act of naming it, they shroud it in a vapor of praise. We want this vapor cleared away. We wish to see the praised *something* plainly. We want to know in detail what the phrases mean. We want them translated into terms of life and action. For it is according to the value of the exact meaning of them that the system they belong to stands or falls. We know what self-sacrifice and unselfishness mean well enough. In the world's "better self" we find no meaning but what we bring. "Beauteous order" is of course "beauteous." But we do not want it to be thus named by others; we want to be shown it, so that we may be forced so to name it ourselves. Whilst as to "undying music," we want to hear it first before we know whether its continuance would be a blessing or a torture. And here in passing we may notice another hallucination of our moralists. They seem to think that the excellence of their end is guaranteed and heightened by the trouble which, they tell us, must be taken to arrive at it. They forget that music fit for an orgy may be just as hard to play as music fit for the Mass. The musician may have to struggle, groan, and agonize as much in one case as in the other. At present the unbeliever's system of morality is like a rugged Ararat, which we are bidden climb and help others to climb, for the sake of an Ark that is said to rest on the peaks of it. But the peaks are hidden by clouds, the ark can be seen by none below; and those who profess to have reached it, can give no distinct account of the treasures they profess to have found in it. Why should men then not remain on the level plains, and live at will there quietly with the flocks and herds, if there is nothing to assure them but a vague bewildered rumor that they will gain anything better by the pains and perils of mountaineering?

Once again let me repeat it is the ultimate end of action we want to know about, which is quite distinct from our painful efforts to secure it. What is this precious *something*, this peculiar kind of happiness, that we ought to live for? What is it that we gain by virtue and seriousness, and lose by vice and frivolity? It must be something, and it must be something definite. Else why is the moralist pleased with the serious, and why is he angry with the frivolous? He can only tell us why, by presenting to us this end of action; and by presenting it to us in such a way that we see it to be its own justification, that we realize it to be attainable, and that we feel it to be attractive.

I am quite aware that it is easy to state these things on paper, and to win from the reader a certain kind of assent to them; but that it is quite a different matter, and often a very difficult one, to produce a really fruitful, a really living con·viction. I will therefore adduce a very singular example to prove that what I have been saying about atheistic ethics is the simple sober truth—true not only on paper, but in actual life and practice. And I shall take the example from the confessions of one of the atheists themselves; one of the most distinguished, the most earnest, the most influential among their number: he shall be my witness.

"From the winter of 1821," writes John Stuart Mill in his Autobiography, "when I first read Bentham . . . I had what might truly be called an object in life; to be a reformer of the world. . . . I endeavored to pick up as many flowers as I could by the way; but as a serious and permanent personal satisfaction to rest upon, my whole reliance was placed on this . . . . But the time came when I awakened from this as from a dream. . . . It occurred to me to put the question directly to myself: 'Suppose that all your objects in life were realized ; that all the changes in institutions and opinions which you are looking forward to, could be completely effected at this very instant, would this be a great joy and happiness to you ?' And an irrepressible self-consciousness distinctly answered 'No!' At this my heart sank within me ; the whole foundation on which my life was constructed fell down. . . . The end had ceased to charm, and how could there ever again be any interest in the means? I seemed to have nothing left to live for. . . . The lines in Coleridge's *Dejection* . . . exactly describe my case :

> "'A grief without a pang, void, dark, and drear,
> A drowsy, stifled, unimpassioned grief,
> Which finds no natural outlet or relief
> In word, or sigh, or tear.
>
> . . . .
>
> Work, without hope, draws nectar in a sieve,
> And life without an object cannot live.'"

And the teaching of this account is pointed by the following comment on it: 'Though my dejection, honestly looked at, could not be called other than egotistical, produced by the ruin, as I thought, of my fabric of happiness, yet the destiny of mankind in general was ever in my thoughts, and could not be separated from my own. *I felt that the flaw in my life must be a flaw in life itself; and that the question was whether if the reformers of society and government could succeed in their objects, and every person in the community were free, and in a state of physical comfort, the pleasures of life, being no longer kept up by struggle and privation, would cease to be pleasures.* And I felt that unless I could see some better hope than this for human happiness in general, my dejection must continue."

Surely this passage must speak for itself. It can need but little comment. Here is the truth of all that I have been saying, confessed by one of the unbelievers themselves; and confessed not as an abstract, not as a theoretical truth, but as a truth whose full bitterness he has himself felt. He has acknowledged it by months of misery, by intermittent thoughts of suicide, by years of recurring melancholy. Some ultimate end of action some kind of satisfying happiness—this, and this alone, can give any meaning to work, or make possible any kind of virtue. Without this we must be content to live as the beasts, or we can never be content to live at all. All this Mill distinctly acknowledges. What is the end—the last end of action? That is the vital question. Any answer that stops short of this will be but postponing the difficulty, not meeting it; and will leave us in no better condition than that of the Eastern cosmogonists, who first explained the earth's stability by saying that it rested on an elephant; and being asked on what the elephant rested, answered, on a tortoise.

Mill, however, though he fully felt the difficulty in question, did not long succumb to it. He was determined that he would conquer it, and he at last persuaded himself that he had done so. He contrived to make life again bearable, and to convince himself that it contained something worthy of his self-devotion. It will be instructive to see how he does this, as a further light will be thus thrown on those subtle deceptions which the unbelievers practice on themselves, and their contrivances for veiling that question whose naked face they seem even afraid to look at. The process, then, of Mill's moral convalescence, as he himself understood it, took the form of two new discoveries. In the first place, he tells us, that though he never " wavered in the conviction that happiness is the test of all rules of conduct, and the end of life," he now thought that this end was only to be attained by not making it the direct end. "Those only are happy . . . who have their minds fixed on some object other than their own happiness; on the happiness of others, on the improvement of mankind; even on some art or pursuit, followed not as a means, but as itself an ideal end." Now what does Mill gain by this? Is he meeting the difficulty? Not in the slightest; he is simply wriggling out of it. For firstly, as to any "art or pursuit, followed not as a means, but as itself an ideal end," if happiness is the test of all rules of conduct, the following of these arts or pursuits can only be justified because they promote happiness. Every path in the ethical labyrinth leads back to that. Nor, next, is any difficulty overcome by bidding us follow the happiness of others instead of our own. For the question still remains unsettled, what kind of happiness for others is it, that it will be worth our while to promote? We are merely thus removing the matter to a little distance, in the hopes of gaining a clearer view of it. But that no clearer view of it can ever be got this way, the following pithy passage out of More's *Utopia* is sufficient to remind us; " For a joyful life, that is to say a pleasant life, is either evil; and if so, then thou shouldest not only help no man thereto, but rather as much as in thee lieth withdraw all men from it, as noisome and hurtful ; or else if thou not only mayest, but also of duty art bound to procure it for others, why not chiefly for thyself? to whom thou art bound to show as much favour and gentleness as to others." And Mill with a curious inconsistency seems to have admitted and felt that this was really true. For no sooner had he come to the conclusion we have been just considering, that men should not seek their own happiness, than he went on to inquire, with the utmost anxiety, in what this happiness consisted. He took some time in discovering this, and was at first not a little perplexed about it. But at length light broke upon him ; the discovery at length was made. And what, according to his own account, was it? The " perennial " happiness, for which men are to live, which is to make life desirable " when all the greater evils . . . . shall have been removed," consists, he tells us, " in states of feeling, and of thought coloured by feeling, under the excitement of beauty." This is the only description, the most accurate and complete description, he can give us of the one thing by which all conduct is to be tested, and the hope of attaining which is alone to make life liveable. Mill is as vague as George Eliot. His answer is just as worthless. If some special kind of happiness is the one thing we are to work for, we must know so exactly what this happiness is, that we can, without error, distinguish it from all other kinds. It must be such, too, that we shall be prepared to admit that all acts will be moral that conduce to it; and that no act will be immoral that does not keep ourselves or others from the possession of it. Now are " states of feeling, or thought coloured by feeling, under the excitement of beauty," an end so def-

inite that any man can work for it? Or could they form a
test, even were they so, by which we could condemn any
gratification, however base or abnormal, which we might
passionately and persistently long for? Or granting even
that such longings did stand condemned as distracting us on
our course, should not we in this case best conquer temptation by yielding to it? Mill, it is true, thought this vague
happiness definite enough, and attractive enough. But then,
let us remember, he was determined to do so. He was an
ethical Don Quixote in search of a mistress ; and we should
find probably, could only this Dulcinea be identified, that
her charms existed nowhere but in the imagination of her
knight.

Here, then, is a fact which is surely not without significance ; here is a lesson which he that runs may read, and
which may well give pause to our voluble modern teachers.
Mill's experience should at once show us that the very possibility of an atheistic morality is at least not self-evident ; that
even the earnest and benevolent, who long to give life a serious meaning, are bewildered when they try to discover any
source for its seriousness ; nay, that bounded as our teachers
bound it by itself, the chances are that all ere long will grow
to acknowledge its vanity.

What ! it will be asked, and do they all go for nothing, the
utterances of our eminent teachers ? Our modern atheistic
moralists have been men of blameless life, of set and solemn
purpose, of subtle and of powerful intellects. They have
worked, and thought, and written. They have won the ear
of the world. All these men tell us confidently that life is ·

serious. And shall not their confidence be some assurance to us? In this matter of opinion is not these men's authority of the greatest weight?

I answer, No; and for a reason that we shall do well to consider.

Nearly all our great modern unbelievers, the men on whose speculations and discoveries unbelief in our days has based itself, have been men of letters, of research, or of science. They have won their eminence in the study, or the laboratory, or the dissecting room; and they have there come to conclusions which they proclaim loudly to the world as fatal to all religion. But the knowledge which has qualified them to destroy religion, has no bearing whatever on the knowledge that will qualify them to replace it. They have taken away the happiness of heaven. They replace it by the happiness of earth. But if heavenly happiness be a myth, may not earthly happiness be a myth also? No eminence gained in the laboratory or the study will make a man an authority upon this question. If he be an authority upon it at all, he will have acquired his qualifications in very different places; and he will have acquired them not in virtue of his success as a specialist, but in spite of it. Would we judge about the happiness that life can yield, life is the one thing we have to study. We must study men and women as they are around us, and the varied impulses under which they act. Now not only will lonely thought and study necessitate in general a certain withdrawal from life, and a consequent ignorance of it; but devotion to any special pursuit, that is possible only for the few, will tend to distort the judgment, and will lead a man to put the personal *motive* of his own career in place of the ultimate and general *justification.* Such men, indeed, live surrounded by *idola specûs.* Interests which absorb them and give their lives a meaning, they imagine will affect the world at large in a like way; unconscious that the world at large has other interests which they know of but by empty names; that it is allured by pleasures, and that it has to battle with passions, to which education and temperament have alike made them strangers. There is indeed something grotesque in the notion of a *savant* emerging from an examination of a beetle's wing, or a speculation upon parallel lines, before men and women of the world, flushed or embittered with the joys, the passions, or the pains of life, led by the bright or dark allurements of ambition, or of vanity, or of love, to instruct them on the strongest motives to action, and the real secret of making the most of this life. Men of science for instance, talk continually about moral matters as though scientific research were the great thing to live for. But when they talk like this, it is plain they cannot know what they are saying. It would be attributing a too unworldly simplicity to them, to fancy that they supposed really that the mass of men would ever follow science for its own sake, or that even could they, they would ever wish to do so. Nor, granting even that this were possible, can we imagine any one bold and blind enough to accept the conclusion that would inevitably follow. For if scientific research be the true end of life, and the test of conduct, nothing can then be immoral that does not interfere with scientific research. It is hard to see what fabric of ethics could be reared upon this foundation: it is hard to conceive that the world in general could desire to raise any. And the end of action which we demand, is an end of action for the world in general. It must be that, or it can be nothing. It must be an end that will attract equally the politician and the professor; the fashionable *femme incomprise* famishing for some mad distraction; and the shy profound student, as incapable of understanding passion as he is of inspiring it. It must be an end that will inspire the passionless and restrain the passionate. It must, when we are once within the sphere of its attraction, be the strongest magnet of our lives, of power to counteract the force of all our selfish instincts, and of all the fierce desires which many of the holiest men have hardly resisted, and to which most of the world's greatest men have notoriously yielded.

That such an end as this is possible for the world in general, those only who know the world can be in a position to say. The religious moralist might well be a recluse, for the source of his morality was essentially without this life. The atheistic moralist must emphatically be a man of the world; for the source of his morality is essentially within it. He must, indeed, enter into the pursuits of men, with the same diligence as that with which the other avoided them. A knowledge attained thus is an absolute necessity for him. That he may be qualified to deny the necessity of a first cause, will not qualify him to assert the possibility of human happiness, or to understand its nature. And in refusing to believe in this matter any mere thinkers or discoverers, however morally good, or however intellectually eminent, we are refusing them none of that deference which they may so justly claim. Frederick the Great we may think contemptible as a poet; but we do not for that reason think him the less extraordinary as a man of action.

· And I now come to the last point that I have here to notice; a point which is really the source of the whole confusion. Our atheistic moralists do, as we have seen, name certain things in life, which when looked at from a distance, and not examined too closely, have for many the appearance of adequate moral ends. · But there is this great fact to be remembered. Our moralists, when they deal with life, profess to exhibit its resources to us wholly free from the false aids of religion. They profess, if I may coin a word, to have *de-religionized* it, before they deal with it. About this matter, however, they betray a most strange ignorance. They seem to think that religion exists nowhere except in its pure form, in the form of distinct devotional feeling, or in the conscious assents of faith. These once got rid of, they think that life is *de-religionized*. The process, however, is really only begun; indeed, as far as immediate results go, it is hardly even begun. For it is really but a very small proportion of religion that exists pure. The greater part of it has entered into combination with the common acts and feelings of life, thus forming, as it were, a kind of amalgam with them, giving them new properties, a new color, a new consistence. To *de-religionize* life, then, it is not enough to condemn creeds, and to abolish prayers. We must also sublimate the beliefs and feelings, which prayers and creeds hold pure, out of the lay life around us. Under this process, even if imperfectly performed, it will soon become clear that religion in greater or less proportions is lurking everywhere. We shall see it yielded up even by things in which we should least look for it—by wit, by humor, by secular ambition, by our daily light amusements; and as it leaves them, their whole aspect will change. Much more shall we see it yielded up by heroism, by purity, and by love of truth—by all those great things which our Atheists name with praise. Professor Tyndall calls theologians "Jacobs," who "have deprived matter of its birthright." He had best beware lest he and his fellows be found out to be Rachels, who have run away with the gods of theology, and, sitting on them in their tents, have quite forgotten the theft. Life at any rate must be searched and purified of the faiths we are relinquishing, as none of our atheists have yet searched it. Then, but not till then, shall we be able to estimate its resources, when bounded by itself, and cut off from every hope beyond; when all its ports, so to speak, are blockaded, so that no treasure can be smuggled into them from any foreign country. Then, and not till then, shall we be in any way fit to judge as to whether it contains materials for any kind of happiness which can give it a serious and universal meaning, and make any system of morality possible.

Here is the real matter at stake. Here is the real issue that is trembling in the balance. Here is the real question about which we pride ourselves upon being tolerant, or, in other words, about being calm and quite indifferent. For unless, let our Atheists remember, we can find such an end in life as that which we have been demanding; unless we can find some supreme, some universal, some attainable

end to strive for whose beauty shall outshine passion, and
withstand the dissolving force of reason, that shall be for
ever urging us onward like a steady pilot star, and for ever
urging us onward like a favorable wind, we shall be like dis-
masted ships, without sail and without rudder, left to welter
on a sluggish sea of small and weary impulses, with no escape
from the shoreless accursed surface, till at last, and one
by one, we sink forever under it.

II.

I AM writing for practical people ; I am dealing with practical matters.   When I speak of life, and of the worth of it, I
am referring to common things, to things of daily experience.
I am referring to the joys, the sorrows, and the occupations
that give their quick color to the hours ; and to the loves,
the ambitions, and the interests, that slowly give their color
to the years.   These are the things that surround all of us.
We cannot escape from them.   In them we live and move and
have our being ; and all science and wisdom, and all the pursuits of intellect, must either culminate in teaching us how to
deal with these, or else must humbly take their place amongst
them.   Be we men of thought or action, be we saints or liber-
tines, we have each of us a daily course to shape through a
throng of conflicting impulses.   And unless we are to be the
passive prey of these, some plain principles must be ours to
guide us.   Now, hitherto, such a set of principles we have
had, all of us.   They were readily understood ; they were
readily applied.   Amongst the choices and refusals that beset

us momently, they left us little in doubt as to the right course ; and if we refused to take it, we refused with our eyes open. But times are changed. The old principles, we are told, are obsolete ; they are no longer of the least use to us. Principles, we are told loudly, we need just as much as ever ; but we are offered a new set of them. Now it is plain that the new set will be useless, unless it can take the place of the old. The difficulties we want help in, remain just the same ; they are just as definite as ever. We shall want our new rules of life to be just as definite as our old.

Here comes a pressing and practical question. Are they so ? or can they ever be made so ? Vaguely stated they may sound well enough. But vaguely stated, they are practically useless. Let our modern moralists give them some definite meaning. Let them show us some particular rules deduced from their general principles. We have heard their principles often enough. What I am now to consider is the detailed application of them. We want no more vague messages sent to us out of the study or the laboratory, about the nature of right and wrong. Let the senders themselves come out to us, and illustrate their meaning by examples in the world at large. Let us confront them with men and women as they appear in action. Let us select for them a variety of particular instances. Consider this man, let us say, or this woman ; consider this mood of mind, this pursuit, this pleasure, this way of spending the day or night. Put your finger upon this case, and on that case ; tell us which is wrong, and which is right ; and when you condemn any voluntary human action, tell us exactly why you condemn it from your own point of view, and how you would persuade the offender to condemn it also from his.

Now I have pointed out, in my former paper, that all possible answers to this question are reducible to' one simple form. If they have any meaning at all, they must mean this —an act, a habit is wrong ; a pleasure, a mood of mind is wrong, because by it we are robbed of *something*, or hindered in attaining to *something*, which we can all discern, unless we close our eyes to it, as the one thing that is indeed desirable—the one thing that will make us really happy. And the first task of the moralist is to put this *something* before us.

That this is at least one way of stating the case, has been often acknowledged by our modern teachers themselves. I have already quoted J. S. Mill as an instance ; and the doctrines of to-day are being couched perpetually in this very form. Thus Professor Huxley concludes one of his late addresses by solemnly telling us that the last end of education is to promote " morality and refinement, by teaching men to discipline themselves, and by leading them to see that the highest, as it is the only content, is to be attained, not by grovelling in the rank and steaming valleys of sense, but by continually striving towards those high peaks where, resting in eternal calm, reason discerns the undefined but bright ideal of the highest good—'a cloud by day, a pillar of fire by night.' " [1] And these words are an excellent specimen of the moral exhortations of our new school of teachers.

Now this is all very well as far as it goes ; and were there

[1] *Critiques and Addresses*, p. 32.

not one thing lacking, it would be just the language that the occasion craves. But the one thing lacking is enough to make it valueless. It may mean a great deal. But there is no possibility of saying exactly what it means. Before we can begin to strive towards the "highest good," we must at least know something of what this "highest good" is. We must make this "bright ideal" "stand and unfold itself." If it cannot be made to do this, if it vanishes into mist as we near it, and takes a different shape to each of us as we recede from it still more, if only some can see it, and to others it is quite invisible—then we shall simply set it down as an illusion, and waste no more time in pursuit of it. But that it is not an illusion is our moralists' great claim for it. Heaven and the love of God, they say, were illusions. The "highest good" they offer us stands out in clear contradiction to these. It is an actual attainable thing, a thing for flesh and-blood creatures ; it is to be won and enjoyed by them in their common daily life. It is, as they distinctly and unanimously tell us,[1] some form of happiness that results in this life to us from certain conduct ; it is a thing essentially of the present ;[2] "and it is obviously," says Professor Huxley, "in no way affected by the abbreviation or prolongation of our conscious life." This being the case, then, it is no unreasonable demand to ask for some explicit account of it. When Professor Huxley speaks of the highest happiness, what meaning does he attach to the word? Has he ever enjoyed it himself, or does he ever hope to do so? If so, when, where, and how? What must be done to get it, and what must be left undone? And when it is got, what will it be like? Is it something mystical, rapturous, and intermittent, as the language often used about it might seem to suggest to one? Is it known only in brief moments of Neoplatonic ecstasy, to which all the acts of life should be stepping-stones? It certainly cannot be that. Our modern moralists are essentially no mystics, and their highest happiness must be something far more solid than transcendental ecstasies. Surely, therefore, if it exists at all, we must somewhere be able to lay our hands upon it. It is a pillar of fire by night; it will be surely visible. It is a city set on a hill, that cannot be hid. It is to be lifted up, and is to draw all men unto it. It is nothing if not this; and if, after a careful search, we fail to find it, there will be nothing left us but to conclude that it is nothing, or that, at any rate, this life does not contain it. If we are still resolved to find it, we must seek elsewhere for it. We must once again have recourse to religion, and import it into the natural order from a supernatural order that we postulate.

I have stated, as plainly as I can, the question I want answered. I shall now go on to point out how utterly unsatisfactory are the answers that have hitherto been given to it. These answers divide themselves into two classes, which, though continually confused by confused thinkers, are really quite distinct and separable. And what I must first do is to show that one of these classes consists of what are really no answers at all, and that we must put them altogether aside before we can consider the matter clearly.

Professor Huxley shall give us an example of both. He

is going to tell us, let us remember, about the "highest good" —the happiness, in other words, that is the secret of our life's worth, and the test of all our conduct. This happiness he divides into two kinds. He says there are two things that we may mean when we speak about it.[1] We may mean the happiness of a society of men, or we may mean the happiness of the members of that society. And when we speak of morality, we may mean two things also; and these two things must be kept distinct. We may mean "social morality," of which the test and object is the happiness of societies. We may mean "personal morality," of which the test and object is the happiness of individuals. And the answers which our modern moralists make us, I divide into two classes, according to the sort of happiness they refer to. It is before all things important that this division should be made, and be kept quite clear in our minds, if we would see honestly what our modern moral systems amount to. For what makes them at present so difficult to deal with is the fact that their exponents are perpetually perplexing themselves between these two sets of answers, first giving one and then the other, and imagining that, by a kind of confusion of substance, they can both afford solutions, of the same question. Thus they continually speak of life as though its crowning achievement were some kind of personal happiness; and then, being asked to explain the nature and basis of this, they at once shift their ground, and talk to us of the laws and the conditions of social happiness. Thus, Professor Huxley, starting[2] with the thesis that *both* sorts of morality, personal and a social, are

---

[1] *Nineteenth Century*, No. 3, p.536   [2] *Ibid*, pp. 536, 537.

strong enough to hold their own, he conceives he has established this by simply proving that *one* is. "Given," he says, "a
society of human beings under certain circumstances ; and the
question whether a particular action on the part of one of its
members will tend to increase the general happiness or not, is a
question of natural knowledge, and as such is a perfectly legitimate subject of scientific inquiry. . . . If it can be shown by
observation or experiment that theft, murder, and adultery do
not tend to diminish the happiness of society, then, in the
absence of any but natural knowledge, they are not social
immoralities."

Now here is a clear and complete epitome of one of those
two classes of answers that our modern moralists give us.
And what I am going to point out is, that these answers are
really no answers at all, and to offer them to us creates simply
useless confusion. It is as if we asked for a fish, and were
offered a scorpion. The scorpion might distract our attention ; it certainly would not satisfy our appetite. The question we ask is, what is the test of conduct? in other words,
what is happiness ? And what are we answered ? That happiness is the happiness of men—that it is the general happiness—that it is the happiness of men in societies—that it is
happiness equally distributed. But what does this avail us ?
The word *happiness* is still a locked casket. We know nothing
as yet of its contents. A happy society neither does nor can
mean anything but a number of happy individuals. Granted
that we know what will make them happy, then we shall know
what will make society happy. Then social morality will be,
as Professor Huxley says, a perfectly legitimate subject of

scientific inquiry. Then, but not till then. When we say that a society is happy as a body, we can only mean that it secures for its members their happiness as individuals. What do the individuals want? We must know that, before we can try to secure it for them. But this is what our moralists are perpetually losing sight of. The reason of this confusion is not far to seek. Observation and experiment, it is quite true, will guide us to certain clear and constant rules with regard to conduct. They will show us that there are certain actions which we must never tolerate, and which we must join together, as best we may, to suppress. But what sort of actions are these? They are simply such as disturb the negative conditions of all happiness. They touch neither the loss nor gain of any kind of happiness in particular. Of this class are theft and murder. If we are to be happy in any way, we must, of course, have our lives secured to us, and, next to our lives, our possessions. But to secure us these does not secure us happiness. It simply leaves us free to secure it, if we can, for ourselves. Once let us have some common agreement as to what this happiness is ; we may then be able to formulate other rules and other laws, by which we may be helped in attaining it. But, in the absence of any such agreement, the only possible aim of social morality is not to promote any kind or kinds of happiness, but to secure the conditions without which all happiness would be impossible. Suppose the human race were a set of canaries in a cage, and that we were in grave doubt as to what seed to give them—hemp-seed, rape-seed, or canary-seed, or all three mixed in certain proportions. That would represent accurately the present state of our case. That is the kind of question we are now in doubt about. Surely it is evident that in this perplexity it is absolutely nothing to the point to tell us that the birds must not peck each other's eyes out, and that they must all have access to the trough that we are ignorant how to fill. The real fault, then, of our moralists, that I am now dealing with, is this. They confuse the negative conditions of happiness with the positive materials of it. Professor Huxley, in the passage I have just now quoted, is caught, so to speak, in the very act of committing it. " Theft, murder, and adultery," all these three, it will be remembered, he classes together, and seems to think that they stand on the same footing. But from what I have just pointed out, it is plain that they do not do so. We condemn theft and murder for one reason. We condemn adultery for quite another. We condemn the former, because they are incompatible with any form of happiness. We condemn the latter, because it is a supposed violation of one particular form of happiness, or rather, perhaps, the substitution of a supposed lower kind for another supposed higher kind.

We may observe accordingly, that if happiness be the moral test, what Professor Huxley calls " social morality "— the rules, that is, for producing the negative conditions of happiness—are not in themselves morality at all. They only become so when the inner sense that we are conforming to them becomes one of the positive factors of our own personal happiness. Then they suffer a kind of apotheosis ; they are taken up into ourselves, and become part and parcel of our personal morality. But to tell us simply that happiness is social happiness is to tell us nothing at all.   Social happiness is a mere set of ciphers till the unit of personal happiness is placed before it.   A man's happiness may of course depend on other beings, but it is still none the less contained in himself.   If our greatest delight were to see each other dance the *cancan*, then it would be morality for us all to dance, that we might enjoy the sight of each other.   None the less would this be a happy world, not because we were dancing, but because we each rejoiced in the sight of such a spectacle.   The happiness of the individual, as I have said, must be ever the unit of happiness.   We may talk as much as we like about distributing it in the present, but we must first be clear as to its present value.   We may talk as much as we like about increasing it in the future, but we must first be clear how its present value is capable of expansion.

Surely one might have thought that this was plain enough —that even a child could understand it.   And yet it would seem that it is not so.   For here are all our modern English moralists making daily the same blunder ; and not only making it, but proclaiming it aloud with ever-increasing vehemence.   Thus Professor Huxley, not long since, said that that state of man would be " a true *civitas Dei*, in which each man's moral faculty shall be such as leads him to control all those desires which run counter to the good of mankind "— a sentence which means nothing, unless the " good of mankind " be defined first of all as the divine good of each individual man.   We shall never get to a *civitas Dei* from mere order and co-operation.   These will take us some way, it is true, but it is a part of the way only ; and that they will take us as far as they do is perfectly self-evident, and has no need of all this emphatic reassertion. There must be order amongst thieves, as well as amongst honest men. Let an army be sent on a holy war or an accursed one, the discipline will be the same that we shall need in it. There can be an orderly brothel as well as an orderly nunnery; and all order rests on co-operation. We presume co-operation; we require an end for which to co-operate.

Let us then, once and for all, set aside all this talk about social morality, as at present nothing to the point. Let us remember that the end we are asking for is, in the first place, a strictly personal end. Can our moralists show us any one highest personal good, towards which, as Professor Huxley says, we may be "continually striving?" That is the one question that really calls for an answer. What shall I do?— and I?—and I?—and I? What do you offer me?—and me? —and me? This is the great question that mankind is asking. "You must promise something to each of us," it says, "or very certainly you will be able to promise nothing to all of us." Nor is there the least loophole left for escape in telling us to work for others, and to find our happiness in that. The question merely confronts us with two other facets of itself. What sort of happiness shall I procure for others? and what sort of happiness will others procure for me? What will it be like? Will it be worth having? Let us be sure about that first. For it will certainly give me no delight to procure for others what I should feel no delight in if procured by others for me. The coin itself must have some intrinsic value. It will never acquire it by being merely shuffled about from one hand to another. A million dull individuals will not make a happy state; nor will a million million dull individuals make a glorious humanity, any more than, as we often know to our cost, twenty dull individuals will make a brilliant dinner party, or a hundred average churchgoers a fervent congregation.

We have thus arrived, then, at the true heart of the question. When I am inquring into life's value, I am inquiring into the highest kind of personal happiness that life can be made to yield to us.

I must now examine the answers that our moralists have made to this. It is with these answers that our real concern lies. With the former class it was easy enough to deal. They were not false; they were simply not to the point; and we had nothing to do but to put them on one side. But the fault that vitiates these is far subtler. The question here is no longer evaded. The answers are straight-forward and are singularly plausible; and until we look at them very narrowly, it is hard to say that they are not in a great measure satisfactory. The problem, let us remember, is to give us something worth living for, some goal to work towards when the very notions of a God and a future life shall have left us, and have evaporated even out of our imaginations. Now many of our new teachers begin by frankly admitting to us that the loss of a belief in God, and the hope of a future life, may be some real loss to us. Others again contend that this loss is a gain. Their views on this point, however, are not much to the present purpose. What we have now to remember is that, even according to those who admit life to have lost most in this way, the loss is not a very important, still less is it a fatal one. It will still leave us a life that is worth living. The character of our aims and pleasures will not be radically changed by it. The *good* is still to be an aim for us ; and our devotion to it will be more valuable, because it will now be quite disinterested. Thus Professor Tyndall tells us that, though he has now rejected the religion of his earlier years, yet, granting him proper health of body, there is "no spiritual experience," such as he then knew, "no resolve of duty, no work of mercy, no act of self-renouncement, no solemnity of thought, no joy in the life and aspects of nature, that would not still be (his) ; and this without the least regard to any purely personal reward or punishment looming in the future." [1] The same is the implicit teaching of all George Eliot's novels. So, too, Professor Huxley tells us, that come what may to our "intellectual beliefs and even education," he "sees no reason to doubt" that "the beauty of holiness and the ugliness of sin" are, for those that have eyes to see them, "no mere metaphors," but "real and intense feelings." [2] And Mr. Sully tells us in his late work on Pessimism, that "lives nourished and invigorated" by a purely human ideal, "have been and still may be seen amongst us, and the appearance of but a single example proves the adequacy of the belief." It is plain that such utterances as these enunciate practically no new system at all. They merely redirect our attention to the old one ; they again point to the old practical ends and courses of action, and tell us that these in themselves are their own reward and

[1] *Fragments of Science*, p. 562.   [2] *Nineteenth Century*, No. 3, p. 537.

their own sufficient motive. Such is the teaching of our
modern moralists. There is, too, another school of teachers
to be dealt with, though at present not openly popular, who
would give us a rule of life, but who would yet hardly call
themselves moralists at all. These would still distinguish
probably between vice and virtue, and admit that the pleasures they give us are of a different quality. But they would
deny that one practically was better than the other. They
would call nothing common or unclean ; they would make us
free to eat any fruit in the garden ; and the greater variety,
they would say, we could enjoy of these, so much the better
for us. This teaching is at present more often implied than
stated. But at least one of this school, in our day, has been
clear enough on the matter ; and he explicitly bases his
teaching on the teachings of modern science. " Each moment," says Mr. Pater, " some form grows perfect in hand or
face ; some tone on the hills or sea is choicer than the rest;
some mood of passion, or insight, or intellectual excitement,
is irresistibly real and attractive for us." And thus, "while
all melts under our feet," he goes on, " we may well catch at
any exquisite passion, or any contribution to knowledge, that
seems by a lifted horizon to set the spirit free for a moment,
or any stirring of the senses, strange dyes, strange flowers,
and curious odors, or the work of the artist's hand, or the
face of one's friend."

Here then are two sets of teachers, who profess, without
any aid from religion, to secure for us some real value in life.
The one finds this value in one set of pleasures only, and
maintains that the art of happiness is to renounce all other

pleasures for these. The other finds this value in all pleasures alike, and maintains that the art of happiness is to select as many of all kinds as is possible. And it will be necessary for us to consider both of these views. For, supposing we can show that morality vanishes with the vanishing of religion, still it does not follow that happiness does. And if men can be really thoroughly happy without morality, nothing will convince them that they are losers by having ceased to be moral.

And now what I am about to point out is this—that both these classes of teachers have committed hitherto one radical fault, by which all their after conclusions, be they never so accurate, are of necessity completely vitiated. They both profess to give us a rule of life without religion—without a God whose will we may do here, and whose vision we may enjoy hereafter. But they think that the task is far simpler than it is. They think, it would seem, that they have but to kill God, and that his inheritance shall be ours. Accordingly they strike out the beliefs in question, and then turn instantly to life ; they sort its resources ; count its riches ; and then say " Aim at this,—and this,—and this. See how beautiful is holiness ; see how rapturous is pleasure. Surely these are worth seeking for their own sakes, without ' any reward or punishment looming in the future.'" They find, in fact, the interests and the sentiments of the world's present life—all the glow and all the gloom of it—lying before them like the colors on a painter's palette ; and they think they have nothing to do but to set to work and use them. But let them wait a moment. They are in far too great a hurry. The palette and its colors are not nearly ready for them. One of the colors of life—religion, that is—a color which, by their own admission, has hitherto been an important one— they have swept clean away. And let them remember exactly why they have done this. It may be a pleasing color, or it may not. This is a matter of taste. But one thing all our modern teachers assure us—it is not a fast color. It is found to fade instantly in the new sunlight of knowledge. It is rapidly getting dim, and dull, and dead. It is worse than the "flying colors," as Peter Pindar called them, of Sir Joshua Reynolds. When once it is gone, we shall never be able to restore it ; and all future pictures of life must be tinted without its aid. They therefore profess loudly to us that they are going to employ it no longer. But there is this point—this all-important point that has quite escaped them. They have rejected the color in its pure state, and they think that they have altogether got rid of it. They seem not to suspect that it may be mixed up with the colors they retain, and be the secret of much of their depth and lustre. Let them analyse these colors before they use them. Let them see whether religion be not lurking there, as a subtle coloring principle in all their pigments, even one grain of it being perceptible in its effects. Let them only begin this analysis, and it will very soon be clear to them that to cleanse life of religion is not so simple a process as they seem to have fancied it. Its actual dogmas may be readily put away from us ; not so the effect which these dogmas have worked during the course of centuries. In disguised forms they are round us everywhere ; they confront us in every human interest, in every human pleasure. They have beaten themselves into all life; they have eaten their way into it; like a secret sap they have flavored every fruit in the garden. There are as a powerful drug that has got into our whole system.

But there is this great fact to remember. There have been always forces in the system working this drug out of it; only hitherto fresh doses have been continually administered. Once, however, let us destroy our stock of the drug, and what must follow will be evident. The drug will in time work altogether out of the system, but it will not work out immediately. Its effect will not stop suddenly the moment we cease to administer fresh doses of it. The result will be very gradual, though very sure.

If then we would appraise the vigour and value of life, independent of religion, we must not draw conclusions from it while religion is yet in its system. Our modern moralists, therefore, in taking life as it is, are building on an utterly unsound foundation. A fatal error is the kernel of their first premises. Mr. Sully is thus emphatically wrong when he says that a single example in the present day (or, for the matter of that, any number of examples) either goes or can go any way towards proving the adequacy of any non-religious formula. Equally wrong, too, are the other writers I have quoted. Let them analyze what they mean by the " beauty of holiness," " resolves of duty," and " solemnity of thought ;" or by " insight," " passion," and " intellectual excitement." And let them bring to this spiritual analysis but a little of that skill that has been attained to in the analysis of matter. In our late experiments

on spontaneous generation what untold qains have been taken !
With what laborious thought, with what emulous ingenuity,
have we struggled to completely sterilize the fluids in which
we are to seek for the new production of life !   How jealously
have we guarded against leaving there any already existing germs !   Surely spiritual matters are worthy of an
equally careful treatment.   For what we have here to
study is not the production of the lowest forms of animal
life, but the highest forms of human happiness.   These
were once thought to be always due to religion.   The new
doctrine is that they are producible without such aid.   Let
us treat, then, the "beauty of holiness" and "intellectual
excitement " as Professor Tyndall has treated the infusions in
which life has been said to originate.   Let us boil them down,
so to speak, and destroy every germ of religion in them, and
then see how far they will generate happiness.   And let us
treat in this way vice no less than virtue.   Having once done
this, we may honestly claim whatever yet remains to us ; then
we shall see what materials for happiness we can, as atheists,
call our own ; then our atheistic ethics, if any such be possible, will begin to have a real value for us—then, but not till
then.

Such an analysis must be naturally a work of time.   And
it is indeed more my purpose to point out its necessity, than
to attempt myself to perform it.   But a certain part of it is a
work of comparative ease ; and even this will yield us results
that will be very suggestive to us.

The things of life as they appeal to us, either singly or
woven together by the imagination and the memory, would be

separable naturally into two groups, according as they repel or please us. And a merely natural happiness can be measured by nothing but by what we obtain of the naturally pleasant, and by what we avoid of the naturally painful. But if we examine life as we actually now find it about us, we shall see that this natural classification has been traversed by another. Many things naturally repellent have received a supernatural blessing; many things naturally pleasant have received a supernatural curse. Thus in what at present passes muster as the highest happiness, there are many elements of pain; and in what passes muster as the profoundest misery, there are many elements of pleasure. Thus, whereas happiness naturally would be the test of right, right is now supernaturally the test of happiness. And so completely is this notion ingrained in the world's present consciousness that in all our deeper views of life, no matter whether we be saints or sinners, right and wrong, not happiness and misery, are the conceptions that first appeal to us. A certain supernatural moral judgment, in fact, has become our primary faculty; and it mixes its voice spontaneously with every estimate we form of the world around us.

Now here we have religion in its commonest concrete form. I shall show this more fully by-and-by. But I must first exemplify the fact on which I have just been dwelling— I must exemplify how everywhere and in everything, let us turn where we will, let us fix our eyes on what we will, this supernatural sense is always with us; and that to it is due every keener pleasure and every deeper interest that we at present find life.

This might seem at first sight a hard task to perform—the interests we have to deal with are so varied and so many in number. But there is one special interest that will here assist us, an interest which forms, as it were, an epitome of all the rest, and through which we shall be enabled at once to deal with them. I mean art. For let us consider what art is and why it pleases us. Its pleasures are strictly relative to the pleasures of life. We must care, for instance, for the human face, or we should never care for portraits of it. We must care for living womanhood, or we should never care for marble goddesses. We must care for love, or we should never care for love-songs. And so on with all the rest of life's resources. Art may send us back to these with an intenser appreciation of them; but we must bring to art from life the appreciations we want intensified. Art is a factor in human happiness, because by its means ordinary men are made partakers in the vision of exceptional men. Great art is a speculum reflecting life as the keenest eyes have seen it. All its images are of value only as this. Taken by themselves, "the best in this kind are but shadows." In examining a work of art, then, we are examining life itself, and not life merely, but, as it were, a quintessence of life—life with its resources magnified and intensified to their utmost.

And now remembering this, let us turn to some of the world's greatest works of art—I mean its dramas; for poetry is the most articulate of all the arts, and the drama is the most comprehensive form of poetry. Let us turn, for instance, to Sophocles, to Shakespeare, and to Goethe, and consider some of their greatest plays, and how they present life to us.

If we do this, it will need but little thought to show us that all these are addressed primarily to the supernatural moral judgment; that this judgment is perpetually being expressed explicitly in the plays themselves ; and still more, that it is always presupposed in us. In other words, these plays are all of them presentations of men struggling, or failing to struggle, not after natural happiness, but after supernatural right; and it is always presupposed that we, on our part, recognize this struggle as the one supreme thing that gives life its importance. And this importance, primarily and essentially, is based not upon the social consequences of conduct, but upon its personal consequences. In *Macbeth*, for instance, the main incident, the tragic coloring-matter of the drama, is the murder of Duncan. But in what aspect of this does the real tragedy lie? Not in the fact that Duncan is murdered, but that Macbeth is the murderer. What appals us, what purges our passions with pity and with terror as we contemplate it, is not the external, the social effect of the act, but the personal, the internal effect of it. As for Duncan, he is in his grave ; after life's fitful fever, he sleeps well. What our minds are made to dwell upon is not that Duncan shall sleep for ever, but that Macbeth shall sleep no more. We see in *Hamlet* precisely the same thing. The action that our interest centers in is the hero's struggle to conform to an internal personal standard of right, utterly irrespective of use to others or of natural happiness to himself. In the course of this struggle, indeed, he does nothing but ruin the happiness around him ; and this ruin adds infinitely to the pathos of the spectacle. But we are not indignant with Hamlet as being the cause of it.　We should have been indignant rather with him if the case had been reversed, and, if instead of sacrificing social happiness for the sake of personal right, he had abandoned personal right for the sake of social happiness. In *Antigone* again we have an explicit statement of the supernatural moral axiom on which that whole marvellous tragedy rests—that the one rule we are to live by, and not to live by only, but to die for, is no human rule, is no standard of our own, nor can it be altered by what will make either ourselves or others happy; but it is "the unwritten and the enduring laws of God, that are not of to-day or yesterday, but they live from everlasting, and none can declare the mystery of their generation."　Would we see the matter pushed to a yet narrower issue, let us turn to *Measure for Measure* and to *Faust*. In both these plays, we can see at once that one moral judgment, not to name others, is presupposed before all things. This is a hard and fixed judgment with regard to female chastity and the supernatural value of it.　It is because we assent to this judgment that Isabella is heroic to us; Margaret is unfortunate in our eyes for the same reason.　Isabella has kept, Margaret has lost, her "eternal jewel."　Let us for a moment suspend this judgment, and what will become of the two dramas?　The terror and the pity of them will vanish all at once like a dream.　The fittest name for both of them would be "Much Ado about Nothing."　The deepest feelings that such works could then arouse in us would be pity for people who were so disturbed about trifles, or wonder at people who, having pleasure before them, deliberately refused to take it, or, having taken it, deliberately made it bitter by cursing it.

It will thus be seen—and the more we consider the matter the more plain will it become to us—that the supernatural moral judgment is the first faculty in us that art appeals to ; that in all great art the suppressed premiss is this : The grand relation of man is not first to his brother men but to something beyond humanity ; to this first, and to his brother men through this. We are not our own ; we are bought with a price. Our bodies are God's temples, and if these are profaned, some unimaginable ruin is sure to overtake the profaner. Such are the solemn and profound beliefs, whether conscious or unconscious, on which all the great art of the world has based itself. All the profundity and solemnity of this art is borrowed from thèse, and is in exact proportion to the intensity with which men hold them.

Nor is this true of sublime and serious art only. It is true of cynical and profligate art as well. It is true of Congreve as it is true of Sophocles. The supernatural moral judgment is essential to the character of the libertine as it is to the character of the saint. The libertine is the spirit who denies. But he must have some affirmation for the denial to prey upon. He hates the good, and its existence piques him ; but he must know that the good exists none the less. "I'd no sooner," says one of Congreve's characters, "play with a man that slighted his ill-fortune than I'd make love to a woman who undervalued the loss of her reputation." In this one sentence lies the whole secret of profligacy. We have here the exact counterpart to the words of Antigone that I have already quoted. For just as her life lay in conformity to "the unwritten and enduring laws of God," so does the life of the profligate lie in the violation of them. To each the existence of the laws is equally essential. For profligacy is not merely the gratification of the appetites, but the gratification of them at the expense of something else. Beasts are not profligate—we cannot have a profligate goat. Nay, even in cases where men do their best to sink below the level of profligacy, and to plunge deepest in the pleasures that are most entirely animal, the supernatural element, unsuspected by themselves, is still present, and is really what gives the mad rage to their passion. We may detect its presence even in such abnormal literature of indulgence as the erotic work commonly ascribed to Meursius. It is perfectly evident that such pleasures as are there dealt with are supposed to enthral men not in proportion to their intensity (for this would probably be pretty nearly equal), but in proportion to their lowness—to their sullying power. Degradation is the measure of enjoyment ; or rather, it is an increasing numeral by which one constant figure of enjoyment is multiplied. Such pleasures are sought only in " twilights," where virtues are vices and their votaries are ever ready to ask—

> Ah, where shall we go then for pastime,
> _f the worst that can be has been done ?

Thus, if we look at life as it is, in the mirror of art, we shall see how the supernatural is ever present to us. If we climb up into heaven, it is there ; if we go down into hell, it is there also. We shall see it at the bottom equally of two opposite sets of pleasures, to one or other of which all human pleasures belong. The source of one is an impassioned struggle after the supernatural right, or an impassioned sense of rest upon attaining it ; the source of the other is the sense of revolt against it, which flatters us in various ways. In both cases equally the primary sense appealed to is the supernatural moral judgment. All the life about us is colored by this ; and if this is destroyed or weakened, the whole aspect of life will change to us.

I will now explain why I call this judgment supernatural. I call it so because natural sense cannot supply it ; because no interrogation of nature can either support or verify it ; because, tested by scientific tests of reality, it at once melts into air like the vainest of vain dreams. To see that this is so, we have but to consider two of its essential characteristics. In the first place this judgment is absolute. It discriminates between right and wrong with a menacing and imperious dogmatism, from which there is no appeal ; and it applies the same standard to all men. In the second place, the difference it asserts between right and wrong is one not of degree but of kind ; and the difference is thus in its nature infinite. Let us take for example, the moral judgment on purity. In the first place this judgment asserts that purity is better than impurity for all men, making no allowance either for taste or temperament. In the second place it asserts that the choice between this worse and this better is of an importance that is quite incalculable. These two characteristics, our non-theistic moralists, on their own admission, are utterly unable to supply. But throughout their whole teaching they are perpetually forgetting this acknowledgment. They have explicitly reduced virtue to a taste, but they are for ever speaking of it as if it were more than a taste. They have evidently a meaning and a feeling for which they can find no place in their reasoned system. They have a feeling that not the greatest happiness is the real test of conduct ; and they hold this highest good up to men, as though no one existed who might not grow to discern its goodness. Thus Professor Huxley, as we have seen, absolutely condemns the " rank and steaming valleys of sense." He speaks as if he had some canon of happiness, independent of all the various and veering tastes of those whom he addresses. And such is the language, and such is the position, of all our atheistic moralists. Their meaning is clear enough ; their reasoning is clear enough ; but their reasoning is utterly incapable of giving any support to their meaning. And they are themselves, in a confused way, conscious of this confusion. For let them be only pushed hard enough, they surprise us, one and all, by a sudden desertion of their own premisses, and they clutch convulsively at a support of which hitherto they had made no mention. They start one and all with the axiom that happiness is the test of conduct, that happiness is the object of morality. But as soon as this test shows signs of failing them, they directly quit it for another. Thus Professor Huxley admits that the belief in a God always by us, to see that we are faithfully seeking after our own happiness, might be doubtless very useful, if we could ouly believe it to be true. But, he goes on, if no proof of its truth be forthcoming, and if, in its absence, the human race lapse below the beasts in their beastiality, we shall at least, he says, have one comfort in knowing that men will " not have reached the lowest depths of immorality," so long as they hold to the plain rule of not pretending to believe what they have no reason to believe, because it may be to their advantage so to pretend." Now, by a simple substitution of terms, we can see what an utter absurdity is contained in this sentence. According to the modern definition, immorality can have no conceivable meaning but unhappiness, or, at least, the means to it, which in this case are hardly distinguishable from the end. And thus, according to this rigid reasoning, the human race will not have reached its lowest depths of misery so long as it rejects the one thing which, *ex hypothesi*, might render it less miserable.

The reason of this confusion is plain. Our moralists are beginning with one test of conduct; they are ending with quite another. They are beginning with subjective happiness; they are ending with objective truth.

And now here is a plain question, which may be answered in one of two ways, but which, on the atheistic hypothesis, cannot possibly be answered in both. Is truth valuable only because it conduces to happiness? or is happiness only valuable when it is based on truth? If the latter, truth, not happiness, is the test of conduct. If our teachers really mean this, let them explicitly and consistently say so. Let them keep this test, let them reject the other; for the two cannot be fused together. Apparently they have some dim superstition that the attainment of truth will, in some unexplained way, coincide with the attainment of happiness. But, as we have just seen, the moment this notion is really brought to the test, its falsehood becomes apparent. Truth may sometimes subserve happiness, but at other times it is absolutely opposed to it. Never at any time are the two to be identified

ὄξος τ᾽ ἄλειφά τ᾽ ἐγχέας ταύτῳ κύτει
διχοστατοῦντ᾽ ἂν οὐ φίλοιν προσεννέποις.

And if we do but consider the matter a moment, it will be plain that this not only is so, but that it must be so. For , what does truth mean as our modern teachers speak of it? It means the apprehension of the facts, the sequences, of the natural order, as observation and experiment reveal them to us. It means the knowledge of Nature. But, viewed from a natural stand-point, what is Nature? Nature, as Mill has so well pointed out, is a thing that can have no claim either on our reverence or our approbation. Judged of by any human standard, Nature is a monster. There is no crime that men abhor or perpetrate that Nature does not commit daily on an exaggerated scale. She knows no sense either of justice or of mercy. In what way then can it be a holy, a noble, a moral thing to study the ways of this monster, unless, the test of all morality being human happiness, we can lay it down as an axiom that an intimacy with this eternal criminal will make us happiest? I am speaking of this purely from the atheistic stand-point. The believer, of course, admits that truth is a sacred thing; and he believes that truth will never militate against the highest happiness, but will always guide him to it, when apprehended fully. But his belief rests on a foundation that has been renounced altogether by his opponents. He values truth because, in whatever direction it takes him, it takes him either to God or towards him. He sees Nature to be cruel when viewed by herself. But behind Nature he sees an all-merciful God, in whom mysteriously all contradictions are reconciled. Nature for him is God's, but it is not

God. " Non enim vasa," he says in the words of Augustine, "quæ te plena sunt, stabilem faciunt; quia etsi frangantur, non effunderis. . . Ubique totus es, et res nulla te totum capit." "Though God slay me," says the believer, "yet will I trust in him." This trust can be attained to only by an act of faith like this. No observation or experiment will be enough to give it; nay, without faith observation and experiment will do nothing but undermine it. Thus a belief in the essential value of truth is as strictly an act of religion as is the belief in any article of an ecclesiastical creed. It is simply a concrete form of the beginning of the Christian symbol, "I believe in God, the Father Almighty." It rests on the same set of proofs, neither more nor less. Nor is it too much to say that without a religion, without a belief in God, no fetish worship was ever more ridiculous than this cultus of natural truth. There are many true facts, of course, which it is plainly good for us to know; and the discovery and publication of these are of course praiseworthy from the utilitarian stand-point. But this electicism in the search for truth is not devotion to truth for its own sake. It is devotion to it for the sake of its consequences, not in scorn of them; and we are thus simply sent back again to the place we came from. We are sent back to happiness—to that test which we found so shifting. It is only in the devotion to truth for its own sake that we find anything absolute. And this devotion is, as I say, in its very essence religious and supernatural; or if not that, it is utterly mad, aimless, and irrational, nor can it possibly long continue to hold its own in the world.

Thus again we come to religion. As it was embodied in

our praise of purity, so is it embodied also in our praise of truth. Let us struggle in what way we will to produce a moral judgment, we shall find that without religion it is impossible for us to do so. This being the case, the moral judgment is a thing of which we must in imagination rid ourselves ; we must look on life uninfluenced by it, if we would see what life can offer us out of its own resources, and what prospects we can hold out to the world when it has got rid of all that reason can rid it of, and when it believes nothing but what it can support by proof.

It is absolutely necessary that this should be done, and that it should be done thoroughly. What the new school of teachers are now introducing amongst us is the reign of reason, or it is nothing : it is a reign of reason, as opposed to a reign of faith. But they seem to forget somewhat what reason is. Reason will do much for us ; but what will it do ? Reason itself is nothing but a mill. If we bring grist to it, it will grind. If we bring no grist to it, it can but turn and turn ; it will never bring any grist to itself. It will manufacture conclusions out of premisses that we supply to it ; but we must get our premisses from elsewhere. Natural science gets these from the senses, and bids reason grind out of them what happiness it can. But the senses themselves are not reason. It is not reason that tells us that sweet is sweet, and that sour is sour. Still less is it reason that discerns the beauty of holiness, or " the undefined but bright ideal of the highest good." The lower goods are discerned by the senses. The highest good is discerned by faith. And here we see the great difference between the two. The lower goods are indisputable. The higher goods are disputable. No one can talk us out of our five senses ; but the value of truth and holiness has been disputed and denied by millions all through the world's history. If, therefore, we are to believe in nothing but what cannot rationally be doubted, reason at once tells us thus much, that the absolute good is a thing we are not to believe in. Accordingly, were one of our new teachers to talk to me about his highest good, I should answer him with his own arguments. I should tell him that no doubt it might seem as fine a thing as he said it did, but that my first step was " to ask for a proof of its existence," and that if no such proof were forthcoming, I had his own authority for setting it down as a dream. Can he bring, I should ask, any better proof of his " highest good " than the believers can of their " most high God ? " It is evident that he cannot ; it is evident from his own admission, and from the admission of all his school. And what will be the result of this ? By the same warrant by which theism is taken from us, the right to our moral judgment is taken likewise. We cannot keep the last, if we are resolved to get rid of the first. Our moralists will intercede in vain for it with the judge they have chosen. They have appealed to reason. To reason they must go. Nor will reason let them out of its presence till they have rendered up to it the very uttermost farthing. They go to it saying " We will assert nothing, we will be certain of nothing, but what we can prove and verify." And reason at once answers that in their eyes God must be a dream, a fancy. But reason does not stop there. When they say before it that love is better than lust, that truth for its own sake is better than falsehood, or that it is a higher pleasure to look at a beetle through a microscope than at a ballet-girl through an opera-glass, reason again answers, " This is a dream and a fancy too. If a few men happen to think some pleasures better than others, there is a fact to notice. It is not worth much ; still it is a fact. But if you mean that such tastes have any claim on men who do not possess them, or in whom they are counterbalanced by other tastes,

> This is the very coinage of your brain.
> This bodiless creation ecstasy
> Is very cunning in.

This is simply disease—hysteria ; and on your own ground, men will attach no more worth to it than you do to the stigmata on hysterical peasant girls, or to the visions ot the blessed Margaret Mary."

And now having seen what reason will take away from us, let us see what it will leave to us. It will leave us, as I have said, the natural senses ; and it will guide us to the production of such social order as may leave us free for these senses to serve us as we will. It will always be a delicious thing to drink when we are thirsty, and to sleep when we are tired. The cool wind will be always grateful to hot foreheads. The smell of flowers will please us ; and animal spirits may come to us in the spring. But over all these enjoyments that will be left to us a heavy change will come. In the absence of the super-natural moral judgment, they will all be reduced to a dead level. The heights of life will be lowered ; its valleys will be filled up. There will be no hollows full of shadow, and no summits gleaming, as at present,

with lights from another land.   The chiaro-oscuro will have
gone from life; it will present to us no more moral scenery,
at least none such as we know at present.   The same thing
will happen to life that we have seen will happen to art.
Take away the moral judgment, and all its interests fall to
pieces, just as the interest does of *Faust* or of *Measure for
Measure*, and just as the wit does of Congreve.   Laughter
and gravity become silent side by side.   " We say of laughter
it is mad, and of mirth, what doth it ? "   The same blow is
fatal both to the sublime and ludicrous.

Thus, therefore, .without reference to any prejudice in
favor of either vice or virtue, here is one effect of atheism
that will be of equal import to all.   The first thing now to
impress on the world in general is not that these new principles will inaugurate a reign of immorality—that, to half the
world, would be no bad news—not that, but that they will inaugurate a reign of dulness.   Vice and virtue will deaden
down to one neutral tint ; every deeper feeling either of joy
or sorrow will lose its vigor, and will cease any more to be
resonant.   There will be no contrast ; there will be no variety ; there will be no solemnity of thought for the Tyndalls;
there will be no levity of thought for the Voltaires.   The
worn curate toiling hard to save souls in the East End, the
intriguing wife toiling hard to ruin her own in Belgravia, will
each find a sustaining power gone out of their lives.   The
object that each sighed for and that excited each will be
gone.   Indeed the state of things that modern thought seems
to promise us, and which it is in some degree actually even
now bringing upon us, is one· that was long ago predicted,

with an accuracy that seems little short of inspired, at the end of Pope's *Dunciad.* All that he says of dulness may be said of our modern atheism. Its teachers are one and all the precursors of this new kingdom ; they are preparing the way before it. They may deny this as loudly and as honestly as they please. They may pit as they please the practice they have inherited from their fathers against the principles they are bequeating to their children ; but it will be

> In vain, in vain. The all-composing hour
> Resistless falls : the muse obeys the power.
>
> Before her fancy's gilded clouds decay,
> And all the varying rainbows die away.
> Wit shoots in vain its momentary fires :
> The meteor drops and in a flash expires.

Such literally is the effect with which atheism threatens the present resources of life. In our own day, about us in England, we may see the prophecy beginning to fulfil itself. We may see in many quarters dulness and lassitude already setting in, and the very notion of content and happiness vanishing. And yet we are being told that our new aim in life is happiness, and that even if we cannot procure it for ourselves, we can help to procure it in a brighter future for others. We are told that the happiness of heaven was an idle dream, a vapid figment ; that it vanished when we tried to conceive it ; but that this human happiness is something that is solid and certain. If so, what is it? Even at present it is hard to procure, with all the interests of life at their present intensity. Much more will it be hard to procure when these interests lose their strongest hold upon us, and when all life's finest flavors shall have gone from it, as I have shown they must go with the final going of religion. When therefore our moralists talk about humanity, and the glory of its earthly present, and still more of its earthly future, I reply to them in the very words that one of themselves has used with regard to its heavenly future. I say to them as Mr. Frederic Harrison says to his opponents, "*My position is this. The idea of a glorified energy in an ampler life is an idea utterly incompatible with exact thought; one which evaporates in contradiction—in phrases which, when pressed, have no meaning.*" What, I ask, will the ideally happy man be like? What will he long for? What will he take pleasure in? How will he spend his days? How will he make love? What will he laugh at? Let us have some picture of this nobler, ampler, glorified being of the future. Let him be described in phrases which, when pressed, do not evaporate in contradictions, but which have some distinct meaning, and which are compatible with exact thought. Perhaps such a being *may* emerge in the future. I can only say that I defy any one to imagine him, or seriously to hope for his production. If we really do believe that he is in store for us, the belief is as much an act of faith as the belief in heaven; it is as vague; it is even more grotesque; and what discredits the one equally discredits the other. For myself, I can conceive no more ludicrous spectacle than any possible picture of one such radiant being, except it were a whole race of them. In a life bounded by itself, in a life with no hope, no outlook beyond itself, in a life from which religion, the present salt of the earth (and I mean here, by salt, the *flavoring* as well as the *preserving* element), has been taken, it is impossible to imagine what any such radiance could be about. If a heaven with God is a state of blessedness that is unthinkable, a Utopia on earth without a God is much more so.

As far, then, as observation and experiment will carry us, the one conclusion that we come to is this :—All the higher, indeed all the strictly human, pleasures of life—human as distinct from animal—depend, and have always depended, on the supernatural moral judgment ; on the sense not that we are doing our own will, but the will of a Power above us, who is greater and more sublime than we, and yet is, in a sense, akin to us. Nor in saying this do I confine myself to the Christian centuries, nor to nations nor to ages that have risen to any higher kind of theism at all. The same tending towards a personal God is to be traced in all the great civilizations of the world. There has been the same moral passion, though it has been utterly unable to explain itself to itself. To understand this, it is enough to hint a comparison. This longing for God, man's strongest spiritual passion, has its analogue in his strongest physical passion. And as the latter is a mystery to itself in the youth of the individual, so is the former a mystery to itself in the youth of race.

Our present school of moralists are men who would still retain the moral passion, but at the same time they deny the existence of its only possible object, and set up others that are utterly inadequate either to excite or to appease it. Such is the enthusiasm of humanity, which is now offered as an explanation of it. This is really nothing but the desire of God, which will not confess itself. George Eliot's books, to turn to a striking instance, are really instinct with a latent theism,

with an unacknowledged religious dogmatism of the most
absolute and severest kind. George Eliot is really, as Spinoza
was, a person intoxicated with God. Mr. Frederic Harrison
is another case in point. He, too, like George Eliot, is a suppressed theist. He is full of a longing for God that declines
to own itself ; and when he tells us that all his fine feelings
are due to the teachings of Positivism, the best reply we can
make to him is in the lines of Byron, with the alteration of a
single word :

> If you think philosophy 'twas this did,
> I can't help thinking *theism* assisted.

I am not speaking at random. I am simply calling attention to a fact as capable of investigation and proof as any
other—that is, the intimate connection of morality and religion, or rather their essential identity, not their mere connection. They are, in fact, but different aspects of the same
thing. " I desire to be pure in heart " is only another way of
saying " I desire to see God." Neither the value of purity
nor the existence of God is a thing that can be proved ; but
this fact can be, that they stand and fall together. We can
get rid of both if we like, but we cannot keep the one and
reject the other. What destroys one will destroy both.

The practical question, then, that is really before us is
this :—Has life, as we have hitherto viewed it, been viewed
under a false aspect, a deceiving glamour? Are all its pains
and pleasures but a mixture of a nightmare and an ecstasy,
giving to everything an exaggerated value both of joy and
sorrow? Is the moral life only a dream we have been

dreaming, and from which, in groups less or larger, we are now at last awakening?

This is a question that reason cannot answer. The answer must be sought in a deeper part of our nature. The choice is between premisses, not between conclusions. Shall we set our affections on nothing but what cannot be doubted? If so, we shall set them on nothing but the pleasures of sense. And this is what the entire science of the last three centuries has been schooling the world to do, though the real import of its teaching is only now at last slowly becoming apparent.

At present, beyond a doubt, it is the world's tendency to accept this teaching. Indeed, in a great measure it has already accepted it. What I am trying now to point out is the certain practical result of this acceptance. That result is a paralysis of the moral judgment—the paralysis, that is of the sense by which all life's keener interest has been hitherto apprehended.

And what will be the state of those on whom, one by one, in the world now about us, this paralysis seizes, as it is seizing day by day? They will be men looking before and after. They will see the life that the world has lived hitherto, but is now leaving behind it. They will see the life that the world is drifting into. The old *feeling* for virtue will still remain with them. They will still carry with them the importunate notion that life might have some high and worthy meaning. They will still have the wish to struggle after righteousness. Personally, very likely, they will still continue to do so. But all the while the conviction will haunt them, corroding their whole nature, that this struggle is, after all, an unmeaning one ; and they will feel that to other men they can give neither blame nor praise. They will be forced to look with a desponding impartiality on the higher impulses that are yet surviving, and on the lower impulses that will always remain a constant quantity. They will not call the virtuous foolish, nor the vicious wise. They will praise one set of men no more than the other. They will merely say to each with the same listless impartiality : "Do as you please, so long as you do not interfere with your neighbors. If a man has principles, let him live by them. The principles are a dream, but no matter—to him practically they are facts." They will say the same to the man with no principles : "Follow your vices ; follow your passions ; be a beast if you choose to be—do just as you like."

They will not deny that to many life may have a balance of pleasures. But this they do say—that if this balance be not realized here, and on this side the grave, then life has no meaning for us, and can have none. To the unsuccessful they will have no word of comfort. They can only say to such, "The end will come soon. Then draw the curtain ; the weary farce will be over."

No denial of life's worth can be more complete than this. It is all the more forcible, because it affects no impossible universality. It will leave life the worth of a toy for those that care to play with it ; but to those who have outgrown toys it will leave nothing. This pessimism is very different from that of Schopenhauer. Schopenhauer's has been attributed to some form of mental disease—to some abnormal depression of spirits that made all life look black to him. But

this pessimism is of a different kind. It will be possible
for the most healthy and most joyous temperaments, as
well as for the most morbid. It will darken the brightest
moods as well as it will harmonize with the darkest. It
will be ready to assail us in all our business and in all our
pleasures, touching us with ever-recurring qualms of life-
sickness. It is so simple that all can accept it. It is a
kingdom into which even little children may enter. It may
leave us mad; but to get a hold on us, it assuredly will not
need to find us so.

CONSTANTINOPLE. By Edmundo de Amicis, author of "A Journey through Holland," "Spain and the Spaniards," &c. Translated by Caroline Tilton. With introduction by Prof. Vincenzo Botta. Octavo, cloth.

A trustworthy and exceptionally vivid description of the city which, in the present reopening of the Eastern question, is attracting more attention than any other in the world. De Amicis is one of the strongest and most brilliant of the present generation of Italian writers, and this latest work from his pen, as well from the picturesqueness of its descriptions as for its skilful analysis of the traits and characteristics of the medley of races represented in the Turkish capital, possesses an exceptional interest and value.

THE GREEKS OF TO-DAY. By Hon. Charles K. Tuckerman, late Minister Resident of the U. S. at Athens. Third Edition. 12mo, cloth, ... $1.50

This work attracted special attention at the time of its publication, in 1872, as giving a trustworthy and interesting picture of life in Greece, and of the character and status of the modern Greek. At this time, when public attention is so generally directed towards the scheme of practically re-establishing a Greek empire and Greek supremacy in the East, it is thought that a new edition will prove of interest and service.

" The information contained in the volume is ample and various, and it cannot fail to hold a high rank among the authorities on modern Greece."—*N. Y. Tribune.*

" No one can read this book without having his interest greatly increased in this brave, brilliant, and in every way remarkable people."—*N. Y. Times.*

" We know of no book which so combines freshness and fullness of information."—*N. Y. Nation.*

ENGLAND; POLITICAL AND SOCIAL. By Auguste Laugel. Translated by J. M. Hart. 12mo, cloth, ... $1.50

" It is written with a tone of confidence and force of expression which captivate."—*Buffalo Commercial.*

" Affords a clear, distinct, and comprehensive view of the political institutions of England."—*N. Y. Nation.*

" Here, in every sense, is a charming book. * * * * So full of thought, that, like the best of Macaulay's Essays, it will bear reading more than once. * * * * We have rarely met with more picture-like descriptions of what seems to have dwelt most upon his mind—English landscape scenery and rural life."—*N. Y. World.*

THE SILVER COUNTRY; or, THE GREAT SOUTHWEST. A Review of the Mineral and other Wealth, with the attractions and material development of the former kingdom of New Spain, comprising Mexico and the territory ceded by Mexico to the United States in 1848 and 1853. By Alexander D. Anderson. 8vo, cloth, with Hypsometric Map, ... $1.75

" Just at the present moment everything which affords reliable information on the question of silver, its uses and production, is of almost paramount interest."—*Washington National Republican.*

" A very useful book for those who wish to study the silver question in its fundamental feature."—*Chicago Journal.*

" The book will unquestionably become the authority on the subject of which it treats."—*St. Louis Republican.*

www.ingramcontent.com/pod-product-compliance
Lightning Source LLC
Chambersburg PA
CBHW021714110726
47902CB00005B/1181